THE MUSIC MAKERS

By the same author

CRY ONCE ALONE
BECKY
GOD'S HIGHLANDER
CASSIE
WYCHWOOD
BLUE DRESS GIRL
TOLPUDDLE WOMAN
LEWIN'S MEAD
MOONTIDE
CAST NO SHADOWS
SOMEWHERE A BIRD IS SINGING
WINDS OF FORTUNE
SEEK A NEW DAWN
THE LOST YEARS
PATHS OF DESTINY
TOMORROW IS FOR EVER
THE VAGRANT KING
THOUGH THE HEAVENS MAY FALL
NO LESS THAN THE JOURNEY
CHURCHYARD AND HAWKE
HAWKE'S TOR

The Retallick Saga

BEN RETALLICK
CHASE THE WIND
HARVEST OF THE SUN
SINGING SPEARS
THE STRICKEN LAND
LOTTIE TRAGO
RUDDLEMOOR
FIRES OF EVENING
BROTHERS IN WAR

The Jagos of Cornwall

THE RESTLESS SEA
POLRUDDEN
MISTRESS OF POLRUDDEN

As James Munro

HOMELAND

THE MUSIC MAKERS

E.V. THOMPSON

ROBERT HALE · LONDON

First published in Great Britain 1979
This edition published 2013

ISBN 978-0-7090-9843-0

Robert Hale Ltd
Clerkenwell House
Clerkenwell Green
London EC1R 0HT

www.halebooks.com

Printed in the UK by the Berforts Group

We are the music-makers,
   And we are the dreamers of dreams,
Wandering by lone sea-breakers,
   And sitting by desolate streams;
World-losers and world-forsakers,
   On whom the pale moon gleams:
Yet we are the movers and shakers
   Of the world for ever, it seems.

A. W. E. O'Shaughnessy

Chapter One

The small isolated fishing village of Kilmar has grown up on that stretch of Ireland's coastline where the turbulent Irish Sea is squeezed through the narrows of St George's Channel on its way to the vast Atlantic Ocean.

Viewed from the sea, the land hereabouts has the shape of a giant crouching dog, tailless rump rising high above County Wicklow, its nose nudging a rounded bone in County Wexford. The bone is the lone hill of Kilmar. Here, Dark Age missionaries once looked eastward, hoping to catch a distant glimpse of a heathen land wherein lay canonisation and the promise of immortality. Just below this hill, on the water's edge, the missionaries built simple huts and prayed to the one true God to still the angry waters and allow His dedicated servants to set forth on their perilous journeys. When their pious patience was rewarded, each aspiring saint stepped into his curragh – a frail craft of animal skins stretched over a frame of saplings – and, setting a precedent for millions of fellow-countrymen yet to be born, crossed the sea into nostalgic exile.

The huts these men of God left behind were soon occupied by their followers, who waited hopefully for the return of the saintly evangelists and fed themselves with fish they caught from the sea.

The saints never returned to Kilmar, but the fishermen remained. The wood-and-grass huts became houses and the village extended up the slopes of Kilmar hill. When a stone wall was built to give Kilmar its own little harbour the picture was complete. A ten-mile-long reef of rock and sand half a mile out from the harbour entrance ensured that nothing larger than a fishing boat would ever come to Kilmar, but it afforded additional protection from the fury of the sea and fishing gave the villagers a good, albeit dangerous, living.

In this year of 1845, the fishermen still used the traditional curragh, constructed in the same fashion as the flimsy shells used by the Celtic saints, but now canvas was stretched over the light wooden frame in place of the less manageable animal hides. To the people of Kilmar the future lay ahead of them as comfortably predictable as their past. But already changes were beginning to nibble at the fabric of their lives, spreading a disease for which there is no known cure. The disease known as Progress.

With the wood of the fishing boat's stem pressing in his stomach, Liam McCabe leaned far out and plunged his hands into the sea. Just below the surface he gripped the water-stiffened rope from which hung a small-meshed fishing net. Above the rope a long line of cork floats extended seaward from the boat.

Liam's arm muscles tautened and protested as he began slowly heaving the net hand over hand into the boat. Suddenly, a long low wave passed on its way to the shore and lifting the boat slewed it sideways on to the line of the net.

The agony of maintaining his grip on the rope showed on Liam's face as he fought against the boat's movement. Looking over his shoulder quickly, he saw his younger brother leaning on the heavy wooden oars, his eyes fixed upon the shore but seeing only faraway places of his mind.

'Dermot! Stop dreaming and hold the boat steady. There's enough to do without having you fall asleep over the oars.'

Dermot McCabe started guiltily and dug the oars deep into the water, leaning back from them as he pulled the boat around to face toward the horizon once again.

'This damned boat is too heavy for just the two of us,' grumbled Dermot in an attempt to divert attention from his lapse of concentration. 'She's a cow to hold in a swell.'

'Perhaps we should sell it and go back to using a curragh again.'

As another yard of dripping net cleared the water Liam glanced again at his brother and grinned at the indignation he saw on his face. Their twenty-feet-long, clinker-built wooden boat was the subject of fierce pride for both of them. In order to buy it they had worked desperately hard for three years, spending every daylight hour fishing from an old and much patched curragh, putting to sea in stormy weather when every other boat was drawn high up on the beach. With the help of their mother they had salted most of their catches and, once a week, one of them would pull a home-made cart laden with salted fish to Gorey market and stay there until every fish was sold.

At the end of those daunting three years Liam took the money they had saved and set off for Wexford Town. There he sought out the best boat-builder and ordered the craft that had been a dream for himself and Dermot for so long. There was only one other wooden boat in Kilmar, a second-hand English coble, owned by the red-haired Feehan family.

'You must be out of your mind,' snorted Dermot. 'I'd manage the boat single-handed rather than sell her – and so would you. But there must be an easier way to earn a living. We slog our guts out catching fish – and for what? Nobody has the money to buy.'

'They'll have money when the potatoes are dug. Meanwhile we carry on salting. Anyway, what would you rather be doing? Bending your back on somebody else's land? Eating nothing but potatoes, morning, noon and night?'

While Liam was talking, silver-bodied fish were twisting and flapping in the bottom of the boat. The brothers had a good catch. Bringing it into the boat would be hard work. A light breeze was blowing toward the shore and, pulling the oars inboard, Dermot moved to the stern of the boat. Swiftly and skilfully he rigged a small mizzen sail. It would hold the boat steady and prevent her riding over the net as they hauled in the catch.

Liam made way for his brother, and shoulder to shoulder they hauled on the net in practised unity, concentrating on the work in hand. Then Dermot said, 'We've got a meeting of the Association at the inn tonight, Liam. Why don't you come along and give us the benefit of your superior learning?'

The good humour left Liam's face for a moment. He did not approve of Dermot's involvement with the All-Ireland Association. Liam believed that a fisherman had nothing to gain by involving himself with the political aspirations of any of the many associations in the land. Politics had brought nothing but misery to Ireland. He doubted whether the All-Ireland Association would improve upon that sad record.

But Dermot had not finished talking. 'Eugene Brennan is going to be there. You should hear him speak, Liam. He means every word he says. You won't find a finer man anywhere. He's done more to unite Irishmen than any man for centuries.

The best day's work County Wexford ever did was to elect him to Parliament. Oh, I know he's getting on in years now, but he is a great man. They listen to him in London, I can tell you. If it wasn't for him, we'd still be paying tithe duties on the fish we catch. One day he'll have union with England repealed and we'll have our own parliament in Dublin again. You wait till we rule ourselves, Liam—'

'Enough!' growled Liam. 'Keep your spiel for the meeting and your breath for the fish. If we don't get this net in, you'll be out here talking politics to the moon. Bend that strong arm of yours and heave.'

Dermot obeyed his brother's order, but not without a rueful shake of his head, and he continued to express his views while hauling in the net. 'I despair of you, Liam. To hear you talk no one would dream that your own grandfather was a leader in the ninety-eight rising – that he marched on Dublin at the head of half the county—'

'And left behind a widow and eight small children when they hanged him for it,' retorted Liam. 'Will you shake out that net – or shall I put you back on the oars?'

Dermot fell silent, but Liam knew that nothing he had said to his younger brother would make any difference. Dermot was fired with the need to free Ireland from England's domination. It had been the dream of hot-blooded young men for centuries, urged on by the religious fervour of their womenfolk. The vast majority of the Irish were Catholics. Those who ruled over them were Protestants. For generations Catholics had been barred from representing their people in Parliament and unable to hold public office or even vote. Eldest sons could not claim the estates of their fathers unless they renounced their religion. True, much had been done in recent years to right such gross injustices, but the changes in the law had been made with such obvious reluctance that the resentment of the Irish people remained and would smoulder for many years to come.

Liam knew much about the history of his people. The village priest, Father Clery, had given him a thorough schooling, grateful to have found a boy with such a thirst for knowledge; but Father Clery had not taught Liam how he might persuade his brother that changes in Ireland did not have to come about through violence.

Liam wished, as he had on many occasions through the years, that their father was alive to take the responsibility from him. Liam remembered the quiet strength of the pipe-smoking man who had taught him to fish and to handle a boat. Eamon McCabe had been a thoughtful and patient father, a rock against which all the troubles of a small boy might break.

But Liam's childhood had been brutally brief. He had been a ten-year-old boy, waiting on Kilmar jetty with his five-year-old brother for their father's return from a day's fishing, when a sudden storm swept off the land and fought its destructive way out to sea. When it moved on, seven Kilmar fishing boats had disappeared without trace. Eamon McCabe's boat was one of them.

Holding Dermot's hand so tightly that the small boy cried out in pain, Liam had fought back his own tears and taken his young brother home. From that day he had been the man of the family, fishing by day and learning all he could from Father Clery's books at night. He still spent many of his evenings reading the village priest's books, but now Liam was a serious young man of twenty-seven – and a fisherman who owned a wooden boat.

For an hour Liam and Dermot were kept busy hauling in their net and disentangling the larger fish from its mesh. Before long the baskets in the stern of the boat were full to overflowing and the deckboards in the bottom of the boat slippery with feebly flapping fish. They were mostly herring, although they had also netted a shoal of some two hundred mackerel, frightened up from the depths by a larger fish.

When the whole of the net was lying in an untidy heap in the bottom of the wooden boat, all the smaller and lighter fishing curraghs were already well on their way back to Kilmar with their catches. Only the Feehans were still hauling, a quarter of a mile farther out to sea.

'Let's have the mast up and sail home in style, Dermot,' said Liam.

It was only a matter of minutes before the boat was heeling over away from the wind with the sea slapping noisily against the wooden planking. Liam headed the boat toward the small harbour. Behind them, Tomas Feehan and his two burly sons finished hauling in their nets and prepared to row back to Kilmar. The Feehans had followed the McCabes' example in buying a wooden boat, but had struck such a hard bargain with the seller that he had 'forgotten' to include the mast and sails.

From the glassless window of a tumble-down sod-and-thatch cottage, perched high on the slopes above the village, Kathie Donaghue watched the last of the curraghs nose into the small stone-walled harbour. Reaching for a faded black shawl, she threw it over her hair and shrugged the edges about her shoulders.

Kathie had almost reached the door when a man's voice called querulously from the shadows in the corner of the room.

'Is that you, Kathie? Are you going out, child? Where would you be off to at this time of the day?'

The girl crossed the room as the man struggled to a sitting position on the misshapen straw pallet. The movement caused him to belch noisily, and Kathie wrinkled her nose as the odour of stale ale and whiskey reached her.

'So you're awake, are you? It's not before time. I'm away to the jetty to see if I can do some fish-gutting in return for a few fish.'

'Is that the truth of it, girl? You wouldn't lie to your own father? You don't have a sweetheart among those good-for-nothing fishermen?'

When Kathie made no reply, he went on, 'You'd best be careful, Kathie. These fishermen are all for getting young girls into trouble.'

'I know exactly what you're talking about, Father—and the "young girls" they've been getting into trouble is *one* young girl of fourteen. If it's of any interest to you, she's marrying the father of her unborn child on Sunday.' Kathie threw up her head angrily. 'I'm no young child. You may not have remembered it, but I turned twenty last week.'

The thought that he had forgotten his daughter's birthday embarrassed Tommy Donaghue. 'Ah well! I'm just saying you should be careful, that's all.'

'No, that's not all. I may be reduced to wearing clothes that are more patches and darns than material, but the body inside them has never belonged to anyone but me—and it won't until I'm good and ready.'

Kathie swung away to the door and, opening it, called back, 'Will you be here when I return, or shall I look for you in the ale-house?'

'Now, is that the way to be talking to your own father?' Tommy Donaghue spoke with the flat unmusical accent of the north of Ireland. 'Anyone would think I went to the ale-house for my own pleasure. You know very well it's where I earn my living, Kathie.'

He reached out an unsteady hand and plucked a string of the fiddle that lay on the broken chair beside the rough bed. The note hung on the air in the small room.

'Being a fiddler is hard on a man with responsibilities, girl. Do you think I enjoy spending long hours away from a daughter who is all the family I have? You'll never hear me complaining about it, Kathie, but I do expect you to understand.'

'Understand what? That you'd sell your soul for a drink? That you've sold everything we ever owned to satisfy your thirst? You play your fiddle in an ale-house for as long as there's a man left to buy you a whiskey – or until you're too drunk to hold your fiddle. Is that what you're asking me to understand?'

'Now, Kathie.' The words came out as a pathetic whine.

'All right, then, so it's your "work". Will you let me have some of the money you've made from this "work"? If there's no gutting to be done, I'll have to buy fish and I'll need money.'

Tommy Donaghue sank back on to his rough bed. 'Ah well, that's not quite so simple as it sounds.'

'Just as I thought. You collected your pay in a pint pot again.'

Tommy Donaghue looked across the room to where his daughter was framed in the doorway of the tiny one-roomed cottage. She stood with feet planted firmly apart, her hands resting on hips as slim as a young boy's.

'Kathie, when I see you angry you're the spitting image of your poor dear mother . . . the spitting image! If she had lived to see you today, she'd be a proud woman, God rest her dear soul.'

Kathie held on to her anger for another minute, then her hands dropped helplessly to her side and she shook her head, acknowledging defeat. 'Father, you're an impossible man. Why do you have to go and say something like that just when I'd got good and angry with you? You'd charm the blemishes from an apple. Oh, you needn't worry about giving me money. I've got some here.'

'You've got money? Where did you get it?' The words were out before Tommy Donaghue could check the ridiculous suspicion that leaped to his mind. He well knew that there were still ways for a pretty girl to earn money, even in these hard times. But he should have known his daughter better.

'I earned it. Six pennies for weeding potatoes on the Earl of Inch's lands, while you snored your head off in bed. Will you need to see my hands before you believe me?'

She spread fingers before him that were cracked from hard work and stained from weeds and earth.

'Now, Kathie. . . .' As Tommy Donaghue struggled up from the pallet his daughter drew the shawl tight about her shoulders.

'It's time we moved on from Kilmar. You're beginning to think more like a fisherman than a music maker.'

Kathie slammed the door behind her and hurried down the pathway from the ramshackle hut, leaving her father sitting on the edge of the home-made mattress, head in hands, feeling sorry for himself. Kathie knew she had upset him but she did not turn back. She had done so on too many occasions and it invariably ended with her parting with some of her hard-earned money for Tommy Donaghue to spend on drink. His drinking was at the root of all their troubles and one day it would kill him for sure.

But, with or without money, Tommy Donaghue would never go short of a drink of whiskey while he could play the fiddle – the drinking and making music were his whole life.

When Tommy Donaghue tucked a fiddle beneath his chin and drew a bow across the strings, he entered a new and glorious world of his own making. He was no longer a pathetic failure, an itinerant musician earning a precarious living for himself and his motherless daughter. Lost in his music, Tommy Donaghue became a man among men. When he played men sang and women danced. When he stopped they slapped him on the back and begged for more, thrusting drinks into his ready hands. The fact that many of his evenings ended in unconsciousness these days mattered little to him. Drunk or sober, Tommy Donaghue was a fine fiddle-player.

True, it was a precarious way of earning a living, especially since Kathie's mother died. Kathie had been thirteen then, and Tommy Donaghue took to the road soon afterwards. It had not been so bad while they remained in the north of the country – there was some industry – but Tommy Donaghue was restless. There was always another town, another village, another hill.

Somehow they had made their way here to County Wexford, where money was scarce. A fiddler could rely on being given as much ale or whiskey as he could drink, together with a dish of potatoes and salt fish, but he received few coins. Little of the fish from this small and isolated fishing community found its way to a market. It was bartered on the quayside for whatever was needed. Exchanged with the cottier for potatoes and with the farmer for corn and butter. A new pair of trousers or a coarse linen shirt would ensure a whole season's supply of fish for the tailor. The barter system had worked well for centuries, and most fishermen resisted the call for change.

Only the Feehans and the McCabes had made any attempt to advance with the changing world about them, but even they made little effort to widen the market for their catches.

By the time Kathie arrived at the stone jetty the cobblestone quayside was crowded with people and raucous gulls. The curraghs had landed their catches, and the fishermen's wives were noisily but efficiently gutting the harvest of the sea. About them swarmed dozens of hungry cottiers, the poor peasants from the inland potato holdings. It was late summer, the worst part of the year for them. The potato was their staple diet. It was boiled, baked, mashed and made into soup. In good years the men made a rough but potent alcoholic brew from the potato and traded off any surplus, but in every year there came a time when the previous year's crop was gone and the new season's potatoes were not yet ready. During these in-between weeks the poor cottiers roved the countryside and haunted the fishing villages, begging, stealing, and pleading to be fed.

Pushing her way through a crowd of children who were squabbling over a discarded dogfish, Kathie reached the top of a flight of stone steps leading down to the water of the harbour. Below her Liam and Dermot had just secured their boat and were preparing to stack their full fish-baskets on the lower steps, away from the quick hands of the cottier youngsters.

'Will you be needing someone to do the gutting for you when you've finished unloading?'

Her words were directed at Liam, who was scooping fish from the bottom of the boat into a basket. Without looking up, the perspiring fisherman replied, 'We do our own gutting and salting. We need no help.'

When the basket was full, Liam swung it on to the steps with the others and, looking up, saw Kathie for the first time.

She was a tall dark-haired girl who held herself very erect, and from her thin face a pair of very green eyes returned his stare and made him feel obliged to explain his refusal.

'Our mother helps with our gutting. She'll be here any minute now—but if you're hungry you're welcome to a couple of fish.'

At any other time Kathie might have accepted the offer gratefully, but there was something in the frank appraisal of this fisherman that stopped her. Her chin went up and she said, 'The Donaghues are not yet reduced to begging. I have money to buy food but I prefer to work for it.'

Liam was aware of Dermot grinning at him from the steps, but at that moment there was a bump against the side of the boat that knocked him off balance. It was the Feehans' boat coming alongside, and Liam turned as Sean, the youngest of the two red-haired boys, scrambled across the McCabe boat, a mooring-rope in his hand.

'You – girl. Are you looking for work, or making some private arrangement with Liam McCabe?'

The brusque question came from Tomas Feehan, head of the Feehan family. A thick-set, coarse-featured man, he scowled up at Kathie, ignoring Liam McCabe.

'I'm looking for work – gutting fish.' Kathie qualified her reply for the benefit of Eoin, the remaining Feehan, who leered at her from the stern of the family boat.

'Then help my boy to push the McCabe boat back out of the way. We've got a catch here that will busy you for a couple of hours and send you away with enough fish to keep a family for two days.'

A gross bull of a man, Tomas Feehan had spent most of his

fifty years proving he could outfish, outfight and outswear any man in this corner of County Wexford.

'Eoin!' Tomas called upon his eldest son. 'Get up top and clear a space for us. Make sure it's at the edge of the quay where we won't need eyes all about us to see thieving hands.'

Eoin Feehan, a good-looking, dark-eyed young man of Dermot McCabe's age, had eyes only for Kathie Donaghue as he scrambled across the McCabe boat.

'Watch your boots on that paintwork, Eoin. I haven't spent hours painting my boat for some big-footed fisherman to scrape it all off again. If you're in such a hurry you should have got into harbour earlier. Now you can wait for a few minutes until Dermot and I have finished unloading. When we've done that *I'll* move my boat and allow you to come alongside.'

Liam spoke to Eoin, but his glance took in the scowling Tomas and the young man at the top of the steps.

As Tomas Feehan glared at Liam, Dermot tensed, wondering how this strange violent family would take his brother's words.

'It's all right, Liam. We're in no hurry. Here, I'll give you a hand with those baskets.'

It was seventeen-year-old Sean Feehan who broke the moment of tension. Stepping carefully into the McCabe boat, he took a newly filled basket from Liam and swung it ashore.

Dermot breathed a sigh of relief. 'Will you be at the meeting tonight, Eoin?' he called.

'We'll all be there, the *whole* Feehan family.' Tomas Feehan looked pointedly at Liam, who missed neither the glance nor the implication.

'Then Ireland need not tremble,' Liam said. 'At least, not while there's talking to be done in an ale-house.'

Turning his back on the older man, he swung the last basket ashore and jumped out of the boat. Unfastening the mooring-rope from the steel ring on the jetty, he passed close to Kathie. She smelled and looked clean, unlike the majority of the cottiers who came to Kilmar. To Dermot he said, 'Mother should be here to help you soon. She'll have seen us coming in. I'll take the boat to the beach and lay out the nets to dry; there's no space to do it here.'

As Liam rowed the heavy fishing boat away he looked back at the landing-steps he had just left. His mother had arrived and she waved a hand to him before she and Dermot began carrying their loaded baskets up the steps. Then Liam watched Kathie as she helped the Feehans. Her body strained against the patched dress as she swung the heavy baskets up to Eoin. She was a shade too thin for good health, but she was a willing worker and doing more than her share of the work. Liam thought she was not like the usual cottier girls who came down to the fishing villages from the hills at this time of the year. He wondered who she was and why he had not seen her before.

Liam's interest was shared by Tomas Feehan's elder son. Eoin Feehan considered himself to be something of an expert on the merits of the impoverished cottier girls. He was a good-looking young man and could claim a high degree of success in his brief encounters with them. It was nothing to his credit. The cottiers stayed on their tiny plots of land until their situation became truly desperate. By the time they reached Kilmar they were weak from starvation. When hunger and chastity came into direct conflict the needs of hunger invariably won the battle, but it seemed less degrading when a carnal arrangement was made with a good-looking young man.

Eoin Feehan said nothing to Kathie until, with the gutting half-completed, Tomas Feehan followed Liam's example and took his own boat to the beach.

'I haven't seen you here before,' Eoin Feehan opened the conversation. 'What's your name?'

'You haven't seen me here because I haven't been in Kilmar long,' said Kathie. 'And my name doesn't matter to you or anyone else just so long as I gut your fish for you.'

Kathie's reply was far blunter than Eoin had expected, but he did not allow it to deter him.

'You're a good worker. The gutting is coming along well.'

'I've done it before.'

'Yes, I suppose you have. Times are hard between crops.' Eoin still thought Kathie was a cottier girl, and she did not correct him.

'I wouldn't argue with that.'

'You know, there's an easier way for a pretty girl like you to earn a few coppers than gutting fish.'

Kathie's knife flashed faster, and the fish she was gutting

lost its tail in a swift accident. She said nothing, but her silence encouraged Eoin to continue.

'You meet me tonight behind the old salting-house and you won't have to gut fish for a few days.'

'Oh? Since when has fishing made a man so rich?' Kathie stopped gutting and looked Eoin Feehan in the face for the first time. He saw fire and passion and a deep darkness in her eyes, and Eoin Feehan knew he wanted this girl as he had never wanted any girl before.

'I may not be rich, but I'll give you as much as a family man earns for a day's work on a farm. I'll give you ten pence.'

Kathie's eyes never left his face, and suddenly Eoin Feehan felt uncomfortable.

'Well . . . ? Do we have an arrangement?'

Kathie spat in Eoin Feehan's face. He was taken completely by surprise. Then his anger flared and he took a step toward her. He stopped just in time as a razor-sharp fish-knife slashed the air an inch from his nose.

'You come one step closer and you'll take no girl behind the old salting-house – or anywhere else. I've never lifted my skirt to any man for love and I'm damned if I'll do it with you for money. Ten pence indeed!'

Furiously Kathie shouted the words at him, and Eoin Feehan was aware that the Kilmar fishermen and their women had stopped work to enjoy the incident. He tried to calm the angry girl, but she addressed her next words to the watching and listening crowd.

'Did you hear his offer to me? It's a great opportunity for any girl amongst you who would like to earn herself ten pence. All you have to do is to meet him behind the old salting-house tonight.'

She slashed the knife dangerously close to Eoin Feehan's face, and he took an involuntary step backward, infuriated by the laughter that rose from the fishermen and their helpers.

'You've done yourself no favour,' he hissed at Kathie. 'There will come a day when you'll be down here begging for fish with the rest of the cottiers. I'll see you starve before you get anything from a Feehan.'

'I'd willingly starve before I took it,' retorted Kathie. 'And my father is a fiddler, not one of your bog-cottiers. You'll never have the pleasure of seeing me beg for food – or for anything else. Now, I've gutted more than half of your fish, so half a basket is a fair payment. I'll take it now and you can gut the rest of your fish yourself.'

Helping herself to no more fish than she believed she had earned, Kathie Donaghue picked up the basket and made her way from the quay, the grinning fishermen moving back respectfully from her path.

'I don't know who she is,' said Dermot McCabe to his mother as Kathie passed by without looking to left or right, 'but she's just saved Eoin Feehan the trouble of going to confession on Sunday. I wish Liam had been here to see what went on. He offered to give her some fish when we came in.'

'Did he now?'

Norah McCabe looked after Kathie with renewed interest, and frowned. Until now there had been little opportunity for Liam to take an interest in women, but this girl was both attractive and strong-willed. She would have little difficulty in getting any man in Kilmar. Norah McCabe felt an uneasy stirring within her. Her instinct told her that this unusual and high-spirited girl would bring trouble to the village.

To Dermot she said, 'Liam is lucky not to have felt her tongue. That girl carries a pride that doesn't go well with an old patched dress.'

Chapter Two

The meeting of the All-Ireland Association had been in progress at the Kilmar ale-house for longer than an hour, but had not yet been called to order. Men stood around in noisy, sweating, drinking groups and tobacco smoke hung from the low-beamed ceiling thicker than a November fog. In a far corner Tommy Donaghue drew tune after tune from the strings of his fiddle as a wide variety of drinks came his way. Gin, ale and local whiskey followed each other down his throat in quick succession.

'Where has Eugene Brennan got to?' asked Dermot for the sixth time. He ran a coloured handkerchief over his glowing face. 'We've got men from all over Wexford in here to hear him speak. If he doesn't arrive soon, we can forget the All-Ireland Association in this part of the county. No one will want to know us.'

'Don't you worry yourself. Eugene Brennan will be here. He's said he'll be coming, and Eugene Brennan is a man of his word.'

The reassurance came from Patrick Meahey, the leather-aproned landlord of the ale-house. His shirt was wet with perspiration, and beneath the bottom edge of the apron his trousers were soaked with spilled ale. He had never before been quite so busy and secretly hoped County Wexford's Member of Parliament would be delayed for another hour. Impatient, waiting men drank more than men who were listening to a good speaker.

'Father Clery went to meet Brennan,' said Sean Feehan. 'I saw him leaving the village before I came in here.'

'Then they've more than likely gone to the big house at Inch.' Tomas Feehan wiped froth from the tip of his nose with a large grubby hand. 'Eugene Brennan will not be worried about keeping a few fishermen waiting while he's looking at an earl over the top of a glass of good brandy.'

'Brennan cares more for the likes of us than he does for the land-owners,' said Sean Feehan hotly. 'He could have had a good living as a lawyer if that was all he wanted. Instead, he's spent a lifetime working for Ireland – and pauperised himself in the process.'

'I don't know why I let this young terrier have schooling,' growled Tomas Feehan. He emptied his tankard and banged it down upon the rough wooden table. Glaring at his younger son, he said, 'If you want to air your learning in grown-up company, then tell us something about the ninety-eight rising right here in County Wexford. It was the ordinary people who rose against the English then and it will be the same next time. You can forget all about your lawyers and good talkers. Not one of them will risk his neck if there's the slightest possibility of it ending up in a noose.'

'Pa's right,' agreed Eoin Feehan. 'We should forget about Eugene Brennan. He's an old man now. He's spent fifty years talking about things and we're more under the rule of the English now than we were when he started. We haven't even got a parliament in Dublin. That's what his talking has done for us.'

'I'll hear nothing against Brennan.' Dermot's face was flushed with the heat of the room and the amount he had drunk. 'He's a good man . . . a great man. But I agree that it's time we showed the English that the All-Ireland Association means business. We should take over the land belonging to absentee English landlords and give it back to the Irish people, for a start.'

'What for? So that the cottiers can grow more potatoes?' Tomas Feehan took a stubby clay pipe from the corner of his mouth and spat on the sawdust-scuffed floor. 'No, boy. That's not a cause that will make me march on to an English bayonet.'

He stabbed the end of his pipe toward Dermot.

'I'm not saying anything against our Member of Parliament. He's done his best. I'll give him that. I'm just saying that he'd do as well to stay in London . . . talking. That's what he's best at doing. When it comes to fighting, then we've got to organise ourselves. We'll get little help from outside when the time comes – and none from the likes of them at the big house where Eugene Brennan most likely is at this very moment.'

'There's nothing wrong with the Earl of Inch.' The landlord panted to a halt beside them. 'He's as Irish as the rest of us. If every land-owner looked after his people half as well as the Earl, there would be no hungry cottiers down on the quay – and no need for meetings like this.'

'Then it's as well for you that such a state of affairs will never come about or you'd lose all your business,' retorted Tomas Feehan. Reaching out, he knocked his empty tankard over on the table before him. 'Now you've given us the benefit of your opinion perhaps you'll fill this and bring it back before I choke to death in this smoke.'

From the far corner of the room there was a loud cheer as Tommy Donaghue climbed upon a chair and began scraping out the music of a well-known tune about Kelly the pirate and the pirate queen Grannaile.

'I thought this was supposed to be a meeting,' grunted Tomas Feehan. 'Whose idea was it to turn it into a ceilidh?'

Further talk became impossible as voice after voice took up the words of the popular folk-song.

The singers were well into the last verse when the ale-house door was thrown open and a small grey-haired priest pushed his way inside. He made his way to the centre of the room, holding up his hands for silence. The singing faltered and then broke as men were nudged into an awareness of Father Clery's arrival.

Moments later Tommy Donaghue was playing to a silent audience. With eyes tightly closed and a happy faraway expression upon his face he tapped his foot on the chair in time to the tune, unaware that the mood of the room had changed.

'Shut the fool up, someone.'

Tomas Feehan's voice boomed out in the room and hands reached out to drag the protesting fiddler from his chair.

Father Clery looked about him, aware of the puzzled looks of the men who had come here to hear their Member of Parliament.

'Eugene Brennan will not be here tonight.'

The meeting erupted in protest, and the priest waited until the noise had died away to a disgruntled murmur before he attempted to speak again.

'Before you begin blaming Eugene Brennan you'd best hear me out. He's not here because . . . he's been arrested.'

There was a moment's stunned silence and then an angry roar burst from a hundred throats.

'What for? Why has he been arrested?'

The voice was Dermot McCabe's.

Father Clery shouted above the din, 'He's been accused of treason. The English are charging him with inciting the country to rebellion.'

'We'll show them what rebellion means! The country will rise for Brennan. We'll march on Dublin and set him free.'

Dermot's words brought an enthusiastic response.

'We'll throw the English out of Ireland while we're about it.'

Both suggestions received noisy support, but Father Clery waved his arms wildly until the crowd heeded him and quietened down.

'No! That's just what the English are hoping will happen. They know we are not ready for a rising. We have no weapons, and Dublin is crawling with soldiers.' The priest had a powerful voice for such a small man and it boomed out in the room. 'If we take to the roads now, we could destroy the All-Ireland Association for all time.'

'Then what action *do* we take?' demanded Dermot. 'We're not going to stand back and do nothing.'

'We'll start by having a collection toward Eugene Brennan's defence—'

'That's right, take up a collection. What tune do you want me to play for you this time?'

There was a shocked silence as, clutching his fiddle, Tommy Donaghue pushed his way through the crowd about the priest and stumbled drunkenly to one knee before him.

'I'm all right . . . all right,' the fiddler mumbled as Father Clery caught his arm and prevented him from falling on his face.

'Who is this?' The priest released his grip as Tommy Donaghue regained his feet and stood swaying before him.

'He's quite harmless,' called Patrick Meahey. 'Tommy Donaghue is just an old fiddler who plays for me in the evenings. Come on, Tommy. Away back in the corner with you.'

'Not until I've played something to earn me collection.'

Tommy Donaghue shook off the landlord's hand. 'What will it be—a marching song to carry you to Dublin? I'm your man for that. Many's the time Tommy Donaghue has set the feet of the Orangemen swinging off on a march through Ulster. . . .'

Tommy Donaghue beamed stupidly about him. oblivious of the effect of his words on the stunned men who had heard them. The All-Ireland Association had been formed with the object of gaining independence for Ireland but, although it claimed to represent the whole of the country's people, it was predominantly Catholic, as was every man in the ale-house. The Orangemen mentioned by the drunken fiddler were militant Protestants. Staunch supporters of Protestant supremacy, they had played a major part in putting down the rebellion of 1798. Here, where the fighting had been bloodiest, the events of less than half a century before were still fresh in the mind of every County Wexford man. Many local men had been summarily executed by militiamen from the Protestant north, and hatred for them festered on. Tommy Donaghue had made a monumental drunken blunder.

'Did you hear that? The man's a Protestant! He must be a spy,' spluttered Eoin Feehan.

'Nothing of the sort. He's just a drunken old idiot, that's all. He means no harm to anyone.'

Patrick Meahey was alarmed. He knew these men. Knew their tempers when they had been drinking. 'Throw him outside if he's offending you – but give me his fiddle first. By tomorrow he'll have forgotten every word he's heard tonight and be back playing for all of you.'

'Yes, throw him out,' agreed Father Clery, and others took up the cry. The fiddle and bow were passed over the heads of the crowd to the landlord of the ale-house, and a feebly protesting Tommy Donaghue was manhandled to the door and pitched headlong out into the night.

He stayed on his feet for half the width of the rough road before tripping and pitching into a deep ditch, dug to carry away the storm water from Kilmar hill.

The ale-house door closed to the sound of laughter, and soon only the muffled voices of excited men could be heard from inside.

But one man had not gone back inside the ale-house with the others. An oblique shaft of dull yellow light fell from a half-curtained window on his heavy boots as he walked quietly to the storm drain. Unnoticed, he looked down into the shadows as Tommy Donaghue grovelled helplessly below him.

'Oh, Mother of God! Where am I? What did they have to do that for? Help! Help me, someone!'

'Tommy Donaghue?'

'Who's that? Thank the Lord you heard me. Will you help me up, sir? Give me a hand out of here.'

Two muddy hands were held up pleadingly above the darkness of the ditch, but when the unseen man made no move to help him the fiddler lowered them to rest upon the hard-packed earth at the edge of his deep prison.

'Help me out . . . please!'

The heavy boots came a pace nearer. For a few moments the only sound was Tommy Donaghue's heavy breathing. Then, without any warning, one of the heavy boots was raised above him and before Tommy Donaghue's befuddled mind signalled the warning it crashed down upon the fingers of his right hand.

Eoin Feehan let the old man's scream die away to an agonised sobbing before he opened the door of the ale-house and slipped inside. Tomas Feehan's firstborn son felt a fierce satisfaction. When Kathie Donaghue was making a fool of him she had boasted that here father was a fiddler and she had no need to beg like a cottier girl. Now she would see how much fiddling could be done by a man with broken fingers. He would see her begging yet, and the thought pleased him.

The meeting in the ale-house was still in full spate when Liam passed by. The wind had freshened, veering easterly, and he had been down to the water's edge to put an extra mooring-line on his boat. It was not really necessary, but he knew he would sleep easier should a storm blow up.

Liam recognised Father Clery's voice raised in political argument and he smiled. The priest was a little gnome of a man with a cheerful disposition and a generous nature, but politics was his weakness. It was said he would interrupt his blessing on a dying man to straighten out his politics before sending him on his way to a better, albeit non-political, world. Father Clery was in good voice tonight, and as his views coincided with those held by the others in the room he had a noisy and enthusiastic audience.

Liam was about to pass on his way when he heard another sound that brought him to a halt. It was muffled crying that appeared to come from the deep ditch opposite the ale-house. At first, Liam thought it must be the whimpering of a dog, but as he moved closer he recognised it as the soft crying of a man.

Peering into the darkness, Liam could see nothing for a few moments, then there was a movement in the mud at the bottom of the ditch and a dirt-streaked face was raised toward him.

'Help me, sir. For the love of God help me out of here.'

Tommy Donaghue had been in the ditch for an hour, but the smell of drink was still powerful on his breath and Liam smiled at the drunken man's predicament.

'Give me your hands and I'll pull you out.'

'Bless you, sir. But I've only one hand to give you. The other is hurting so much I feel sure it's been broken.'

Liam took the one hand that was offered to him and, bracing himself, took the weight as Tommy Donaghue's feet scrambled against the sheer side of the ditch, seeking a foothold. It took three attempts before the fiddler emerged from the ditch and he promptly collapsed to the ground at Liam's feet.

Tommy Donaghue stayed on the ground, trying to tuck his injured hand beneath his left armpit. In the light from the ale-house window, Liam could see the fingers crooked and swollen.

'You'd better get that hand seen to quickly. Come along, I'll take you to Bridie O'Keefe. She'll straighten out your fingers and set them for you.'

'No, I'll be all right if you can help me home. My own daughter will tend to me.'

Liam looked at the man in surprise. He had not seen Tommy Donaghue in the village before and had assumed he was a cottier from the potato fields. Now he looked more closely and saw that beneath the dirt of the ditch this man was better dressed than any cottier.

'Where do you live?'

'Up the hill a way. I'll show you if you just let me rest on your arm.'

Tommy Donaghue was in great pain from his injured hand and by the time they arrived at the tumbledown cottage it was only Liam's arm about him that kept him on his feet.

Kathie answered the knock on the door and she, too, smelled the alcohol on her father's breath as Liam led him past her. In the restless light of the single candle that lit the room Liam recognised her as the girl who had wanted work on the quay.

He led the old man to the blanket-covered pallet in a corner of the room and gently lowered Tommy Donaghue down on to the crude bed.

'I hope you and your friends are proud of yourselves for getting my father in this state,' Kathie said bitterly. 'You'd be better putting the money into his pocket if you really appreciated his playing. There'll come a day when he won't be able to hold a fiddle because of the drink and you're doing him no favour by buying it for him. You should be ashamed of yourself—'

'The only favour I've done is to pull an old man out of a ditch and bring him home,' interrupted Liam. 'As for playing a fiddle, you'd better do something with his hand or I doubt whether he'll play again.'

For the first time Kathie noticed the fingers of her father's right hand protruding at unreal angles. Snatching the candle, she dropped to her knees beside him. Gently lifting up the injured hand to look at it more closely, she gasped at what she saw.

'How did he do this?'

'I don't know. I suppose he must have landed on them when he fell in the ditch.'

'I didn't fall into any ditch. I was thrown there.'

'Why would anyone want to do that?' Liam did not believe the drunken old man.

'I don't know. We were all enjoying ourselves in the alehouse and I heard someone speak of taking up a collection. Then they shouted that they were going to march to Dublin and I offered to lead them, just as I have led the Orangemen on many a march. You remember, Kathie? Me walking down the middle of the road in Belfast and a thousand men with banners marching behind me. . . .'

Liam's mouth fell open in disbelief. 'You spoke of marching with Orangemen at a meeting of the All-Ireland Association? Good God, man! You're lucky it wasn't your neck that was broken. The men of County Wexford have little reason to like Orangemen. They made many widows and orphans hereabouts in ninety-eight.'

'But all that happened nearly fifty years ago!' protested Kathie.

'Kilmar men have long memories. You'd be wise to remember that.'

'How was I to know?' asked Tommy Donaghue. 'I was just trying to please them. . . .' His voice broke as he held up his hand. 'There was no reason for them to stamp on my fingers. There was no call for them to do that, was there?'

Liam was sceptical, despite the other man's very real distress. '*Stamped* on your fingers? Who would do a thing like that to you?'

'I don't know. I could only see his feet. I put my hands on the edge of the ditch and asked him to pull me out. He stamped on my fingers.'

Tommy Donaghue's eyes brimmed with tears and he sank back on the bed. The whole incident was beyond his understanding.

Liam had been crouching down by the fiddler. Now he stood up and found himself looking down at Kathie's face. She had been preparing for bed when Liam had knocked on the door and her hair hung long and black about her brown shoulders.

'Who would deliberately hurt an old man?' she demanded fiercely.

Liam shook his head. 'The only person who might have answered that question is your father – and he did not see the man's face.'

Kathie smelled as fresh as she had when he had passed close to her on the quay. Being so close to such an attractive girl was a new experience for him and to cover his sudden shyness he spoke more gruffly than usual.

'You'd better do something about those fingers if you want him to play the fiddle again.'

Kathie nodded. 'I'll splint them up now. They will be all right, in time.'

A long heavy silence descended upon them until Liam said awkwardly, 'I'll be going now, then.'

'Thank you, Liam McCabe. My father and I are grateful to you.'

Liam was startled out of his unaccustomed shyness.

'How do you know my name?'

'Sean Feehan mentioned it when I was working on the quay.'

It was only a small lie. Sean Feehan *had* told her – but she had asked him first.

Liam nodded his head. 'Sean is the best of a bad family.' He turned to go but paused at the doorway. 'Your father won't be playing his fiddle for a while, but there's no need for you to go hungry. You can have the job of gutting the McCabe catch every day if you need work.'

'I thought your mother always did that?' Her eyes were large dark shadows in the shabby ill-lit room.

'So she does, but we need to be getting on with salting fish and she hasn't time for both.' Now it was Liam's turn to tell a lie.

'I thank you, Liam McCabe. You are a kind man.'

The All-Ireland Association meeting was still in progress. Someone had opened the ale-house door to allow the eye-tingling smoke to escape, and the noise of argument and counter-argument spilled out into the night.

On impulse, Liam went inside.

Before his eyes had accepted the smoky yellow light in the room, his arm was firmly gripped by his brother.

'It's good to see you here, Liam. Have you come to join our Association at last?'

'No, I'm not here to join anything – and I'll have nothing to do with an organisation that condones the crippling of old men.'

Liam's angry voice was loud and the conversations about him died away as men looked at him.

'I'm talking about the old fiddler.'

Dermot's face lost its startled expression. 'Oh, him! We didn't hurt him, Liam. He was drunk and being a nuisance so we threw him out.'

'You threw him out because he mentioned Orangemen,' corrected Liam. 'I thought you were supposed to be the "All-Ireland" Association – or have you changed the name?'

Liam had the attention of most of the men in the room now and some of them had begun to mutter angrily, but Liam went on, 'How many times have you told me that the Association is working for a united Ireland, free from English rule? I thought "united" included everyone. Catholics, Protestants and Presbyterians. Am I wrong?'

'He was interrupting the meeting.' Eoin Feehan was flushed

and dangerous with drink. 'And so are you. You're not a member of the Association. This is a closed meeting.'

'So what are you going to do about it – throw me out and stamp on my fingers, as someone did to the fiddler?'

'No one hurt his fingers, Liam,' insisted Dermot. 'He was being a nuisance so he was put out, that was all.'

'No, that wasn't all. I've just helped him to his home. He has two fingers broken on his right hand and he was sober enough to know they were stamped on by someone from this room. If that is your way of uniting Ireland, then I want none of your association.'

The angry murmuring began again, louder this time, but as Liam glared defiantly about him Father Clery came across the room and took him by the arm.

'Dermot is telling the truth, Liam. I was here when the fiddler was put out. If his fingers are injured, then it happened after he left here. But where are my manners? I've been trying to get you to a meeting for years. Now you're here you'll at least stay for a drink and I'll try to persuade you to join our association. We need men like you, Liam. You have a good head on your shoulders and would be a great help on our committee.'

'Thank you, Father. I'll accept the drink – but I don't need your talk about the Association. You gave me schooling so I could make something of myself. It won't come from arguing politics in an ale-house.'

On the far side of the room, Sean Feehan had lost the taste for his ale. Pushing it away from him, he stood up and left the room without a word to his half-drunk brother. He alone of those in the ale-house had noticed Eoin Feehan return after Tommy Donaghue had been ejected.

Chapter Three

The grim high walls of Dublin Jail cut off sunshine and light from the narrow street in front of the prison gates, causing the visitor to shiver involuntarily as he approached. Inside it was even more forbidding. Sallow-faced jailers with noisy rings of heavy keys at their belts looked suspiciously at the intruder into their harsh and secretive world. Reluctantly they swung open the huge barred doors ahead of him.

It was exactly a week since the All-Ireland Association meeting at Kilmar, and Father Clery was paying a visit to Eugene Brennan.

As the heavy iron door of the narrow cell crashed into place behind him, Father Clery shook hands warmly with the frail white-haired old man who stood up from the single bunk.

Eugene Brennan looked more like a scholar than a revolutionary and, indeed, he was a very learned man. A brilliant lawyer. Only his eyes betrayed him for what he was – a man with a vision. An all-consuming purpose in life. Eugene Brennan had fought the English, within the law, for five decades. He had founded the All-Ireland Association with the declared aim of separating Ireland from England and giving his country a free and independent government. But, for all the passion of his beliefs, Eugene Brennan had always preached against violence. He had been a young man when Ireland rose in rebellion against English rule in 1798 and the bloody slaughter he had witnessed then haunted him even now.

'How very kind of you to come all this way to see me, Matthew.' The two men were old friends. 'Time drags in here, with little to brighten the day.'

'A man of your age should be at home in his own warm house, not in a damp prison cell.'

Father Clery was genuinely concerned at the appearance of Eugene Brennan. He looked listless and weary, as though his seventy years were beginning to weigh heavily upon him.

'I must agree with you, Matthew. Perhaps between us we might persuade the Lord-Lieutenant of Ireland to imprison me in more salubrious surroundings.' A smile passed briefly across his face. 'But enough of my comfort. Our country sleeps less easy than I. What news do you bring?'

Father Clery reached inside his coat and pulled out a thin sheaf of papers. 'I have brief details here of all meetings held throughout the country. They all tell much the same story. Strong protest at your arrest and demands for action to free you. Collections have been made for your defence and the usual subscription receipts have been trebled – and there's more promised.'

'I am deeply grateful for the contributions, Matthew.' The emotional old politician abruptly began pacing the length of the narrow cell to hide his feelings. 'But there must be no talk of action to free me – or of any other form of violent protest. Not only would it defeat my lifetime's work but it would also seriously jeopardise an acquittal and be playing right into the hands of Sir Robert Peel.'

Sir Robert Peel was the Prime Minister of England and a lifelong opponent of Eugene Brennan and the aims of his association.

'Pass the word to all branches of the Association, Matthew. There must be no trouble.'

He swung around to face his friend. 'Tell them the English brought troops to Dublin in preparation for my arrest. There are five thousand more than there were three months ago.'

Eugene Brennan ran his fingers through his long white hair. 'God! We can do without another bloodletting. You are nearly as old as I am, Matthew. You can remember ninety-eight. Irishmen killing Irishmen and English soldiers sacking the countryside. I'll not have history say I was responsible for another such time of carnage.'

Eugene Brennan stopped and looked up wistfully at the small barred box of blue sky high up in the cell wall.

'Ireland's the most beautiful country in the whole world, Matthew – God's own land – but He has put in some hot-headed tenants to look after it for him.'

He turned back to Father Clery with tears in his eyes.

'Don't let them wreck everything I've worked for, Matthew. Have the rules of the Association read out at every meeting. I want to be sure that each man there knows what they mean. It's an association for every man and woman born in Ireland – a united Ireland. That's our aim and we'll achieve it through peaceful means. Through the English Parliament. What happens to me is unimportant. There can be no personalities in this matter. When I go, however I go, someone else will take my place, and I pray he will have more success than I. But whoever is leading the Association must have Ireland first and foremost in his mind at every moment. Ireland and our people. The people of the mountains and the fields, the villages and the cities, whether they be in the north, the south, the east, or the west. Tell them, Matthew. Make sure they know.'

Eugene Brennan turned back to the barred sky again and his shoulders sagged.

'What's happening out there, Matthew? Is the sun shining on the corn in the fields? Are there children playing games in the streets of Dublin? And what of your own village, Kilmar? Ah! I can almost smell the sea and the wet sand and the fish on the quay.'

The politician returned his attention to the priest and produced a weak smile. 'Memories are a great comfort to an old man, Matthew. He is able to see faraway things more clearly than can a young man.'

'You'll soon be seeing everything for yourself,' said Father Clery, alarmed at the depressed state of the great man before him. 'Have they fixed a date for your trial yet?'

'No, and they won't for a while. They have no evidence against me that would stand up in a properly constituted court. They will bide their time in the hope that our young men will lose patience and do something foolish. Then the prosecution will be able to point to it as an example of what my speeches have brought to pass.'

'All the more reason to keep our members under control,' said Father Clery firmly. 'I'll make sure that every one of them is fully aware of his responsibilties.'

'Then this has been a very successful visit. I thank you, my friend,' said Eugene Brennan, clasping Father Clery's hand in both his own. 'Leave your notes for me and I'll look through them. They will make better reading than the English newspaper they bring me here.'

'Goodbye, and may God remain with you,' said Father Clery to his old friend.

'He will, Matthew. He will. Go now.'

Turning the corner, away from the shadow of the high grey

walls, Father Clery felt the evening sunshine warm upon his face and thought of Eugene Brennan's tiny square of daylight. He determined to petition Eugene Brennan's fellow-MPs in a bid to gain his release, or at the least a speedy trial. The ageing politician needed friends now as never before.

At about the time Father Clery was walking into the sunshine of a warm Dublin evening, two men sat down to dine together in London. One was Sir Robert Peel, Tory Prime Minister of the uneasy union of Great Britain and Ireland, the other Sir James Graham, Peel's Home Secretary with responsibility for the administration of Ireland.

Peel was talking.

'. . . I have no wish to exaggerate the importance of Brennan's association, or to give the Irish another martyr. Pass the word along to the judge that I am looking for a light sentence to be given to Brennan. Who knows, it might gain us a friend or two in Ireland.'

Sir James Graham leaned well back in his chair and shook his head slowly.

'We will make no friends in Ireland, Sir Robert. Clemency would be a serious mistake. The members of Brennan's All-Ireland Association would interpret it as weakness. Either we drop the charges or pursue them with the utmost vigour. Personally, I favour the latter course. Brennan has been a thorn in my flesh for as long as I care to remember. I can make no statement to the House on Irish affairs without suffering his interruptions. At least once every day he accuses me of not understanding his countrymen and demands self-rule for Ireland with monotonous regularity. I confess there are many occasions when I feel like giving him the damned country. They deserve each other. Ireland has little but mist and bog and argumentative peasants.'

Sir Robert Peel smiled wryly. 'There is a great deal of truth in what you say, James – but Ireland is a part of Great Britain, albeit a troublesome part, and so she will stay. A light sentence, if you please, Home Secretary.'

The Prime Minister had issued an order that Sir James Graham would disregard at his peril, but Sir Robert Peel had already passed on to other matters.

'Try some of this wine, James. The French ambassador

has it brought in from his own vineyards in the Loire valley. I fancy it lacks the body of a Bordeaux, but I'm sure you will find it quite palatable. With the current state of things in France we are lucky to have any wine at all. The country is ripe for another revolution. . . .'

Ireland's problems were thrust to one side as the two most powerful men in the land discussed France, its problems . . . and its wine.

Father Clery reported back to a noisy and divided meeting of the Kilmar branch of the All-Ireland Association. The older men accepted Eugene Brennan's instructions, seeing the wisdom of taking no action whilst their leader was held in prison, but the younger men were bitterly opposed to a period of inactivity. They argued, quite rightly, that Brennan could be held for many months before he was brought to trial. During that time the Association would be totally lacking in direction.

'Not necessarily,' argued the priest. 'We'll gather signatures on a petition to the Lord-Lieutenant in Dublin, calling for an early trial.'

'He'll give it to his servants to light fires,' retorted Dermot. 'I say we take positive action, to frighten the English into releasing Brennan.'

'I'm with Dermot,' said the eager young Sean Feehan, and around him other young men murmured their agreement. 'Unless we show we mean business the English will do as they like with Eugene Brennan.'

'The English don't frighten so easily,' said Father Clery patiently. 'You can't fight them with hot words. They have at least ten thousand well-armed troops in Dublin right now. Would you face them with a few hundred men armed with knives tied to poles?'

'We'll find a way – but not if we agree to do nothing. The men of Wexford will rise to help Brennan, and others will come with us.'

'Don't be so hasty, Dermot.' Father Clery put a hand on the young man's shoulder. 'Eugene Brennan knows more about this than we do. When the time is right he will tell us to make our move and, if need be, the men of Kilmar will have all the arms that are necessary. Until then we must just bide our time.'

'We've been biding our time for seven hundred years. I

for one think it's time to be doing something to change things. If no one else takes the lead, I'll do it myself. Who'll come with me?'

Dermot McCabe's plea brought an enthusiastic response from the young men of the All-Ireland Association.

'Your way will help no one, least of all Ireland, and I'll have no part of any of it,' declared Father Clery. 'If you take the path to violence now, you'll be going without the blessing of the Church.'

Dermot glared defiantly at the priest. 'Then so be it, Father. We'll make our plans without involving either you or the Association.'

Chapter Four

When Liam broke the news to his mother that Kathie Donaghue would be helping with the fish-gutting on the quay, Norah McCabe was not pleased.

'I need no one to help me—on the quay or in the fish-cellar. I've done the work for all these years by myself and I'm not old or helpless yet.'

'No one is saying you are, Ma, but we are doing so well with the new boat that I want to find a market for our salted fish in Gorey. If I can do that, we'll need to catch more fish and you'll have to salt more. You'll be glad enough then of the help. Besides, her father has broken his fingers and can't play his fiddle. I'd rather she worked for us than begged for them both.'

'Oh?' Norah McCabe was full of sudden interest. 'And are we to have all the cottiers working for us now to keep them from begging? I can't wait to meet this girl; I think she's bewitched you.'

Liam's growled reply was unintelligible, and Norah McCabe watched him stamp from the house with very mixed feelings. Her son was twenty-seven years of age now and had been the breadwinner in the McCabe family for more than half of his life. He had taken on his responsibilities when a young boy without a protest and she had never heard a complaint from him since. But there had been many nights when Norah McCabe had cried herself to sleep because of his lost childhood. She had suffered agonies whenever the wind freshened while Liam was fishing a mile from land, only a piece of stretched canvas between him and the sea that had taken his father.

She could do nothing to make up for those lost hard days now, but Norah McCabe believed her son deserved something special from life. She was determined that no cottier girl was going to use Liam as a stepping-stone to a comfortable home and a secure future. But, for all her expressed opposition and personal misgivings, Norah McCabe took to Kathie immediately. By the end of the first week, she was a welcome visitor to the McCabe cottage after she had finished her work. Quite often Tommy Donaghue came with her. He kept the whole family amused with his exaggerated stories of incidents he claimed to have witnessed during his travels through Ireland. Since the night of his injury he had not been back to the ale-house and it did Kathie's heart good to see her father again as the man he had once been.

Kathie, too, enjoyed working with Norah McCabe, but most of all she liked to be on the quay with Liam and Dermot when they returned from a day's fishing.

Liam was quiet, almost shy, yet he had such a strength of purpose and a faith in his own ability that Kathie found herself a little in awe of him.

Dermot lacked his brother's seriousness. To Kathie he was fun. His carefree nature deserted him only when Kathie goaded him about the All-Ireland Association.

'One day I'll take you to a meeting,' he declared finally. 'Then we'll see what you have to say when you're there.'

'I'll keep you to that promise,' said Kathie. 'I'm for a free and independent Ireland – and so is my father – but I'm particular about who I have to speak on my behalf. I've never heard Eugene Brennan or Father Clery – only Dermot McCabe – and you don't make a great deal of sense with some of your ideas.'

Then, early in September, came news that temporarily overshadowed even the high aspirations of the All-Ireland Association and its members. Rumours began to circulate that a blight had hit the Irish potato crop. A week later the grim rumour was confirmed.

For anyone not familiar with the Irish economy it would be difficult to understand the seriousness of such a situation. Even the English Government was slow to accept the stark truth.

In Ireland, the vast majority of farm labourers were not employed on a regular wage-earning basis. Indeed, the majority of farms were too small to support a labourer. Instead, in return for work in the appropriate seasons, farmers and landowners would grant a plot of land to a man and his family, for an agreed rent. On his small plot the cottier would build a tiny cottage and plant potatoes over the whole of the remaining land. Often it was not suitable for any other crop, but from this tiny patch of land a man had to feed his family for the whole year with sufficient potatoes left over to sell to pay the rent. This unsatisfactory system was spread over the length and breadth of Ireland, and in 1845 at least three million people depended entirely upon the potato. If it failed, they starved. The economics of the matter were as starkly simple as that.

And, in 1845, the potato crop failed.

It was almost a total failure, the tubers rotting as they were brought above ground. Soon the once pure air of Ireland was fouled with the stench of rotting potatoes, and death beckoned every man, woman and child in the countryside.

To the fishermen of Kilmar, the blight made little difference, at first. The begging of the cottiers lasted longer than usual, and they were unable to exchange fish for potatoes, that was all.

Then, starving thousands from inland made their way to the coast and crowded the quay when the fishing boats came in. Women and children begged for every scrap of the fish, and even heads and guts were scooped up hungrily. More serious to the fishermen was the thieving. If a fisherman were foolish enough to turn his back on a basket of fish, it would be emptied by the time he looked at it again.

In the village itself a host of homeless hungry cottiers roamed the narrow streets. Children, dirty, ragged, barefooted and bewildered, clung to the tattered dresses of their mothers, all respectable clothing long since sold or pawned for food. Starving families would 'adopt' a fisherman's household and squat for hours outside the back door, hoping someone would come out and empty a few scraps of food on the ground for them.

For the cottier life became a deadly duel with death and all over the land he was the loser.

As winter approached, the situation became even more desperate. The worst gales for years hit the coasts of Ireland, and for weeks even the McCabe and Feehan boats were unable to put to sea. Gradually, the cottiers drifted away from the village, hopelessly seeking food elsewhere.

The winds blew mainly from the north, and some days the people of Kilmar saw the sails of great merchantmen and passenger-ships from Canada and America, blown miles off course, seeking an Irish landfall to set themselves back on course for Liverpool, or making for an Irish port until the storms blew themselves out.

One evening, Liam was in the house with the rain lashing against the rattling windows when there was a sudden pounding on the door. Before he could rise to his feet the door crashed open and a number of young boys spilled into the room. One of them, the son of a fisherman drowned in a storm two years before, picked himself up and said excitedly, 'Mr McCabe! There are wreckers out along the hill a way. Me mam said I should come and tell you about it.'

'Wreckers?' Liam was on his feet reaching for his waterproof coat in an instant. 'Are you sure?'

'We've seen them,' answered one of the other boys, his wet hair hanging about his face. 'They've got a fire going, and lanterns – and there's a ship out there.'

'Get down to the ale-house and call out all the men you can find. Tell them I'm going up the hill to find out who it is.'

'Liam, take care. . . .'

Norah McCabe's cry was snatched away by the wind as Liam ran out into the night, shrugging on his coat as he went.

Once clear of the houses the storm gathered new strength and, head down and leaning into the wind, Liam was upon the would-be wreckers before he saw them. Their fire was not large, but to the captain of a storm-tossed ship, trying desperately to find a haven, it might easily have been mistaken for the Arklow beacon, some miles to the north – and that was exactly what had happened. A large passenger-ship was edging closer in toward the coast.

Beside the fire, two men were standing waving lanterns from side to side with long sweeping movements of their arms, further convincing the stormbound captain that people on shore were aware of his plight and were signalling for him to bring his ship in to safety.

Faces turned toward Liam as he stumbled into the firelight. There must have been at least thirty men, but Liam recognised none of them. From their ragged garb he thought they must be cottiers, starved into desperation.

'What the hell do you think you are doing?' Liam demanded of the men who stood between him and the dancing flames of the fire.

'This is none of your business,' growled one of the men,

and his accent was not that of a Kilmar man. 'Go home and forget you've seen anything. What you don't know about you can't be blamed for.'

'There will be no deliberate wrecking on this part of the coast,' said Liam bluntly. 'We all live too close to death from the sea without bringing it upon others. Put that fire out.'

As he went to push past the man in front of him, others moved forward to bar Liam's way and he knew the time for talking was past. Without more ado, Liam swung his fist at the man nearest to him. The wrecker staggered backward to fall amidst the blazing timbers of the fire, scattering the deadly beacon more effectively than Liam might have done.

The fallen man screamed and rolled clear of the fire, his saturated clothing saving him from serious burns. In the sudden confusion, Liam fought his way through the other men and began kicking out the fire as best he could in the strong wind that kept blowing renewed life back into the scorched wood.

His efforts lasted no more than a few seconds before the wreckers fell upon him and dragged him away.

Liam fought desperately, punching and kicking about him, but he did not see the upraised timber above his head. It was brought down as Liam was in mid-punch, and Liam pitched forward on his face, unconscious before he hit the ground. Blood flowed from a deep gash in his head and the rain sent it coursing along half a dozen paths down his face as he lay upon the ground.

To the wreckers it seemed he must be dead, but it did not prevent the man he had knocked in the fire from kicking the prostrate Liam viciously in the ribs with heavy iron-tipped boots and cursing him for his interference.

Fortunately, the vanguard of the fishermen called from the ale-house arrived at that moment and fighting broke out all around the remains of the fire.

The battle did not last for long. As more fishermen reached the scene, the foiled wreckers disengaged themselves and fled into the night.

Out at sea, just beyond the reef, the bewildered captain of the passenger-vessel and his look-outs had watched the shadowy figures battling in front of the fire before it was finally extinguished. Realising that something was seriously amiss, the captain put his ship about, his shouts goading the seamen to unaccustomed speed as the large sailing ship heeled over, every timber groaning, and headed out to sea, missing the waiting reef by less than two fathoms.

'Someone bring a lantern over here – quickly!'

Dermot kneeled beside the still body of his brother, cradling his blood-soaked head in his arms. When a lantern arrived and was held down toward Liam, Dermot sucked air through his teeth noisily. The wound was serious, and Liam's pale face was an indication of how much blood he had already lost.

'One of you run with all speed to the village. Get Bridie O'Keefe to our house and prepare my mother. A couple of you help me to lift Liam up. Come on, hurry! God help us all if it's a corpse we carry in through the door.'

Chapter Five

Liam lay unconscious on a bed in the McCabe kitchen for six days. Bridie O'Keefe was a frequent visitor to the house, forcing medicine down his throat and applying foul-smelling poultices to the slow-healing wound in his head. As the bruises came out on his body the full extent of the beating he had taken became apparent, but Bridie O'Keefe assured his distraught mother that he had no broken bones.

About the main wound she was not so certain. The old woman shook her ugly head and muttered aloud to herself in the ancient language still used by some of the older folk in more remote corners of Ireland. To Norah McCabe, the old crone expressed confidence that Liam would survive.

'But I will not say that he will return to us with all his senses,' she added gloomily. 'He's taken a blow hard enough to make a simpleton of the strongest of men.'

Fortunately, the strange old healer's gloomy prediction proved ill-founded. Liam regained consciousness late in the evening of the sixth day. At first he found it difficult to focus his eyes upon anything. Then the haze in front of them cleared, his bruised brain co-ordinated his senses, and he realised where he was. Turning his head, he saw his mother bending over the peat fire, stirring a fish stew that bubbled noisily in a large black cauldron.

He made three attempts to speak before a hoarse croak escaped from his throat. The painful sound caused Norah McCabe to turn around sharply. When she saw his eyes were open she dropped the ladle she was holding and rushed to her son's bedside.

'Liam! Oh, thank God you've come through. . . .'

Liam ran the tip of his tongue over his dry lips and gave his mother a weak grin.

Tears sprang into Norah McCabe's eyes as she laid a hand gently against his face.

'You've had us worried sick, Liam. Dreadfully worried. But the Lord heard me, and I thank Him for it.'

She took her hand away before the tears of relief overwhelmed her and she made a fool of herself. Moving to more familiar ground she said, 'And now I suppose you'll be wanting something to eat?'

His mother had to hold him up in the bed in order to feed him, but Liam emptied a full bowl of soup before sinking back gratefully to the comfort of his pillow, his head as noisy as an anvil in a busy smithy.

'What am I doing down here?' Liam's tongue felt thick and lazy, but the words were intelligible.

'Bridie O'Keefe said I was to keep you in the warm. Besides, Kathie has your room. We've been taking turns in sitting up with you all night.'

Events of the past were slowly dropping into place, and the mention of Kathie jogged many memories. The thought of her living under the same roof and sitting by his bedside all night brought a warm feeling of pleasure to Liam. But he also remembered that he had responsibilities.

'The fishing . . . ? What's happening?'

'Hush, now! There's nothing for you to fret about. You get yourself well again before you begin to worry about any fishing. Tommy Donaghue is helping Dermot with the boat. Sure, he's a landsman, but he's willing. He's learning well, and the exercise is good for his poor fingers.' Tommy Donaghue's fingers had healed, but one of them would be permanently crooked and he would never be quite the fiddler he had once been.

'The two of them are catching enough for us to eat and I've been salting some away.'

Liam relaxed. The thought of the little old fiddler out in a boat, fishing, amused him, but he knew Tommy Donaghue was a willing enough worker.

'Where is Dermot now?'

'He's away to a meeting of his association – and Kathie has gone with him.'

'A woman at an Association meeting?' It was unheard of in Kilmar.

'Dermot says there is no rule against it. He has heard that women go to meetings regularly in Dublin.'

'This isn't Dublin,' commented Liam. 'But I don't suppose any harm will come from it. If Kathie keeps quiet, she'll hardly be noticed.'

Norah McCabe gave him a quick smile. 'Kathie isn't a girl to stand by and keep quiet. If she disagrees with what they are saying, she'll tell them so. Her tongue is often ahead of her thinking; it's a fault she shares with her father – though I'm saying nothing against either of them. Kathie is a good girl. I don't know how I'd have managed without her. Tommy has done his best, too, bless him, but he's a better fiddler than he is a fisherman.'

Liam hardly heard his mother's comments about Tommy Donaghue. His mind was conjuring up pictures of Kathie standing at Dermot's side at an Association meeting. The thought made his head ache more than ever, and he was glad when Bridie O'Keefe arrived to cluck over his return to consciousness and give him a draught of evil-tasting medicine that put him back to sleep once more.

The All-Ireland Association meeting was being held by torch- and lantern-light in the clearing behind the old salting-house. It had been called as a routine meeting to give the members details of the progress of the fund to help Eugene Brennan.

The Association members formed a large loose-knit group in the centre of the clearing. Outside the lamp-light, drawn there by curiosity and the lack of anything else to do, were a number of cottiers from inland. They stood in a shadowy silence, the only sound from them an occasional hollow tubercular cough.

Father Clery opened the meeting, and the usual routine was followed until it was time to ask if there was any other business to be brought before the meeting.

'Yes.'

The voice was Eoin Feehan's. He stood in the crowd somewhere behind Dermot and Kathie.

'There is someone here who is not a member of this association. She should be removed before the meeting goes on.'

As Kathie was the only woman present there could be no doubt to whom Eoin Feehan was referring.

'I have a better idea,' Dermot called above the buzz of excitement that had been set off by Eoin Feehan's words. 'I propose that Kathie Donaghue be made a member of this association.'

Every man attending the meeting turned to look at him, and Dermot defended his proposal.

'There's nothing unusual about a woman member. There are any number of them in Dublin – and a few in Wexford Town, so I've been told.'

'That may be so.' Father Clery cleared his throat noisily. 'But she would be the first here in Kilmar. Is there a seconder for the motion?'

'Yes.' The clear young voice of Sean Feehan rose from where he was standing beside his father and brother. 'I second the motion.'

'May I take it you are a dissenter, Eoin Feehan?' Father Clery asked.

'He was keen enough to get me here a while ago,' said Kathie to Dermot in a whisper loud enough to be heard by most of the men attending the meeting. There was a roar of laughter from the fishermen, who were aware of the argument that had taken place on the quay.

Eoin Feehan flushed angrily, and his father, frowning at his younger son's support for Dermot McCabe, called, 'And I'm against allowing a Protestant woman to join this association, too. We'll have a vote on it, if you don't mind, Father.'

'Very well. Will all those members against the motion please raise their hands?'

Five men supported the Feehan father and son.

'Now, those in favour?'

A forest of arms waved above the crowd.

'Welcome to the All-Ireland Association, Kathie Donaghue.'

'Heaven help us, we'll be having children joining us next,' growled Tomas Feehan and he spat at the ground, not looking at his son Sean.

The younger men of Kilmar crowded about Kathie, offering their noisy congratulations until Father Clery called the meeting to order and announced that they would proceed with Association business.

For another half-hour the meeting continued uneventfully. Father Clery had just ended a stirring speech stressing the need for patience, reiterating Eugene Brennan's call for restraint in their dealings with the English, when a tall broad-shouldered man stepped from beyond the perimeter of burning torches. Wearing tattered knee-breeches and a buttonless shirt, he carried a soft-brimmed hat respectfully in his hands and walked forward to stand before the Kilmar priest.

'Excuse me, Father. May I have a word with you?'

'This is a meeting we are holding here. Will your business wait a while?'

'No, Father. I would like what I have to say to be heard by everyone here tonight.'

His voice was surprisingly soft for such a big man, and Kathie had to strain to hear him above the fidgeting of the crowd.

'This *is* a meeting of the All-Ireland Association?' Without waiting for a reply, the newcomer continued, 'Does that name mean what it implies, Father? Or is it just a name given to a fishermen's association?'

He had said enough to arouse the little priest's interest. 'It means exactly what it says. It is an association for every Irishman.'

'Then will you tell me why you are talking about nothing more important than spending money on posters to hand out in Wexford Town? Eugene Brennan has been put in prison unjustly – no one would argue with you about that – but he is being well fed there. Don't you know that only a mile or two from here women and children are dying from hunger? Their menfolk have no work and little hope for the future. Does no one care at all about them, Father? Will you leave them out there to die like animals?'

'Do you deserve any better when you cottiers behave like wild animals?'

Tomas Feehan pushed his way to the front of the crowd and stood facing the tattered man. 'Your people came here and tried to lure a ship on to the rocks only a week ago. Did you have the same concern for the women and children passengers on board? You weren't content to let them die on a stormy sea; you tried to wreck the ship and make *certain* they died. Whatever Father Clery might say, this is an association for *responsible* men – and to me that means *fishermen*.'

'I don't know anything about this incident you are talking about, so I don't know whether the men involved were cottiers. It was a terrible thing to have happened, a terrible thing – but so is the great hunger that is upon us. If you were to ask me whether I would kill a fellow-man in order to save the lives of my own children, then I could only answer, in all truthfulness, "Yes, I would". And I would offer my own life for the same cause. Wouldn't you, sir?'

Tomas Feehan was man enough to realise that this unknown peasant had destroyed his own argument with his complete honesty and he was grateful when Father Clery came to his rescue.

'I don't think I have seen you about Kilmar before. What is your name?'

'Nathan Brock, Father.'

Father Clery took another careful look at the big man standing before him, eyeing the broad shoulders and bulging arm muscles. 'Nathan Brock the prizefighter?'

The big cottier acknowledged the question with a quick nod of his head. 'The same, Father. But I had to give up fighting when I did this.'

He held up his left hand, and the priest saw that the third and fourth fingers were missing.

'What are you doing here? You are not a County Wexford man.'

'That's quite true, Father. I had a small piece of land and a cottage up in the Wicklow mountains, but I was owing rent when the potato crop failed. I was put out by the landlord and my cottage torn down. I was left with a wife and three children and nothing with which to feed, clothe or house them. My youngest, the little girl, died of a chest cough, but I've managed to get the others in a poor-house while I look for work and a place where they can join me.'

'Wouldn't it have been better for you to stay in Wicklow where you are known, rather than come so far from home?'

Nathan Brock's impassive face showed a trace of sadness. 'No. You see, my daughter meant a great deal to me. When she died I was mad with grief. I went looking for my ex-landlord – and I found him. My left hand isn't what it once was, but there is nothing wrong with my right. I broke a bone or two, so County Wicklow is no place for Nathan Brock for a while.'

'No, indeed. The law is a remorseless force when it is used to protect the landlords. But come home with me after the meeting. I'll give you a meal and we will talk some more.'

'Is that all the members of this Association ever do – talk?'

Kathie pushed her way to the front of the crowd and, after a moment's hesitation, Dermot followed her.

'Nathan Brock is quite right. You – every one of you – believe that Ireland begins and ends right here in Kilmar. You come to your meetings and find fine words behind which you can hide. Maybe this is what Eugene Brennan has taught you. I don't know. But I do know that when I walk out of this village I am still in Ireland and among Irish people. You heard what Nathan Brock said. There are women and children out there dying. What are you going to do about it?'

Kathie glared about her defiantly, but no one answered.

'All right, I'll give you a chance to do more than talk. I'm coming round to make a collection to buy food for starving Irish women and Irish children – and I don't expect anyone to be mean.'

Kathie turned to Nathan Brock. 'I'll need something in which to collect the money. Give me your hat.'

The big ex-prizefighter passed his hat to her without a word, and Kathie moved away into the crowd.

'Dermot McCabe, did you know you were introducing a virago to the Association this night?' Father Clery rubbed his round chin ruefully. 'I fear the Association will never be the same again!'

'There are many who will say it should have changed long ago, Father. There's a time for talking, and a time for action. Until now we've done nothing but talk. Now it's time to try something else.'

Liam was awakened by the sound of laughter and he heard his mother whisper belatedly for Dermot and Kathie to 'Be quiet!' He opened his eyes to see Kathie looking down at him and he smiled.

'Liam, it's good to see you with your eyes open again.' Kathie took one of his hands and drew it to her. 'I despaired of ever having you look at me again.'

Norah McCabe thought there was little fear of that now. Her elder son could hardly take his eyes from the girl.

'Can a brother get a word in and say that he's pleased, too?' Dermot moved to stand beside Kathie and grinned down at Liam. 'You've been a worry to everyone. Now you're back with us perhaps we'll be able to get down to some serious fishing again. Me and Tommy aren't catching enough to keep Kathie busy for more than an hour a day.'

Dermot chuckled. 'You should have been at the Association meeting tonight, Liam. Kathie told them a few home truths. Then she went around and made a collection. Some of the men dug out coins that hadn't seen the light of day for years.'

The smile that passed between Dermot and Kathie hurt Liam far more than the throb of the drum that had begun to beat in his head.

'Did no one object to Kathie being there?'

'How could they? She has been voted in as a full member. Tomas and Eoin Feehan opposed her membership, but the vote went overwhelmingly for Kathie.'

Dermot chuckled again. 'Mind you, I don't think they expected her to come up with such a tongue-lashing as she gave them. Father Clery was flabbergasted. You'll have to come to the next meeting, Liam.'

'Will there be a next time for you?' Norah McCabe asked the girl.

'Oh yes! There is much the Association can do once its members lose the love of their own voices.' Kathie tucked Liam's hand back inside the bedclothes. 'Dermot is right, Liam. You must come to a meeting when you are completely well. I am sure you could do a lot of good there.'

Liam smiled weakly; the sound of voices was beginning to tire him. 'Dermot is the revolutionary in this family. I have to keep my mind on the business.'

A few minutes later Norah McCabe ushered Dermot and Kathie from the kitchen, and before sleep took him Liam could hear Kathie's laughter from the next room. It sounded right in the McCabe home, but Liam wished he was well enough to be able to share her happiness.

Chapter Six

It was two weeks before Liam was sufficiently recovered to resume his place in the boat. By then Kathie had returned to the old cottage on the hillside above the village and the starving cottiers were begging on the quay in their hundreds. For some days after the attempted wrecking the fishermen of Kilmar had been in no mood to tolerate the inland beggars, but time and the pinched faces of the hungry cottier children eventually sapped the fishermen's anger.

In early November the disastrous potato harvest enabled Liam to bring forward his plans to expand his fishing enterprise. He was able to buy a horse and a small cart at a give-away price from a ruined farmer. He paid for it with what little money he possessed and the promise of a season's supply of fish for the farmer's family.

Soon Liam had Tommy Donaghue making a twice-weekly journey with the horse and cart to Gorey, a small town about seven miles distant. There a trader bought all the fish Liam could provide and gave him a very good price.

Tommy Donaghue enjoyed his trips to the market town. The slow-plodding horse needed only an occasional flick of the reins to keep him moving, and Tommy was able to exercise his fingers in practice on his fiddle, serenading the birds and the startled animals of the hedgerow.

Tommy Donaghue had adapted to his new way of life very well. He again spent a couple of evenings a week playing to the customers of Kilmar's ale-house, but now Patrick Meahey paid him in coin instead of drink. Kathie had made her father insist on this, just as she had persuaded him to work for the McCabes. Tommy Donaghue had raised many objections at first. He was a fiddler, a musician, and musicians could not be expected to do menial work. But Kathie had accepted none of his arguments and, once he had started, he was forced to admit that he quite enjoyed himself. Riding along behind a slow-moving horse gave a man time to think about life. To remember what had been, and to ponder upon the future. It was the future, Kathie's future, about which he was most concerned.

She had reached an age when most girls were already married. Kathie gave no hint that she was ready to settle down yet, but her friendship with the McCabe boys had raised Tommy's hopes. The trouble was, he did not know which of them she would settle for. The girl spent a lot of time with Dermot, perhaps because he was more her own age, but Tommy Donaghue had never seen her look at him the way she looked at Liam. Yes, he thought it would probably be Liam, and she could not have made a wiser choice. Liam had a good head on his shoulders and would make a fine son. He was also good-looking enough to keep the interest of a young girl.

These were the thoughts that were going through Tommy Donaghue's mind as he rode the last couple of miles to Gorey on one of his regular trips, when suddenly a man rose from the tangled grass beside the road and stepped out in front of the horse.

The startled fiddler heaved on the reins and brought the horse to a halt only inches away from a large man he remembered seeing on a number of occasions about Kilmar.

'What do you think you are doing?' he asked angrily. 'You came mighty close to being knocked down by the horse.'

'I'm sorry if I startled you,' said Nathan Brock easily. 'But I stopped you because I am in need of a small donation from you.'

'If you're a robber, then you've stopped the wrong man,' said Tommy Donaghue. 'I've not a penny in my pockets and nothing but salt fish on the cart.'

'Salt fish will be manna from heaven for some people I would like you to see,' replied Nathan Brock. 'Will you come no more than half a mile out of your way to meet them?'

'The fish doesn't belong to me.' Tommy Donaghue was alarmed at the prospect of leaving the main road in the company of this large man. He seemed mild-mannered enough, but Tommy Donaghue had met quiet villains before. 'Besides, I'm late already.'

'The McCabes are reasonable men . . . and Gorey won't run away while you are with me. Are you coming, now?'

Tommy Donaghue shrugged. He really had no choice. He had put up a token argument, but if Nathan Brock had made up his mind, then he would have to go along with him.

'I'll lead the way,' said Nathan Brock. 'I appreciate your co-operation.'

It was a long half-mile along a bumpy track that rattled Tommy Donaghue's teeth and made the asking of questions impossible. The track ended in a mud-hard clearing, around which were built six sod huts. There was a disgusting smell in the air and it took Tommy Donaghue only a few moments to locate its source in heaps of putrid potatoes, liquefying in the small fields around the clearing.

There was no sound from the mean hovels and there was such a forlorn neglected look about the place that Tommy Donaghue eyed his companion uneasily, wondering why he had brought him here. Without a word, Nathan Brock strode to the door of the first sod house and beckoned for Tommy Donaghue to follow him.

There were no windows in the building, and it was a moment or two after he had stepped over the threshold before Tommy Donaghue's eyes became accustomed to the gloom. He immediately wished he could have remained blind to the scene he saw before him. Lying upon dirty rags strewn about the floor of the hut were five people, four children and their mother. Each of them was no more than a skin-covered skeleton with ugly swollen joints.

'The Lord preserve us! Have they all starved to death?'

'Only one of them,' replied Nathan Brock grimly. 'The others are still dying.'

Tommy Donaghue took a step closer to the emaciated bodies, and the eyes of two of the children followed him. The others continued to stare blankly at the turf roof of the hut above them and he could not tell which one of them was dead.

'Why are they so quiet?' The silence and the unreality of the whole situation caused him to talk in a hoarse whisper. 'Why aren't they crying out with pain . . . hunger . . . anything?'

'Crying demands strength. I doubt if they have enough energy to both cry and live. And what is crying but a call for help? These people have learned that there is no help for them – or there wasn't, until you came along.'

'But the fish doesn't belong to me. . . .' Tommy Donaghue's glance fell on the emaciated bodies and he found himself looking into the eyes of one of the children. 'How much fish do you want?'

'One small barrel will be enough to put life back into these bodies for a few days.'

Tommy Donaghue looked at Nathan Brock in consternation. A small barrel contained a large quantity of fish, even for a family as starved as this one.

'There are more cottiers in the other cabins,' explained Nathan Brock. 'Many of them children.'

'I'll get the barrel and start a fire going,' said Tommy Donaghue. 'Find me a pot from somewhere and we'll soon put some life back in these poor souls.' The old fiddler was clearly shaken at the thought of there being still more people so near to death.

'No, you've done your part. Drop off the barrel and I'll attend to the rest. Go on to Gorey about your business; then return to Kilmar and tell the McCabes what I've done. I'll come in to see them tonight.'

The big man put a heavy hand upon Tommy Donaghue's shoulder. 'You'll remember what you've seen here today, but cottiers are dying from starvation all over Ireland. These were luckier than most, even before you came along. They are at least dying with a roof over their heads.'

Eugene Brennan's long-delayed trial was staged without any prior warning to the accused man. Breakfast was brought to the County Wexford MP at the usual time, but only half an hour later a key grated in the heavy cell-lock and a flustered deputy governor entered. He informed Eugene Brennan that his trial had been fixed for that day.

It was no use arguing that he needed more time to prepare to go into court. He had already been waiting for months. Besides, the deputy governor of the the prison had received his orders direct from the Lord-Lieutenant of Ireland. He could do nothing but obey them.

For the same reason, the protests of Eugene Brennan's barrister were equally unavailing. The judge cut his arguments short and curtly informed him that there had been sufficient time for him to prepare a defence. The trial would proceed as arranged.

But the unhelpful judge was unable to prevent the barrister from exercising his right to challenge prospective jurors. The procedure brought some angry exchanges between judge and barrister, but the beginning of the trial was delayed sufficiently long enough for the defence to round up most of its witnesses.

The case lasted for two days and drew to a close with a summing-up by the judge weighted heavily against the man in the dock.

Now came the proof that Eugene Brennan's barrister had picked his jurors with more success than he realised. The 'twelve good men, and true' retired from the court-room for no longer than twenty minutes before filing back and announcing their verdict.

They found Eugene Brennan 'Not guilty' of the charges against him.

So unexpected was the acquittal that the prosecution was stunned and the judge furious. But justice had been seen to be done, and Eugene Brennan left the dock a free man.

His followers were exultant – and there were a great many of them in Dublin. Within minutes the news had spilled into the streets and was being shouted above the street noises of Ireland's capital city. Workers downed tools and flocked to the law-courts to cheer the good news, and Irish housewives forsook their baking and followed their menfolk.

By the time the County Wexford MP left the court-building, traffic in the vicinity had been brought to halt by the cheering throng. Not all Dubliners supported Brennan and his All-Ireland Association, but this was more than the acquittal of an innocent man. It was a victory for Ireland in her fight against England. The English Government had ordered Brennan's arrest and trial. An Irish jury had set him free. Eugene Brennan was the hero of the day.

It was impossible for the MP to pass through the crowd, and the constabulary could do nothing to make the people move. Eventually, he made a speech from the steps in front of the court-building. It was a rambling, sometimes feeble speech. The voice that of a tired old man overcome by emotion. It did not matter; the cheers would have drowned his words whatever was said. When the applause reached fever pitch, Eugene Brennan went back inside the court-building and was smuggled out of a door at the rear of the cell-block.

The months spent in prison, followed by the strain of the last two days, had taken their toll on the old politician, and he did not feel he could face the rigours of parliamentary life in

London immediately. Yet he knew that if he stayed in Dublin the All-Ireland Association would place him under an even greater strain. They would want to capitalise on his current popularity and have him address committees and meetings and giant outdoor gatherings.

All Eugene Brennan wanted was to be able to rest and relax for a while. To cast off the burden of his country's problems and enjoy just being an old man. The feeling would only last for a few weeks. By then he would be ready once more to lead his country out of the union with England.

Seeking a refuge, Eugene Brennan's thoughts turned to his lifelong friend, Father Clery, and the peaceful fishing village of Kilmar.

Chapter Seven

Kilmar was little more than fifty miles south of Dublin. Eugene Brennan arrived in the late afternoon of a sombre November day, after a tiring ride in his own carriage. But he found little of the peace he was seeking.

Tommy Donaghue had returned to the fishing village only a few minutes earlier, and Liam had not yet recovered from the initial anger he felt at the news that Nathan Brock had appropriated some of his fish. Father Clery was quickly drawn into the argument, and tempers had not cooled when the old MP arrived on the scene.

When the excitement caused by the news of Eugene Brennan's acquittal had died away, the politician asked the cause of the angry scene he had just witnessed. He listened in silence during Tommy Donaghue's explanation and his description of the appalling state of the cottiers.

'Could you find this place again?'

'I could. And if I got lost my nose would lead me to those cabins.'

'Then climb up with my coachman and guide him there. You had better come with us, Matthew – and you, young man.' He pointed to Liam and then looked at Kathie, who was standing beside him. 'Who are you?'

'Kathie Donaghue – and a member of your association.'

Eugene Brennan smiled fleetingly. 'That singles you out as a girl of sound sense. Come with us. We may have need of you.'

After making it clear early in the journey that he was not a member of Brennan's association, Liam said very little. Father Clery, on the other hand, was eager to hear every detail of Eugene Brennan's remarkable acquittal and the two older men remained deep in conversation until the carriage turned on to the rough track leading to the collection of cottier huts and talk became almost impossible.

Nathan Brock was in the clearing, squatting before a fire on which stood a huge pot-bellied saucepan exuding steam and a strong smell of boiling fish. Propped up against the wall of a hut on one side of the fire were three children, their heads appearing abnormally large on their skeleton-thin bodies. On the far side of the clearing six newly dug graves of varying sizes, topped by rough-tied wooden crosses, testified to the ex-prizefighter's industry.

In answer to a question from Father Clery, Nathan Brock waved wearily toward the nearby huts.

'Go and see for yourself, Father. If I have to dig graves for less than half of those who are left, it will be a miracle.'

The whole party from the carriage went on a tour of inspection of the huts and Liam returned to the fire shaken by the scenes of suffering and squalor, all thoughts of his missing fish completely forgotten.

'How can such a thing happen?' he asked of no one in particular. 'Only a few miles away there are fish in the sea for the taking and beyond Gorey the corn is still stacked in the fields. How is it that people can starve to death in this way?'

'They are starving because the potato has failed and many of these cottiers have never eaten anything else. They wouldn't know how to set about catching a fish and they have no money to buy any. Besides, all the fishermen in Ireland couldn't catch enough to keep the cottiers alive. As for the corn, it's being shipped out of the country to make a profit for the landlords. They have never cared that much for the cottiers.' Nathan Brock snapped his fingers angrily. 'Go to Wexford harbour and you'll see corn being brought in from the countryside guarded by troops to prevent starving cottiers from getting at it.'

'But the whole thing is scandalous. Something must be done to help these people.'

Nathan Brock shrugged his shoulders. 'What do you suggest – that everyone follows my example and steals for them? They certainly can't do very much for themselves. As you will have noticed, there are only women and children here. Their men are in Dublin, or in the north, seeking work. There isn't a poor-house in this part of Wexford, and the Government in England has yet to be convinced there is a famine in Ireland. For the rest of it you'll need to speak to your All-Ireland Association friend. He is the one who sits in the Parliament in London and knows what is going on in their minds.'

Eugene Brennan returned to the fire in time to hear Nathan Brock's last words.

'Do you know of any more cottiers in a similar plight to these poor people here?'

'I could take you to many who are worse off, but unless you can take food with you it would be better to spare you the agony of watching them die. Three miles from here two cottier families were unable to pay their rents because disease had taken their potato crop. They were dragged from their homes, too weak to stand, and left to die by the side of the road while the landlord's men put torches to their houses.'

'I can do little about the power of the landlords,' said Eugene Brennan. 'But while Irish women and children are dying of starvation I can make damn sure that the conscience of the English Government never rests easy.'

'The mother of a dying child will surely thank you for that,' said Nathan Brock so evenly that not one of his listeners could be certain he was being sarcastic. 'But stop corn from being exported and have it distributed to those in need and she'll give you her blessing, too.'

'Supply me with facts and Parliament will have them,' promised the MP.

To Father Clery he said, 'I've changed my mind about staying, Matthew. I must go to London and get relief action under way immediately.'

Eugene Brennan turned to Liam. 'Can you promise the support of your fellow-fishermen in helping to feed these poor people? I'll call a meeting of the Association before I go and see what money can be raised toward the cost involved.'

'It's late in the year and there will be few fishing days during the next few months. Only the Feehans' boat and my own can put to sea for most of the winter. But I'll come to your meeting and speak to the fishermen myself. I can promise you they will not allow women and children to die if fish will keep them alive – and it will be given without payment.'

'I wish our people were always as ready to solve the country's problems,' said Eugene Brennan despondently. 'Will you come back to Kilmar and arrange a meeting for us, Matthew?'

Father Clery looked about him and wrung his hands helplessly. 'I should stay here. . . .'

'You can pray for them as well from Kilmar,' said Nathan

Brock. 'Organising a meeting to provide food is something no one else can do. I'll stay here with them for tonight. Perhaps by the morning one or two of the women will be feeling stronger and can give me some help.'

'I'll stay here with you,' said Kathie firmly. 'And so will my father.'

'The matter appears to be settled,' said Eugene Brennan. 'Now I think we should go. I am impatient to return to London and put this matter before the Prime Minister. I will not allow him to use death by starvation as a means of solving his government's Irish problem.'

The hurriedly called All-Ireland Association meeting was held in the Kilmar ale-house late that same night. News of Eugene Brennan's presence had travelled fast and the room was packed to capacity with many of the latecomers standing outside in the roadway, listening at the open windows to what was being said. A good speech was expected and their Member of Parliament did not disappoint them. He produced all the fire and forcefulness that some of his followers had secretly feared he had lost for ever. Eugene Brennan castigated a government that ruled from beyond the sea and allowed its people to die of starvation. The fiery politician promised his audience that, while he had breath left in his body, he would fight the injustice that allowed the Irish people to be treated as a conquered people.

One day, he said, their country would control her own destiny and not have to rely upon uncertain charity to keep their fellow countrymen and women alive. Then Eugene spoke of the plight of the cottiers, starving in the fields and hills around them. He begged the fishermen of Kilmar to help them in every way possible and called upon Liam to tell them of what he had seen.

Liam gave the grim details without embellishment, a fisherman talking to fishermen. He spoke of the skin-covered skeletons that were children. Of dried-up mothers holding dying babies to their emaciated breasts. Of those in pain, yet without the strength to cry. He spoke of shallow graves and unlettered crosses that were all the cottiers could look forward to at the end of their miserable lives.

As Liam spoke, the picture of the mean huts and their occupants rose before him to haunt him as it would for the remainder of his life – even though he would see far worse sights before the famine ended.

Every fisherman in Kilmar promised to contribute a portion of his catch. Tomas Feehan was one of them, even though he knew he and Liam would be expected to contribute more than the others.

'You speak well,' Eugene Brennan complimented Liam when the meeting ended. 'You have simplicity and honesty, the very things a seasoned politician lacks. Would you come and speak at some of the public meetings I arrange in aid of the cottiers' relief fund?'

'Come where – to Dublin?' Liam was startled by the suggestion; he had never travelled beyond the borders of County Wexford.

'No – to London.'

When Liam was quite certain the MP was serious, he said, 'Why would Englishmen want to listen to anything I have to say?'

'Because you have first-hand knowledge of a tragedy that will make the headlines of every English newspaper before I am done. You tell them what you have just told the men of Kilmar and they will empty their pockets for you.'

Liam was far from convinced. 'I'd probably get tongue-tied at seeing so many people I didn't know and end up by making a fool of myself, and you.'

Eugene Brennan looked at Liam's broad shoulders and dark good looks and thought of the women's meetings at which he would introduce him. For a moment he had an uncharacteristic twinge of conscience. This innocent young fisherman would stand no chance against the sophisticated women of London. Quickly the MP pushed such thoughts to the back of his mind. The cottiers' plight was desperate. He would raise money for them in every way possible.

'Neither of us will look fools and you will be helping to save hundreds of lives. Can I take it that you will come?'

Liam sensed that he was being backed into a corner from which there was no escape. 'But I'm a fisherman, not a speaker. I have a living to make.'

'Me and Tommy Donaghue managed quite well while you were lying injured. We'd do it again. Anyway, there's little enough fishing can be done in winter – you've said so yourself.' Dermot had been listening to the conversation enviously. He wished such a chance would come his way.

'We wouldn't go out in normal times,' agreed Liam. 'But we'll need to brave the weather if we are to feed hungry cottiers. No, Mr Brennan, I'll be of more use to you staying here and catching fish rather than trying to do something that is best left to others.'

'Come to London and you'll bring in enough money to feed more cottiers than all the fishermen in Kilmar. You'll come, Liam. You'll come because the thought of all those starving people won't allow you to do otherwise. But first I would like you to do something else for me. Go to Inch House and tell the Earl what you have seen. Say I asked you to call on him. If he could possibly provide work for a few of the cottier men, it would help.'

The thought of calling upon the greatest land-owner in this corner of County Wexford was almost as alarming as going to London, but Liam could hardly refuse.

'Good man!' Eugene Brennan clasped Liam's hand warmly. 'I think the cottiers might have found the champion they so desperately need. I will send for you to come to London just as soon as I have arranged a few meetings. In the meantime ask Nathan Brock to take you to visit more cottiers. It won't be pleasant but it should convince you of the need to help them and give you facts to shock more money from the purses of the ladies of England. Now, if you will forgive me, I must go to Father Clery's house and take some rest. I intend making an early start and I fear the excitement of the last few days is catching up with me.'

Walking home with Liam through the darkness, Dermot could not hide the envy he felt for his brother.

'There must be half a million men in Ireland who would do anything for Eugene Brennan and he chooses you. Why, you're not even a member of the Association.'

'Perhaps that's *why* he picked me,' said Liam thoughtfully. 'Eugene Brennan has just spent months in prison because he leads your association. That means it is not popular with the English Government. He needs someone from outside to help raise money for the cottiers. If he used one of you, he could be accused of trying to increase the Association's popularity among the cottiers. Once labelled as a political move his relief fund would be doomed.'

Dermot did not fully follow Liam's thinking, but he was acutely aware that, while his brother helped Eugene Brennan in England, the Association in Ireland would be doing nothing. He became more determined than ever to do something to enhance the Association's flagging prestige.

It needed to be a bold and imaginative scheme.

An action to prove to every Irishman that the Association had the strength and ability to carry their hopes for the future.

Chapter Eight

Walking between the high stone pillars at the entrance to Inch House, Liam was regretting his promise to visit the Earl of Inch on Eugene Brennan's behalf and it came as a great relief to him when the lodge-keeper informed him that the Earl was away.

'You won't find his Lordship at home very often,' the man volunteered. 'Things is much more exciting in those foreign parts. Why, I remember when I was in France with the Duke of Wellington—'

Liam hastily interrupted the man's reminiscing. He had no wish to be treated to the campaign experiences of a garrulous lodge-keeper.

'Who is in charge of the estate in the absence of the Earl?'

'Ah now! Had you asked me that a week ago I could have told you straight away. It would have been his estate manager. But he's gone now . . . dismissed. And not before time, either. Living better than the Earl himself, he was. I suppose the person in charge now would be Lady Caroline, his Lordship's sister.'

'Then I will go and see her,' said Liam impatiently.

'I'm not so sure I should let you go up to the Great House,' said the lodge-keeper, gnawing his lip in an agony of indecision. 'The last thing his Lordship said to me was that no one was to go up to the house I wasn't sure about. "There's a lot of good-for-nothing beggars about", he said. Not that I'm saying you're a beggar,' the lodge-keeper hastened to add as he saw Liam's chin go up. 'I can see that plain enough, but I don't know you, and I have a job to do.'

'I was asked to call on the Earl by Eugene Brennan,' said Liam, with far more patience than he felt.

'I don't know no Eugene Brennan. I'm not sure his Lordship does,' said the lodge-keeper ponderously. 'He certainly hasn't come visiting through these gates.'

'Then I expect they met in Dublin, or London. Eugene Brennan is the Member of Parliament for County Wexford.'

'Is he, now? Ah, then that must be where they've met. His

Lordship is often across in London, at the House of Lords. Are you a friend of this Mr Brennan?' He looked curiously at Liam's rough-cut Sunday-best serge suit.

'No – but it doesn't matter. I'll go up to the house and make my explanations to Lady Caroline.'

'Just a minute! I'll come up there with you.' The lodge-keeper was offended. 'It's not that I'm trying to keep you out, but I have a responsibility here, you know.'

Liam said nothing and set off along the treed driveway. The lodge-keeper, struggling into his coat, caught up with him a hundred yards farther on.

The great house was a truly magnificent building, and Liam counted no fewer than forty-two windows at the front of the house alone. There were terraced lawns, each separated from the other by a stone balustrade, and a profusion of shrubs and trees such as Liam had never seen before. For a few moments, Liam was in danger of being completely over-awed by such magnificence. Then he remembered the hovels of the dying cottiers, only a few miles away, and his mood changed. The owner of this house could afford to save the lives of many of the cottiers who would otherwise die.

As the two men approached the house the path divided, and here the lodge-keeper was faced with another dilemma. He was not sure whether he ought to take Liam to the front entrance, or guide him to the tradesmen's entrance at the rear of the house. After two or three surreptitious glances at the fisherman's clothes, the lodge-keeper decided that the rear door would be more appropriate and turning off the main drive he led Liam along a wide path that went past the stables.

Once inside the house, Liam was subjected to more questioning, this time by a haughty English butler who made it plain he thought Liam had no right to be in the house at all. Only when the butler began to question Liam about his business with the Earl did Liam show annoyance. He curtly informed the butler that his business was between Eugene Brennan and the Earl of Inch himself. Since he was not in the house, Liam would pass his message on to the Earl's sister – and to no one else.

Liam was left standing in the servants' hall while the head servant went off to find Lady Caroline. He returned with the news that the Earl's sister would see Liam in the library.

Liam was shown to a magnificent room, two walls of which were filled from floor to ceiling with shelves of leather-bound books. To Liam, the sight was more impressive than his first view of the house itself. Liam had an insatiable appetite for reading, but beyond the family bible and the few dozen ragged books in Father Clery's house there had been little opportunity to satisfy his hunger. He quickly took in the leather-covered chairs in the room, the polished cabinets and the heavy logs burning in the grate on the dog-headed andiron, but once more his attention returned to the books.

Finally, plucking up the courage to take down one of the books from the shelf, Liam chose Bunyan's *The Pilgrim's Progress* and so deeply engrossed did he become in the classic that he did not hear the door open softly behind him.

Lady Caroline Dudley was a woman of about Liam's own age. Tall, slim and blonde, she wore her long hair drawn up on her head, the style showing off to great effect the lines of her delicate features.

'I see you are a great reader, Mr McCabe.' Her voice was softened by just the trace of an Irish accent, and at the sound of it Liam swung around guiltily.

'I – I – I'm sorry, ' he stuttered. 'I don't see many books.'

Liam tried to replace the book without taking his eyes from Lady Caroline. He had been thrown completely off balance by her appearance. If he had thought about the Earl's sister at all, it had been of a vague elderly woman. He was not prepared for a confrontation with someone who was undoubtedly the most beautiful woman he had ever seen in his life and who now stood smiling in gentle amusement at his confusion.

'There is no need to apologise; the books are here to be read – though I doubt whether Edward, my brother, ever takes one from the shelves. Here, allow me.'

Liam's clumsy fumbling had caused the book to drop to the floor, and Lady Caroline bent down to pick it up as Liam did the same. Their head brushed together briefly, and Liam caught the delicate scent of her perfume.

She laughed and, placing the book in its place, crossed the room and sat down in a wide-armed easy-chair, inviting Liam to sit down opposite her.

'I believe you have a message from Eugene Brennan for my

brother? If you care to give it to me, I will ensure it is passed on to him.'

Hesitantly at first, still over-awed by the young woman who sat watching him intently, Liam told his hostess of the potato famine and of the things he had witnessed in the huts of the cottiers. As he told of the misery of the women and children his voice gained in strength and conviction. He forgot the Earl's sister, the tapestries and pictures in the room, the walls of magnificent books. He was carried back to the mud-floored hovels, looking down at living skeletons lying on beds of stinking rags.

When he stopped talking, a heavy silence hung in the room for a long time.

'The whole thing is quite unbelievable,' whispered Lady Caroline at last. 'Are you telling me this state of affairs exists only a few miles away from this house?'

'The potato famine has hit the whole of Ireland. I doubt whether you could travel anywhere in the country without meeting with starving cottiers. We have hundreds of beggars in Kilmar and I've heard there are mobs of a thousand strong scouring the countryside farther inland.'

Lady Caroline stood up abruptly and looked down at Liam. 'What is your interest with the cottiers?'

'Only that of a man who has seen their misery at first hand. I believe they have a right to live and I'm prepared to do my best to see that it is given to them. Eugene Brennan wants me to go to London to help him raise money for the fund he is setting up.'

'You are going?'

Liam nodded, although he had not been sure until this moment.

'How did Eugene Brennan think my brother might help?'

'He suggested the Earl might find work for some of the cottiers on his estate.'

'I see.' Lady Caroline began pacing the room with long boyish strides as she thought.

'Edward has been talking of having a wall built all the way around the estate. I think now would be a good time to have it done.'

She stopped in front of Liam. 'It might also be the right time to build a house on the few hundred acres of the estate belonging to me. Can you send word to the cottiers that work is to be had here?'

'Yes. There is a man who seems to know where every cottier is to be found. I'll tell him.'

'Good. Work can start immediately. Thank you for bringing this matter to my attention, Mr McCabe – but what is your christian name?'

'Liam.'

He was not sure whether he should call her 'Ma'am', or perhaps 'My lady', so he used no form of address, even though it made his words sound more abrupt than he would have wished.

'Liam McCabe.' She said it as though she was thinking aloud. 'It is a good name. How do you earn your living, Liam?'

'I'm a fisherman. I own a wooden boat.'

He immediately wished he had said nothing about his boat. Among Irish fisherman, to say he owned a wooden boat would immediately have raised him above his fellows, made him a man of substance and standing. Here, in such opulent surroundings, it sounded childish and foolish.

'Really? Surely that is most unusual in this area? I thought fishermen still use curraghs.' To Liam's surprise Lady Caroline seemed to know a great deal about fishing. She also knew a great deal about Ireland and asked Liam many questions about Kilmar and life in the surrounding countryside.

At one stage during their conversation Lady Caroline rang the bell and requested the butler to bring a whiskey for Liam. The fisherman saw the shock on the servant's face at the thought of serving him with the Earl's whiskey. But the butler was careful to conceal his feelings from Lady Caroline and the drink was duly produced.

Not until the early gloom of a November evening began to settle over the room did Liam reluctantly announce that he would have to leave. He had an unfamiliar road to travel from Inch House and wished to be closer to Kilmar by the time darkness fell.

'Of course. I should not have kept you talking for so long . . . but it has been such a long time since I had someone interesting with whom to talk. Before you go I would like to give you something for Eugene Brennan's fund. Wait here. I will not be a moment.'

Lady Caroline left the room and returned with a handful of dully gleaming coins.

'Here are twenty guineas. Use them as you will. You may decide to spend them upon the immediate needs of the cottiers around Kilmar. That is for you to decide.'

Liam began to thank her, but she cut his words short.

'It will take more than twenty guineas to see the cottiers through this famine. I will be leaving for London later this week and I will raise what money I can for them among my friends.'

She held out her hand to Liam. 'Perhaps I will see you there. In fact, I insist. You must stay at my London house during your fund-raising. I will ask Eugene Brennan to arrange everything.'

Liam released her soft hand and turned to go, not sure what he should say to her generous offer.

'Liam?'

He turned to see Lady Caroline taking a book from the shelves.

'Here, this is the book you were reading earlier. Take it with you. Bunyan wrote it to be read, not to gather dust on a bookshelf.'

Not until he was well on his way home to Kilmar village did Liam make an interesting discovery. Whenever he thought about Lady Caroline Dudley there was something he had seen in her eyes that bothered him, something that did not accord with the luxury surrounding her. Even when she had smiled it had been there.

Now he realised it was unhappiness. Lady Caroline was a desperately unhappy woman.

Chapter Nine

'Oh Liam! You are so lucky to be going to London. I wish I could come with you. They say it is such a huge city that all the people in Ireland could live there.'

Kathie gave Liam an envious sideways glance.

'So I have heard.'

Liam was doing his best to appear nonchalant, although his stomach muscles contracted uncontrollably every time London was mentioned. He, Kathie and Nathan Brock were riding on his cart, returning from one of the remote cottier settlements. They had delivered food while Kathie attended to the needs of some seriously undernourished women and children.

The previous evening a message had been received from Eugene Brennan. The MP wanted Liam to travel to England the following week and begin the campaign to raise money for the victims of the potato famine.

'Don't be believing all you've heard about London,' said Nathan Brock in his soft voice. 'Sure, it's big enough for a countryman to have trouble breathing there, and it is easy to become lost in its streets, but it is just another place where people live and earn a living.'

'Have you been there, too, Nathan?'

Kathie was on the seat between the two men and she looked up at Nathan Brock in surprise.

'Yes, I've been there.' The big man grinned at his memories and flexed the remaining fingers of his left hand. 'I lost a good purse at Hampstead Heath in 1838, and won a better one at London Fields a year later.'

'Yet here you are with no money at all and your wife and children in a poor-house. What happened to all your winnings?'

The animation left the ex-prizefighter's face and his shoulders drooped as he thought of his family. He had become increasingly concerned about them of late. He had tried to get word to them without success. Very soon he would have to take a chance on being arrested and go to the Rathconard poor-house in County Wicklow to reassure his wife that he was still alive. Hopefully, he would be able to bring them here to County

Wexford. In the meantime, there was much to be done for the cottiers.

He spread his hands wide in a hopeless gesture in answer to Kathie's question.

'What happens to the rain in a puddle when the sun comes out? The money just went. I had many friends and we enjoyed a fine time drinking together. Once I put some money into a business with one of them, but it came to nothing. I was a fighter, not a merchant. I never used to worry overmuch. There were many more years of fighting left in me. I could always earn more money. Then I did this.'

He held out his disfigured hand.

'How did it happen?' Liam flicked the reins casually at the slow-plodding horse. It was the first time the subject of Nathan Brock's missing fingers had come up in conversation.

'I couldn't tell you exactly how – only when. I tried to stop a runaway horse and carriage in Dublin a couple of years back. I managed to get a grip on the reins of the horse but he dragged me along the street with him until the reins broke. I fell under the horse and was knocked silly between the wheels of the carriage. When I sat up the horse and carriage had gone – and so had two of my fingers. Taken off so cleanly a surgeon might have done the job himself. Naturally enough, no one was fool enough to back a one-fisted fighter and that was the end of my prizefighting days.'

Kathie shuddered at the thought of the accident, and Liam became very quiet. Suddenly, a dirty and ragged boy ran out from the tangled hedgerow and stood waving his arms on the road in front of them.

'Hey, mister!' He addressed himself to Liam. 'Will you come and help my mother? She's awfully sick.'

'Where is she – and what is wrong with her?'

The boy pointed to an overgrown track leading away at a right-angle from the road. As he moved, Kathie could see the finger-thin ribs protruding from his skin beneath the tattered shirt.

'She's along there. The hunger's upon us.'

It was an expression that Liam and the others had heard many times during the last weeks. The cry of a starving nation. 'The hunger is upon us.'

'All right, jump up on the cart. We'll have a look at her.'

'No, I'll go on to tell her you're coming. You can't miss us if you follow the track.'

With that the ragged boy turned away and ran along the track as though there was a devil at his heels.

Liam turned the reluctant horse from the road and goaded it into a bone-rattling jog along the rough-surfaced track. They had not gone more than two hundred yards when Nathan Brock pointed to a lightning-blackened tree standing conspicuously alone in the hedgerow ahead of them.

'I thought I remembered this lane,' he said quietly. 'There is no hut to be found along here and no reason for anyone to build one. The track ends in a peat bog a little way farther on.'

Liam pulled the horse to a halt.

'You think the boy was lying? Why?'

Nathan Brock shook his head, but his eyes were searching every possible place of concealment ahead of them. 'I don't know. But we are wearing good clothes and have pockets that might hold money. There are many with neither.'

'But what if you are wrong and there really is a sick woman along there?' asked Kathie. 'We can't go away without finding out.'

'You are quite right,' agreed Liam. 'But it might be safer if I turn the cart around and leave you here. Nathan and I will go along the path a way on foot.'

They had no need to go anywhere for Nathan Brock's suspicions to be confirmed. The ex-prizefighter was right. There was no cottage along the track. Only half a dozen ruffians who had sent the boy out as a decoy while they waited in hiding not fifty yards farther along. When they saw Liam begin to turn the cart in a field gateway they let out a concerted howl of frustration and ran at the trio, each ruffian armed with a heavy cudgel.

There was no opportunity to escape. The track was too narrow for Liam to turn the cart in a hurry. Even had he done so, the horse would not have been able to outpace the men on the rough surface.

Liam kept a stout wooden bar in the cart to push between the spokes of the wheels when he had to leave the cart on a slope. Ordering Kathie to stay on the high seat, Liam took up the bar and jumped down to join Nathan Brock, who was already preparing to meet the first of the ruffians.

The encounter was brief but decisive. Ducking beneath a raised club, Nathan Brock gripped the man's right wrist with his own mutilated left hand and brought his right fist up in a short uppercut that landed flush on the other man's chin.

Without a sound, the attacker slipped face-down to the ground, unconscious.

The ex-prizefighter turned to meet the next of the robbers, but Liam had already taken his legs from under him with a mighty sweep of the brake-pole.

Then the fighting became confused as Nathan Brock used his fists to great effect and Liam jabbed and swung at the attackers with his heavy wooden pole.

At the height of the battle, Kathie could remain inactive no longer. Jumping to the ground she picked up the cudgel dropped by a fallen robber and wildly swinging it about her head advanced into the fray.

She was still swinging when the last of the attackers fled from the scene and only then did Liam realise that her eyes were tightly closed.

'Kathie! Kathie! It's all right. They've gone. It's all over.'

Kathie stopped her wild gyrating and opened her eyes, lowering her ineffective cudgel. She was madly giddy and, as she staggered, Liam caught her and she collapsed into his arms both crying and laughing at the same time.

It was a minute or two before the excitement died away and Kathie regained her composure. Not until then did either of them realise how close Liam was holding her to him. Reluctantly he released his hold and she slowly pushed herself away. They were each searching the other's face hoping to read something of their thoughts when Nathan Brock broke the spell.

'Look what I've just found hiding behind a bush. What do you think we ought to do with him?'

He had the young decoy's ear held fast in a painful grip, and the boy's head twisted to one side as he sought to lessen the agony.

'By the look of him I would say he could do with a bit of fattening up,' commented Kathie. There was no denying that the boy was painfully thin.

'I doubt if he would stay around for long enough to put on any fat,' said Liam. 'The moment you turned your back he'd be away – taking everything he could lay his hands on away with him, no doubt.'

'So what do we do – turn him over to a constable?'

Kathie did not see the wink that passed between the boy's captor and Liam. She looked at the two men in alarm.

'We can't do that. He'd be hanged, or at the very least transported.'

The boy was in wide-eyed but silent agreement.

'What else can we do – release him to go straight back to his thieving ways?'

'No, I'll take him back to Kilmar with me and feed him up a little. He'll be no trouble in our house: we have nothing worth stealing.'

'It's hardly worth the trouble,' said Nathan Brock. 'I agree with Liam. You won't keep him for a day. At the first opportunity he'll run off to rejoin his friends.'

'I won't try to stop him from such foolishness,' said Kathie, looking into the boy's rebellious brown eyes. 'But he'll leave with a full belly and will have seen how decent folks live.'

Nathan Brock gave the boy's ear a final tweak before releasing his grip.

'What's your name?'

'Jeremy.'

'Jeremy what?'

'Jeremy nothing. I'm just Jeremy, that's all.'

'Where is your family, Jeremy?'

'I've got no family.' The boy rubbed his ear vigorously with the palm of his hand in a vain attempt to drive away the pain.

'You have no family . . . or you don't know where they are?'

Jeremy shrugged his thin shoulders. 'I've got none. I don't think I've ever had any.'

Nathan Brock estimated the boy's age to be about ten. He alone of those watching the youngster knew exactly how the boy was feeling. He understood and sympathised with every resentful thought in Jeremy's head. This dirty, lying, thieving child could have been himself thirty years ago. He knew what it was to fight a lone battle against a hostile world. By the time he reached the age of ten an orphan in Ireland knew he could trust no one and must rely upon his own resourcefulness. If he wanted anything, he would either have to steal it, or fight for it with both hands – and win. Nathan Brock had been big and determined. He had learned to fight. This young man could only steal. To him it was neither wrong, nor a good way of life. He knew no other way.

'Get in the cart,' said Liam to Jeremy. 'It's time we were on our way.'

'You're not going to hand me over to a constable?'

'No,' replied Kathie. 'You are coming to stay with me and my father. You are far too young to be running with a band of cut-throats. If you behave yourself, perhaps Liam will take you out in his boat and teach you how to fish.'

Jeremy jerked a thumb at Nathan Brock. 'Will he teach me to fight as good as he does?'

Kathie smiled. 'I'm sure he will – once you have some strength in your body.'

'All right, then, I'll come with you.'

Jeremy clambered into the back of the cart, and the others took their places on the seat and resumed their interrupted journey to Kilmar.

'I recognised one of those men back there,' said Liam. 'He was with the wreckers up on Kilmar hill.'

'Then the cottiers were not involved,' said Nathan Brock. 'These men are footpads who roam the countryside in good times or bad.'

He turned back to the boy. 'Where will your friends go when they stop running?'

The boy remained silent and, putting on a ferocious expression, Nathan Brock growled, 'Tell me, boy. If you don't, I'll screw your ears from your head.'

'The Wicklow mountains.'

'Then we have little hope of finding them. You could hide an army in those mountains.'

They rode in silence for a while, then Nathan Brock gave Liam a cheerful lop-sided grin. 'I thought you handled your shillelagh well today. Some of those rogues will be hobbling long after they reach the Wicklow mountains.'

'They will be spitting teeth, too. You swing a mighty punch, Nathan.' Liam's answering grin widened. 'But we must not forget Kathie. She fought as well as either of us – and with her eyes tight closed!' They laughed, and the girl on the seat beside Liam remembered the feel of his arms about her. She thought that the attack by the six footpads had turned out to be a very satisfying experience.

Before they reached Kilmar, Liam tried to persuade Nathan Brock to come to England with him. Liam had grown to like the big man and he enjoyed his company. Nathan Brock knew London and was known to many of the sporting gentlemen there. He could attract a great many additional guineas to the cottiers' relief fund.

But Nathan Brock had other ideas. He felt he was doing more good travelling around the countryside locating cottiers before they were beyond any help. He also intended returning to County Wicklow for his wife and children very soon and he wanted nothing to interfere with that.

Kathie wished that Liam would try to persuade her to accompany him to London. It was not only that she wished to see the great country on the far side of the Irish Sea. Kathie felt that a new warmth had come into their relationship and she was frightened that if Liam went away from her now it would be lost for ever.

Without trying to analyse her feelings for him, Kathie admitted that Liam had come to mean a great deal to her.

Chapter Ten

Jeremy ran away from the Donaghue cottage two days before Liam left Kilmar for London. One of the fishermen said he had seen some men resembling the footpads close to the village on the day the boy disappeared but, although a number of the villagers helped Liam and Nathan Brock to search the surrounding countryside, no trace was found of Jeremy or his former companions.

Then the boy's not entirely unexpected escape was quickly forgotten as the time for Liam's departure drew near. It was an event in which the whole village took an interest. It was rare indeed for anyone from Kilmar to travel so far abroad, and when Eugene Brennan's carriage entered the village, sent from Dublin for Liam, there was not a man, woman or child remaining indoors.

They witnessed the kisses Liam exchanged with Kathie and with Norah McCabe, and then anyone who could push close enough shook his hand before he climbed into the carriage and set off, waving to them all in the manner of departing royalty.

The journey to Dublin was without incident, the carriage conveying Liam to the dockside and the paddlesteamer that would carry him to the port of Liverpool. The crossing itself turned out to be a twenty-four-hour nightmare. The weather was stormy, the sea rough, and the boat hopelessly overcrowded.

There were many cottiers among the passengers on board. Irish landlords were quickly learning that it was cheaper to ship their unwanted tenants to England with a couple of shillings in their pockets than to contribute to their indefinite stay in a poor-house. The cottiers were bad sailors and as they fell victim to sea-sickness they became convinced they were dying. Soon conditions between decks became so appalling that Liam found himself a nook on the leeward side of one of the deckhouses and spent most of the journey huddled in the cold, but fresh, air.

When Eugene Brennan met Liam on the dock at Liverpool, the fisherman pointed out the cottiers who stood on the quay in bewildered shivering groups. Their thin cheap clothes were as unsuited to the weather as they themselves were to a new life in this strange foreign land. Most of them were from the remote estates in the west of Ireland and few of them spoke or understood English.

Eugene Brennan talked to the new arrivals before directing them to a part of the city where they would find other Irish immigrants to help them begin their new and bewildering life.

'I fought against the Irish Poor Law when it passed through Parliament in 1838 because I knew it would lead to just such a situation as this,' muttered the MP as he and Liam watched the cottiers pick up their children and few meagre possessions and move off toward the city. 'Nobody would listen to me then, but, by God, they'll have the problem dumped on their doorstep now, right enough! Come, Liam, we are travelling to London by the railway. It is a noisy, draughty and dirty means of travelling, but we'll be in London a damn sight quicker than if we went by road.'

They did not have to go far to board the railway carriage that would convey them to Manchester, the first of two changes on the railway line to London. The interior of the first-class carriages was totally enclosed, and not so very different from the inside of the horse-drawn mail coaches that still criss-crossed England and Ireland. The seats were hard and uncomfortable and, as Liam was to find later, jolted and swayed alarmingly when in motion.

But it was the long-boilered locomotive that impressed Liam most. An awesome wheeled engine of black steel, it stood as tall as two men – three, if the long chimney was included – and hissing steam escaped from so many different places that Liam feared that it was about to explode at any moment.

Not until Liverpool was far behind them did Liam begin to relax, and Eugene Brennan confessed to sharing the fisherman's fears of the modern means of transport.

'A man knows where he is when there's a horse in front of him,' he said. 'Even if something scares the beast and it runs away with you there's a fair chance of bringing it to a halt before it does any damage – but how do you stop a runaway steam engine, eh? Tell me that, if you can. All the same, it will have us in London soon after dark, and the sooner we begin holding our meetings the better. There is much interest in your forthcoming talks. Lady Dudley – I believe you met her in Ireland – insists that you become a guest in her town house while you are in London. It's a splendid beginning, Liam. Lady Dudley is accepted in London society as I could never be. Her support will be of inestimable value in our fund-raising activities.'

Liam nodded half-heartedly. He was tired after his journey across the Irish Sea and until this moment had all but forgotten the Earl of Inch's sister. Remembering disturbed him. Her cool polished beauty was in direct contrast to the fiery dark-haired girl he had left behind in Kilmar. Liam dropped into a disturbed sleep thinking about the two women.

At first sight, London was something of a disappointment. The houses beyond the edge of the railway line seemed small and unimpressive, and the myriad lights Liam had expected to see illuminating the great city were hidden in a cold clinging fog that rolled up-river with the incoming tide. Even the magnificent tall columns of Euston railway station were lost from Liam's view. Although he could not fail to be aware of the noise and bustle all about him, he caught only phantom glimpses of muffled men and bonneted women in the spluttering light from the lamps of the torch-boys. It was a great let-down, but Eugene Brennan told Liam the fog would clear by morning.

'It is a terrible city at this time of the year,' he added. 'I am surprised anyone can breathe at all.'

They caught a hackney carriage from the station, and the MP announced that he would take Liam for a meal before going on to Lady Caroline Dudley's house.

They ate in a high-class inn on one of the main thoroughfares in central London, sitting at a quiet table close to a roaring log fire. Liam was dismayed at the bewildering array of cutlery surrounding his plate, but he soon realised that the thoughtful Irish MP had entertained him to a meal in order to teach him the basic etiquette expected of him during his time in London.

'You'll get used to it – everyone does.' Eugene Brennan smiled at his protégé at the end of his brief instruction. 'If you're ever in any doubt, then keep talking until someone else starts and follow whatever they do. That shouldn't be too hard for a true Irishman. Now, it's time we were getting on to the Dudley house.'

The square where Lady Caroline lived was illuminated with London's latest refinement: gas lighting. The blue flames hissed and popped noisily, but they cast enough light on the surrounding houses to show Liam that this was an expensive area and differed greatly from the houses he had seen adjoining the railway line.

The two men were shown to a room that was in every way as impressive as the library at Inch House. The high ceilings and general air of luxury threatened to overcome Liam. Lady Caroline Dudley was not at home, and Liam had a brief moment of panic when Eugene Brennan announced that he was leaving. It passed quickly enough, and when the MP had gone Liam retired to the upstairs room that had been prepared for him.

Here, Liam felt more comfortable. A warm fire burned in the hearth, and he no longer had the feeling that a servant was hovering just out of sight, waiting for one of Liam's heavy boots to catch on the thick carpet and catapult him against one of the many priceless knick-knacks in the room. He felt even better when he saw that a pile of books had been thoughtfully left for him on a fireside table.

Seated in front of the crackling fire with a book in his hand, Liam felt a long way from Kilmar and everything he knew and loved. There would be fires there, too, of course. Aromatic, smoky, peat fires and low white-washed walls.

Abruptly, Liam stood up and went to the window. Drawing aside the heavy curtains, he looked down at the street. The fog had thinned, and life was going on outside as though it were still day. Coaches and carriages rumbled past, and there was much coming and going from the fine houses with their black-painted railings and wide fan-shaped steps. Men rode high-stepping horses and occasionally raised a hat to friends strolling arm in arm along the stone-slabbed pavements. Where the blue light from the fluctuating gas-jets of the street-lamps met the yellow light from the open doors, it provided a green binding, joining the two.

Suddenly, London became an exciting reality to Liam. A vast wonderland, a thousand years removed from Kilmar. Here, Liam thought, a man could probably find all that life had to offer – or lose himself in the seeking.

He slept well between the fine linen sheets of the large bed and was startled to wakefulness by a servant girl who drew the curtains and flooded the room with daylight.

''Morning, sir.' She gave him a cheeky grin. 'Breakfast'll be ready in 'alf an hour. Lady Caroline says she'll see you then.'

Lady Caroline Dudley was already at the breakfast-table by the time Liam made his way downstairs. She motioned for him to take the seat opposite her and smiled at him, but again he was aware of the sadness in her eyes.

'Well, Liam, here you are in London at last. Do you think you will like it here?'

Liam replied that he had not been able to see much of the city because of the fog.

'Never mind. You have plenty of time, and London is a city to be tackled when you are fresh and at your very best. You must have been tired last night after your long journey. I looked in your room when I came in and you were snoring like a drunken cook.'

'You came into my room while I was asleep?'

Lady Caroline Dudley had an attractive laugh. 'Why, yes, Liam. Have I offended your morals?'

She saw the colour rise to Liam's cheeks and her smile became gentler. 'Now I have embarrassed you. I can see I will need to protect you from the more outrageous of my friends. We will also need to call upon the services of a good tailor. Your suit is fine for the rigours of the Irish countryside, but London calls for something rather more . . . fashionable?'

Liam had realised when he was eating with Eugene Brennan in the inn the previous evening that his suit of coarse serge fell far short of the quality of the clothes worn by the other diners, but he stubbornly told himself he had not come to London to dress up for English society.

'My clothes will serve for the short time I'll be here,' he said ungraciously. 'I'm a fisherman and I have come here to tell people of the plight of starving cottiers in Ireland. I've not come to learn how to become an English gentleman.'

Lady Caroline was taken aback for a moment but, quickly realising she had said the wrong thing, she reached across the table and rested the tips of her long fingers on the back of Liam's broad hand. 'You are quite right, of course, Liam. To dress you up for a meeting would detract from the tremendous impact I know you will make on everyone. But we will need to show you off at various evening functions, too. You will need to dress for them. Eugene Brennan would agree with that, I am quite sure.'

The Irish MP did agree. He called that morning and, brushing aside Liam's protests, took him to see his own tailor. Liam was measured for suits and coats, and Eugene Brennan impressed upon the tailor the need to have them ready as soon as was humanly possible. When Liam asked where the money for the clothes would be coming from the old MP replied, 'We receive special donations for just such necessities as this. The few pounds it needs will be money well spent. You're a fine-built young man, Liam. Put you in a good suit of clothes to set off those shoulders and there is not a lady in the city will be able to refuse you anything – and, remember, it is the ladies you need to charm if you'd find a way to the pockets of their husbands.'

That afternoon Eugene Brennan had some business to attend to, and Lady Caroline took Liam in her open carriage on a sight-seeing tour of London. Together they saw St Paul's Cathedral, Westminster Abbey and the grim Tower of London. They rode through the royal parks and watched river traffic on the busy Thames at the very heart of the capital.

But it was the people who held the greatest fascination for Liam. They were an ever-changing visual experience. In some of the back-streets traders ran alongside the carriage offering for sale everything from baubles to bread, while in the more fashionable thoroughfares dandies with exaggerated movements flicked their velvet cloaks and fluttered the lace at their wrists. On street-corners stood high-hatted constables, sternly aloof from their fellow-beings. There was the constant noise of street-cries, and small boys with more fat on them than Liam had ever seen on an Irish child ran beside the carriage, begging for pennies.

Most of all, Liam found he enjoyed the company of Lady Caroline Dudley. She showed him London, pointing out sights that were familiar to her with all the enthusiasm of a young girl seeing them for the first time. In the Regent's Park she clutched at his arm in an agony of excitement when they both glimpsed the huge grey bulk of an elephant through the fence of the zoological gardens. Later, when a dog scrambled from the muddy waters of the Thames and shook water over a fastidiously pompous gentleman, she laughed and touched her cheek briefly against the sleeve of Liam's rough serge jacket in unforced amusement.

Only when they were once more driving through the fashionable streets near her home did Lady Caroline lose some of her gaiety, although she still talked more than was usual for her, and more than once touched Liam's hand to emphasise a point she was making.

When they arrived at her home some of Lady Caroline's friends were awaiting her, and Eugene Brennan was there to take Liam to meet some of his own circle. There was not time to tell her how much he had enjoyed the day.

The next day was a busy one for Liam. Eugene Brennan called for him early, before Lady Caroline had risen, and to Liam it seemed that the whole day was spent shaking limp hands and holding meaningless conversations with flat unemotional people.

That evening, Liam gave his first talk on the condition of the Irish cottiers to a small audience of Members of Parliament and senior government officials at Eugene Brennan's club. The meeting was to set the pattern for those to follow. The Irish MP gave a speech explaining the cottiers' total dependence upon the potato and the dire consequences that followed a crop failure. He commented bitterly upon the present government's irresponsibility toward the famine. So far, their contribution to the desperate needs of the cottiers had been a few tons of condemned naval biscuits.

Then Eugene Brennan called upon Liam to describe the misery, poverty and death he had seen in the sod cabins around Kilmar.

The audience listened in a shocked and tight-lipped silence as Liam told them of skeletal children, hollow-eyed and swollen-limbed. Children who were too weak to cry and who died when they were given food because their stomachs had ceased to function; of mothers, able to beg or steal barely enough food to keep a single child alive, having to decide which of their families they must allow to die; of women, fighting like wild animals over a scrap of putrid meat that would turn the stomach of any of the men present in the London club.

Liam painted a remarkably vivid word-picture of the horrors of the Irish famine, yet inside he still felt a deep frustration because he was unable to bring home to those listening the sheer desperation and hopelessness of the poor cottiers. Whatever was donated here would not be enough. Men, women and children would still die because they needed aid on a massive scale.

Eugene Brennan sensed Liam's melancholy mood and on the drive back to Lady Caroline's house told him that his talk had brought promised donations of more than two thousand pounds for the fund.

But still Liam could not shake off his depression. For some reason, the sights he had seen about Kilmar were haunting him badly tonight.

After Eugene Brennan had left him, Liam helped himself to Lady Caroline's whiskey and sat slumped in an armchair, gazing broodily into the dying fire in the drawing-room.

He was still there when Lady Caroline returned to the house shortly before midnight. The Earl's sister had been to an excellent dinner party at the house of a close friend and her face was flushed with the wine she had drunk.

When she saw the obvious unhappiness of her guest, Lady Caroline was immediately full of concern.

'My dear, what has happened? What has gone wrong? Surely you weren't given a bad reception at Eugene's club?'

Liam dragged his thoughts back to his present surroundings. It was not easy; he had taken far more whiskey than he was used to drinking.

'No, Eugene thinks we did very well.' Liam told her how much they had been promised for the fund.

'Why, that is an absolutely marvellous start for you. Two thousand pounds from such a small gathering is excellent! You should be celebrating, not sitting here looking the picture of misery. In fact, I insist! No, stay there, Liam.'

She gently pushed Liam back in the armchair as he attempted to rise, then went to the drinks cabinet and poured two very large whiskeys.

Carrying them to the fire, she handed one to Liam and raised her own glass to him.

'I am told that drinking whiskey is not ladylike, but I happen to enjoy it and this is a very special occasion. Here's to all the money you are going to raise for the victims of Ireland's potato famine.'

Liam looked into his glass and said morosely, 'And here's to the souls of the thousands who will die before any relief can reach them.'

He took a large mouthful of his drink and it burned its way down his throat. He felt light-headed, but the whiskey was helping his mood.

When Liam stood up abruptly and walked over to look down at the fire Lady Caroline was there with a hand on his arm.

'Liam, you cannot take all the troubles of the Irish cottiers upon your shoulders.'

'No? No, perhaps you're right, but there is something very wrong with the world. Here I am with a glass of expensive whiskey in my hand. Tonight I stood in a room thick with tobacco smoke, talking to men who were bloated with good food and brandy. I was trying to tell them of a people who are starving . . . dying. Do you think they really understood what I was saying? As I spoke I couldn't see the faces of the men there. All I could see were the filthy sod cabins and the faces of children who look like little old men. Three score years and ten the Lord gave them to live. Who took it away from them? Can you tell me that? When I picked up a pencil from the table tonight I did not see it. Instead, it became the thin brittle fingers of a dying little girl I had found one day – a little girl who wanted desperately to live, though God only knows why.'

Liam took another mouthful of whiskey.

'I carried that child out of a stinking cabin and laid her in a grave beside her mother and three brothers. She was six years old but no heavier than a cat in my arms. Do you think any one of the men in the club tonight really cared about that little cottier girl? Oh, sure, they gave promises of money. But what is money to them? They reach into their pockets, hand out a few coins and go away feeling good. Do they know that I am telling them about men and women and children who talk to one another just as you and I do? Who feel things just as we do? People who once had dreams for themselves and their families and who are frightened at what is happening to them now? No, they don't want to think about things like that. It just isn't nice. . . . God, but I'm drunk!'

Liam reached for the mantelshelf over the fire for support

and turned away from Lady Caroline. But it was not the whiskey alone that was affecting him. The drink had merely tapped a deep well of sorrow and emotion within him. He *felt* for the cottiers. His whole being lived and died with them.

'Liam, you must not let the thought of what is happening to our country tear the heart out of you. You can't hold yourself responsible for our people.'

Lady Caroline wanted desperately to comfort Liam. The hard shell of the man had peeled away from him and tonight she had witnessed his vulnerability. Tomorrow he would feel ashamed because he had bared his soul to her in this manner – and she did not want him to feel shame.

She came close to him – close enough to raise a finger and trace away the thin line of perspiration that had formed above the line of his upper lip.

Her finger was light and soft. It stopped suddenly and rested upon the corner of Liam's mouth as Lady Caroline looked up and saw him looking at her with a strange expression upon his face.

'Liam, what is it, my dear?'

With a feeling of unreality, as though he was watching someone else's actions, Liam reached out for her and felt her body slim and firm beneath the silk of her dress. Then her mouth was upon his, her hand moved up behind his neck and her body came hard to him.

Her mouth moved hungrily. His body was aroused and his right hand slid beneath her arm, caressed her breast, then moved down her body.

'No, Liam. No, please. Not here. Not here.'

She gripped his hand in hers and, still not believing this was really happening, Liam allowed himself to be led from the room, across the hall and up the wide staircase.

He walked behind her into a room that breathed the perfume worn by Lady Caroline. Then her silk dress was lying on the floor and he was stepping over it, following her to a wide soft bed. Cool sheets caressed his naked body and long fair hair brushed his face as he kissed her lips, her neck.

Minutes later her body was responding to his own and her hands upon his back cajoled and kneaded, fought him and drew him to her. His body no longer belonged to him but moved in a primeval rhythm he had never before known. Finally, Liam sank down into a state of ecstatic weariness, his lungs roaring for oxygen.

'Oh, my darling! Liam! Liam! Liam!'

Lady Caroline held him fast in the well of her body as her lips brushed like a butterfly against his mouth, his eyes, the tip of his nose. Liam felt as though his body was floating away from him.

'Go to sleep now, my darling,' she whispered and he slept, his face against hers, while she gently stroked the back of his neck.

Liam woke early, as the old lamp-lighter, with his long brass-hooked pole, whistled his way along the street beyond the window, turning off the gas-lights.

He had not yet reached the light outside the house and, starting up, Liam looked down at the face on the pillow beside him.

A wedge of light came through a broad gap beside one curtain and lay diagonally across the bed, not quite touching Lady Caroline's face, but showing the dark smudges beneath her eyes and the trace of a worry-line across her forehead.

Liam believed there could be no other woman quite so beautiful – and last night he had made love to her. The memory had the impact of a physical blow. He felt both elated and frightened. She was a lady, the sister of an earl. He was a fisherman. Then a frightening thought came to him. He had been drinking. Had he forced her?

Lady Caroline's eyes flickered open just before the light went off outside the window, plunging the room into darkness. Before Liam could say anything, could mumble a confused apology, her arms reached out for him and she drew him to her, finding his mouth with her own.

They made love again, until the grey dawn touched the rooftops of London and outlined the windows of the bedroom. Then, with sounds of movement elsewhere in the house, Liam left Lady Caroline's bed and made his way silently and secretly to his own room.

When they met at the breakfast-table, Liam found it almost impossible to behave as though nothing had happened between them. He felt an overwhelming urge to touch her, to hold her to him and ask about the future, but Lady Caroline was behaving as though nothing out of the ordinary had occurred, as though the world might even go on as before. Liam was hurt and bewildered, but he took his cue from her.

He returned the friendly smile she gave him, and Lady Caroline said, 'You are certainly happier than you were last night, my dear. When I came in I thought you looked almost suicidal.'

'It was Eugene's club. The contrast between what I was saying and the luxury I saw there.'

'I am afraid you will have to learn to accept such contrasts, Liam, if you wish to raise money for your cottiers. People who live in humbler surroundings would undoubtedly give your cottiers more sympathy, but that will not feed a hungry child.'

Liam knew she was right. He would remember her words when he gave his next talk.

She put her napkin on the table before her and stood up. 'I am afraid I must leave you now, Liam. An aunt of mine is passing through London on her way to Italy. I have to spend the day with her.'

Liam's spirits sank. He had hoped they might spend the day together, just the two of them, as they had on his first day in London.

'Will you be home when I return from my talk tonight?' he blurted out.

Lady Caroline pretended to be shocked. 'Oh dear! What slumbering beast have I awakened in you, Liam McCabe?'

Liam coloured up, and when she laughed it embarrassed him even more. The realisation came to him once again that he was an inexperienced and clumsy fisherman from Kilmar who had stepped out of his own world into another that he neither knew nor understood.

'I'm sorry. . . .'

Lady Caroline leaned over him as he sat at the breakfast-table and put a finger to his lips.

'Shh! You have no need to apologise – for anything. Of course I will be here when you return from your meeting.'

She removed her finger and kissed him quickly. 'While I am getting ready you can try on your new clothes. The tailor sent them round this morning.'

A note with the clothes stated that they were intended merely to give him something to wear while he waited for the bulk of his order to be fulfilled, but the suit of fine-quality cloth fitted tolerably well. Liam was particularly pleased with the heavy overcoat; there was bitterly cold wind blowing through the London streets with an occasional flake of snow escaping from the morose grey-clouded sky.

Eugene Brennan was as pleased as Liam with the clothes. He was taking Liam for lunch with some of his fellow-Irish Members of Parliament and few of them cared to be reminded of the rough-serge-and-corduroy-knee-breeches image the British had of the Irish. It was not snobbery. Each of them had fought a hard and bitter battle for many years to gain equality for their electors and to prove the Irishman as good a man as his fellows in England. Their efforts had not been helped recently by the enforced exodus of the dispossessed cottiers. Practically penniless, and ignorant of the ways of what was, after all, an alien country, they had set up a wave of anti-Irish feeling that would soon surge through Liverpool and other large cities in the land, counteracting the sympathy around by their country's plight.

Some of this feeling had already reached London. That night's meeting was the only public meeting of Liam's tour. It was held in a hall in the City of London, the small business heart of the capital. Here, for the first time in his brief experience of speaking, Liam encountered hecklers.

The jeers and catcalls began when Eugene Brennan was speaking, but the old MP was far too wily to allow them to distract him. He ignored most of their interruptions and scored points from those he chose to answer.

For Liam it was different. He had come to tell his story to what he had believed would be a sympathetic audience. He could not understand why men would bother to come to a meeting to protest against helping people who would otherwise die. When the heckling became too persistent and Eugene Brennan would have stood up to intervene, Liam expressed his surprise to the crowd.

Immediately, there were cries of 'Why can't the Irish feed themselves, the same as we have to?'

'Because the potato crop has failed,' said Liam simply. 'The potato is the sole food for hundreds of thousands of cottiers.'

'Then let them eat the grain they're sending to England,'

demanded a voice. 'I have seen three shiploads of Irish grain pass through the docks this week.'

'No doubt it came from the farm of an absent English landlord,' retorted Liam. 'We have many such people in Ireland and they use the Army to make sure starving cottiers don't steal so much as a handful of the grain they bring here to you.'

'What about all the Irishmen who come to England to take our jobs from us?' called another unseen man. 'If they don't give a damn about us, why should we help them?'

'If there was work or food in Ireland, they wouldn't need to come here. The men you see here are the lucky ones. They will live. Left behind in Ireland are wives and little children who will not – and I have watched them die. That is why *I* have come to England. I am just an ordinary fisherman who is giving a share of his catches to help those who are starving – but it is not enough. I am here to ask for your help, too.'

When Liam went on to tell his audience of some of the harrowing sights he had seen, the hecklers allowed him to speak without further interruption and when he sat down Eugene Brennan took the opportunity to give one of the few political speeches of the tour. He slated the unfair Corn Laws that encouraged Irish farmers and land-owners to ship their corn to England for resale, at the same time preventing cheap corn from being allowed into Ireland. He berated the Tory administration of Sir Robert Peel for doing nothing to provide governmental aid to the Irish. Finally, he spoke against the union of England and Ireland which had taken the control of Irish affairs out of the hands of the Irish and left them at the mercy of politicians who neither knew nor cared about their problems.

The meeting broke up in an uproar of cheers and counter-cheers, and the collection was hastily abandoned when one of the collectors was badly man-handled by a small group of ruffians. When the noise had gone on for ten minutes and showed little sign of abating, one of the hall officials helped Eugene Brennan and Liam to slip away through a side door.

In the carriage on their way from the hall, Liam expressed incredulity that a meeting held to raise money for starving people – British people – should attract such violent opposition.

Eugene Brennan gave a short humourless laugh. 'When you have been politics for as many years as I have there are few surprises left. The men who were carrying out the heckling were in the pay of Sir Robert Peel's party, have no doubts about that.'

'But why should our appeal attract the attention of politicians?' Liam was puzzled. 'The cottiers have nothing to do with politics.'

'No, but I have. The hecklers were in the hall tonight to discredit me. Sir Robert Peel's mismanagement of the famine has gained me many supporters. Certain men of influence are beginning to realise that Ireland can only be successfully administered from Dublin. Peel's position as Prime Minister is far from secure. If he loses any more popularity, he may well find himself out of office.'

The old MP sat back in the carriage seat and looked appraisingly at Liam.

'I was impressed with the way you handled Peel's men at the meeting tonight. I almost wish I had arranged a few more public meetings so that you could perfect your technique. You could easily become a very effective speaker with your directness and lack of guile. But I realise you have not come all this way to help my political career. You are here to get money for the cottiers – and, by God, that's what we'll do, Liam.'

Eugene Brennan shrugged the carriage blanket about him and gave Liam a wry smile.

'We may not have made much money tonight, but it did me good to tell an English meeting what years of direct rule has done to Ireland. They will go home with something to think about, at least.'

Liam shook his head sadly. 'I understand little of all this. I only know that people are dying in Ireland while you play games here. Perhaps Dermot should have come to London instead of me. He claims to understand politics.'

But Liam was glad he had not missed the opportunity to come to London, although for the remainder of the drive his thoughts were not of politics, or of the money he would help to raise for less fortunate countrymen. Looking out of the carriage window at the snow beginning to fall in silent heavy flakes upon the London streets, he was thinking of Lady Caroline Dudley, of her touch, her kisses and the feel of her slim body.

As the iron-clad wheels of the carriage rumbled along a narrow alleyway and the hoofs of the horses struck sparks from the cobbles, Liam lapsed into a contemplative silence and dreamed of sharing his hostess's bed.

Chapter Eleven

In Kilmar, a week of appalling weather had prevented any fishing. The wind howled off the sea and brought angry waves crashing on the shore sending spray high over the stone wall of the fishing quay. The two wooden boats were dragged to safety, high up on the beach, and the curraghs lay upside down along the narrow village streets or were tilted against sheltered cottage walls.

Because of the severity of the weather, more and more dispossessed cottiers were pouring in from the surrounding countryside. The promise of work on the Earl of Inch's estate had brought salvation to a hundred families, but only misplaced hope and ultimate despair to a thousand more. In a last desperate bid for life men brought their starving families with them and begged that they, too, should be given work.

The Earl's man appointed by Lady Caroline tried to apportion the work to different men each day, in an attempt to spread relief farther, but it only resulted in the cottier men fighting bloody battles for the right to work. Since the famine the price of foodstuff in Ireland had risen alarmingly. A day's wage was barely enough to feed a small family for two careful days, and the men had to work regularly to keep their families alive.

As the fights grew daily more desperate, the Earl's man had no alternative but to sign on a regular labour force and order the others from the estate.

The cottiers without work descended upon Kilmar, begging piteously by day. At night the more agile amongst them braved the high wind on the steep seaward slopes of Kilmar hill, snaring sleeping seagulls for the cooking-pot.

The Kilmar branch of the All-Ireland Association held an emergency meeting to discuss the latest development in the situation, but broke up without arriving at even a temporary solution. They felt there was nothing to be done until money from Liam's fund-raising tour in England began to arrive.

The decision did not please the younger members of the Association.

'The whole business is appalling.' Dermot McCabe was in a small back room of the Kilmar ale-house with Kathie, Eoin and Sean Feehan and half a dozen others. 'All that anyone ever says at these meetings is "Wait, wait, wait" – and at the end of the waiting they will no doubt talk some more. All the talking in the world won't save a single cottier.'

'In the meantime the landlords are still shipping grain from Wexford Town,' growled Eoin Feehan. 'They have been holding it back waiting for the price to rise as high as they think it will go. Two ships left last week, and I've heard there's another waiting to be loaded at this very moment.'

'That's quite true,' said one of the young men. 'My father was in Gorey today. He said they are gathering corn-wagons together and by tomorrow will have thirty wagons of grain and two hundred head of cattle to take to Wexford Town with an escort of soldiers.'

'Did he say how many soldiers there were?' asked Dermot eagerly.

'About twenty, he thought. Why?'

'This could be the opportunity we've been waiting for. A chance to do more than talk. It will take the wagons two days to reach Wexford Town. During that time it would be easy enough to steal a couple of wagonloads of grain and a few head of cattle.'

There was an instant build-up of excitement in the room. Only Kathie raised a doubt about the practicality of Dermot's startling idea.

'And how will we perform this miracle? The soldiers will have muskets. There are only ten of us here in this room and we don't have a gun between us.'

'We don't need guns,' said Dermot excitedly. 'We'll use a trick the Irish have used for centuries and the soldiers will not even see us. No, Kathie, don't be asking any more questions just now. We've got plans to make. Now, this is the way I see things. . . .'

Dermot explained his plan, and when the others gave it their wholehearted support the idea that had been born out of a spirit of bravado became a reality. Each young man in the room was given a specific task.

Kathie, who felt as fully committed as any of the others, was indignant that she was not included.

'I have a special task for you,' declared Dermot. 'If we are to succeed, we will need to slow the wagons and keep them as close to Gorey as possible by nightfall tomorrow. That's when we will take the wagons, and we will need to be back here in Kilmar before daybreak. If a Kilmar fisherman is stopped that far from his village at night, the soldiers will know for sure who is responsible. Your task will be to delay the soldiers for as long as possible – and you will need as many cottiers as you can find to help you. I don't care how it is done – the cottiers can all lie down in the road and claim they are dying, if need be – *but the soldiers must be slowed.* They will be going along the coast road; that's the only way they will find enough water for the cattle, and it will be easier for the grain-wagons. After dark, tell the cottiers to go back along the road for about half a mile and wait there. They are to be ready to receive as much grain as they can carry off with them and must be off the roads by daybreak. Don't tell them exactly what is going to happen, Kathie. It's better they don't know – whatever they may guess.'

Kathie had a great many doubts about Dermot's scheme. With so many people involved in its execution there was so much that could go wrong. But she said nothing – and would bitterly regret her silence for the remainder of her life.

The English soldiers ran into trouble when they were only half a mile from Gorey. Soon after taking the coast road they found it blocked by a large crowd of cottiers. There appeared to be a celebration, with everyone joining in the singing and dancing.

The officer in charge of the soldiers was a young untried ensign. His uncertain requests for the cottiers to clear the road were met with smiles and unintelligible replies in Gaelic, a language understood by none of the military men.

The wagon drivers were no help. They gave the officer a number of widely differing interpretations. The cottiers were celebrating a wedding . . . a saint's day . . . the departure of a family group to the Americas.

Not until the column had been delayed for almost four hours did a long-serving soldier, Corporal William Garrett, take a hand. His experience had told him something unusual was afoot as soon as the cottiers began their delaying tactics. He had waited impatiently for the young ensign to take some positive action. Now he felt the farce had gone on for quite long enough. These stupid peasants were making the English Army look foolish – and to Corporal Garrett there was no greater crime.

Calling upon half the soldiers to follow him, he began physically clearing the road ahead of them, pushing the protesting cottiers out of the way and using the toe of his army boot on more than one occasion when a cottier was slow to move.

The corporal had gained a slow half-mile for the column when an old woman, severely weakened by weeks of near-starvation, dropped dead only yards ahead of the advancing troops. There was an immediate and angry reaction from the cottiers, some of whom had not seen the old lady fall and who genuinely believed she had been struck by the soldiers.

The situation began to look ugly when the Irish men moved forward to face the soldiers and the women and children dropped back to form up behind them.

The young ensign realised he had to take command again and, believing that he and his men were in imminent danger, he ordered his soldiers to load their muskets.

A bloody clash was averted by Kathie Donaghue. She had tried to remain in the background, out of sight, but now she had to come forward and tell the cottier men to back off, explaining that the old lady had died from the excitement of the moment. Reluctantly, the men backed away.

Corporal Garrett urged the ensign to take advantage of the momentary confusion to take the wagons and cattle through the cottiers at speed. While the young officer hesitated, the opportunity passed. A young cottier woman went into labour by the side of the road and any attempt to pass her was out of the question. Angry cottier men the young ensign might have dealt with. Threatening, determined women totally defeated him.

The birth proved to be long and difficult, and the screams of the young mother-to-be unnerved the soldiers. They donated some hastily cooked meat to her, and the ensign sent his own water-bottle. But the young Irishwoman needed more than well-intentioned sympathy and a little food and water. Not until the weak winter sun was sliding down into night did she give birth. The child, a girl, died within seconds of taking her first breath of cold air, and the cottiers buried her in an unmarked grave within a few feet of her birthplace. But it could be said her brief life had served the cottier cause well. It was too late for the soldiers to move on. As the cottiers finally dispersed from the scene, the soldiers prepared a camp for the night, driving the cattle into a nearby field.

The wagon drivers made their own fire some distance away from the soldiers and spoke in low tones about the events of the day. They knew the cottiers had deliberately held up their progress and were sure there was a motive behind the cottiers' actions. The wagon drivers agreed among themselves they would not become involved in any trouble that might occur. They had been employed by the corn-owning landlord for this one trip. None of his huge profit would come their way and they had no intention of fighting the cottiers on his behalf.

The soldiers were detailed for sentry duty in two-man shifts during the hours of darkness, but it was a cold and blustery night and, as part of their duty entailed keeping the fires of the camp burning, they took care to ensure that this chore occupied most of their time.

The first intimation that all was not well came with the alarmed blowing of the cattle as Dermot and his Kilmar companions drove half their number from the field in the darkness.

Shouting to waken their companions, the sentries ran toward the field, unslinging muskets from their shoulders, only to meet the close-packed cattle spilling from the field toward them.

Dermot and the others were driving the cattle on with sticks, and as the animals jostled each other to squeeze through the narrow gateway they panicked.

The two sentries were fortunate to escape with their lives. One stumbled into a shallow water-filled ditch by the side of the road, losing his musket but saving his life. The second crouched trembling behind a tree that was little more than a narrow sapling as the hundred crazed cattle thundered past without so much as a heavy breath falling upon the terrified soldier.

Their companions in the camp were less fortunate. Half-stupid with sleep, they were hardly on their feet before the cattle overran them, scattering men, equipment and fires in all directions, the ground trembling beneath their pounding hoofs.

When the last of the cattle thundered off into the night three soldiers lay on the churned-up earth. Miraculously, none of the soldiers was dead, although the young ensign was unconscious and they all had broken limbs.

Bootless and quivering with rage, Corporal Garrett called the survivors to him and tried to bring some order to the situation.

Dermot chose that moment to drive the remainder of the cattle through the shambles that had been an army camp. This time the men from Kilmar were right behind them, leading the wagon-horses. By the time the ensuing confusion was over, three wagonloads of corn and a great many cattle were heading back toward Gorey to be handed over to the hungry cottiers who had played their part in the operation.

Within the hour, cottiers would be straggling across the countryside in every direction, weighed down with corn and great joints of hastily slaughtered beef.

But the young men of Kilmar paid a high price to fill the bellies of the cottiers.

Had the young ensign not been trampled and badly injured by the cattle, the outcome of the raid on the Wexford-bound column might have been a total victory for the men of Kilmar. Under his leadership the soldiers would have spent the remainder of the night running around in the darkness, uselessly trying to round up the missing cattle. As it was, Corporal Garrett assumed command.

Unlike the more inexperienced soldiers, Corporal Garrett slept with his musket at his side, and it was for this he reached the moment he was awakened. He guessed immediately the real motive behind the stampede. As a young boy-soldier he had listened to the old campaigners tell of their days in Ireland. The use of cattle as a diversion had always been a favourite tactic with Irish partisans.

When the second wave of cattle overran the camp, he made straight for the wagons as soon as he was able. He was in time to see the third wagon being driven away and snapped off a quick shot at the two indistinct figures on the high wagon-seat. He heard a loud cry of pain, and Corporal Garrett knew his musket-ball had found its target. Then the soldier heard the frightened blowing of horses and the jangle of harness from the darkness nearby. He surprised two men backing a horse into the shafts of a fourth wagon. Wielding his musket as a club, Corporal Garrett struck one of them to the ground.

The second man immediately took to his heels, but the Corporal ran after him and brought him down with a hard tackle.

The two men rolled over and over on the ground, exchanging wild punches until some of the soldiers, attracted by the noise, came to the aid of their corporal and helped him subdue the violent fisherman.

'There is another one over by that wagon,' panted the Corporal, rubbing his bare foot where he had caught it on a rough stone. 'Bring him over here, then fetch a torch so we can have a look at them.'

A torch was quickly lighted, but the soldiers who went to the wagon returned empty-handed.

'Damn!' swore the corporal. 'I thought I'd put him out for good. These Irishmen must have heads like cannon-balls. Never mind, we've got this one. Let's have a good look at him.'

The prisoner was on his knees, held by two soldiers. Corporal Garrett took a savage grip of the man's hair, jerked his head back and in the wind-distorted light of the flaming torch looked down at the mud-streaked face of Eoin Feehan.

'Well, my beauty, your days of raiding and thieving have come to an end. You'll trample no more English soldiers with your wild Irish cattle.'

'What will we do with him, Corporal? Tie him up and take him back to Dublin?'

'What for? So some smart-talking lawyer can get him off with transportation and a better life in Botany Bay than he's ever known before? Oh no, my lad.' The Corporal jerked his head into the darkness. 'How is the Ensign?'

'He's still unconscious.'

'Then we'll deal with this Irish bog-trotter in our own way. Who's got a bayonet to loan me?'

A shocked silence followed, till the Corporal said, 'Come on! What's wrong with you? Don't tell me you've become squeamish all of a sudden. This Paddy tried to kill us – or do you think he sent two hundred cattle charging over sleeping men to give us a big laugh? Here, you – give me that.'

Corporal Garrett seized the handle of a bayonet from the belt of one of the soldiers and withdrew a two-foot-long blade from its scabbard. Twice slashing the air in front of him, he pushed the point of the bayonet against the skin beneath Eoin Feehan's chin as the squirming fisherman tried to force his head back from the cold steel blade. Turning to the others, the Corporal said, 'He was killed during the fight for the corn wagons, are we all agreed?'

There was neither agreement nor disagreement from the soldiers, but one or two of them licked their lips nervously.

The Corporal turned back to Eoin Feehan.

'If you've got a prayer you want to say, then you had better make it a quick one, Paddy. I'm going to count to ten silently, then the point of this bayonet will come out through the back of your neck. Right, start praying. . . . I'm counting.'

The silence lasted for only a few short seconds and then a hoarse tortured sound came from Eoin Feehan's throat.

'Wait! I'll do a deal with you.'

'A deal? What do you have that you think I want?'

'Names. I'll tell you the names of the others who were with me tonight, if you let me go.'

The Corporal looked with disgust at the face of the man before him. Eoin Feehan's eyeballs were rolling back in terror and his whole body trembled uncontrollably.

The soldier shrugged. 'Names are no good to me. One Irishman is much the same as another as far as I'm concerned. You can give me all the names you like; there are too many of you cottiers on the roads of Ireland for us to stop every one of you and ask for names.'

'We are not cottiers. We are fishermen, and I can tell you where to find the others.'

For the first time Corporal Garrett showed interest in what Eoin Feehan was saying.

'Fishermen, eh? How many of you were here tonight?'

'Eight. There were eight of us.'

'So you'll give me seven names and tell me where I can find them.'

'Yes, if you'll only let me go. Please. . . .'

Eoin Feehan was breathing with difficulty now, fear paralysing the muscles of his diaphragm.

Corporal Garrett turned to his men. 'Well, what do you say, lads? Do we make it seven for one? Or is it better to kill the goose we've got?'

Eoin Feehan's hope of survival lay in the fact that the soldiers were reluctant to see a man killed in cold blood. One of them said, 'Let him go, Corporal. We know his face. We'll find him again if he's lying to us.'

'*Are* you lying?' The point of the bayonet drew blood as the Corporal leaned on the weapon.

'No. I swear it!'

'All right.'

The bayonet was eased back, and the Corporal casually wiped the bloody tip of the blade on Eoin Feehan's shirt-front as the reprieved man slumped before him, aware that he had been within five brief heartbeats of death.

Tapping the flat of the blade against the palm of his hand, Corporal Garrett said, 'Before we begin, what is *your* name.'

'Feehan, Eoin Feehan.'

'Right, Eoin, my name is Corporal Garrett and I want us to understand each other from the very beginning, because if you lie to me there will not be a rock in the whole of Ireland large enough for you to hide under. Do you understand that?'

Eoin Feehan nodded, fighting to keep the fear from his voice. 'I won't lie.'

'Good. Who are the men who were with you tonight, and where can we find them?'

Eoin Feehan gave him the name of every man who had been on that night's raid, leaving out only one. His brother, Sean.

When he had ended, the Corporal frowned.

'Why should fishermen get themselves mixed up in something like this? They aren't starving.'

'We belong to the All-Ireland Association. We thought we ought to do something to help the cottiers. We didn't mean for anyone to get hurt—'

'Shut up!' Corporal Garrett's contempt for the man before him hid the excitement he felt at the disclosure Eoin Feehan had just made.

'Isn't this All-Ireland Association led by Eugene Brennan,

the MP – the man who was acquitted in Dublin on a charge of treason?'

'Yes.'

Corporal Garrett looked at Eoin Feehan thoughtfully. He regretted giving his word to set him free. His evidence against the All-Ireland Association would be welcomed by those in authority. However, if he, Corporal Garrett, could arrest members of the Association for an attack on the Army, it might lead to fresh charges being laid against the Irish MP. It might even lead to the outlawing of the All-Ireland Association. Such a coup should result in Corporal Garrett rapidly becoming Sergeant Garrett.

There was a sudden commotion from nearby and one of the soldiers cried out that he had caught one of the raiders sneaking back.

As other soldiers went to his aid, a white-faced Eoin Feehan snatched at the sleeve of the Corporal in alarm.

'He must have seen me here!'

'Probably. So what?'

'He'll know I've told you everything. He'll get word back to Kilmar, telling them.'

'That's your problem. Nothing to do with me.'

'Yes, it is. I've kept my word to you. You've got to protect me. You must kill him.'

Corporal Garrett looked at Eoin Feehan in disgust and spat at his feet. 'Are you telling me your life is worth something and his isn't?' He looked at Eoin Feehan until the fisherman turned his head away.

'All right, Eoin Feehan. It just so happens that I don't think any Irishman's life is worth very much. For that reason alone I will kill him. Not to please you.'

With the bayonet glinting in his hand, the corporal walked to where the soldiers held their struggling prisoner.

Eoin Feehan heard the harsh bark of the corporal's voice. Then there was a sudden silence that brought him out in a cold sweat. The silence was broken by a stifled scream that died away in a bloody gurgling as Corporal Garrett cut the prisoner's throat.

Eoin Feehan looked up as two of the soldiers dragged a limp body face downwards through the dirt toward him and deposited it at his feet.

Corporal Garrett said, 'Before you go you can tell me which of your friends this was.'

He turned the body over with his foot and Eoin Feehan looked down at the wide-eyed slack-jawed face of his brother Sean.

Chapter Twelve

The raid on the escorted wagons had gone terribly wrong for the young men from Kilmar.

The turning-point had been the moment Corporal Garrett put his musket to his shoulder and pulled the trigger. Until then, everything had gone exactly as it had been planned. With two loaded wagons already on their way to the cottiers and another about to pull away behind the one he was driving, Dermot knew the exhilaration of success.

He felt the blow from the musket-ball without even hearing the sound of the shot. It was as though someone had punched him low down on the right side of his body. Seconds later the fire from the wound flared up inside him. Gasping that he had been shot, Dermot passed the reins of the horse to his companion and gave way to the nauseous darkness that roared inside his head and poured out to engulf him.

At the handover point a rough dressing was put on Dermot's wound and a makeshift stretcher constructed to carry him home.

Anxiously, the fishermen waited for the fourth wagon, but it did not come. Eoin Feehan and one other man were missing. When the fishermen agreed that they dared wait no longer, Sean Feehan declared he would return to search for his brother while the others hurried Dermot to Kilmar.

Shortly before they reached the village, the man who had been detailed to steal the fourth wagon with Eoin Feehan caught up with them and told of Eoin's capture. He told them he had given Sean Feehan the same information.

The fishing village was not asleep, despite the lateness of the hour. The raid on the grain-wagons had been a well-kept secret, but with so many young men missing from their homes it quickly became apparent that something was afoot.

When the men carrying the unconscious Dermot entered the village, doors banged open and heads appeared at windows. As questions and answers were called back and forth across the narrow street, men began pulling on their clothes to follow the small procession.

It was a grim-faced band of adventurers who trooped into Norah McCabe's house and laid her son on his own bed. He had regained consciousness intermittently along the way, and the aggravation of the pain by the bouncing of his stretcher had brought him bolt upright, screaming in agony. Now he was so weak he seemed to be hardly breathing.

Norah McCabe looked at Dermot's bloodless face and as she examined the wound sent one of the young fishermen to fetch old Bridie O'Keefe to the house.

'While she's coming the rest of you can tell me exactly what has been happening.'

The fisherwoman listened in tight-lipped silence as she busied herself removing Dermot's clothing and cleaning the ugly inflamed area around the blue-edged bullet-wound.

While she was working, Kathie Donaghue entered the room. She had been waiting in the small cottage on the hill for news of the raid and had seen the sudden increased activity in the village. Now she stood in silence beside the bed as the water in the bowl used by Norah McCabe became red with Dermot's blood.

When she heard the full story of the night's events, Norah McCabe shook her head in incredulous disbelief. 'Did you honestly believe you would get away with such stupidity without something like this happening?'

When none of the men replied, she turned to Kathie. 'Did you know about this?'

Kathie nodded unhappily, unable to meet the unhappiness in the older woman's eyes.

'You disappoint me, Kathie. It's well known that the young men of County Wexford have more brawn than brain, but I would have credited you with more sense than to encourage them.'

'If others in years past had acted instead of talked, it wouldn't have been necessary for us to do what was done tonight,' said one of the young men defiantly.

'Talked, you say? Talked? Take a walk through the graveyards of Wexford with your eyes open and you'll soon see what talking has been done in years past. You'll find my grandfather's name there and many more besides. They were hanged for doing more than talking – and a fat lot of good it did anyone. Don't you speak to me of things you know nothing about, young man. A little more talking and my son wouldn't be lying here with a musket-ball inside him. Now you can all get out and leave me to get ready for Bridie O'Keefe. I only hope to God she can do something to right your folly.'

'I'd like to stay,' said Kathie in a strangely subdued voice.

'Then get some water boiling and keep it going while Bridie O'Keefe is here. There will be plenty for her to do up here, and she is not a patient woman.'

As Kathie moved to go downstairs she was obliged to stand back for a short but heavily built old woman with a face as wrinkled as a walnut. Bridie O'Keefe wheezed her way to the bedroom stair by stair, passing Kathie without a sideways glance. The girl wrinkled her nose in distaste. Bridie O'Keefe smelled as though it had been many months since she had last taken off any of her dirty black clothing.

Despite her unprepossessing appearance, Bridie O'Keefe did what needed to be done with speed and great efficiency. Kathie was kept busy running to and fro with boiling water and torn-up linen. Finally, she had to clean a wickedly sharp knife that had been worn to a fine point on a grindstone.

An hour after she arrived, an ugly lead-grey musket-ball lay in a bowl in the kitchen and Dermot slept in less pain than before in his room upstairs. The operation was over.

'He'll need plenty of rest,' declared Bridie O'Keefe, wiping her hands on a blood-stained cloth before the kitchen fire. With a feeling of revulsion, Kathie saw that the old hag's fingernails were broken and black. 'But he's not likely to get it in this house.'

'Why?' Norah McCabe was startled by the old lady's remark.

'On the way here I heard it being said that the two Feehan boys were missing from tonight's raid.'

Kathie drew in her breath sharply; she had known nothing about the missing men.

'I hope for the sake of the young men of Kilmar that they return safely – Eoin Feehan in particular. Like all bullies he is not the bravest of men. The soldiers would only have to threaten him with violence for him to break down and tell them all he knows.'

'He and his brother might be dead,' said Kathie.

'Then Tomas Feehan will claim their bodies and the soldiers will search this village for their friends. Dermot will be hard to hide with a hole in his side. Dead or alive, the Feehans will bring no good to this house – and none to you, girl. Don't you forget that.'

Abruptly, Bridie O'Keefe turned to Norah McCabe. 'I will be back in the morning. I doubt whether anything will happen before then.'

When Bridie O'Keefe had left the house, Kathie asked Norah McCabe, 'What did she mean about the Feehans bringing no good to this house, or to me?'

'It's no use trying to understand Bridie O'Keefe's sayings, but you'd best heed what she said. Bridie hears voices that speak to few humans – and she is rarely wrong.'

At dawn, Eoin Feehan returned to Kilmar in a state of near-collapse and rendered almost speechless with shock. All he was able to say to those who gathered about him was that the soldiers had killed Sean.

When Tomas Feehan arrived on the scene, Eoin broke down completely and sobbed out a disjointed story of being captured, of a rescue attempt by Sean and escape in the ensuing chaos. He told how he had hidden in some bushes until he had seen the soldiers carry Sean's body into the firelight at their scattered camp.

'There was nothing I could do. . . .' Eoin Feehan sobbed bitterly as, helped by his grieving father, he was led away through the crowd of sympathetic listeners.

There were many questions Kathie would have liked to put to the surviving Feehan, but they would have to wait. For a few days she was kept busy helping to nurse Dermot. Now fully conscious, he was impatient at being confined to bed. He felt that things were about to happen in the world outside Kilmar village and he wanted to be involved in them.

He made Kathie repeat Eoin Feehan's story to him twice and then lay back on the pillows, his hands clenched as he thought again of the abortive raid.

'Poor Sean.' He thought of the eagerness of the seventeen-year-old to be included in the raid. 'But his death won't be forgotten. We'll avenge it before we're through.'

Kathie looked at him in alarm. 'Don't be stupid, Dermot. You are lucky to be alive yourself. Besides, the soldiers will probably come here to Kilmar looking for Sean's friends. You try to think of ways to elude them, not of avenging Sean.'

Dermot struggled to sit up, fighting the pain in his side. 'The soldiers coming here? Then I can't stay in this house. I've got to talk to the others. We must make plans. . . .'

'What is all this foolish talk of making plans?' demanded Norah McCabe, entering the room. 'I would have thought you and your friends had had quite enough of "plans". Sean Feehan is dead and you've come as near to it as matters. If there are any plans to be made now, then you'd best leave them to someone who has the sense to think them out first. Liam is the only one in this house who is to be trusted to make sensible "plans".'

'But Liam isn't here. He's a few hundred miles away, in England.'

'Not for long, he isn't. I've asked Father Clery to send word for him to come home.'

'You can't do that. He's there raising money for Eugene Brennan's distress fund – for the cottiers.'

'This family has already done enough for cottiers. With no man about the place I'll soon need a fund started for me – and I can't see any of your potato paupers lining up outside my door to help me. They are all up in the hills filling their bellies with the food you and your friends were stupid enough to steal for them.'

'You don't have to worry, Ma. I'll be up and about again in a few days.'

'I hope so, but not for fishing. You'll need to have strength enough to run from the soldiers – and they will be here, you mark my words.'

A few minutes later, when both women were downstairs in the kitchen, Kathie asked, 'Have you really sent for Liam?'

'Yes.'

Norah McCabe was on her knees, cleaning out the ash from the fire.

'How long do you think it will be before he arrives?'

Norah McCabe looked up at Kathie but was unable to read her expression.

'Why? Are you frightened of what he will have to say about this stupid escapade?'

'No. Well . . . a little. More than a little. . . . But it isn't that. I feel safe when Liam is around. Somehow it doesn't matter what has gone wrong; Liam always manages to sort things out.'

Norah McCabe snorted. 'Things have gone beyond the sorting-out stage this time. But I have no doubt that Liam will do his best.' She brushed as though she would wear the stone away. 'You think a lot of him, don't you?'

'Yes.'

'Does he know how you feel?'

'I don't know.' Kathie remembered how Liam had held her after the fight. Each of their bodies had responded to the other in that brief exciting moment, but he had not attempted to repeat the experience before leaving for London. 'I don't know,' she repeated.

'Liam has had little time to think about girls,' said Norah McCabe. 'He has spent far too long thinking about his brother and me. When he returns from London you make sure he understands your feelings for him. You both have a deal of happiness owed to you.'

Chapter Thirteen

Eugene Brennan was becoming concerned about Liam's relationship with Lady Caroline Dudley. He had seen the way Liam looked at her when they returned to her house after the disrupted public meeting and it was hardly the look a fisherman should give to an earl's sister.

Since then there had been other occasions to worry him. At a fund-raising party arranged by Lady Caroline and attended by many of her London society friends, he had watched Liam's face as the hostess joked with the men present. Once, when she laughed and touched the arm of the man with whom she was talking, Eugene Brennan was afraid Liam was about to stride across the room and strike the other man.

Lady Caroline paid Liam no obvious attention at the party, but his artless devotion to her was not missed by the gossip-hungry women at the gathering.

'But, *darling*, it is so terribly *touching*,' said one acid-toned dowager, within the MP's hearing. 'I had intended buying one of those delightful little Maltese poodles, they become such *devoted* pets, but now I feel I simply *must* find myself an Irish fisherman.'

Eugene Brennan told himself it was probably no more than the admiration of an impressionable young man for a beautiful woman; nevertheless, he felt it wise to mention the matter to Liam.

The old politician chose the day when he and Liam left London together to attend a meeting in the university city of Cambridge. Liam was as miserable as a young swain parted from his sweetheart, but when Eugene Brennan brought up the subject of Lady Caroline Dudley he pretended to fall asleep in the swaying carriage and the opportunity passed.

The Cambridge meeting was a huge success and afterwards, much to Liam's relief, Eugene Brennan stayed on to take part in a political discussion, leaving Liam free to return to London alone.

Liam saw none of the winter beauty of the English countryside. The patchwork of green and brown fields, the woods and gently sloping hills passed by unnoticed, so eager was he to return to Caroline.

He arrived at the house in the early afternoon only to find that his hostess was not at home. In answer to his questions, the servants would only say Lady Caroline was 'out', although he felt sure they were keeping something back from him.

He settled down in the drawing-room to await her return and was still there when the marble clock on the mantelshelf chimed the hour of midnight. By now Liam was having great difficulty in staying awake. Feeling thoroughly miserable, he decided to go to bed.

Last night, in the hard bed at the Cambridge inn, he had lain awake wondering whether Caroline was missing him as much as he missed her. He had thought of the words he would say to her when they were together once more in the warm and exciting intimacy of her bedroom. They were loving words. Words he had never spoken to any other woman. He was going to tell her how much he loved her . . . of the change she had brought to his life. True, she had a title and he was only a fisherman, but he no longer thought of her as *Lady* Caroline, and he would work hard to better himself. He would read books of the kind kept on the shelves of her own library, would study the social graces. He would learn to dress well – his knowledge in this direction had already improved tremendously since coming to London. Eugene Brennan had told Liam he spoke well and had the gift of holding an audience's attention. One of his friends had jokingly suggested that Liam should be in Parliament himself. Well, why not? Liam was sure the old Irish MP would give his support. One day Liam could take his place at Caroline's side, and she would be proud of him.

They had been the dreams of yesterday and now they stuck in Liam's throat like a herring-bone as he made his way up the elaborate staircase to his room. His dream of a tender reunion with Caroline had no more substance than the romantic notions of an immature boy. The hurt he felt was entirely of his own making.

As he undressed, he was ready to accept what Eugene Brennan had tried to tell him in the carriage on the way to Cambridge. Liam and Caroline came from two irreconcilable backgrounds. Yet they had found a way to each other in the darkness of a bedroom. Liam would never forget their nights together. Could never fully accept that the fire that had burned then might be so utterly extinguished by convention.

As he climbed into his bed and pulled the blankets up about his body, Liam thought he had never been so miserable in his life.

He heard the carriage turn into the square and the steel-shod hoofs of the horse slide to a halt on the stones of the road outside the house. Liam heard Caroline's voice, and his jealousy flared up anew when he heard the deeper tones of a man's voice answer her. Liam could not hear what was said. Then the hoofs clattered noisily upon the road and the leather-sprung carriage creaked away into the night.

The door from the street slammed shut and there were running feet on the stairs. They stopped outside his door, and after a brief pause – perhaps a moment of indecision – the door swung open quietly.

'Liam . . . are you awake?'

The question came in a hoarse whisper.

'Um . . . ?'

The answer came reluctantly. Liam had decided he would pretend to be asleep.

Caroline slipped into the room, closing the door behind her, and crossed the room to the bed.

'Oh, Liam, I am sorry I was not here when you arrived. But I had a long-standing engagement that could not be broken. Darling, please say you forgive me. I have been so unhappy all evening, sitting with dreary people, wanting all the time to be here with you.'

There seemed to be a brittleness in her, a taut nervousness. Suddenly, for no apparent reason, Liam was reminded of the deep unhappiness he had seen in her eyes when he had first met her at Inch House. Liam wanted her, needed her desperately, but he was hurt and confused.

'I heard a man's voice, when the carriage drew up outside. . . .'

'A man? That must have been the cabbie. I caught a hansom cab home, to be here as quickly as possible. Oh Liam . . . darling. Tell me you have missed me. Tell me you want me. Tell me. . . .'

Liam's chest and throat constricted so much that he was

hardly able to speak. When the sound came out he did not recognise it as his own voice.

'I want you, Caroline. God, but I want you.'

Her mouth came down to cover his as she wriggled out of her clothes. A few moments later she was in bed with him, her body against his, demanding to be taken.

Except for the words that would not now be said, the reunion after their brief parting was all that Liam had hoped for. Much later, Liam lay in the happy half-real world between waking and sleeping, Caroline's head resting on his shoulder and his arms about her.

Then he felt her tears upon his shoulder and, reaching up a hand, he followed their trail to touch her open eyes.

'What is it? What's the matter?'

'Nothing.'

The long body-juddering sob that escaped from her belied the word, but when Liam pressed her for an explanation she turned to him fiercely and they made love with an abandonment that left no room for conversation. Afterwards, Liam fell into a deep and exhausted sleep.

He awoke suddenly with the feeling that he was alone and reached out for Caroline. The bed was empty, but he heard a noise in the room.

'Caroline, is that you?'

'Yes, Liam.'

He lay back with a contented smile, waiting for her to come to the bed and put her arms about him. There was only the continued rustling of clothing and it was then he remembered the tears of the night.

'Is something wrong?'

Again there was only silence and Liam threw back the untidy bedclothes, intending to go to her.

'No, Liam. Stay there. I have something to say to you.'

Liam frowned but made no further move to go to her. He leaned back on the pillows and clasped his fingers behind his head.

'I won't be here with you tonight.'

'Why?' It came out as a cry of distress. 'Do you have to go away somewhere?'

'No . . . yes . . . I really don't know. It is quite possible I may have to go to a house I own in Oxfordshire.'

Liam smiled and relaxed. 'Oh, that's all right. Eugene will be back today. I'll persuade him to go to Oxford. I'm quite sure your friends there will donate to the cottiers' fund.'

'No, Liam!' Caroline gave an agonised cry of despair. 'I am trying to tell you everything between us must end. My . . . my husband has returned to England. He will be coming here today.'

'Your *husband*?' Liam sat upright in the bed, his mouth dropping open with shocked surprise. 'Your . . . your *husband*?'

'I . . . I am sorry, Liam.' She was crying, and the sound distorted her words. 'I thought you knew. He is leading a Treasury Commission on army expenditure and has been in India for some months. I did not expect him home quite so soon but I had a message yesterday, from Falmouth. His ship arrived there on its way to London.'

In the long silence that followed, Liam thought the thudding of his heart would waken the whole household.

'I didn't know. . . . I never dreamed. . . . Will he be coming here? Staying here tonight – with you?'

'Only if his ship is late docking. Otherwise we will leave for Oxfordshire today.'

'Then I had better leave the house this morning.'

'That won't be necessary, Liam.' Her sudden laugh was shaky. 'Richard is a civilised man. You are a guest in this house, here to raise money for a charitable cause. There is no question of you leaving.'

Liam sank back on the pillow, his thoughts in utter confusion. He was in another man's house, a man he had cuckolded, yet was expected to remain as a welcome guest while everyone tried to pretend nothing had happened. He did not believe that such a secret could be kept from Caroline's husband. It was unthinkable that he should even try.

'Richard is a lot older than I, Liam.' Caroline broke in on his thoughts.

'You must have accepted that when you married him.'

'It was an arranged marriage, Liam. Richard had money and my father had very little. He thought he would have to give up the estate in Ireland. Then Richard offered to settle my father's outstanding debts. In return, my father would obtain a title for Richard from his old friend Lord Melbourne, who was Prime Minister at the time. I think marrying me was an afterthought, to ensure that my father did what was required of him. He was well known for forgetting his debts. Well, Richard married me and Lord Melbourne obtained a baronetcy for him.'

Caroline came closer to the bed. 'I have never been a real wife to him, Liam. Richard enjoyed having me as a hostess for his friends and that was all he required of me. It was not what I either expected or wanted from marriage, but there was nothing I could do. When I pleaded with Richard to take me with him on one of his frequent trips abroad, he told me his duties took him to the world of men, where women had no place. I did not know it when we married, but there is no place for a woman in Richard's personal life. To him they are a social necessity, nothing more.'

She spoke quietly but with more firmness now.

'On our wedding night Richard told me what was expected of me – as a wife – before he went to his own room. He told me I might do as I wished – but with discretion, of course. There must be no hint of a scandal. That might injure his career.'

Caroline tried to laugh, but it collapsed and became a stifled sob. 'Can you imagine that, Liam? To be told on your wedding night that you can have affairs with other men, providing you are discreet? No, it was not what I had expected from marriage.'

She stopped speaking and Liam knew she waited for his sympathy, for his understanding, but he could think of no words to say. Eugene Brennan had been right to worry about him; Liam could not comprehend this world of double standards. He was not and never could be a part of it.

'Liam, I'm sorry.'

Liam believed her, but he could say nothing. A moment later she was gone.

Caroline did not come downstairs for breakfast, and Liam did not see her before he left the house. He wished now that Eugene Brennan was not in Cambridge. He felt utterly dejected and alone but he could not remain in the house, expecting the arrival of Caroline's husband at any moment

As Liam walked the streets of London, the day was as gloomy as his thoughts, the sky overhead heavily overcast, a cold drizzle putting a dark coat on the slate rooftops and polishing roads and pavements.

He walked along the Strand, stopping to look in shop windows bright with beribboned merchandise and decorated with branches of evergreen trees. With a sudden sense of shock, Liam remembered that today was Christmas Eve. He had bought a present for Caroline, the figurine of a young girl embracing a swan, created in fine Dresden porcelain. He had been looking forward to giving it to her on Christmas morning and it lay, carefully wrapped, at the back of a drawer in his room.

Liam turned away from the shop windows and made his way aimlessly along the edge of the pavement. The wide road here was busy with every form of transportation: brewers' drays, farm carts laden with produce, heading for Covent Garden market; high-seated hackney carriages; horse-drawn omnibuses and a myriad carts and barrows threading through the traffic with a skill inherited from generations of costers.

Along the wet pavements, unsmiling men with coat collars turned up against the wind and hands thrust deep in overcoat pockets pushed on their way determinedly, elbowing aside other unsmiling men and long-coated women with umbrellas who endeavoured to keep their long impractical skirts clear of the mud and dirt underfoot.

Here a man could be part of a crowd and yet remain alone. There was not a single word of greeting, or the face of a friend. It was exactly what Liam needed and he lost himself among the citizens of London, isolated from them by his thoughts.

Later in the day he found himself walking by the side of the Thames. It was too far up-river for deep-sea ships, but the surface of the water here was alive with smaller vessels and oared boats. It reminded him of Kilmar and his own boat. It was the first time since he arrived in London that he had given any real thought to the little fishing village and those he had left there. Strangely, he found that he felt more guilty when he remembered Kathie Donaghue than he did when he thought of Caroline's husband.

He wondered whether Kathie and her father would be spending Christmas with his mother and Dermot. Suddenly, Liam was sick of London and everything here. He wanted to be home in Kilmar.

Liam turned his footsteps toward Caroline's house as the tide began to move up the river, bringing with it heavier rain and a prolonged early twilight.

The house was the scene of great activity and there were lights on in almost every room. Luggage was being carried indoors from a mud-spattered carriage, and Liam threaded his way through piles of trunks and cases in the hall. He had intended making his way straight to his bedroom, but the door to the drawing-room opened and Caroline came out

Seeing Liam, she exclaimed, 'Why, there you are, Liam. I have been looking for you everywhere. Richard is dying to meet you.'

She took his hand without a trace of embarrassment and led him to the drawing-room. He would have wished to look his best for this meeting. Instead, he was soaked through, his trousers clinging to his legs, wet and cold, and his dark hair plastered down on his head, water trickling from it inside the collar of his shirt.

Sir Richard Dudley stood with his back to the fire, legs astride, an outsize glass of brandy in his hand. A small man, he was immaculate from his highly polished black boots to the top of his sparse grey hair. He was even older than Liam had expected and was exceedingly ugly. The discovery boosted Liam's flagging confidence momentarily.

Caroline introduced the two men, and her husband eyed Liam with one eyebrow raised in surprise at the younger man's appearance.

'So this is your young fisherman who has taken London by storm. It rather looks as though he has been out pursuing his calling.'

It did not escape Liam's notice that the baronet addressed his wife and did not speak directly to him.

'Richard is right, Liam. You are absolutely soaked through. Where have you been? You look as though you have been walking in the rain all day. Here, you must have a glass of brandy to warm you and then go straight upstairs and change, before you take a chill.'

'I am quite sure he will be all right, my dear. Irish fishermen are a hardy breed, quite used to being out in all weathers. They are not fragile flowers, as you and I are.'

Sir Richard Dudley was smiling with his mouth but there

was no humour in his eyes. They were as cold as the London rain outside and suddenly Liam's guilt fell away from him. He did not care that he had made love to this man's wife. Perhaps the baronet's feelings had never been important. Liam realised that his hurt had been at not knowing, coupled with the thought of losing Caroline and the torment of thinking of another man possessing the right to touch and know her body.

That part of it still hurt, but not as much as before. Liam knew instinctively that what Caroline had told him about her relationship with her husband had been true. This man would never know his wife as Liam had.

Liam felt as though he had laid down an intolerable burden. He became a whole man again. There was a pain inside him that would remain for a very long time, but he had survived.

'Your husband is quite right, Caroline.' The smile disappeared from Sir Richard Dudley's face at Liam's use of his wife's name. 'We fishermen are a tough crowd; but, yes, I will have a brandy – a large one, please.'

Liam's accent had never sounded out of place in this house before, but now, with the immaculate Sir Richard Dudley standing before the pink Adam fireplace, Liam felt his tongue thicken in his mouth and his words came out wrapped in an accent as thick as that of any west-coast bog cottier. It did not worry Liam. When Caroline handed him a half-full brandy-glass, Liam raised it to her husband.

'Here's health to fishermen and fragile flowers, Sir Richard. May the sun bring its blessings upon us all.'

He downed his drink quickly and placed the empty glass upon a nearby table. The brandy burned a path down his throat and exploded in his stomach with a satisfying raw heat, and Liam remembered he had not eaten since breakfast.

'Now I will go and change out of these wet clothes. Eugene will probably be taking me out to dinner tonight. If you'll excuse me . . . ?'

'Of course.'

Sir Richard Dudley was icily correct, but he had an angry glint in his eyes and Liam knew he had made an enemy.

Later, when Liam had changed, he returned downstairs. The bustle in the hall had ended and there was not a servant to be seen. Liam thought Caroline and her newly returned husband had gone to their own rooms, but as he approached the drawing-room the door was open and he could hear them inside. They were talking about him.

'. . . the man is a nobody, an ignorant lout. Why you allowed him to have the run of the house and treated him as a guest I will never know. He would have been far happier accommodated in the servants' quarters.' Sir Richard Dudley's voice was high-pitched and peevish.

'He is in England at the invitation of Eugene Brennan, Richard, and his talks are very well received. He has already raised thousands of pounds for famine relief. Every house in London is open to him. Could I do less than treat him as a guest?'

'I really do not know why he has to stay in this house at all.'

'He is here because I invited him to stay after meeting him at Inch House.'

Sir Richard Dudley snorted derisively. 'The damned Irish are a thorough nuisance. If they were to put in a good day's work for themselves, they would not have these incessant famines. They are for ever screaming for help from England. I am surprised Peel listens to them. Left to their own devices they would discover a remedy quickly enough.'

'Richard! We cannot allow women and children to starve. You must come to one of Liam's talks and hear of the appalling suffering he has seen—'

'I have no intention of listening to any Irish fairy stories,' Sir Richard Dudley snapped. 'You must do whatever amuses you, but do not expect me to waste my money on any of your misguided charities – and I must ask you to arrange for that fisherman to leave this house at the earliest opportunity. Why is he mixed up in such a cause at all? The potato famine does not affect fishing. Is he one of Brennan's rabblerousers?'

What Caroline's reply would have been, Liam never knew. As he listened, poised to enter the room, there came a hammering at the front door of the house. As it was only a few paces away, Liam opened the door and Eugene Brennan swept into the house clutching Liam by the arm.

'Thank heaven you are here. I was afraid you would be out gallivanting this Christmas Eve.' He waved a letter in the air. 'You'll need to go straight back to Ireland. That fool brother of yours and his friends have attacked the English Army and taken grain and beef for the cottiers. One of them got himself killed, and all hell has broken loose.'

Perspiration stood out on the old man's face as though he had run all the way to the house, although Liam had seen his carriage waiting in the street outside.

'Well, well, Mr Brennan. It sounds very much as though you have lost control of your followers yet again. After what my wife has been telling me about conditions in Ireland I must admit I am surprised. I hardly thought the poor starving masses would have the strength to cause trouble.'

Sir Richard Dudley spoke from the doorway of the drawing-room.

'There is always strength in a man's heart to fight injustice,' retorted Eugene Brennan. 'But by the time England has a prime minister who understands that it will be too late.'

'Oh? For whom, England or Ireland?'

'For both our countries, Sir Richard. Now, if you will excuse me, I will help Liam to pack. He will need to return to Ireland immediately.'

'How sad.'

Sir Richard Dudley's expression belied his words. He looked happier than Liam had yet seen him. But Caroline was genuinely concerned for Liam and a short while afterwards she stopped him in the corridor outside his room.

'Liam, if there is any way in which I might be of help, please let me know.'

'Thank you.'

Liam's curtness was due to concern for his brother. Eugene Brennan's letter was from Father Clery; it gave details of the raid and told of Dermot's wound. The MP had told Liam there would be serious repercussions for all of them. Dermot would certainly be arrested, and some of Sir Robert Peel's party were demanding that the All-Ireland Association be banned.

'I am sorry to hear the news of your brother . . . and I am even more sorry for hurting you. That was the last thing I wanted to happen, believe me.'

Liam said nothing; it had all been said.

'You will come to see me if you return to London?'

He looked at her and saw she was very close to tears. He did not want to hurt her any more.

'I won't be returning to London.'

'Then I will come looking for you in Kilmar.'

Suddenly she rested her hands upon his shoulders and, standing on tiptoe, kissed him quickly on the lips.

'Goodbye, my dearest, and take care. I will think of you often, and always with great fondness.'

With that she left him, and Liam felt as empty as he had that morning. This had been the worst day he had known since the death of his father.

Chapter Fourteen

Christmas Eve in Kilmar was no happier for the McCabe family than it was in London. It was the day the soldiers came.

The young men of the All-Ireland Association had been maintaining a watch on the Gorey road for them since the day Tomas Feehan brought the body of his youngest son home for burial. Even so, they were almost taken by surprise, for the soldiers came not from Gorey, but from the north. From Dublin.

In company strength, there were more than a hundred men of the 92nd Foot Regiment – the Gordon Highlanders – commanded by a stern and experienced captain. They entered the fishing village as arrogantly as only professional soldiers can, with bayonets fixed to their muskets and a single piper leading them.

With the soldiers, but considerably less arrogant, was the district magistrate. He had been summoned at great haste from his dinner the previous evening and, acting upon the orders of the Lord-Lieutenant of Ireland, had ridden to join the soldiers. He had spent a cold, comfortless and sleepless night in a draughty tent and was a most unhappy man.

With guards posted at every exit from the village, the magistrate stood on the quayside, surrounded by silent Highlanders, and called upon the citizens of Kilmar to come from their houses and hear the proclamation he was about to make.

Kilmar ignored him. A few curious children, a deaf hag, and an old ex-fisherman too crippled by rheumatism to move from the bollard on which he was sitting were all the audience the magistrate could command.

The day was bitterly cold, his teeth were chattering, and the magistrate was in a hurry to return home and join in the Christmas festivities. In consequence, his proclamation was scarcely audible, even to the soldiers about him.

'Whereas it has been represented to me that divers persons took part in an attack upon Her Majesty's subjects . . . inflicting injuries upon forces of the Crown . . . stealing cattle and corn

. . . I call upon all the true and loyal subjects of the Queen to arrest these men . . . I declare them to be outside the protection of the law . . . persons aiding or succouring them shall be guilty of an offence.'

The proclamation ended with the names of seven of the men who had been on the raid. Eoin Feehan was not one of them. This omission did not pass unnoticed in Kilmar, but it was assumed that, before Sean Feehan died, he had been forced to give the names of his fellow-conspirators, and had balked at giving the name of his own brother.

The proclamation was made in the name of Lord Heytesbury, Lord-Lieutenant of Ireland. His reading completed, the shivering magistrate pinned the document to the locked door of the weighing-shed on the quay and looked about him at the village of Kilmar.

The only sound was the hissing of the tide on the shingle and the mocking cry of a seagull hanging on the wind above him.

The magistrate hurried to the warmth of the Kilmar alehouse, leaving the Captain and his kilted soldiers to search the houses of the fishermen systematically for the men named in the Lord-Lieutenant's proclamation.

They were a full hour too late.

Nathan Brock had been digging graves in a cottier settlement a couple of miles to the north of Kilmar when the soldiers approached along the road from Dublin and he quickly took the news to the villagers.

The initial reaction in Kilmar was one of panic, the Scots had earned a bloody reputation in Wexford, fifty years before. It was agreed that the men who had been on the raid would have to leave Kilmar immediately. The problem was knowing which way they should go. At this very moment more soldiers could be closing in on them from the south and west.

'There is only one place where you can be sure of being safe,' declared Nathan Brock. 'That's in the Wicklow mountains. You need to go no more than twenty-five miles to be in country where no Englishman dare set foot. There are hills and forests and streams and a mist that would hide Ireland itself.'

'And there are a hundred soldiers between us and the mountains,' retorted Eoin Feehan. He knew he had to throw in his lot with the others. If the Army did not find any of the men he had named in Kilmar, they might take him back with them instead – and he had no wish to sample more of Corporal Garrett's questioning.

'You will have to travel by the one route the soldiers won't be guarding,' said Nathan Brock patiently. 'You must go by sea. The weather isn't too bad, and there is nothing more natural than for the Kilmar fishermen to be at sea. When the soldiers search the village without finding anyone they are after they will wait until evening when the boats return. By that time, if you use the Feehan or McCabe boat, you will have landed a few miles up the coast and be well on your way to the mountains.'

Raising her voice above the noisy enthusiasm that greeted Nathan Brock's idea, Kathie cried, 'That is all very well for everyone else, but what about Dermot?'

The shouts about her died away.

'Can he walk yet?' asked the ex-prizefighter.

'No. He'll have to be carried – and he'll need someone to look after him properly for a week or two.'

'We can't take Dermot with us! We'll find it difficult enough to take care of ourselves in the mountains.'

'Would you have the soldiers find him, then, Eoin Feehan? Let them give him the choice of dying in prison, or recovering so that they might hang him? Oh no, Dermot goes with you – and I'll come along myself to make certain he's properly looked after.'

'You can't do that, Kathie,' Tommy Donaghue protested. 'It wouldn't be decent for one girl to be up there with so many men – and who would look after me?'

'You'll get by. No doubt Mrs McCabe will give you a meal or two. As for being decent, I'd be less than that if I stayed here doing nothing while Dermot died up in those mountains for lack of care. You go and tell the fishermen to get their boats in the water while I help Mrs McCabe to get Dermot ready.'

Norah McCabe was no more taken with the idea of Kathie going to the mountains than was Tommy Donaghue.

'It would not be right, Kathie. Besides, Dermot is not fit enough to go anywhere just yet. We'll find somewhere in the village to hide him.'

'There is nowhere in Kilmar where the soldiers won't look,'

insisted Kathie. 'If you keep him here, you'll be sentencing him to death yourself. I *know* Dermot shouldn't be moved, but it's his only chance and I am going with him to see that it isn't wasted. It's the only way, Mrs McCabe, really it is. You see, I feel I am as much to blame for what happened as any of the men who went on that raid. I had been goading Dermot for weeks, telling him that the Association was able to do nothing but talk. If only I'd had more sense, Dermot wouldn't be lying wounded now. I *must* go with him; I owe him that.'

'But what about Liam, Kathie? What shall I tell him when he comes home?'

For the first time, Kathie's resolution faltered. Then she looked directly at the other woman.

'Tell him the truth, Mrs McCabe. Tell him why I am going to the Wicklow mountains – and tell him I won't come home until Dermot is able to come back, too.'

High in the Wicklow mountains, on Christmas Day, Nathan Brock led the small band of Kilmar outlaws through wooded valleys and up gorse-covered slopes until they eventually arrived at a wild remote area of tumbled granite ridges, springy heather-carpeted uplands and coarse-tufted peat bogs. Here he suggested they should set to and construct dug-out cabins, roofing them with peat turfs cut from the bog about them.

Nathan Brock had decided to bring the party to the mountains himself when he learned that Kathie and the wounded Dermot would be travelling with them. Had he not made this decision, he knew that such an inexperienced and handicapped group would never reach the safety of the mountains undetected.

'You'll be as safe here as anywhere,' he said, looking across the empty miles to where a solitary hen-harrier beat its lazy progress above the heather, in search of an unwary bird or small mammal. 'The soldiers rarely find their way into these parts.'

'But how will we live?' asked Eoin Feehan. 'There is nothing up here.'

'You will have to follow his example,' said Nathan Brock, pointing to the harrier, which suddenly plummeted to the ground in a tumbling dive. 'Hunt. If things get too bad, you will find fish in the rivers, and food can always be stolen from the soldiers who camp near the towns. There are farmers, too, and they are sympathetic toward men on the run from the English – but be careful how you approach them. Thieves and cut-throats also hide in these mountains, and the farmers have their own ways of dealing with them.'

'It sounds a real home from home,' commented Dermot, smiling weakly between shivers. He had stood up to the journey well enough, thanks to Kathie's constant bullying of the men who took it in turns to carry him, but he could not get warm. The cold up here in the mountains worked its way to the very marrow of a man's bones. It was as persistent as the mist that lived upon the high ridges.

'Before we think of doing anything else we'll get a fire going,' declared Kathie firmly. 'The rest of you can stamp around to get warm; Dermot can't. As for food, we'll have to make do with salt fish for another day or two until someone organises the hunting.'

'What a way to spend Christmas Day,' complained one of the Kilmar men. 'You would have thought the soldiers might have waited for a few more days.'

'They no doubt expected to catch you off guard,' said Nathan Brock.

'And so they would, had it not been for you,' said Kathie. 'How long are you staying with us, Nathan?'

'Only until tomorrow. I will show some of you the nearest roads and farms and then I have a call to make before I return to Kilmar.'

'Your wife and children, Nathan?'

'Yes.' The big man grinned like a child anticipating a church party. 'They are in the poor-house at Rathconard, only a couple of miles from here. I have decided to take them back to Kilmar with me. There are a few derelict cottages on the hill behind the village. I can do one of them up and Liam has said there will always be work for me, either helping him with the fishing, or helping Tommy Donaghue on his trips to Gorey.'

'He'll need all the help you can give him now,' said Dermot. 'And I would like to think you were there helping him and Ma.'

'Right now we'd better be helping you,' said Kathie. One

of the Kilmar men put a flame to a small pile of furze and twigs as she and Nathan Brock helped Dermot to the shelter of a rock. Gratefully, the wounded fisherman held his hands out to the crackling, spitting fire.

'With any luck you'll not have to be up here for more than a few months,' said Nathan Brock. 'Unlike the constabulary, the Army has a short memory. Soldiers come and go quickly in Ireland and the new ones seldom take over old troubles. They make their own soon enough. Now, while you two get yourselves warm I'll show the others where to make the dug-outs. When they are completed you'll be as comfortable as fleas on a dog up here.'

He set the Kilmar outlaws to working hard, hoping to make the most of the few remaining hours of daylight. Temperatures would drop rapidly at nightfall and it was wise to have some shelter from the strong westerly winds which ripped across the exposed mountain slopes stripping bushes and bending trees.

'I would be happier if he were staying with us,' said Kathie to Dermot as she watched the big man bullying and cajoling. He made the men put up low turf walls among the granite outcrops, taking advantage of the natural landscape for shelter and concealment.

'And I would be happier if you returned to Kilmar with him,' commented Dermot, repeating the words he had said to her on a number of occasions since they had left the fishing village. 'This is no place for a girl.'

'We will discuss it when you are well.'

'What is your reason for coming away with us, Kathie? If it was Liam lying here wounded, I could understand it, but I don't believe you did it for me.'

'There has been nothing said between me and Liam,' declared Kathie quickly. 'I am as free as anyone else to do just as I please. We are all members of the same association and I didn't join just to pass the hat around at meetings.'

'But a woman living up here among so many men is bound to create difficulties, unless. . . .'

Dermot fell silent, and Kathie looked at him with a puzzled frown on her face. 'Unless what?'

'Unless you marry me.'

Kathie did not know whether or not he was serious, and she

did not want to know. Standing up from the fire, she said, 'This mountain air has blown away your senses, Dermot McCabe. I'll start some fish cooking while you still have enough wits about you to eat.'

Watching her walk away from him, Dermot himself wondered why he had made the offer of marriage. It was not something about which he had been thinking. But he did not regret having made the proposal. If Kathie had accepted him, he would have been proud to marry her.

Chapter Fifteen

Nathan Brock set off for the poor-house at Rathconard late the following afternoon. He had done all he could for the Kilmar fishermen and now he was his own man once more. A man with a family and hopes for the future. A happy man. He would get news into the poor-house tonight, and tomorrow his wife and the boys would meet him outside the town. Then they would all go on together to their new life in Kilmar. It was not the soft turf alone that put a spring in his steps.

It was easy enough to pass unnoticed, even when he reached the old military road that had been built for the soldiers involved in putting down the 1798 uprising. It was a bitterly cold day and the few people he saw had their coat collars turned up about their ears and their heads down against the wind.

He arrived at the outskirts of Rathconard before it was quite dark and huddled in a ditch at the side of the road, impatiently waiting for the slowly advancing darkness to settle over the town. When he was satisfied that he could not be recognised, Nathan Brock climbed from the ditch and made his way through the near-deserted streets to the poor-house.

But even here his suspense was not over. He hid in the shadows near the poor-house door for more than half an hour before he saw an old woman, bent against the wind, approaching.

As she turned in to enter the dimly lit doorway, he slipped out from his hiding-place and took her thin arm. Her immediate reaction was to snatch it free but, as gently as he could, Nathan Brock guided her to the shadows beside the doorway.

'It's all right. It's all right, mother. I'll not hurt you. I want you to do a small favour for me, that's all. Do you know Shelagh Brock?'

He released the old woman's arm but stood between her and escape into the poor-house.

'Eh? You'll have to speak up. I'm a bit deaf.'

The last thing Nathan Brock wanted was a shouted conversation here in the centre of Rothconard, but it seemed he had little choice. This old woman might be the only person entering the poor-house that night. He raised his voice as much as he dared.

'Shelagh Brock and her two boys. Do you know them?'

She cupped a hand to her ear and stood slack-jawed before him, lips drawn back from toothless gums.

Nathan Brock was unable to stifle his exasperation and, throwing away all attempts at caution, shouted his question in the old crone's ear.

'Do you know Shelagh Brock?'

'Shelagh Brock? Mrs Brock, d'you mean?'

Nathan Brock nodded his affirmation, elated at his belated success.

'She's not here, me dear. She's gone.'

'Gone? Gone where?'

The old woman shrank back from him, having no difficulty in hearing his last two shouted words.

'She's left. The master put her out.'

The old woman shook her head until she saw that the angry man in front of her was waiting for a reply. Her brow wrinkled and she thought hard.

'I don't know. . . . A month, maybe more.'

'Where did she go?' Nathan Brock had hold of the old crone's arm again, but seeing her wince in pain he hastily let it drop.

'Where does anyone go when they leave this place? The lucky ones are carried to a grave. The others . . . ? I don't know.'

'Then you had better stay outside for a while, mother. I am going in there to find out a thing or two.'

Anger had taken the place of discretion. Pushing past the old woman, Nathan Brock strode to the door of the poor-house and flung it open. Inside he entered a long ill-lit corridor with dormitories on either side. There was a strong smell of unwashed bodies and boiled cabbage. The sound of spoons scraping against earthenware bowls came from beyond a door at the far end of the corridor. When Nathan Brock opened it he found himself in the poor-house eating-room.

The large gloomy room was hopelessly overcrowded, with inmates packed shoulder to shoulder at long wooden tables, a bowl in front of each of them. Those at the nearest tables to the door looked up at him with a dull interest. Nathan Brock recognised the resigned expressions on the faces of every one of them, men, women and children. Here, in this room, were Ireland's failures – and each of them was thoroughly defeated. Even the smallest child accepted that life owed him nothing at all.

'What do you want?' The question was shouted across the room at Nathan Brock by a thick-set balding man who wore a dirty green waistcoat over a colourless shirt, and knee-breeches that rode over thick grey woollen socks.

'I am looking for the master.'

Those listening heard only the softness and none of the menace in his voice.

'You're looking at him. If you're thinking to find a place in here, you're out of luck. I turn a hundred away every morning. Away with you and shut that door as you go, I haven't got money to spare on heating.'

'I am not after lodging in your poor-house,' said Nathan Brock. 'I am seeking Mrs Brock.'

The poor-house master gave a derisive snort. 'You won't find her here. I turned her out. It's hard enough finding room for genuine distress cases, without harbouring the wives of criminals.'

Peering short-sightedly across the room, the poor-house master asked, 'Who are you, anyway? What do you want with her?'

'I am her husband.' Speaking as quietly as before, Nathan Brock advanced determinedly across the room toward the other man. 'Unless you can tell me where she has gone I intend cracking your head for you. A man who turns out a woman and her children in winter has no right to be in charge of a poor-house.'

The poor-house master backed away across the room, feeling his way with one hand behind him, not daring to take his eyes from Nathan Brock. As he went, he mouthed noiselessly, until the words escaped, his voice as high-pitched and squeaky as a young girl's, 'Seize him! Take him! He's a wanted criminal.'

Not one inmate moved. Even the spoons were stilled as the occupants of the room watched the unusual scene before them. Never before had anyone challenged the life-or-death authority of the poor-house master in this famine-hit area.

'Seize him, I say! I'll give a reward to the man who takes him,' the poor-house master squeaked as he backed away, trying to keep a table between Nathan Brock and himself.

One man, braver or more foolish than the others, moved to stand up just ahead of the ex-prizefighter. Placing his big right hand on the top of the other man's head, Nathan Brock sat him firmly back on his seat and in so doing almost pushed the pauper's chin through his breastbone.

With a quick agile move that scattered startled inmates and half-empty bowls, Nathan Brock vaulted across the long table, causing the poor-house master to scurry hurriedly behind another.

'You won't get away with coming in here and terrorising people who can't defend themselves.'

Nathan Brock said nothing and, as he circled the table, the poor-house master tried a new plea.

'I was only doing my duty when I put Mrs Brock out. I have to obey the rules laid down by the Board of Guardians. They say that the families of convicted criminals must not be housed here. I had to send your wife away.'

'When was I convicted?' Nathan Brock's voice hissed angrily at the other man. 'Or are you judge and jury of all men now?'

The two men stood facing each other, separated only by the width of the table. With a swift movement that took the poor-house master by surprise, Nathan Brock swept the people at the table aside and, gripping the edge of the table, heaved it over, scattering pots and bowls. The paupers on the far side scrambled away as the heavy table came over on them. Stepping through the confusion, Nathan Brock reached out and grabbed the front of the poor-house master's shirt with his good right hand. With his left he cuffed the squealing man into silence.

'Where did my wife and boys go?' he demanded.

'I don't know. How could I? I have more than enough to do looking after the inmates here without following what happens to those who leave.'

'I have no doubt you make more than your share of profit out of doing it.'

They were standing beside a small table upon which stood a huge cauldron, half-filled with lukewarm soup. It was water-thin, and the smell rising from it gave evidence that the vegetables used in its making had been in an advanced state of decomposition.

'How many others have you turned out to die?' asked Nathan Brock. When he had first burst into the eating-room to seek out the poor-house master he had wanted only to feel the man's neck between his hands and choke from him his reasons for turning out Shelagh and the two boys. Now the violent anger had been soaked up in the silent misery about him.

The poor-house master's eyes had not left Nathan Brock's face and he, too, had seen the black anger ebb away. 'I do my duty as I see it,' he declared. 'No one can do more.'

'Do you eat your own disgusting food, too?'

Nathan Brock banged the cauldron, disturbing its contents, and a foul aroma escaped from it like gases from a bog.

Some of Nathan Brock's anger returned. The poor-house master was given money enough to purchase better food than this.

Gripping the other man's hair, Nathan Brock bent him double and dunked his head into the soup. He held it there until the man began choking, thrashing the air desperately with his arms. When he thought the poor-house master had swallowed as much of the foul concoction as a man could reasonably take, he withdrew the man's head and allowed him to fall to the floor where he lay choking and retching.

Looking about him, Nathan Brock saw smiles on the faces of the inmates of Rathconard poor-house for the first time. But he was in no mood for humour. Somehow he had to find Shelagh and his two boys. It was a near-impossible task. There were hundreds of thousands of starving women and children on the roads and byways of Ireland.

The thought that they might at this very moment be lying somewhere out there, cold, hungry and desperate, hit him harder than any physical blow and he reeled blindly out of the room, crashing along the corridor and into the street outside.

'Mr Brock?'

A woman's voice brought him to his senses and he turned as a ragged woman ran from the poor-house toward him.

'It's about Shelagh, Mr Brock. We were friends. She was good to me when my child died.'

The voice was that of a young woman but the face turned up to his was lined with care and defeat.

'You know where she is?' Nathan Brock's hopes soared.

'No . . . but I know where she was going. She said she would go to Wexford, to seek you. I work in the kitchen here. I managed to get some food for her to take to eat along the way.'

'Bless you! But did she say where in Wexford she was going?'

'I'm not sure. It might have been Wexford Town.'

Behind them a door slammed inside the poor-house and noise spilled out on the street.

'You'd best be getting far away from here as quickly as you can, Mr Brock. The master is a spiteful man. He'll have the constabulary out looking for you in no time.'

'The constabulary know better than to search the countryside for a man in the dark. When did Shelagh leave?'

'It will be four weeks ago on Tuesday. She was hoping to find you before Christmas. She had told the boys you would all be together again by then.'

'God help them all.' Anything could have happened by now. Nathan Brock felt sick inside at the thought of his family wandering for a month, friendless and without money.

The woman standing before him shivered uncontrollably in the night air, and Nathan Brock put a big hand on her shoulder.

'Thank you for telling me . . . and for helping Shelagh when she needed a friend. You had better go inside before the master misses you and suspects you of talking to me.'

'I'll pray that you find Shelagh and the boys, Mr Brock. She was the only friend I ever had in this place.'

The woman turned and ran for the poor-house door. As she reached it she was engulfed in a crowd of complaining inmates. The enraged poor-house master had turned them all out of the building to search for Nathan Brock.

The noise quickly roused the whole town. Men holding lighted torches advanced on the poor-house, and Nathan Brock thought it was time to make his escape. Slipping into the dark shadows between two houses, he ran silently away from the scene of chaos behind him.

He was about to begin a search that would test the power of prayer, and his own determination, to its limits.

*

Nathan Brock followed the road southward until a late dawn broke over the hills. The road had been constructed during an earlier famine, when men had been employed on such public works. Because there would be no more work when it was completed, the road swung this way and that, covering twice as many miles as it might otherwise have done. Even so, Nathan Brock had put a considerable distance between himself and Rathconard.

He left the road and plunged into the forest that came down to the road on either side, pushing his way through the clumps of hazel and blackberry that tangled the forest floor.

Finding a dry nook in the shelter of an ancient oak-tree, he settled down to sleep away the daylight hours. A mile ahead the forest gave way to rich farmland and, as he was still in County Wicklow, Nathan Brock preferred to pass through this area unnoticed.

Sleep was long in coming to him. He tried to put himself in Shelagh's place and work out where she might go. It was impossible. She could be anywhere south of where he lay. She might even have changed her mind and gone north to Dublin. He tried not to think of the other alternative, but once, when he dozed off, he dreamed that he found them in one of the cottier communities of death that he had so often seen.

Eventually, Nathan Brock slept, but it was only for a couple of hours. He was brought awake by the high-pitched protest of an ungreased cart-axle. The horse was labouring up the hill from the unwooded valley, and Nathan Brock could hear the cursing of the farmer as he goaded the beast to greater effort.

He could hear another, younger voice, too, speaking in plaintive tones, but could not make out what was being said.

Curious, Nathan Brock left his bed of dry leaves and made his way to the top of a high ivy-covered bank beside the road as a farmer's cart passed by. It was laden with swedes and bundles of green kale—but that was not all. Lying uncomfortably balanced on top of the nobbly swedes, bound hand and foot, was Jeremy, the boy who had run away from Kathie and Kilmar a few weeks before. It was he who was doing the pleading. As Nathan Brock watched, the boy struggled to a sitting position and said something to the man holding the reins. The farmer turned around and with a backward cuff of his hand knocked Jeremy to a prone position once more.

The farmer's cart squeaked on its way for another quarter of a mile until it reached one of the steepest sections of the road through the hills. Here the road twisted to and fro across the slope in a bid to lessen the gradient. On one of the sharp bends the farmer saw a man reclining on the grassy bank beside the road, apparently asleep. As the cart drew nearer, the resting man moved and a hand rose to push back the soft-brimmed hat from his eyes and look upon the approaching farmer with exaggerated surprise.

The reclining figure was Nathan Brock. Just before the cart reached him, he rose to his feet and stepped out to the centre of the road, brushing himself down with great care.

The farm vehicle creaked to a halt as Nathan Brock completed his grooming and gave the farmer a beaming smile.

'Good day to you, sir. It's a fine day for this time of year.'

'Get off the road and let me pass. I'm late enough for market as it is.'

'Market, you say?' Nathan Brock walked around the cart and gave the incredulous Jeremy a cheerful wink. 'You have a fine load of swede and kale, but I can't see you getting much for the young boy. He's far too thin.'

'He's on his way to the constable. I caught him stealing. Caught him red-handed.'

'Did you, now? And what was he stealing? Cattle? Sheep? Your valuables?'

'He was stealing ducks. He crawled into their house during the night and wrung the necks of two of them.'

The farmer moved a bundle of kale to one side and exposed the corpses of two plump white ducks.

'I've brought the evidence to show the constable.'

Nathan nodded seriously. 'Nothing is safe these days. You must have a hard time with so many hungry cottiers ready to steal food wherever they can.'

The farmer snorted. 'They are no problem to me. I threw them off my land when the potato failed and I had the Army behind me. They know better than to come back and try anything.'

'But take this youngster, now. Wouldn't it save you a lot of trouble to give him a whipping and send him on his way with a sore backside to remind him of the virtues of honesty?'

'Not him! You only have to look at his face. He's a vicious

young rogue if ever I saw one. A few months in prison will do him a power of good.'

Jeremy looked pleadingly at Nathan Brock. 'It won't just be a few months in prison. I've been caught stealing before. I was whipped then. Now it will be transportation for sure.'

'There! I told you he was a rogue,' said the farmer triumphantly. 'Perhaps they'll hang him this time. A good riddance to him, too, I would say.'

'You would have them hang a hungry boy for stealing two ducks?' Nathan Brock's voice had dropped to little more than a whisper. 'Yes, I believe you would. A man who would turn out poor cottiers to certain death would not care about one more young boy.'

'I am running a farm, not a poor-house.... But you have held me up for long enough. Stand aside, if you please. Get up there!'

The farmer raised his short whip above his head, but before he could bring it down upon the flanks of his horse Nathan Brock reached forward and took a grip of the farmer's long coat. With a single jerk of his powerful arm he lifted the farmer from his seat and stood him on the road.

'Why, you. . . .' The farmer brought his whip down hard on Nathan Brock's shoulder.

The ex-prizefighter released his grip on the farmer and, bringing his fist back no more than six inches, he jabbed it almost casually up to the other man's chin.

The farmer slumped to the ground without a sound and, stepping over him, Nathan Brock swung himself up on the cart. Leaning over the boy he quickly released his hands, leaving him to untie his own ankles.

'That was a beautiful punch.' There was hero-worship in Jeremy's eyes.

'Never mind the talk. Hurry up and free yourself. The farther we get from this road, the happier I shall be.'

'Just a minute.' Jeremy freed his feet but stopped to delve beneath the kale. When he leaped from the cart he was holding the two ducks by their long white necks, and there was the bulge of at least two swedes inside his ragged shirt. 'I couldn't leave these ducks behind, not after all the trouble they've caused you.'

Nathan Brock and Jeremy were two miles from the road, in

a remote treed valley, before they stopped to light a fire and cook Jeremy's ill-gotten booty.

'What were you doing down among the farmlands?' asked Nathan Brock. 'Where are your friends?'

'They were no friends of mine,' said the boy briefly. 'I left them as soon as I could, and I was down in the valley because I was hungry and there is nothing up here to eat.'

'Nothing to steal, you mean. You'd best stay well clear of farms for a while, my lad. There will be a noose waiting for you one day for sure if you carry on the way you are going.' Nathan Brock tried not to look at the ducks roasting over the fire. 'I must be on my way as soon as I have eaten. Will you be returning to the mountains?'

Jeremy shrugged. 'One way is the same as any other for me. There's no place in particular I want to go. I'll come along with you for a while.'

'Oh no! Trouble follows you around like a tinker's dog. I have enough of my own. I'm off to Wexford to search for my wife and family. I can do it better without your company.'

'Two people can look in twice as many places as one. I'll be no trouble to you, Nathan – and I promise not to steal anything . . . unless we're going hungry. You won't even have to talk to me if you don't want to.'

Jeremy tried desperately to think of a plea that Nathan Brock could not refuse, but nothing would come to him. 'Besides, I've got nowhere else to go,' he ended lamely.

It was this last stark statement that got through to Nathan Brock. It brought back painful memories of his own childhood, unwanted by parish or poor-house.

'If I take you along with me, you look after yourself – and that means getting out of trouble as well as getting into it. I haven't time to worry about you.'

'You won't have to, Nathan, honest you won't. I'll do everything just the way you tell me. Cross my heart and hope to die if I don't.'

Jeremy spat on his finger-tip and made the sign of a cross on his chest where he vaguely imagined his heart to be.

'All right.' Nathan Brock was moved by the boy's desperate bid to avoid being left alone, but he had other things on his mind. 'Just remember that I am not going to wander aimlessly about County Wexford. My family is out there somewhere.

They set off from Rathconard a month ago with no money and very little food. We need to find them quickly.'

Nathan Brock feared it might already be too late, but that was a half-thought he would never put into words.

'We'll find them, Nathan, don't you worry. We'll set off as soon as we've eaten these ducks. Here, this one is ready now.'

Jeremy laid one of the spit-roasted birds on a rock and, taking the knife that Nathan Brock held out to him, cut the duck in two. After only the slightest hesitation, he handed the larger portion of the bird to Nathan Brock.

In this simple manner, Jeremy made the first truly unselfish gesture of his young life.

Chapter Sixteen

A severe storm delayed Liam on the English side of the Irish Sea and he did not arrive in Kilmar until the year 1845 had only a few dark hours to run. He travelled alone. Eugene Brennan had intended returning with him but was forced to change his mind at the last moment. A Coercion Bill was being introduced to an emergency session of Parliament. Once passed it would enable the Lord-Lieutenant of Ireland to impose martial law in any area he wished, giving the Army almost unlimited powers. The Irish MP knew he had little hope of succeeding, but he intended fighting the Bill at every stage of its passage through the House of Commons.

Norah McCabe was sitting in her kitchen with only the flickering flames from the fire lighting the room. Bringing up two boys without a husband, she had long ago learned the futility of tears, but after a week alone in the house her relief at seeing Liam broke her hard-won composure. She clung to him as he comforted her and fought desperately to regain control of herself.

Afterwards, she busied herself with familiar things, cooking a meal for her elder son as she told him of the events that had prompted her to send for him, and of the flight of Dermot and the others to avoid the soldiers.

'This wound of Dermot's, is it bad?'

'Bad enough, but he'd had a few days' rest, and with Kathie to look after him I'm sure he'll make out. But what does the future hold for him, Liam? He's a hunted man and will never be able to show his face in Kilmar again.'

'I doubt if anyone here would turn Dermot over to the soldiers. On the other hand, someone must have given them the names of those who took part in this stupid raid. I can't believe it was Sean Feehan. Seventeen he might have been, but he was as much of a man as anyone else I know.'

Liam looked at his mother. 'What I really can't understand is why Kathie went off with the others. She wasn't involved.'

'She felt Dermot needed her – and she blamed herself for encouraging him to carry out the raid on the wagons.' Norah

McCabe wished her son's thoughts were easier to read; she could tell nothing of his feelings from his face.

'Then she'll be back again when Dermot is well?'

'I don't think so. She said she would not return until Dermot was able to come with her.'

'Does Dermot have an understanding with her?'

'Oh no, nothing like that – and I am sure she will be back in Kilmar as soon as Dermot is well enough to look after himself, for all she has said she won't.'

Norah McCabe prayed she might be proved right. She believed Liam and Kathie would make a fine couple, and it was high time he settled down. Something had happened to him while he was in London, she was sure of that. Something had unsettled him, but Norah McCabe knew her son too well to ask him what it was. She would find out in due course; for now it was enough that he was home.

'Is there anything we can do to help Dermot?' Norah McCabe watched her son tuck into a meal as though he had not eaten during the whole of the time he had been away.

'Not for the moment. As soon as I can I will go to the Wicklow mountains and see how he is, but I would like to know what the Army intend doing first. I doubt if they will simply go away and forget anything happened.'

Liam was quite right. The Lord-Lieutenant of Ireland was furious that no one had been arrested for the attack on the corn-wagons and he ordered the army commander to take retaliatory action against Kilmar.

The same company of Gordon Highlanders as before entered the village at dawn, a week after Liam's return. They had marched from Dublin to carry out a well-planned operation. While some soldiers sealed off the roads from the village, others went to the houses of the men known to have been on the raid against the wagons and unceremoniously kicked in the doors to search for the wanted men.

The Captain in charge of the Highlanders had expected to take the outlaws by surprise and was angry to have failed. Liam was taken from his bed and spent a cold and uncomfortable hour convincing the Captain that he was not Dermot.

Then, when Liam was evidently freed, the officer called him back before he had walked ten paces.

'Your brother has a fishing boat. Where is it?'

'It's a family boat, not my brother's.'

'Where is it?'

'Tied up alongside the quay.' Liam had spent the previous day cleaning the boat and checking his fishing equipment, ready for an expected change in the weather.

'I have been instructed to take and destroy all property of value belonging to those members of the All-Ireland Association involved in the attack on English soldiers and the wagons they were guarding. Sergeant.'

The officer called to a giant of a man who wore three gold stripes on the sleeve of his red tunic. 'Take an axe and go down to the quay. Find the rebel McCabe's boat and destroy it. Then do the same with the boats used by the other men.'

'But I have already told you – it is a family boat. As the elder son it is more my boat than Dermot's. The same goes for the curraghs belonging to the others. They are all young single men. I doubt if there is one of them with his own boat.'

'That makes no difference to me. Let it be a reminder to Kilmar to keep its sons within the law in the future. You have your orders, Sergeant.'

Liam took a step toward the Captain, his fists clenched, and immediately two of the kilted soldiers lowered their bayoneted muskets to bar his way.

'Make one more threatening move and you will find yourself in Dublin Jail,' said the Highland Captain. 'I'm not fussy which McCabe I take. I don't doubt you were both involved.'

'I have already told you I was in London when the raid took place,' said Liam angrily. 'Even an English court would have difficulty in getting around that fact. But you don't really care, do you, Captain? You have been sent out after Irish blood and you don't mind whose it is you spill. Just be careful, Captain. You'll find an Englishman's blood spills as easily as an Irishman's.'

Liam's anger had prompted him to say more than was wise and, turning his back on the officer, he strode away toward the quay.

The Scots officer looked after him thoughtfully, then called to the two soldiers who had barred Liam's way.

'You men go down to the quay and stay where you can help the Sergeant in the event of trouble. If anything does occur, be sure Liam McCabe is the first man you take.'

The McCabe boat was secured to the quay by a bow rope and Liam arrived just as the big sergeant stepped on board. Liam was prevented from going any closer by a number of soldiers who were already on the quay.

'Is this your boat, McCabe?' the Sergeant called to him.

When Liam did not reply, the Sergeant sighed. 'Aye, I can see by the look on your face that it is.' He raised his axe and Liam started forward again, but the soldiers were ready for him and he stopped with the points of two bayonets only inches from his stomach.

As he stood there, unable to go forward and yet unwilling to walk away, the Sergeant went about his business. Each splintering crash of the axe stabbed Liam like a jagged knife. Finally, he could stand it no longer. With a sudden unexpected movement, he side-stepped the bayonet of one of the soldiers and knocked the other to the ground. It was a foolish thing to do, and other soldiers quickly rushed forward to seize him as he tried to fight his way to the quay steps, and his boat.

Liam's arms were pinned to his side, and the soldier who had been knocked to the ground picked up his weapon and raised it to strike the fisherman.

'Stop that!'

The circle of soldiers about Liam parted to make way for the big Scots sergeant. Behind him, in the harbour, Liam could see only the gunwale and stem of his boat showing above the water at the end of a taut mooring-rope.

'Let him go.'

The soldiers looked at the Sergeant in disbelief.

'But he was going to attack you,' said one of them.

'Of course he was,' boomed the big sergeant. 'I've just destroyed his boat and taken his living from him. Now, do as I say and let him go.'

The grip on Liam's arms was relaxed and he shrugged the soldier's hand away.

'Come here with me,' the Sergeant said to Liam, leading him along the quay, away from the soldiers.

When they were out of the hearing of the others, the Sergeant stopped and turned to Liam, his aggressive authority dropping away. 'What happened back there to your boat was not my idea. I was carrying out orders, you understand?' He spoke in a soft Elgin accent.

'You carried them out well,' replied Liam bitterly. 'I worked for three hard years to buy that boat.'

'I don't doubt it,' agreed the Sergeant. 'She's a fine craft. My own father is a fisherman and I have two brothers who earn their living from the sea. Destroying a man's boat is not to my liking, McCabe, and I did not do it as well as I might. If you wait until we are gone, and get some help to pull your boat from the water, you'll find there is only one damaged plank in her. You'll be able to fix it in a day, I dare say. Now, I'll away back and report to my captain. If I'm not mistaken, you have someone coming to see you.'

The Sergeant brushed past Liam before the fisherman could reply and strode away along the quay, calling upon his soldiers to follow him. Halfway to the ale-house, he touched a hand to his tall plumed helmet as he met Father Clery. The priest ignored the soldier's salute and hurried to Liam.

'Are you all right, my boy? I was told you were in a fight with the soldiers and I hurried here right away. You are not hurt?'

Liam shook his head. 'I'm all right . . . but they have sunk my boat.'

He looked to where the boat had been. It had gone right under now, the mooring-rope disappearing beneath the ruffled water of the harbour, strained to breaking-point.

'I'll call some of the men out. We'll raise her straight away, Liam.'

'No, she's safe enough there for a while. We'd better be getting up to the village, Father. The soldiers are going to destroy every boat belonging to the families of the young men who were on the raid. There could be trouble.'

'Dear God! What did the Irish do so bad in the past that the English were sent as a plague upon us? Come, Liam, let's get there quickly.'

They reached the village just in time to prevent a confrontation as a group of angry fishermen gathered to prevent the soldiers from carrying out their task.

After some argument, the priest persuaded the fishermen to disperse.

'You'll be doing nobody any good by trying to prevent the soldiers from doing what they have been ordered to do here. Try it and you'll be playing right into their hands. They have muskets and bayonets and are looking for an excuse to use them. Stay away. Curraghs can be built again; husbands and fathers can't. Remember, the soldiers will be going away without any of the Kilmar men they came here to find. That is our victory. Don't turn it into a defeat. Go on – away to your homes, now.'

The Kilmar fishermen were not convinced, but gradually, reluctantly, their anger subsided and, although they did not all go home, they moved back from the soldiers and watched them from a more discreet distance.

Accompanied by their captain, the soldiers smashed their way systematically through the village until they arrived at the smoke-stained cottage that belonged to Bridie O'Keefe. As the soldiers used the stocks of their muskets to smash the wooden-framed curragh propped against the wall of Bridie's neighbour, the old harridan flung open her door and gave them the benefit of her sharp-edged tongue.

'You'll be proud of yourself, smashing the boat of a widow-woman with five young children to support?'

'This is none of your business, old woman. Go back inside your cottage and close the door, then you won't have to watch things you don't like.' The Captain wrinkled his nose in disgust at Bridie O'Keefe's appearance and the smell that wafted from her.

'Will closing my door make you go away? Will it leave a boat there for someone to catch fish for hungry children? Oh no, Bridie O'Keefe won't go away, soldier. And I'll tell you something for nothing. I'll still be on this earth when you are long gone and your fine uniform is rotting in the ground.

'Ah, you smile all you like,' she added as the officer sniffed his scorn at her prophecy. 'But I'll tell you something else to take the smile from your face. There will be an English mother weeping as a result of today's work. When that happens you'll not smile again when you remember my words.'

With that, the old woman pursed her lips and spat on the ground, only inches from the officer's buckled shoes. Immediately, one of the children in the crowd that had gathered darted forward and did the same. He was followed by another, and then a third. Then one of the Kilmar women walked forward and also spat at the Highland captain's feet.

Liam started forward to stop them, but Father Clery put a restraining hand on his arm.

'No, leave them be,' he said in a quiet voice. 'The soldiers won't harm the women and children, and it will give our men something to smile about. Until this happened I was fearful one of them would lose his temper and do something stupid. It's a miserable victory, Liam . . . but it is better than a blood-letting.'

Liam realised the sense of the priest's words and he watched silently as, one by one, the women and children of Kilmar stepped from the crowd to spit at the feet of the Captain.

The officer was pale with fury, but he did nothing. To move would be to concede a humiliating defeat. He stayed where he was until every woman and child in Kilmar had expressed their contempt for the holder of the Queen's commission.

Not until then did the white-faced Captain order his men to move on to the next house on his list and it was here that the accident occurred which frightened the soldiers and caused the fishermen and women of Kilmar to nod their heads knowingly and whisper about the soothsaying powers of old Bridie O'Keefe.

Earlier, when the angry fishermen had gathered, the soldiers had primed their percussion muskets ready for immediate action. When the fishermen had been persuaded to disperse, most of the soldiers had removed the percussion caps and eased down the hammers of their weapons. One young soldier, only recently posted to Ireland, had not. His musket was still ready for action and it was his ill-fortune to be called upon to help smash the next curragh. He struck at the timber frame of the boat only once, with the heavy butt of his musket. The blow brought the hammer snapping down upon the percussion cap and the charge detonated.

Almost an ounce of lead entered the soldier's body just above his hip-bone and tore its way up through the soft organs of his stomach.

By the time his companions carried him to the shelter of a nearby shed, the young untried soldier was coughing blood. Unable to speak, he could only mouth the words he wanted to say and stare at his captain with panic-filled eyes.

Ten minutes later the young soldier was dead and the others had lost heart for their destructive work. They had heard

Bridie O'Keefe's warning. If the Captain had heeded it, there would not be a dead soldier stretched out among the nets and ropes and floats of a fisherman's shed.

The officer was remembering the other half of the old witch's prophecy and was no more eager than his men to stay in Kilmar. After the half-hearted destruction of one more curragh, the soldiers of the Gordon Highlanders were fallen in. Carrying the body of their comrade, they marched away to the beat of a muffled drum.

Father Clery breathed a sigh of relief; he had expected more trouble from the fishermen, but when he turned to Liam he saw that he was frowning.

'If it's your boat you are thinking of, then we'll away and find some men to raise her. The sooner she's repaired the sooner you'll be fishing again – but I'm not so sure about some of the curraghs.'

'I was thinking more about the Feehans' boat,' said Liam slowly. 'Eoin and Sean were both on the raid, yet their boat has not been touched. Wouldn't you say that was something to ponder on, Father . . . ?'

Chapter Seventeen

Liam's boat took longer to repair than the Scots sergeant had predicted. First, it took two full days to raise from the bottom of the harbour after the mooring-rope snapped. The salvage was not completed until Liam had dived repeatedly into the icy waters and managed to secure a new rope to the sunken vessel.

Then, with a calm sea and wasted fishing days behind him, Liam had to travel the road to Wexford Town to buy a seasoned piece of timber to replace the one the Sergeant had smashed. By the time the fishing boat took to the water again ten days had elapsed and stormy weather returned to prevent fishing.

More than the lost fishing days, it was the injustice of the soldiers' actions that really hurt Liam. He could not understand how they had been able to come to the village and smash boats at will – with the law on their side! He had tried to stay clear of politics and the controversial issue of England's domination over Ireland, but now he felt a burning resentment that soldiers from across the sea were able to behave in such an arbitrary manner in his country.

During these angry and empty days Liam missed the company of Dermot, but at night, when he was alone in his room, his thoughts always returned to London . . . and Caroline. No matter how much he thought about his other problems, she always seemed to be on his mind when sleep eventually came to him.

Norah McCabe's concern was far less divided. As the weeks went by without news, she became increasingly worried about Dermot. Tommy Donaghue did not help. The old fiddler came to the house for a meal most evenings and his talk always turned to Kathie and the way she had left her old father with no one in the whole world to look after him.

Tommy Donaghue had resumed his drinking habits, but as he seemed able to draw nothing but dirges and heart-rending laments from his fiddle he received fewer drinks than before. On fine days he helped Liam in the boat, but his palsied hands proved to be something of a liability when handling nets. He was happier when Liam was able to send him to Gorey market with a cartload of fish.

Liam had expected Nathan Brock to return to Kilmar and tell him where Dermot and the others were in hiding, but the weeks went by and still the ex-prizefighter had not put in an appearance.

Then, in early March, Eugene Brennan returned to Ireland. There were no mammoth meetings on this occasion, no spontaneous gatherings of Irish workers anxious to catch a glimpse of their hero, no crowds straining to hear the words of the man who had fought for Ireland's identity since the abortive rising of 1798.

Eugene Brennan arrived in Dublin on the night tide and by the time the sun began warming the city's sprawling grey streets he was well on his way to Kilmar.

Liam was shocked by the old politician's appearance. Gone was the dynamic fund-raiser he had known in London, the astute lawyer with the ability and rhetoric to cow a hostile audience. Eugene Brennan looked old and tired – and totally defeated. When Father Clery saw him, he was reminded of the man who had been released from prison only a few months before. But on this occasion there was no all-consuming cause to take his mind off all else. The Irish cottiers were still dying in their thousands, but in future the assistance given to them by County Wexford's MP would lack much of its fire.

Sir James Graham, Home Secretary in Sir Robert Peel's Tory government, had called Eugene Brennan to his office and spelled out what the future would hold for the old Irish MP if he held any more mass meetings, or if any of his supporters broke the law. The Coercion Bill had been hurried through Parliament despite the noisy and concerted opposition of the Irish MPs. Sir James Graham told Eugene Brennan bluntly that the Lord-Lieutenant of Ireland would not hesitate to use his new powers and throw him into prison if he believed it to be necessary. It was made clear to Eugene Brennan that, once in prison, he could never expect to walk the roads of Ireland as a free man again.

Much as the Government would have liked to wash its hands of the starving cottiers and their problems, Sir James Graham told the MP he was prepared to ship three thousand tons of

Indian maize to them – but only if he had Eugene Brennan's word that the All-Ireland Association would cause him no more problems. Thus, the Tory Minister laid the responsibility for the lives of thousands of cottiers squarely upon the old Irish politician's shoulders.

It was useless for Eugene Brennan to point out that he could not possibly be held responsible for the hot-headed young men in his association. They had become frustrated by the lackadaisical attitude of the English Government toward the desperate plight of the Irish people. If they decided to take matters into their own hands, who could blame them? Eugene Brennan left Sir James Graham's office with the knowledge that in the future the Home Secretary would lay the blame for much of the crime in Ireland upon the All-Ireland Association.

After fifty years of fighting for the things in which he passionately believed, Eugene Brennan had been beaten into submission by a strange mixture of blackmail and legislation. His situation at Westminster no longer tolerable, he returned to Ireland, an old man going home.

As he sat in Father Clery's house, telling Liam and the priest of the Home Secretary's ultimatum, tears rolled unchecked down the politician's cheeks.

'So God help Ireland now,' he ended brokenly. 'For there is no one in England who will.'

When the terrible winter of starvation finally drew to a close, Liam hoped that, around Kilmar at least, it would be possible to feed the cottiers from the increasing catches of the fishermen. At this moment of hope, a new and terrible affliction fell upon the children of St Patrick.

Black fever.

News that the terrible lice-spread disease had reached Kilmar was brought by Tommy Donaghue. He came to the McCabe cottage unusually early one morning, and was invited to share breakfast with Liam and Norah McCabe.

'No, thank you. I rarely feel like eating this early in the day, and this morning I have had an experience that might well put me off my food for a whole week.'

'What is it this time, Tommy?' asked Norah McCabe. The old musician had not been short of problems, both real and imagined, since his daughter had gone away with the young men of the All-Ireland Association.

'It's some cottiers up on the hill. They took over an old place behind my cottage a week or two ago. There has been a baby crying there for two nights now but I haven't seen a soul out of doors. Last night the baby was crying and whimpering so piteously I hardly got a wink of sleep. This morning I went up there to find out what was wrong....'

'And . . . ?' Liam prompted.

'I didn't go inside,' Tommy Donaghue confessed. 'There was such a foul stench coming from the place that I turned around and came down here.'

'That's not like you, Tommy. We've been inside some pretty unwholesome places taking food to the cottiers.'

'But there was never anything like this. Another step closer and I swear I'd have heaved my heart up.'

'Drinking has weakened your stomach,' snapped Norah McCabe. 'What about the baby?'

'It was still crying when I left.'

'Then there will be no breakfast in this house until we learn what is wrong with the poor little mite. On your feet, Tommy Donaghue, and show me the way.'

'You had better stay here, Ma. There is no telling what might be inside that cottage. I'll go up there with Tommy.'

'No one is stopping you – but I am going, too. Neither of you has the hands to tend to a baby. Come on, now. There has been enough time wasted already.'

Norah McCabe put her shawl about her shoulders and ushered Tommy Donaghue out of the house before Liam could slip a jersey over his head.

The roof of the old cottage on the hill had collapsed at one end and the door hung on only one rusty hinge, but as the three approached the stench coming from inside drove away all other considerations. It was appalling.

'You had better stay outside, Ma,' said Liam. 'Let Tommy and me go in first.'

'We would all do better to stay outside,' replied a grim-faced Norah McCabe. 'I would recognise that smell anywhere. There is black fever in that cabin.'

At that moment a low irregular noise came from within the broken-down building.

'There's also a baby in there,' said Liam, trying the door. 'Come on, Tommy. Hold your neck-scarf up to your nose and help me with this door. Something has been put against the inside to stop it opening.'

The 'something' turned out to be the body of a man, his swollen face choked almost black, lips drawn back from his teeth in a frightening snarl. Other bodies lay sprawled about the floor, their fearful expressions and clawed fingers evidence of an agonised death.

The smell in here was so overwhelming that Liam retched uncontrollably. He located the baby, clutched in the arms of its dying mother. They were the only two left alive in the cabin, and within minutes there was only one. It was as though the emaciated and helpless mother had clung desperately to life until she saw her baby taken to safety. As Liam eased the baby from her arms, her eyes flickered open and looked up at him. Her whole body tensed as she tried to say something. But when her mouth opened it was the result of a sudden obscene convulsion that ended when she relaxed in death, her eyes still staring at Liam.

He recoiled in horror and, clutching the baby, stumbled outside with Tommy Donaghue.

Norah McCabe took the baby from her son and wrinkled her nose at the dirty rags in which it was wrapped. Peeling them off, she threw them to the ground and wrapped her own shawl about the naked cottier boy.

Norah McCabe took the baby home with her, and while Tommy Dongahue scoured the village to obtain some milk Liam sought out Father Clery and took the priest to the charnel-house on the hill.

Together they dragged out the bodies of eight adults from the broken-down cottage, but could find no means of identifying any one of them.

'This is a bad business,' said the priest. 'It's typhus – the black fever – right enough, and I hope for the sake of Kilmar that we can contain it up here on the hill. It is not unknown for this disease to wipe out whole communities. When we have finished our business up here I want you to go home and take off all the clothes you are wearing and put them to soak for a day in strong salt water. Tell your mother and Tommy

Donaghue to do the same. But first we have another duty to perform.'

The priest and the fisherman visited each of the twenty or so derelict cabins on the hill and were horrified by what they found there. Every cabin was occupied by starving cottiers, and the fever was raging in more than half of them.

'Dear God!' exclaimed the priest. 'What is to be done about them? They need a doctor and food urgently.'

'They need someone up here caring for them,' said Liam. 'But we can't ask anyone in Kilmar to put the lives of themselves and their families at risk. Perhaps Eugene can think of something.'

Father Clery frowned. 'It would not be fair to ask him. He is an old man who is sorely in need of help himself; a burden like this might well break him. But we can't deal with the black fever by ourselves. Liam, will you go to see if the Earl is at Inch House? He could send to Dublin for help.'

Liam remembered the last occasion he had been to the great house and was reluctant to agree.

'Please, Liam. Unless something is done urgently the fever will spread through the whole of County Wexford. It will hit fishermen and the Earl's estate workers as well as the cottiers.'

Reluctantly, Liam said he would go to Inch House, but first he went home to put on his London clothes, remembering the suspicious gate-keeper.

Tommy Donaghue had obtained some goat's milk, and Norah McCabe solved the problem of feeding the tiny baby by the simple expediency of dipping coarse linen in the bowl of milk and allowing the child to suck the milk from the cloth. It was messy but effective and, as Liam set off for Inch House, women neighbours were coming to the house with baby clothes and to make foolish noises at the undernourished infant. Their brief joy was short-lived. The baby had been starved for days and its tiny stomach was unaccustomed to such rich fare. It died four hours later, watched by the helpless fisherwomen and attended by Bridie O'Keefe.

The Earl of Inch's gate-keeper seemed not to recognise Liam. Touching his hat and calling Liam 'sir', he came out to escort him to the house, taking him without question to the front door of the great house. If he wondered why a gentleman should come calling without either horse or carriage, he asked no questions.

The butler at the house had a better memory and he retained a tight grip on the heavy front door as he informed Liam that the Earl was out of the country.

'That is all right. I will receive Mr McCabe.'

To Liam's astonishment and dismay, as the butler stepped back out of the way Caroline pushed the door open wide and stood before him.

'Liam, how wonderful to see you again.' She took both his hands in hers and leaned back to look up at him. 'You are looking well . . . as handsome as ever. But what are we doing talking here? Come inside.'

'I came to see your brother . . . the Earl.'

This was a meeting Liam had looked forward to with a confused mixture of anticipation and dread. Seeing her again sent the blood racing through his veins and he thought she must feel his hands trembling in hers.

'My brother is not here, so you will have to speak with me instead. Is that so difficult for you, Liam?'

Still holding one of his hands, Caroline led the way to the library, ignoring the disapproval on the butler's face.

'There! Isn't this better?' Caroline closed the library door behind them, and before Liam could reply she turned quickly to him and kissed him on the lips. Her lips lingered upon his, but when he did not respond she stepped back and studied his face seriously.

'Are you still angry with me, Liam? After all these months? What if I tell you I have missed you desperately?'

Liam tried to think of something to say, something meaningful, but all that came through the turmoil inside him was 'How is your husband?' The question was foolish and childishly cruel. He saw the hurt in her eyes and would have given anything to take the words back again.

'I deserved that, didn't I, Liam? Richard is working in Dublin. I came here to Inch House because I hoped I might see you again. I have been carrying on your good work in London, Liam . . . raising money for your starving cottiers. I have collected thousands of pounds for your fund. Does that please you?'

Liam remembered the reason for his visit to Inch House.

'I came here to see the Earl on an urgent matter. Do you know when he will be back?'

Caroline shrugged. 'Perhaps not until the summer. Is there anything I can do?'

Liam looked at the beautiful and elegant woman standing before him and thought of the cottier women dressed in rags, lying filthy and ill in their stinking hovels.

'No, Caroline. I don't think there is anything you can do. The cottiers on Kilmar hill have gone down with the black fever. I . . . we . . . were hoping the Earl could arrange for a doctor and some help to come in and prevent the fever from spreading.'

Caroline's mood became one of immediate concern. 'Typhus. So close to here? That is dreadful news – but, as it happens, I *can* help you.'

'You? How?'

His disbelief both amused and saddened her.

'I told you I have been working hard for your cause, Liam. Not only have I been raising money, but I have also paid for two doctors from the Society of Friends to come to Ireland and serve where they are most needed. They are in Dublin at this very moment. I will send for them to come to Kilmar immediately. Will you be there to show them where these poor wretches are lying?'

Liam nodded. 'Me or Father Clery. It is very kind of you, Caroline—'

'Kind? Oh no, Liam, I am as selfish as any other woman.'

He thought she was about to reach out and touch him. Instead, she turned away and moved to the window, looking out over closely trimmed lawns toward the sea, visible in the distance through gaps in the Lebanon cedars, planted when the house was built many years before.

'How is you brother, Liam?'

'I haven't seen him since I returned to Ireland.'

Her words stirred up the feeling of guilt that had been nagging at him for some weeks. He ought to go to the Wicklow mountains to try to find Dermot. The last news of his brother had come from a tinker who had passed through Kilmar, and it had been cautious rather than comforting.

'What a mess our country is in, Liam. Oh yes, I am as Irish

as you. I was born in this house and, though I have spent most of my life away, my heart is here. More than ever recently.'

'Then you will be doing your countrymen and women a great service by bringing in those doctors.'

'Of course.' Caroline turned back toward him. 'I will send a horseman with a message immediately. He will be in Kilmar tomorrow.'

'Thank you, Caroline.' Warmed by her ready help, and aware that he had hurt her, he added, 'It has been nice to meet you again.'

'Has it, Liam? Has it really?'

There was an eager pleading in her voice.

'Yes.'

She was watching his face, and now she gave a short laugh. 'Don't say things just to be polite to me, Liam. Spare me that, please. We were lovers – remember?'

She moved closer to him. 'Yes. I can see you remember, Liam. I will have to be satisfied with that for now, but when you wake in the night for no apparent reason think of me, Liam. The chances are I will be thinking of you, too.'

She reached out and touched his face gently. 'And now you must leave me. Your cottiers need help.'

Chapter Eighteen

The following day proved to be an eventful one in Kilmar. In the morning Liam, Tommy Donaghue and Father Clery took food to the sick cottiers on the hill. In return, the cottiers promised to stay clear of Kilmar village, though few of them had the strength to do anything else. Four more typhus victims had died during the night while sharing their blankets with the living. Liam and Father Clery pulled the corpses outside to await burial, then did what little was possible for the others.

Their tasks occupied the whole of the morning, and they had returned to the village and Liam was preparing his boat for half a day's fishing when a small boy came running into the village shouting that soldiers were coming.

The news gave Liam an uneasy feeling in his stomach, but he refused to be panicked. He could have put to sea with Tommy Donaghue, but if the soldiers intended searching the houses once again he did not want his mother to be in the house on her own. Stowing his fishing gear in his boat, he secured it and went home.

He and Tommy had almost reached the cottage when the soldiers entered the village. He heard a shout of 'That's them. That's the two who were with the priest,' and looking back saw a soldier pointing at him.

'Stop, or you will be shot!' the officer in charge called, and to Liam's dismay he saw it was the Scots captain and the same company of men who had paid the last destructive visit to Kilmar. Quickly he reached out and pulled Tommy Donaghue to a halt.

'He means what he says, Tommy. Stand still or they will shoot us.'

'What for? We've done nothing wrong!' Tommy Donaghue argued, but he wisely stayed where he was.

The officer came along the narrow street toward them and his face showed his disappointment. 'It was very sensible of you to do as you were told,' he said. 'Although a musket-ball is far less expensive than a trial.'

'A trial for what? We've done nothing.'

'Nothing you thought anyone could see,' corrected the Captain. 'Unfortunately for you I decided to send a man ahead of us with a powerful telescope. He saw you taking food up the hill to those derelict cottages. I knew if I bided my time I would learn where your brother and the others were hiding.'

Now Liam knew the reason for the officer's strange behaviour he felt greatly relieved.

'I'm afraid you've made a mistake, Captain. There are no fugitives on the hill. Only poor cottiers – and the black fever.'

'There have been no reports of fever in Wexford. Save your breath. You'll need it for the march to Dublin.'

The officer turned to his men. 'Four of you stay here and guard these men. Take no chances. If they try to escape, shoot them. Sergeant, detail two more men to arrest the priest. You come with me and deploy the men around the hill before we move in on those cottages.'

Liam became seriously alarmed. 'Captain, we are trying to contain the fever in those cottages. If your men go searching through them, they are likely to pick up the fever and spread it from here to Dublin.'

Liam's words had their effect upon the soldiers of the Scots regiment and they looked uneasy, but the Captain had already made his decision.

'Take these men inside the house and allow no one to talk to them,' he instructed his men, ignoring Liam's pleas. 'We've got other things to do.'

A few minutes later Father Clery was brought to the McCabe cottage to join Liam and Tommy Donaghue. He, too, was protesting angrily, but all to no avail. The soldiers had their instructions and they would obey them to the letter.

'I only hope Eugene does nothing foolish,' said the priest as he paced the room under the watchful eyes of their guards. 'He went after the officer in an attempt to bring him back and I fear he was in a terrible temper.'

It seemed an age before anything happened to relieve the priest's anxiety. Then one of the guards looked through the window and said the others were returning. The three prisoners were taken outside to meet them, and one look at the faces of the soldiers told Liam that the men had seen for themselves what black fever could do to anyone unfortunate enough to contract the disease.

Eugene Brennan was with the soldiers and he was shaken by what he had seen on the hill. He was angry, too, and his anger was directed against the Scots officer. Liam could see the old MP berating the disbelieving Captain every step of the way along the road.

'Well, are you satisfied?' Liam addressed the Captain as soon as he came within hearing. 'I trust you let your nose tell you the truth of what I said and did not allow your men to come in contact with the cottiers.'

'The damned fool had his men tramp through every cabin. They even examined the bodies they found to be sure they weren't wanted men. Liam, I have seen some awful sights in my life, but nothing to compare with the inside of those cabins up there.'

'If you take the fever back to the barracks in Dublin, you'll be responsible for killing more of your soldiers than any Irishman,' said Father Clery to the Captain. 'And you will not be able to say you weren't warned.'

'I did what needed to be done,' said the officer stubbornly. 'And I am still not convinced that you and these other two don't know where the fugitives are hiding. Mr Brennan has spoken on your behalf and I am releasing you, Father Clery. The others will come back to Dublin for questioning.'

There was an immediate protest from every one of the men involved, with Eugene Brennan's voice booming out that he would vouch for the innocence of Liam and Tommy Donaghue, but the Scots captain was adamant. He was taking Liam and Tommy Donaghue back to Dublin. It mattered not that there was no evidence to link them with the raid on the wagons. The Coercion Bill was being used as Eugene Brennan had predicted it would be. The Irish were being brought to heel.

The argument grew more and more heated, and the officer had just ordered his men to surround the two prisoners when a carriage bumped and swayed its way recklessly along the narrow street, forcing the soldiers to give ground or be bowled over.

Stopping close to Liam and Tommy Donaghue, the carriage door was thrown open before the coachman could climb down from his high seat and Caroline was handed out, followed by two doctors and the district relief organiser for the Society of Friends.

'What is happening, Liam? Why are all these soldiers here?'

Liam took a step toward her, but one of the Scots soldiers immediately barred his way with the thirty-nine-inch barrel of his musket.

Eugene Brennan was taken by surprise by Lady Caroline's unexpected arrival; he had not been told about Liam's meeting with her, but the old MP knew of her affection for Liam and was prepared to take full advantage of it on this occasion.

'This fool of a captain is arresting Liam and taking him off to Dublin. He thinks he had something to do with that raid on the wagons.'

'I'm taking him to Dublin for questioning, ma'am. He's not being arrested.'

'Do not play with words, Captain. You are taking this man against his will, therefore he is being arrested. You will accept my word that Liam McCabe was a guest in my London house when this raid took place and release him immediately.'

'I am sorry, ma'am, but I have given my orders. Captain James Brody, at your service—'

'And I am Lady Caroline Dudley, sister of the Earl of Inch. My husband, Sir Richard Dudley, has recently arrived in Ireland on behalf of the Treasury to check upon the absurdly high cost of maintaining the Army in this country. I am quite sure that he would be most displeased to hear that a captain and – how many men do you have with you . . . a hundred? That so many men are wasting their time and Treasury money when they could be gainfully employed elsewhere in these troubled times.'

The Scots captain hurriedly abandoned all his principles. The officer's mess in Dublin was buzzing with the news of Sir Richard Dudley's arrival. The baronet held a position in the Treasury important enough to wipe out a whole regiment with a single stroke of his pen. During his visit, generals would be running around him as though they were mere messenger-boys. It was unthinkable that he, a junior captain, should go against the wishes of that official's wife. Captain James Brody capitulated unconditionally.

'I am obliged for your kind assistance, my lady. I trust you and your husband will have a most enjoyable stay in Ireland.'

While the Captain and Caroline were talking, the tall Scots sergeant moved closer to Liam. When it became apparent that

Liam and Tommy Donaghue were to be released, the Sergeant moved quickly to Liam's side and pressed a handful of small coins upon him.

'Here, take these. We've had a collection among ourselves. Use it for those people up the hill. We'll not be troubling you again. We are returning to barracks in Scotland next month and there is talk of the regiment going to India later in the year.'

The Scots sergeant moved away before Liam could thank him and, her brief encounter with the captain at an end, Caroline moved through the ranks of the soldiers toward him.

'Come, Liam, this ridiculous misunderstanding has wasted precious time. If you will send someone to show the doctors where the poor cottiers are lying, you and I will have a talk to your priest and Eugene to see what more we can do.'

With Caroline holding his arm and Tommy Donaghue walking on his other side, Liam walked away from the soldiers who had been holding him prisoner and they moved back respectfully to allow him to pass.

'Perhaps we might talk in your cottage, Liam. It is very cold out here.'

Caroline shivered in an exaggerated manner, but she was smiling at Liam and the relieved fisherman returned the smile. He knew that had she not come to his rescue he would have been taken to Dublin and thrown in jail until he was able to prove his innocence.

The sight of her son and this elegant woman smiling at each other in such an intimate way told Norah McCabe much of what had happened during Liam's stay in London, and the knowledge filled her with dismay. Nothing good could come from such a relationship. But now was not the time to pursue the matter. That would have to come later. Doing her best to ignore the way Caroline touched Liam's arm and hand at every opportunity, Norah McCabe thanked her for securing her son's release and welcomed her to the McCabe cottage.

'With luck we have seen the last of the soldiers,' said Liam as the kilted Scotsmen marched from the village. 'But they were not all bad.' He held out the money given to him by the Sergeant and told them what he had said.

It was important news, as everyone in the room was aware.

With this particular regiment gone from Ireland it should be safe for the young men of Kilmar to return to their homes.

As it happened, the Scots Captain and his company would never again bother the people of Ireland and few of them would board the boat taking them to their homeland. They marched from Kilmar carrying with them the seeds of a typhus epidemic that swept through the close-packed barrack-room in Dublin and claimed hundreds of victims. Among them were the sergeant who had proved to be well disposed toward the Irish – and Captain James Brody. So, another of Bridie O'Keefe's prophecies was fulfilled and the cottiers of Kilmar hill wreaked a terrible vengeance for the indignities suffered by their benefactors.

Tommy Donaghue took the two doctors and their fellow-Quaker up the hill to the sick cottiers, leaving the others to discuss ways to help them.

It was not long before the Quaker relief organiser returned to the cottage, alone. He was a much shaken and chastened man.

'I have never in all my life seen such appalling poverty and degradation,' he declared. 'There would be a public outcry in England if animals were found in such a condition. Why has the Government done nothing to help?'

'Because Sir Robert Peel and his Ministers are governing Ireland from comfortable warm offices in Westminster,' said Eugene Brennan fiercely. 'They believe a few maggoty biscuits and a shipload of Indian corn will remove all the problems we have here.'

'Then they must learn the truth,' said the Quaker. 'I will personally lead a deputation of Friends to the House of Commons to inform the Prime Minister of the plight of these poor people.'

'I wish you well,' said the tired old MP. 'I have been telling him of their suffering for more years than I care to recollect, yet the cottiers still starve to death.'

'Are there many cottiers left in the area?' asked Caroline.

'Yes,' replied Liam. 'Many of them have returned to their plots of land in a bid to till this season's potatoes, but we still have more than enough begging about Kilmar.'

'God will that the potatoes do not rot in the ground this year,' said Father Clery.

'Amen to that,' agreed Caroline. 'But first we must do something to keep them alive until the potatoes are ready. Is it possible to obtain food for them?'

Liam shrugged. 'We can provide a certain amount of fish, and there seemed to be no shortage of produce in Gorey market when I was last there – but the cottiers have no money with which to buy.'

'If the Society of Friends will set up a soup kitchen here, in Kilmar,' said Lady Caroline, 'I will guarantee the money to pay for the food. Will the people of Kilmar help?'

'I can promise you there will be no shortage of helpers,' said Father Clery. 'It is a very generous gesture, Lady Caroline. I can assure you I will do my best to ensure its success.'

'I think the soup kitchen should be just outside the village,' suggested Liam. 'Perhaps on the lower slopes of Kilmar hill. We must try at all costs to keep black fever from the village. There will be little sympathy or help for the cottiers if it should break out here.'

The others nodded their agreement and it seemed a good moment to sit back and enjoy the tea Norah McCabe brought into the room for them.

'What a dear little cottage this is,' said Caroline conversationally. 'It has such a happy atmosphere.'

Liam thought of Caroline's London house and the magnificent family home where she had been born.

'It is no more and no less than it was intended to be – a working fisherman's home. As for being happy, it has had its share of happiness and sorrow. It was a happy day when I gave birth to Liam in the big bed upstairs and a terrible one when I lay in the same bed alone, knowing his father would never be beside me again. Then Liam bought the wooden boat and gave us some good years again. Now Dermot is away there is an emptiness in the house once more.'

'There will be happy times again, Mrs McCabe. For you, for Liam – and for Dermot, too. You will see.'

'Maybe you're right. Maybe not. One thing is certain; if you hadn't talked Liam away from those soldiers, things would have been worse – much worse. I thank you for it again.'

'Men like Liam are hard to find, Mrs McCabe. We all need him.'

It was said innocently enough, but of all those in the room

only Father Clery thought Caroline was referring to the cause of the cottiers.

'Lady Caroline, if I went to Dublin to speak to your husband, do you think he might help our cause and appeal to the English Government for funds to help the cottiers?' The question came from Eugene Brennan.

'He has no great sympathy with the Irish people, but I will write a letter for you to take to him. It may help.'

'Thank you,' said the old MP. 'In that case, my brief holiday is at an end. There is work to be done in Dublin and London.'

He smiled ruefully at Father Clery. 'I must remember to go elsewhere for a rest in the future. Whenever I come to Kilmar I end up becoming involved in a cause that cannot be ignored.'

'Aren't you forgetting the Home Secretary's warning? If you push the cottiers' cause again, he will ban the Association and throw you in prison.' Liam was genuinely concerned for the dedicated old man's well-being.

'If something isn't soon done, the Association will be totally discredited and there will be no Ireland left to fight for. At the rate the cottiers are dying the countryside is fast becoming a huge graveyard. If I allow it to go on, then the dreams of a foolish old man will be buried along with the bodies of the children who should be Ireland's future. Should I measure the few years I have left to me – or the name of an organisation – against such a prospect? If the All-Ireland Association is banned, it will quickly be reborn under another name, and there is no shortage of good men to take over from me, Liam. You, Dermot – or Nathan Brock. You each see things in your own way but are all heading in the same direction. One day someone will find the right path to take and lead Ireland to freedom. I am satisfied that I have been able to guide it part of the way and I will continue to do so while there is life left in my body. I was wrong to allow Sir James Graham to frighten me into submission, and he was equally wrong to attempt it. The freedom of Ireland will be written in the history books, one day. Who writes it matters little.'

The long silence that followed was broken by Caroline.

'I think I have just listened to a major political speech, Eugene – but when you meet Richard you had better restrict yourself to pleading the cottiers' cause. He is an Englishman and does not understand the Irishman's love of words. He is also a friend of Sir Robert Peel, so say nothing you would not wish to have repeated.'

Eugene Brennan inclined his head. 'I thank you for the warning. Now, unless I am mistaken, our fiddler friend has news of some importance to impart to us.'

Through the window he had seen Tommy Donaghue hurrying along the street from Kilmar hill, and now the Northern Irishman threw open the door of the cottage and stumbled inside, red-faced and breathless.

'. . . Up behind the top cottage . . . in a shed . . . a woman and two boys with the fever. . . . We've just found them.'

Those already in the room waited for an explanation. There had been so much misery and suffering that three new cases would make little difference.

'One of the boys was able to talk to us,' panted Tommy Donaghue. 'His name is Brock. We've found Nathan Brock's family.'

Chapter Nineteen

Liam set out on foot for the Wicklow mountains the next morning, accompanied by Tommy Donaghue. The old man would slow Liam down, but he wanted to see his daughter again, and, as he pointed out, any soldiers they might meet along the way would be less suspicious of an itinerant fiddler and a companion than of a fisherman travelling alone, miles from his home village.

Liam expected to find Nathan Brock living with the Kilmar fugitives, but he had only the vaguest idea of their whereabouts. He would have to trust to luck and the little information that had filtered back to the village.

At first, it appeared that luck might have deserted them when on the second day they met up with a patrol of militiamen who did not attempt to hide their suspicions of the two men.

Not until Liam informed them he was looking for a man whose wife and children had gone down with the black fever did they cease their questioning and order Liam and Tommy Donaghue to go on their way.

'Mention of the black fever seemed to put an unholy fear into them,' commented Tommy Donaghue as he looked back over his shoulder and saw the militiamen hurrying away.

'Are you surprised?' asked Liam. 'I've seen nothing that I fear more in this life. It could have been sent by the devil himself.'

The two men did not meet up with Dermot and the Kilmar fishermen until the fourth day of their search and then it happened with a suddenness that took them completely by surprise.

Tramping across a wide upland moor dotted with gorse and coarse tufted grass, they were suddenly confronted by two armed men who seemed to rise out of the very ground. For a second, Liam thought he and Tommy Donaghue were to be shot. Then he recognised Eoin Feehan and called his name. Moments later Liam and Tommy Donaghue were surrounded by Kilmar men who thumped Liam on the back with all the wild enthusiasm of exiles meeting old friends.

Liam was concerned that Kathie and Dermot were not with the others, and the first evasive answers to his questions alarmed him even more. Then Eoin Feehan said airily, 'Oh, Dermot is all right. Perhaps not quite as fit as he might be, but he gets about – and he has Kathie to look after him. Find one and you'll find the other. They are as close as two maggots in a pea.'

The Kilmar men took the new arrivals to the place among the rocks where they had their dug-out cabins, questioning them along the way about their own families, the state of the fishing and the latest news of Eugene Brennan and the All-Ireland Association.

They found Dermot sitting outside his dug-out, making the most of the weak spring sunshine. He stood up and held his arms out in a gesture of delight when he saw his elder brother, but Liam was shocked at his appearance. Dermot was painfully thin and had the stooped round-shouldered stance of a man who is in constant pain.

The brothers embraced and Dermot asked after their mother.

'She is well. Missing her younger son, of course, but well.'

Liam stood back from his brother and smiled at him. Then he saw Tommy Donaghue looking about him anxiously.

'But where is Kathie – and Nathan Brock?'

'Kathie!' Dermot shouted. 'Show yourself. You have visitors.

'Kathie has her own dug-out,' he explained so that Tommy Donaghue could hear. 'She keeps herself busy trying to stitch our clothes together. These mountains are hard on fishermen's clothing. But why do you ask after Nathan Brock? He brought us here and then left to collect his wife from the poor-house and take her and his children back to Kilmar. He intended making a new life for himself as a fisherman.'

'His family seem to have found Kilmar,' explained Liam grimly. 'But they are very ill with black fever, and Nathan needs to get to them as quickly as possible.'

'I'm afraid we can't help very much, Liam. We all thought Nathan had returned to Kilmar. . . .'

At that moment Kathie emerged from her dug-out cabin to be greeted by her father with a roar of delight which echoed around the granite outcrops. Tommy Donaghue hugged her to him, swinging her off the ground in his exuberance. When he released her Kathie greeted Liam with a quick hug and looked at him with a shyness that the Kilmar fugitives had not seen before.

'You are looking well, Liam. You have put on some weight.'

'And you have lost some . . . but you, too, are looking well.'

It was quite true. There was a slim fitness about Kathie that came from tramping the mountains in search of food, and from doing more than her own share of work about the camp.

They talked about Kilmar until darkness came down. Then fires were lit, and Liam produced the food he and Tommy Donaghue had brought with them. To the fugitives it was a feast.

The only sour note came when Eoin Feehan asked how his father was faring with his fishing.

'He is doing well,' replied Tommy Donaghue, before Liam could say anything. 'Better than anyone else – but, then, he never lost his boat when the soldiers came to Kilmar.'

Immediately, the others clamoured for an explanation, and Liam told them about the destruction of the boats on the soldiers' first visit. As he spoke his gaze was fixed on Eoin Feehan's face, watching every change of expression there. The red-haired fisherman did not return Liam's look, nor once meet his eyes. Liam became more than ever convinced that Eoin Feehan knew why the soldiers had arrived at Kilmar with the name of every man – except himself – who had taken part in the raid on the wagons.

After they had eaten, the fugitives gathered about Tommy Donaghue. He tucked his fiddle beneath his chin and played for them, giving them all the songs most calculated to bring a lump to the throat of a man exiled from his home and family. Liam took the opportunity to talk to his brother.

'I see you have a few muskets. Where did they come from?'

Dermot chuckled. 'We stole one from a drunken militiaman and then used it to hold up one of his companions. They are old guns but they help to keep us fed – after a fashion.'

'With luck you won't need to skulk up here for much longer.' Liam told Dermot what the Sergeant had told him.

'I wouldn't believe the word of a soldier,' replied Dermot. 'Besides, we are not skulking. We have two guns that each of us has learned to use. When the time comes we will get muskets enough for everyone and lead all Ireland to a victory over the English.'

Liam looked at his young brother incredulously.

'What are you talking about? You are a handful of fugitives with two muskets between you and only your own village on your side. The country is reeling from famine and fear. A rising is the farthest thing from any man's mind. All he can think about is staying alive. Forget such dreams, Dermot. Wait until the Gordon Highlanders have left Ireland, then return home. You have already suffered enough for your cause. Come back to Kilmar and you will be pointed to as a hero for the rest of your life.'

'No, there is no returning home for any of us. This is only a beginning. Until Ireland rules herself we have no homes. On the day we leave these mountains the men of Counties Wicklow and Wexford will flock to join us. By the time we reach Dublin the whole of the country will be behind us.'

Dermot's face burned as though he had a fever and his eyes looked far beyond his brother. Liam was alarmed at his intensity and, reaching out, rested a hand on his shoulder.

'I don't think you are well enough to lead anyone at the moment, Dermot. Come home with Tommy and me tomorrow. We'll find somewhere in Kilmar to hide you. Let Ma look after you for a few months. When you are well again you can begin to plan for the future.'

Dermot shook off his brother's hand angrily.

'You haven't listened to a word I've said, have you? I'm well enough to do what needs to be done. If you are so anxious about me, then come and join us here. We will not go home until the final battle is won, Liam. I swear that. To go before then would be to admit defeat. People would point their fingers, yes, but they would be fingers of scorn. We are none of us going back to Kilmar for that.'

The last few words were flung back over Dermot's shoulder as he limped away to his dug-out cabin, and by the fire the fiddle music died away uncertainly.

'Don't stop now, Father,' Kathie whispered quickly. 'Play something cheerful and get everyone singing.'

As Tommy Donaghue drew his bow across the strings of his fiddle and broke into a song about the fishermen of Connemara, Kathie moved to Liam's side and stopped him from going after Dermot.

'Leave him, Liam. He will be all right again in a while.'

'But he's living in a dream world! He speaks as though he is a modern Moses, with the whole of Ireland waiting for him to come down from the mountains and lead them to the Promised Land.'

Kathie took Liam's hand. 'Come for a walk with me, Liam.'

Aware that only half of the Kilmar men were singing, the remainder listening to what was being said, Liam allowed himself to be led away from the firelight. Sure-footed in the darkness, Kathie took him to the ridge of broken rock that towered above the camp, picking her way between rocks as high as a man. She stopped when they stood on a solid granite platform, with a huge boulder at their backs. Far away in the distance Liam saw a faint flicker of yellow light from the window of a remote farm-house, and all about them the sky was peppered with the dust of a million stars. The camp-fire could not be seen from here, but he could hear the faint sound of the fiddle.

'I often come up here at night,' said Kathie. 'Sometimes I stay here for hours when the others are asleep.'

'Alone – or with Dermot?'

'You are the first person I have ever brought up here, Liam.'

There was a long awkward pause, and then Kathie said, 'Dermot is a sick man, Liam. His dreams are all he has. He can't go with the others when they are hunting, or set out to waylay a militiaman. He is left behind to curse his weakness – and dream up plans for the future.'

'But these dreams are possessing him, Kathie. You would think, from the way he speaks, that the whole of Ireland knew about the raid on the wagons and are just waiting for the call to follow him. It is not true. Only a few cottiers knew about it in the first place – and they have plenty of other things to think about now. Fever as well as the hunger. No one else either knows or cares. The soldiers have not forgotten yet, but the only ones who have taken an interest will be leaving Ireland soon. You can all be home in Kilmar again by the end of the summer.'

Kathie sighed in the darkness. 'You don't know how many times I have sat in this very spot and wished myself back in Kilmar, Liam. I was happy there and your mother was very kind to me.'

'Then come back – now. I never understand why you left in the first place.'

'I couldn't let Dermot go off without someone to look after him. He would have died in the first few days.'

'What is Dermot to you, Kathie?'

'I am very fond of him, Liam. During the time we have been in the mountains we have grown very close. He is just like a brother to me.'

'A . . . *brother*?'

Liam saw her pale face turned toward him. 'I feel responsible for getting him into this mess, Liam. You have said yourself that he lives in a dream world. He has always been a dreamer. After he took me to that first Association meeting he began dreaming of doing something to impress me – something bold and worthwhile. They would never have been anything more than mere dreams had I not urged him on. Had it not been for me he would still be in Kilmar, fishing with you, grumbling about the Association and happily dreaming about things he would never do. Instead, he is here in the mountains, hunted and far from home, and a sick man.'

Kathie's voice broke, and Liam put out a hand to comfort her, feeling her shoulder shake violently beneath his hand as she fought to control her unhappiness.

'Don't, Kathie . . . don't. . . .'

The next moment Kathie was clinging to him and sobbing helplessly against his chest.

Liam felt desperately sorry for her, and her crying cut into him like a knife. He held her to him, stroking her hair as though she were a child and promising her that everything would be all right if only she would stop crying.

Then, suddenly, she reached up for him, her lips pressed hard on his with all the passion that her unhappiness had released, her firm body pressing against his.

Eventually, gasping for breath, her mouth released his and she leaned against his chest, only an occasional sob disturbing the peace that had come to her.

'I feel so safe here with you like this, Liam,' Kathie whispered, and her arms tightened about him as she hugged him to her.

He kissed the top of her head tenderly. 'Then don't move.

We will stay up here all night and you can return to Kilmar with us tomorrow.'

'I can't, Liam. You have seen Dermot. I can't leave him in his present state.'

'Then I'll take him with us, too – by force if I have to.'

'No, Liam. You couldn't do that to him. He would die of shame.'

'But you can't stay here. Not when it is making you so unhappy.'

'I can stay here . . . now. I was not so sure before. Things will be better soon. The warmer months are coming, and Dermot is growing stronger. By the end of the summer he will be strong enough for me to leave him. I might even persuade him to come with me. But, either way, I will return to Kilmar then, Liam.'

She kissed him again and, even as he responded to her, Liam remembered another time, another place – and Caroline.

Kathie slipped from his arms. 'We had better get back to the others before Father comes looking for you and demands that you make an honest woman of me.'

'Then let's stay here until he does. That would settle the question of whether or not you returned to Kilmar with us.'

'No, Liam. We must go back now. It is going to be hard enough staying up in the mountains without you to lean on. Don't give me more problems than I already have.'

'What problems? Tell me.'

'Nothing I can't deal with.'

Kathie took his hand and tried to lead him away, but he did not move and held her hand fast.

'Tell me.'

Kathie tried to pull free, but he held her hand fast and repeated, 'Tell me.'

Kathie shrugged her shoulders. 'It is nothing, really. Nothing serious, anyway. I am alone up here with a crowd of young men – and the Kilmar fishermen are no different from young men from anywhere else. They tease, give my words double meanings, make suggestive remarks and try to involve me in horse-play. It is no more than would happen if I were back in Kilmar, but up here they have no mothers to take them by the ear and give them a shake. It does get difficult at times, but I can get by as long as they don't realise that I, too, have emotions and desires. That is why I don't want you and I to stay away long enough for them to imagine what we might be doing.'

Liam went cold at the thought of what could happen to a lone girl up here in these mountains.

'Is there anyone in particular who is giving you trouble?'

Kathie hesitated too long before finding an answer, and Liam asked, 'Who?'

She tried to laugh the matter away. 'Oh, you know what Eoin Feehan is like. He believes that no woman can be near him for long without falling madly in love with him. But it is nothing to worry about. He is easy enough to slap down when the occasion arises.'

'Eoin Feehan! I might have guessed....'

Liam told Kathie how, of all the Kilmar men who had been on the raid, only the name of Eoin Feehan was missing from the notice proclaiming the men from whom the protection of the law had been removed. He reminded her that only the Feehan boat had been untouched.

'But the soldiers captured Sean,' said Kathie. 'He must have talked before he died. The soldiers would have made him talk, but he would have kept back the name of his brother.'

'Sean would not have talked. He was the one member of that family I would have trusted with my life. I would not say the same for Eoin. We will probably never know the truth of what happened that night, but put no trust in Eoin Feehan. Watch his every movement and question his every word. If he did betray his friends once, he could do it again.'

When they returned to the camp it was Eoin Feehan's hot eyes that followed their progress to the side of Tommy Donaghue. Then Eoin saw that Liam watched him in his turn and, standing up abruptly, he strode wordlessly away from the light.

Dermot had also seen them return, but he said nothing until the following day when Liam and Tommy Donaghue left the camp and the Kilmar fugitives were waving them on their way.

'You spent some time alone with Liam last night.' He put it to Kathie as though it were an accusation.

'Yes.'

When no further explanation followed, Dermot asked, 'What did you talk about?'

'Lots of things. You ... me ... Kilmar.'

'Did he ask you to return to Kilmar with him?'

'Yes.'

'And . . . ?'

'I am still here, aren't I?'

'Are you staying here because of me?'

Tommy Donaghue and Liam dropped from view behind the gorse farther down the slope, and Kathie turned away without replying to Dermot's last question. He stopped her with a hand on her arm.

'What else did Liam say, Kathie? Did he ask you to marry him?'

Looking at Dermot, Kathie saw the torture on his face. 'Of course he didn't!'

'What would your reply have been if he had?'

'Liam has never mentioned marriage to me and I haven't even thought about it.' This was a lie, but Dermot would never know that. 'Come on now. There is a lot of tidying up to be done in camp—'

'No.'

Dermot gripped Kathie's arm so tightly she winced in pain. Dermot immediately slackened his grip but went on talking.

'What would your answer be if *I* asked you to marry me, Kathie?'

'I would tell you that your wound must be more serious than we thought and that it was affecting your mind.'

Kathie did her best to laugh away Dermot's question but she was not successful.

'Don't make a joke of it, Kathie. If Liam has not asked you to marry him, then he's a fool. One fool is enough in any family. I am asking you to marry me.'

'I wish you hadn't, Dermot. Not now . . . or here.'

'Well, I *have* asked you—and I won't take "no" for an answer, so you had best say nothing right now. Think about it, Kathie. Think about it seriously.'

Tommy Donaghue was a happy man on the way back to Kilmar. He had seen his daughter, she was well and he had no doubt that she would be home again very soon. Why shouldn't she be? The Scots soldiers were leaving Ireland, the Kilmar boys would return home—and Kathie would be with them.

Liam was not so sure. More than once he wished he had insisted that Kathie come back to Kilmar with them. He would have liked to bring his brother out of the mountains, too; Dermot was a cause for great concern. He was a sick man and had a sick man's preoccupation with himself. Dermot needed to live among people in more normal surroundings for a while, but Liam was not sure how to set about persuading his brother of the need for a change in his surroundings.

He would have liked to discuss the matter with the man who had taken the Kilmar outlaws to the mountains. Nathan Brock was a very resourceful man and might have thought of something.

That brought Liam to his final problem. Where was Nathan Brock – and where could he begin to look for him?

Chapter Twenty

Nathan Brock searched County Wexford from the Wicklow mountains to Hook Head and from Cahore Point to Mount Leinster without success. There were too many homeless cottiers on the roads of the county. They flowed like a hungry tide from one end of the land to the other, and back again. Few of them had a destination; they knew only that to stop was to die. On the road there was always the hope that something better was around the next bend; but they had long since stopped asking the names of strangers, and Nathan Brock faced a hopeless task.

Jeremy searched as diligently as did Nathan, and more than once they found someone who thought they *might* have seen Shelagh Brock and her two boys. But as winter passed and yellow flowers brightened the grass beneath the hedgerows Nathan Brock was still no nearer finding his family. It seemed they had vanished from the face of Ireland. Slowly, reluctantly, as though accepting defeat, Nathan Brock retraced his steps, heading once more for the Wicklow mountains.

During their months of searching, Jeremy received tuition in the art of prizefighting – and he learned something more. He was able to sample something of the flavour of actual organised fights.

In order to obtain money to continue the search for his family, Nathan Brock took to the ring again. The opposition in this corner of Ireland was not great and he had only two fights, one in Wexford Town, the other in Enniscorthy, winning them both by decisive knock-downs, using his clubbing right hand to devastating advantage.

The purses he fought for were not huge – they were not even large – but they were sufficient to keep the two searchers fed for many weeks.

Jeremy worked in Nathan Brock's corner during the brief intervals between short knock-downs but, unknown to the prizefighter, he indulged in a more profitable activity while attention was fixed on the exciting fight.

Wagers were freely made on the outcome of the fight and

keen sporting men thrust their money pouches carelessly in easily accessible pockets during the excitement of the occasion. For someone as skilful and daring as Jeremy it was a simple matter to relieve the rightful owner of his money and transfer it to his own pocket. Even when the thefts were discovered no one suspected that anyone in the corner of the highly respected Nathan Brock was involved.

But now, with the fights behind him, it was a bitter and desperate man who made his way northward. The only village in County Wexford Nathan Brock had not searched was Kilmar. He did not go there because the people of the fishing village were his friends. They would have given him genuine sympathy – and sympathy was the last thing the fighter wanted at this time. He felt he would have broken down and wept openly.

Secretly, Nathan Brock believed his family must now be dead. The famine was so bad that the hungry cottiers were eating anything that grew – even grass. A woman with two children to support had little chance of survival in the Ireland of 1846.

Nathan Brock and Jeremy trudged wearily back to County Wicklow, with the young boy looking over his shoulder nervously as they passed the farm from where he had stolen the ducks only a few short months before.

They arrived at the mountains safely and found Kathie in the camp alone. As she had predicted to Liam, the warm weather had helped Dermot as no amount of nursing could and he had gone off with the others to cut turf for their cooking-fires.

Kathie was delighted to see the big man again and surprised that Jeremy was with him. Not until Nathan Brock had described how he had met up with the boy and started to talk about some of their experiences together did she realise that he knew nothing about his wife and boys being at Kilmar.

When she told him Nathan Brock suffered an agony of self-recrimination. He cursed himself for his stupidity in not calling at Kilmar. There was nothing for it but to turn round and hurry to Kilmar as fast as he was able, although the news was now more than a month old and he dreaded what he might learn there.

So eager was he to be away that he declined Kathie's offer of a meal.

'I couldn't eat a single mouthful,' he declared. 'Until I learn something about Shelagh and the boys food would choke me.'

'Then I will walk as far as the road with you,' said Kathie. 'There are a few things I would like to discuss with you.'

On the way she told Nathan Brock of what Liam had said about Eoin Feehan.

'And has there been anything more to arouse your suspicions?'

'Yes. Eoin has taken to going off by himself in the evenings and coming back to the camp the worse for drink.'

'Has no one said anything to him about it?'

'Dermot tried, but Eoin replied that he is sick of the mountains and, since he is not a wanted man, there is nothing to prevent him from going to Rathconard and enjoying a drink or two.'

They discussed Eoin Feehan's recent behaviour until they came within sight of Rathconard and then, to Nathan Brock's surprise, Jeremy announced that he would be coming no farther with him.

'But why?' asked Nathan Brock. 'We have travelled all these miles together. Why leave now when we are within a matter of hours of my family?'

'Because you don't need me no more, Nathan. If your family are well, you will want to stay at Kilmar and build a new life for them. If all isn't well, you won't want to share your grief with anyone. Here, take these. You'll probably have need of them.'

Jeremy handed over five gold sovereigns, and the big man looked from the coins to the boy in consternation.

'Where did you get these?'

'I was given them by gentlemen who won a lot of money on your fights. I should have given them to you before, I suppose.'

'You are a young rogue, Jeremy – but we must share these.'

'We have,' grinned the boy. 'That's your half. I've got mine hidden in my sock.'

Jeremy was relieved that Nathan Brock accepted his story so readily. He was sure the ex-prizefighter would not have accepted the gold had he known the gentlemen of whom he spoke had not knowingly parted with their winnings.

'What will you do now? You could probably stay here with Kathie and the others if you wanted to.'

'No,' Jeremy shook his head. 'I don't need them any more

than they need me. I'll go north to Dublin. I might even find another fighter to teach me how to use my fists. Don't you worry none about me, Nathan. I'll make out well enough.'

But an idea had come to Nathan Brock and he was so deep in his own thoughts that he missed the tell-tale trembling of Jeremy's lower lip as he finished talking.

'Jeremy, before you go to Dublin will you do a favour for Kathie . . . and me?'

The boy nodded.

'I would like you to stay hereabouts for a while. Find out what Eoin Feehan gets up to in Rathconard. You know him?'

'I've seen him. But I doubt if he will remember me. Yes, I'll do that.'

'Good boy!'

Nathan Brock clapped a big hand on the boy's shoulder. 'Tell Kathie if you learn anything. If it is something you feel I should know, then come and find me . . . at Kilmar.'

Chapter Twenty-One

It was a very tired Nathan Brock who arrived in Kilmar the next morning. There had been ample time during the walk from the Wicklow mountains for him to consider the news of his family more carefully. During the dark hours the doubts closed in about him. He became convinced that his weakened family could not have survived the onslaught of black fever.

Many of the more morbid thoughts left him when the sun came up to chase away the darkness, but he was prepared for the worst. When he saw not a single cottier on the quayside, or wandering the streets of Kilmar, he felt sure the black fever must have taken them all.

He made his way to the McCabe house and Liam opened the door to him.

'Nathan! We have been enquiring throughout Ireland for you. Where have you been?'

'My family, Liam. Shelagh . . . the boys . . . ?'

Liam saw the agony on Nathan Brock's face.

'They are all right, Nathan. Every one of them. They are fine.'

Nathan Brock's shoulders sagged with relief and suddenly his knees felt very weak. Liam put an arm about his shoulders and led him inside the house to a chair.

'Coming along the road this morning I didn't dare hope. Then, as I neared the village, I saw the empty streets. No cottiers . . . not even a fishing boat out at sea. I thought the fever must have taken everyone.'

Liam laughed. 'Where have you been that days no longer matter, Nathan? It is Sunday. All the good Kilmar people are in church and most of the cottiers have left us for the new soup kitchen in Gorey.'

'Shelagh and the boys, they are in Gorey?'

'No, Lady Caroline has taken them to a cottage up at Inch House. Shelagh still needed some nursing when one of the Quaker doctors died and his companions left Kilmar in a hurry. Shelagh is able to do some light work for her. As for the boys, you would not know they had ever been ill.'

'God Bless Lady Caroline. I'll be leaving you now, Liam. I must go to them.'

'Not so fast, Nathan. You'll have a bite to eat first and tell me all the news. You'd best clean up a bit, too, while I find you a shirt and some trousers. They will be a little tight for you, but they will do. You go up to the house looking as you are and you will never get past the gate-keeper.'

Nathan Brock looked down at his tattered and dirty rags and grinned sheepishly. He was no better dressed than any other wanderer on the roads of Ireland.

'I'll come up to the big house with you,' said Liam. 'Lady Caroline has half the cottiers in County Wexford working on the estate, and I promised to take some fish up there for them.'

Norah McCabe returned to the house before Nathan Brock had finished cleaning up and insisted on cooking a huge meal for him. He was able to repay her generosity by giving her the good news of Dermot's improved health.

On the way to Inch House Liam told Nathan Brock of the demise of the Kilmar soup kitchen. Father Clery had kept it going for a week after the hasty departure of the two Quakers, but the cottiers had poured in from the surrounding countryside in their thousands. It soon became quite impossible to feed them all and, in a desperate bid to secure food for themselves and their families, the cottiers had fought among themselves, the brawls spilling over into the streets of Kilmar and involving the fishermen. This, together with the very real danger of black fever spreading to the villagers, decided Father Clery, reluctantly, to close down his soup kitchen in Kilmar.

The cottiers had immediately moved to Gorey where an English charity had set up a kitchen. Meanwhile, Lady Caroline was feeding the families of the workers on her brother's estate and had taken on twice as many men as were needed. They were building walls and roads, digging ditches and trimming hedges anything to keep them going until the new season's potatoes were ready for digging.

'It sounds as though I and the cottiers of County Wexford have reason to thank this Lady Caroline Dudley,' said Nathan Brock sincerely. 'Without her there would have been little relief in this part of Ireland – and none at all from England.'

'No,' agreed Liam. 'But they were quick enough to send soldiers.' He told Nathan Brock of the visits the Army had made to Kilmar, of the smashing of the boats and the outcome of their last visit, when Caroline had sent them scurrying away.

'The more I hear of this Lady Caroline, the more I like her,' said Nathan Brock. 'Did you get to know her well when you stayed at her London house?'

'Yes.'

Nathan Brock waited for Liam to amplify his curt reply, but he remained silent.

'Is she an elderly woman? She must be, I suppose, to have a husband with such an important post in the Treasury.'

'She is no older than me.'

Liam's reticence began to intrigue Nathan Brock.

'Is she pretty?'

Liam remained silent for so long that Nathan Brock thought he was not going to give him a reply, but then Liam said softly, 'Lady Caroline is not a woman you would refer to as "pretty". Beautiful, she certainly is. Prettiness is for lesser women. Now, tell me more about the fights you had . . . and Jeremy. Can you trust him to keep a close watch on Eoin Feehan?'

Nathan Brock accepted the change of topic, but Liam's reluctance to talk about Lady Caroline Dudley told him almost as much as Eugene Brennan had learned from seeing the two of them together – and he was as concerned for Liam as Brennan had been.

He was even more worried when they arrived at the great house and he met Lady Caroline for the first time. Liam was right: she was a very beautiful woman. Until that moment, Nathan Brock had thought Liam was nursing a secret passion for a woman who, by reason of her station in life, was unapproachable. Now he could see that she had eyes only for Liam. He could foresee serious trouble for his friend. At some time in the future he would find a way to talk to Liam about it – but, for now, Nathan Brock had other matters on his mind.

Caroline was delighted to meet Nathan Brock. 'Shelagh and the boys are all well,' she told him. 'And now you are here they will be the happiest family in County Wexford. But you do not want to listen to my idle chatter. Come.'

The cottage in which Caroline had housed the Brock family was very small, but it was stone-built and had a sizeable garden. In a good year a man could grow potatoes and vegetables for his own family and have enough left over to sell at a small profit.

Shelagh Brock was working in the garden, helped by her two young boys, as they approached. When she saw them, she straightened her back and put a hand to her forehead to shield her eyes from the sun.

When recognition came, her mouth opened to cry out but no sound emerged. Then she began running, leaving her startled children to wonder what was happening.

Liam and Caroline hung back until the emotional reunion had run its course and Nathan Brock stood beaming happily with a small boy in his arms, the other clinging to his hand. Shelagh Brock was streaking dirt across her face as she tried unsuccessfully to wipe away her tears with a dirt-stained hand.

When Nathan Brock began brokenly to thank Caroline, she hurriedly cut him short.

'Shelagh has been a boon in the house – and if only half of what I have been told about you is true you are going to be just as useful to me. I own a four-hundred-acre section of the Inch estate and this would seem to be a good time to build a house. I will, of course, bring in architects and expert landscapers, but I need someone to supervise the labour. I would like you to take on that task – and at the same time help me to run my brother's estate. I fear that at times the cottiers are too much for the present manager to handle.'

Nathan Brock was delighted to accept her offer, and as Liam and Caroline walked back to Inch House from the cottage Liam said, 'You have ensured that there will be no trouble during the building of your house. There is not a man in Ireland foolish enough to risk upsetting Nathan Brock – and he feels he owes you a debt that will never be repaid in this life.'

'I wish it were as simple to solve the cottiers' problems. I fear that many of them will not live to harvest the new season's potatoes. There must be something more we can do for them, Liam.'

He looked at her and saw the strain on her face together with a tiredness he had never seen there before.

'I think you are already doing everything that is humanly possible. This is not a problem that any one person can solve;

it is on far too vast a scale. The English Government will need to send shiploads of grain – and send them quickly.'

'Perhaps Eugene will be able to persuade Richard. If he can impress him with the seriousness of the situation in the whole of the country, I am sure Richard will send a report to Sir Robert Peel and bring help quickly.'

'He might – if only Sir Richard would see him,' replied Liam angrily. 'It seems that your husband is a very busy man. So busy that he has been unable to spare a few minutes for Eugene, in the three weeks he has been trying to see him.'

Caroline stopped and looked at Liam in surprise. 'Are you sure of this?'

'Father Clery has been to Dublin and returned only yesterday. Eugene is so disheartened he is talking of giving up and going to London to speak to Peel himself. Is Sir Richard really so busy?'

'I don't know. I have not seen him for more than a month. But I shall go to Dublin right away. Richard *will* see Eugene if I have to take him into his office myself.'

'Don't push yourself too hard, Caroline. You are doing wonderful work here and the cottiers need you.'

'Only the cottiers, Liam? Not you?'

Her voice was husky with a recognisable longing, and Liam tried not to look at her.

'What either of us needs, or desires, is not important at this time, Caroline. Our people need you – and they need the help of your husband.'

Liam's rebuff was painful, but Caroline accepted it. 'I can give myself, Liam. I cannot make promises on behalf of Richard.'

'Neither of us should make promises that can't be fulfilled, Caroline. You are married and we live in different worlds. You have been to Kilmar. You have seen my home.'

'There is only one world, Liam, and we both came into it in the same way. You are referring to social barriers. They are put up by people who do not care to be reminded that they are no different from the beggar who sits on the street-corner, or the man who cleans out the stables. My grandfather was the first Earl of Inch, Liam. He was given the title and these estates because he was a brilliant soldier at a time when England desperately needed such a man. He was also incredibly reckless, both in his soldiering and in his private life. Had he not been made a peer he might well have been committed to prison for debt. Perhaps it was the thought of this that made him such a brave and fearless soldier. Be that as it may, my own father was once sent home from school because his fees had not been paid.

'Think about it, Liam. Had my grandfather not had Napoleon to fight I would have been born to poverty. I could have been gutting fish on Kilmar quay, or perhaps tramping the lanes, dressed in rags and begging for my food. It is something I remind myself about often when I lose patience with a cottier who quarrels over a scrap of food, or when the sheer enormity of the famine threatens to overwhelm me.'

Caroline spoke with such honesty and feeling that Liam looked at her with a new respect, but words could change nothing.

'I am glad you told me, Caroline. There was a time, in London, when I, too, believed there was no barrier you and I could not overcome. I told myself that the rules had been made for other people and that wanting each other as we did would be enough. Then I learned about your husband and came down to earth with a big bump. You probably think I am a simpleton, but. . . .'

Liam's words tailed away and he made a helpless gesture with his hands.

'Oh no, Liam! I have never thought that – and the last thing I ever wanted was to hurt you. I. . . .' She looked at Liam as though seeking an answer to some unasked question. Her shoulders sagged and she said quietly, 'As you say, I have Richard. And I must go to Dublin to see him.'

They walked on in silence until they reached a place where Liam's way home took him away from the path to the big house.

'Perhaps I should go back to London and out of your life for ever, Liam. You would soon find yourself a good strong Irish girl to give you handsome children and make your mother happy.'

Caroline was watching Liam's face as she spoke, and of a sudden her eyes widened as, inexplicably, her words conjured up a picture of Kathie Donaghue in Liam's mind.

'There *is* a girl, Liam! Who? When? No, I have no right to

ask anything. You have your own life to lead. I have interfered enough. . . .'

With all her sophistication gone, Caroline looked like a little girl who suddenly realises she is lost, but when Liam reached out a hand to her she turned and fled away along the path to the big house, leaving Liam with a strong and bewildering feeling of guilt.

Chapter Twenty-Two

Although Eugene Brennan found Sir Richard Dudley's reluctance to see him increasingly frustrating, the politician did not waste his time in Dublin. He canvassed all the influential men of the city. In addition to the money they donated to his relief fund, he drew promises from them to bring increased pressure to bear upon the English Government to get it to allocate money and food to the cottiers.

Eugene Brennan's task was made easier because it was known that the outbreak of fever in the soldiers' barracks had been caused by contact with the cottiers of Kilmar. The merchants and businessmen of Ireland's capital feared the black fever more than the wrath of government.

The Lord-Lieutenant of Ireland received many unwanted petitions from men of influence, requesting immediate aid for the starving populace. Helpless to act himself, the Lord-Lieutenant passed them on to the Prime Minister.

Sir Robert Peel was himself receiving many such pleas and he realised that the time was fast approaching when he would have to bow to opinion and do something to help the Irish. Yet he was reluctant to spend the money acquired through his recently imposed 'income tax' on such relief. Instead, he announced plans to abolish the controversial corn laws, whereby the crops of English and Irish land-owners were protected by the ridiculously high duty charged on imported corn. By so doing, he hoped to attract sufficient grain to Ireland to alleviate the desperate situation there.

Unfortunately, the Prime Minister seemed unaware that there was a world shortage of grain. Far from bringing relief to Ireland, his action would merely precipitate a political storm that would topple Peel and force his Tory party from office.

But all this was still some weeks away when Caroline's coach left the country lanes behind and clattered along the wide roads of Dublin city.

She went immediately to Eugene Brennan's house, arriving when the surprised MP was in the middle of a late lunch.

Declining an invitation to join him, Caroline came immediately to the purpose of her visit.

'Liam tells me my husband is refusing to see you?'

'Perhaps "refusing" is not the correct word. Sir Richard has made no reply to my request for an interview, even though I sent him the letter you so kindly gave to me. Whenever I go to his office I am informed by members of his staff that he is "engaged" or "busy" or, on occasions, "not available". I realise that his time is valuable, but—'

'Hurry and finish your lunch, Eugene. I will take you to see him. His staff will not refuse to allow me in.'

Caroline was hot, dusty and bad-tempered. Furthermore, she had a headache – the result of urging the coachman to drive faster over pot-holed roads.

'Some things are more important than food,' declared Eugene Brennan, pushing his plate from him and rising to his feet. 'I am ready to leave immediately.'

Caroline's mood did not improve on the road to Dublin Castle, where Sir Richard Dudley had his offices. After two attempts to draw her into conversation about the situation in Kilmar, Eugene Brennan lapsed into silence.

The carriage was halted at the gate to the great grim castle, but Caroline was in no mood for delay and the guard was quick to allow the carriage and its occupants to pass through.

The secretary in charge of Sir Richard Dudley's outer office did not react with the same speed. When Caroline told him to inform her husband she was there, he looked first at Eugene Brennan and then began to explain that Sir Richard was busy.

Without waiting for the man to finish speaking, Caroline swept past him to the door of the inner office, taking the Irish MP with her.

The startled baronet looked up from the letter he was writing as the door swung open without warning. Seeing his wife, he pushed back his chair and rose to his feet as quickly as he could, his mind groping for an explanation of this unexpected visit.

'Richard, I sent a letter with Mr Brennan three weeks ago requesting that you see him. As my request has been ignored I had no alternative but to bring him here myself.'

'My dear, I have been so busy. . . .'

The agitated secretary stood in the doorway wringing his hands and Sir Richard Dudley waved an impatient dismissal.

'I am delighted to see you.' He nodded curtly at Eugene Brennan. 'And you, too, sir. But, Caroline, allow me to offer you a chair.'

'That will not be necessary for me, Richard. I promised Mr Brennan I would arrange a meeting with you and I regret that I had to go to such lengths in order to keep my word. I am sure you are both busy men so I will hold up your business no longer.'

'But . . . Caroline! Where are you staying . . . ? Where can I see you . . . ?'

The baronet started across the room, but Caroline had already reached the door. Opening it, she turned.

'At Inch House, Richard. Where I have been for some weeks. Goodbye.'

The door banged shut behind her and she was gone.

'Upon my soul!' Sir Richard Dudley took a handkerchief from his sleeve and mopped his face. The room had suddenly become unseasonably hot. At a complete loss for words, he shook his head and repeated, 'Upon my soul!'

Then Sir Richard Dudley remembered he was not alone. Tucking the handkerchief back inside his cuff, he returned to his desk and sat frowning for a moment or two before looking up at Eugene Brennan.

'What exactly is it you wish to discuss with me?'

'Death, disease and official apathy,' came the prompt reply.

Sir Richard Dudley leaned back in his chair and gave out a loud exasperated sigh.

'Mr Brennan, I am leading a Treasury Commission investigating army expenditure. Others have responsibility for Ireland – but I doubt whether they have a fathomless sack of money from which to draw unlimited sums to feed out-of-work Irishmen.'

Eugene Brennan pulled his chair closer to the baronet's desk and faced him across the polished width.

'I am not begging for money, Sir Richard. I am asking only that you acquaint yourself with the *true* facts of the situation here in Ireland and pass them on to Sir Robert Peel.'

'Oh? And what are the "true" facts – as you see them, of course.'

'The facts are here for everyone to see, Sir Richard. Your soldiers have reported them – so, too, have the constabulary, the Poor Commissioners and anyone else who has travelled outside Dublin. Ireland is dying, her people suffering from starvation and disease. Unless aid is forthcoming, the Government in London will be directly responsible for the death of a million men, women and children. We need food and doctors – and we need them immediately.'

'Come now, Mr Brennan. You are not addressing one of your meetings, appealing to the emotions of an Irish mob. I asked for facts and you have responded with emotional claptrap. You will need to do better than that if you expect me to exceed my authority by telling the Prime Minister what he should be doing for Ireland.'

Eugene Brennan pulled a tied sheaf of papers from a pocket and threw them across the desk to the other man.

'There are your "facts", Sir Richard. Gathered at first hand by the members of my association throughout the length and breadth of the country. You will find all the "facts" there relating to the dead, the starving and the diseased. All written in so simple a language that no official could possibly misunderstand a single word. The "facts" will shock you, Sir Richard, as they should shock Sir Robert Peel. But they cannot convey the misery or the suffering of a small child who has no food and no hope for the future. There are thousands of such children, dying and with no one to care. That is something you need to go out and see for yourself, as I have on all too many occasions. Facts and figures are necessary, Sir Richard, but they tend to make you forget you are dealing with flesh-and-blood people. People with the same needs and feelings as you and I – and Lady Caroline.'

'Ah yes, Lady Caroline.'

Sir Richard Dudley's fingertips met in front of his face as he gazed speculatively at his uninvited visitor. On a personal level, Sir Richard Dudley did not give a damn for the Irish peasants. They were an ill-mannered and evil-smelling people. If the famine winnowed them out, it would be to everyone's advantage. Much of the Irish problem would disappear with them. It would certainly make his official task easier.

A drop in the population would mean keeping fewer soldiers in Ireland to hold them in check. There would be a substantial saving in army expenditure. On the other hand, if Eugene Brennan's documents provided conclusive proof that the situation was as serious as he stated, then official action would have to be taken. By choosing the right moment to submit a report to the Prime Minister, he, Sir Richard, could take much of the credit for such action, thereby gaining considerable political prestige.

'It would appear that the future of Ireland has been placed in the hands of the Dudley family. Have you no others you can call upon, Mr Brennan? I seem to recall a fisherman who was in London to raise money for the starving Irish. Is he no longer interested in such a worthy cause?'

'Liam McCabe is still working hard for the cottiers' cause but he is a working fisherman and needs to spend much of his time at sea. At least, that is his present way of life. I have other plans for Liam.'

'Indeed? Am I permitted to ask what they are?'

'I intend that he shall become a Member of Parliament.'

Sir Richard Dudley was startled. 'A Member of Parliament – a fisherman?'

'Liam is an exceptional man. He has his own boat, not a curragh, but a fine wooden boat, and has established an inland market for the sale of his catches. He is not just another fisherman.'

'So it seems. He lives at Kilmar, I believe. Not very far from Inch House.'

'He does.'

Eugene Brennan was not happy with Sir Richard Dudley's sudden interest in Liam.

'I met this young man in London. It was only a brief meeting, of course, but I could not fail to observe that the clothes he wore were hardly suited to fishing. They were extremely well tailored, as I recall.'

'Thank you, Sir Richard. They were made for him by my own London tailor. I thought them necessary. Liam addressed a number of meetings while he was in London. He could hardly be presented dressed in an old jersey and fisherman's boots. They are not the clothes for a future MP.'

'But more appropriate for your cause, I would have thought. To show the people a real, live, poor Irishman.'

'The poor of Ireland don't dress in rags because they enjoy

it, Sir Richard. Given the opportunity and the money they would dress as well as you or I.'

'I do not doubt it – and of course this Kilmar fisherman had the opportunity to dress well, did he not? I understand he collected a great deal of money for the famine relief fund.'

Eugene Brennan rose to his feet, suddenly angry.

'Are you suggesting that the relief fund has been defrauded? By God, sir, I wish there was a witness present. I would take you to court for such a slanderous remark.'

'Do sit down again, Mr Brennan. I am accusing you of nothing. Your honesty is not in question. I was talking about the Kilmar fisherman. It is not difficult to understand the temptation for him. He was in unfamiliar surroundings, meeting people far above his own social status. He, not unnaturally, felt the need to improve himself – by buying new clothes with some of the money he had collected. Who can blame him? By his own efforts he was bringing in more money than he had ever seen before. He undoubtedly felt he was entitled to a share in such good fortune. Quite understandable – but hardly the actions of a future Member of Parliament.'

Sir Richard Dudley held up a hand to silence Eugene Brennan before the red-faced MP could splutter an angry reply.

'Hear me out, Mr Brennan, and think carefully of the purpose of your visit here before you make a hasty reply.

'This Kilmar fisherman has ideas above his station in life. He took money from the famine fund to buy the things he felt he needed to achieve his foolish ambitions. It would hardly help you, or your cause, to sponsor him as a Member of Parliament. It would be more to your credit, perhaps, to bring him to justice.'

Sir Richard Dudley leaned forward eagerly, bringing his face close to Eugene Brennan. 'I promise you that if you have your young fisherman indicted for misusing the famine fund, Mr Brennan, I will view your request to me most favourably. Most favourably indeed. Is that understood?'

'But why? Why Liam?' Eugene Brennan was dumbfounded.

'Let us just say that I have an intense dislike of young men who do not accept their lot in life. I have an orderly mind, Mr Brennan. I am made unhappy when things – and people – are not in their correct places.'

The baronet picked up some papers from his desk and

began looking at them. 'Now, if you will please excuse me, I have much work to do.'

The old politician rose to his feet and moved slowly and thoughtfully toward the door, his bemused mind trying to grasp the full implications of what Sir Richard Dudley had just suggested.

'Mr Brennan. . . .'

Eugene Brennan paused, his hand on the door-handle.

'Your countrymen have put their trust in you for a great many years. Many of their lives depend upon your swift action. Do not keep them – or me – waiting for too long.'

Eugene Brennan walked out through the gates of Dublin Castle a troubled man, but the baronet's motives no longer puzzled him. He remembered the glances that had passed between Liam and Lady Caroline when they were in the same house in London. They were very different from the cold look Lady Caroline had given her husband when she swept from his office not half an hour before.

Sir Richard Dudley's orderly mind was not so much concerned with putting Liam in his place as with trying to bring Lady Caroline back to hers.

Chapter Twenty-Three

In the Wicklow mountains, Jeremy was taking his task of watching Eoin Feehan very seriously. It was not difficult to maintain his observation without being seen; he knew the area well. The gang of cut-throats with whom he had once been involved had used these same hills.

Every evening he waited, hidden well back from the track that came down through thinly wooded slopes from the mountains to Rathconard. Most nights Eoin Feehan came along the track, looking neither to left nor right, seeming to be in such a hurry to reach the town that it was all Jeremy could do to keep up with him without giving himself away. Yet when the fisherman reached the small town he did nothing more sinister than enter an inn and sit by himself, drinking steadily for two or three hours.

At the end of the evening, Eoin Feehan would put down his pewter pot, wipe his mouth on his sleeve, and make his way out of the inn without a word to anyone.

On the first few occasions, Jeremy was so curious that he never allowed Eoin Feehan to move from his sight, but when the routine was repeated without variation every evening he became bored. While the fisherman was at the inn drinking, he began making forays of his own.

Rathconard was not a large town, although it was being used increasingly as a stopover on the road between Dublin and the south-western bays of Bantry and Kenmare. The inhabitants had not grown used to the need for locking doors. For a boy of Jeremy's talents, housebreaking was a simple matter. He found a house where the occupants were temporarily absent, opened the door, walked in, and helped himself to anything of value.

So easy was this unlawful source of income, and so predictable were Eoin Feehan's evening activities, that Jeremy became both greedy and careless.

Not far away from the mean back-street tavern frequented by Eoin Feehan was a much larger coaching inn, used by the passengers of many of the cross-country coaches. Jeremy happened to be passing this main-road inn one evening when two coaches drew up. From them alighted a large party of well-dressed men and women. Jeremy was particularly impressed by the jewellery displayed on the fat fingers and wrists of one of the older women. As one of the men handed her down from the coach, the rays of the sinking sun touched her hands and the light scattered in a hundred directions.

Jeremy had never before seen so much jewellery on a single hand. Here were the pickings of a lifetime.

It was not difficult for him to discover which rooms the party were occupying. The rooms were brightly lit, and the laughing and chattering could be heard through wide-open casement windows from the street below.

Jeremy waited outside the coaching inn for almost an hour before, with his nose pressed against the glass of a downstairs window, he saw the party being escorted to a table sagging with food and wine.

In the dusk it was an easy matter to shin up to the low roof of a lean-to stable and thence to a narrow ledge running across the front of the inn only inches below the upstairs windows. From here Jeremy was able to step into one of the rooms occupied by the wealthy coach party.

It was an untidy room with clothing strewn about haphazardly and part-full glasses perched upon bedside tables and mantelshelves. It appeared that the occupants of the room had felt the need for celebration.

Jeremy's attention was immediately directed to the small pile of rings and bangles on the dressing-table, half-hidden by a clutter of small perfume-bottles, brushes and combs. By sheer good luck, he had entered the room of the bejewelled woman, and she had obligingly left her rings and bracelets here for him.

But capricious luck deserted the young thief at the final moment. Even as he reached out a hand toward the heap of gems, the door from the adjoining room opened suddenly and a startled man's voice exclaimed, 'What the devil are you doing here?'

Jeremy grabbed at the jewellery and, grasping what he could, dived for the door leading to the passage outside.

He reached it and had it open when a hand seized his collar from the rear. The man who had entered the room might have been taken by surprise, but his reaction was fast enough.

He held Jeremy in a tight grip, and had he walked the boy in front of him down the stairs to the landlord he would have secured the arrest of the young thief immediately. Instead, he turned Jeremy to face him, the better to see his face.

'So, you young villain, you've been caught. Now I will—'

Jeremy did not wait to hear what the stranger had planned for him. The jewellery was clenched in his right hand, and he brought the closed fist across in a punch that would have done credit to Nathan Brock. It landed squarely on his captor's nose.

Releasing his grip, the man took three unsteady backward steps across the room before sitting down with a hard bump.

Before the man could recover, Jeremy was away along the corridor, a cry of 'Stop, thief!' ringing out behind him. On the narrow inn stairs he bowled over an old man and then careered between startled guests in the lounge and bar below. Seconds later he was outside and running headlong through the window-lit streets of Rathconard.

Not until he had turned four or five corners did Jeremy stop running. He thrust the stolen rings deep inside a pocket and looked about him. He would not be safe until he reached the mountains, but for the moment he needed to get off the streets.

Realising he was close to the inn where Eoin Feehan was drinking, he made his way there. Slipping inside the smoke-filled back-street inn, he bought a portion of fish-pie, the serving-girl insisting upon sighting his money before passing the food across the rough wooden counter. His heart still thudding from his recent exertions, Jeremy pushed his way through the crowded room toward the table where he had last seen the Kilmar fisherman. To his astonishment he saw him talking earnestly to a uniformed soldier with corporal's stripes on his sleeve. English soldiers were not popular anywhere in Ireland, and while Eoin Feehan and the corporal talked two more soldiers sat nervously nearby, their backs to a solid wall and eyes constantly on the move, unable to understand much of the talk about them.

Slipping easily between drinking Irishmen, Jeremy worked his way closer to Eoin Feehan's table and finally sat down beside the smoking fire in the huge fireplace only a few feet away.

Squeezing between a drunken old woman and her daughter, who was viewing each man who entered the room as a prospective customer, Jeremy was almost back to back with the corporal. Both women grumbled irritably, but Jeremy pretended not to notice and within seconds they settled down again.

'. . . you just do your part and leave the rest to me,' the corporal was saying in a low voice. 'And none of your tricks, or you'll not live long enough to regret them.'

'I'll do whatever you say,' said Eoin Feehan hoarsely. 'If anything goes wrong, it will be no fault of mine.'

'Nothing had better go wrong this time,' hissed the corporal. 'I wouldn't fancy your chances if I spread it around that you ordered me to kill your own brother.'

Eoin Feehan blinked nervously about him, his eyes bloodshot from drink and smoke from the listless fire. 'I didn't know it was Sean when I told you. . . .'

'There's them as wouldn't put too fine a distinction on who you *thought* it was,' retorted the corporal. 'Just you keep that in mind and let me know of anything you think I ought to know about. Remember, if you hear nothing more from me, be sure you are not with the others on the night of the next full moon. You'd better come down here again for a few more evenings yet; I may want to speak to you again.'

The corporal straightened up on his stool and his back bumped against Jeremy. 'Now we'll have a last drink together and then you'd best be on your way. Your countrymen don't look too kindly on those who drink with soldiers.'

Corporal Garrett laughed loudly at Eoin Feehan's discomfiture, but Jeremy had heard enough to put his escapade of such a short while before from his mind for the moment. Kathie's suspicions had been fully justified. Now he had to get to her and tell her what he had just learned. He stood up to the accompaniment of more grumbling from the women on either side, but before he could push past them a voice from the doorway shouted, 'There he is! Stop, thief!'

Looking up, Jeremy saw the man he had punched on the nose pushing his way toward him, accompanied by a tall-hatted constable.

There was a door on the opposite side of the room and Jeremy knew it led to a yard behind the inn, but before he could make his escape in that direction a strong hand gripped him by the arm and the corporal's voice said, 'Not so fast, my lad.'

Jeremy struggled and tried to lash out with his fists, but the corporal was tougher than Jeremy's previous captor had been and the two soldiers were quick to come to his assistance. One of them twisted Jeremy's arm cruelly behind his back and he let out a cry of pain, forced to give up the unequal fight.

'Here you are, sir,' said the corporal, releasing a hand to touch his high-crowned cap to the man from the coaching inn. 'It's a good job me and my men was here to catch this young villain for you or he would have been out of that back door and away, for sure.'

'Thank you, Corporal. I am much obliged. Much obliged indeed.'

The man reached inside a waistcoat pocket with thumb and forefingers. Extracting a golden guinea, he handed it to the fawning soldier.

'Why, thank you, sir. I wasn't expecting such generosity, I'm sure. What has this young rogue been up to? That's if you don't mind me asking, sir.'

'He broke into this gentleman's room and made off with a quantity of jewellery,' said the constable. 'And if your soldiers will keep hold of him I'll search him to make sure he doesn't do away with anything on the way to the lock-up.'

While the two soldiers held Jeremy fast, with a circle of curious customers looking on, the constable searched through Jeremy's pockets.

'Ah! I think this is what we are looking for.'

The constable pulled the rings from Jeremy's pocket, and there was a gasp from the onlookers as the precious stones flashed in the light of the lamps. 'There is no doubting that we've got the culprit to rights here.'

'And this isn't the first time he's been caught stealing other folk's property.'

A man pushed his way through the crowd, and with the awful feeling that the whole world was taking a hand in his downfall Jeremy recognised the farmer from whom Nathan Brock had rescued him.

'He stole two of my ducks a few months ago. I was bringing him into Rathconard to face the magistrate when a huge rogue of a man jumped on me, beat me to the ground and made off with this young rascal – and the two ducks I had with me as evidence.'

'Is that so? Then we must be careful none of his villainous friends do the same thing tonight.'

Turning to the corporal, the constable said, 'I shall put handcuffs on him, but I would be obliged if you and your men came with me to the lock-up with this young felon.'

'Willingly, Constable, willingly. Stand back there! Clear a way to the door.'

With the corporal and his soldiers leading the way, the constable led his young prisoner from the inn, while Eoin Feehan slipped quietly away into the night and headed back to the mountains.

As the door banged shut behind the small procession, the inn erupted in a babble of sound as the customers discussed the events of the evening.

The younger of the two women bemoaned her bad luck.

'To think, I was sitting next to the young rascal all that time. Had I known, I would have had my hand inside his pocket and by morning you and I would have been on our way to Dublin Town with enough in our purses to keep us living like ladies for a year or more.'

'Hasn't life always been like that for me?' said the old woman, blinking tearfully into the vast emptiness of a pewter beer-mug on the table in front of her. Haven't the good things always been just out of my reach? A poor widow-woman I was, before you was even out of my arms. It has been a hard life with no man to look after the pair of us. Now you've let a fortune slip through our grasp. If you paid more attention to what a man carries in his pockets and less to what he has inside his trousers, I wouldn't be sitting here with an empty pot in front of me.'

'Hisht, Mother! He was only a boy . . . but he could still do us some good. Didn't they say he'd been thieving around here for a long time? Then where has he put all the things he's taken, eh? He's not going to have any use for them now, is he? Well, then, it's better that he let's them go to someone in need, rather than allow that constable to get his hands on them.'

The young woman drew her shawl about her plump shoulders and stood up.

'Where are you going? You'd not leave me without a drink?'

'Here!' The younger woman threw some copper coins on the table. 'You stay here until the landlord throws you out. I am going to see what I can do to help that poor young boy they have just arrested.'

With a sly wink, she left the old woman grovelling on the litter-strewn floor for a coin that had escaped from her bony grasp.

The constable was not pleased to see Brighid McFall at his lock-up – not that she was by any means a stranger there. He had himself locked her up for being drunk and for prostitution. He had also arrested her for stealing the watch of a respectable visitor to the town, but that good gentleman had refused to press charges and the case against her had been dismissed. Now she stood in the narrow lock-up doorway, an unctuous smile of greeting on her face and a large pie clutched in her grubby hand, asking to be allowed to visit his latest prisoner.

'What is he to you?' queried the constable. 'I have not seen the two of you together.'

'Of course you haven't,' said Brighid. 'I had never set eyes on the boy before tonight. I just feel sorry for him, that's all. I looked at him with those soldiers twisting his arms and everyone set against him. "Brighid," I said to myself, "if you'd had a son he might look just like that poor boy standing there." When you had gone, I said to myself, "That poor child probably hasn't a single friend in the whole of Ireland." So I bought this pie and I'm here to tell him he has one person he can turn to in his time of trouble.'

'Friends are not going to help him where he's going,' said the constable. 'He's an incorrigible criminal, that's what he is. He'll be transported for life and think himself lucky. A few years ago he would have been hung and that would have been an end to it. Them as was hung didn't come back to steal again.'

Brighid McFall laughed because the constable laughed, and he swung the heavy door open wide. 'I suppose you had better come and give him that pie – if you must. He'll have little enough good food where he is going.'

Brighid McFall entered the lock-up and was shown to an iron-barred pen where Jeremy lay back on a bed of none-too-fresh straw. It was dark in here and the constable lit a candle which he stuck to a small shelf with the aid of a drip of candle wax.

'You can give him the pie and have a few words with him through the bars,' he said. 'But don't be too long about it. I'm not paid to stay inside here looking after prisoners and their friends.'

Jeremy sat up on the straw and looked at his visitor with suspicion. He recognised her as one of the women in the inn, but he had never seen her before then, he was quite sure of that.

'Here, I've brought you a pie. I bought it specially for you. I saw you wasn't able to finish yours, back at the inn.'

Jeremy accepted the gift and took a great bite from it, without saying a word.

'This isn't the first time I've been in here,' said the woman, with something that might almost have been pride in her voice. 'I've slept in that straw where you are more than once, I can tell you.'

Jeremy chewed away without a word; the pastry on the pie was tough.

'You know what is going to happen to you, don't you? You are going to be transported. Sent to Australia – for life.'

Jeremy shrugged. He would not think about it. He had been made to fight hard for his very existence in Ireland. Australia could hardly be worse.

'You won't be able to take anything with you. If you've got anything of value hidden away, you'd better tell your friends, otherwise whatever it is will be lost for ever.'

So that was it! Jeremy relaxed. Now he knew what this drab woman was after he was on more familiar ground. He took a big bite of the pie and spoke through it. 'Did he send you in here to see me?' He jerked his head toward the doorway where the constable stood. He had to repeat his question twice before the pie had been chewed sufficiently to make his words intelligible.

'Him? He wouldn't send me anywhere – unless it was to prison.'

Her reaction was genuine, Jeremy was sure of that.

'No, I came because it makes my heart bleed to see a bright young boy like yourself punished so cruelly because you've had to make a living the best way you could. My mother, the dear old soul, felt the same way when she saw those soldiers handle you so cruelly. Fair broke her heart, it did. "Brighid," she said to me, "Brighid, you get yourself down to the lock-up and see if there is anything you can do to help that poor boy. You do what you can and I'm sure he won't be ungrateful." Those were her exact words, and so here I am, just looking for a way in which I can be of help to you.'

Jeremy looked at the woman thoughtfully. There were a few baubles hidden in a ditch on the edge of town, the proceeds of his earlier house-breaking activities; they were worth a guinea or two.

Gulping down the last of the pie, Jeremy wiped the crumbs from the corners of his mouth and leaned closer to the bars separating him from his visitor.

'I do have some things hidden away,' he said, in a conspiratorial whisper. 'But how do I know you will help me?'

'You just ask me to do something – anything. Fetch you food, or drink. I'll do it, you'll see.'

'I want a message taken to someone,' whispered Jeremy. 'It's urgent. You would need to go in the morning.'

'Go where?'

'To the mountains – but only a couple of miles from here,' Jeremy added hastily as he saw the sudden fear come to her face. More than one band of outlaws had found refuge in the mountains. It was no place for a women to venture. 'I would think the property I have hidden is worth a lot of money. Hundreds of guineas, perhaps. You take my message and when you return I'll tell you where it's hidden.'

Brighid McFall hesitated for only a few seconds longer. 'All right, I'll go. Who is it you want me to find, and what do I say to them?'

Chapter Twenty-Four

Kathie saw the two women struggling up the hill toward her the following morning and she went out to meet them, overcome by curiosity. Jeremy had chosen his time well; it was fine weather and the Kilmar men were out digging peat and hunting far from the camp.

The young prostitute had persuaded her mother to come with her, ignoring the old lady's protests that she was too old to go gallivanting around the Wicklow mountains. Both women were in a state of near-collapse by the time they reached the camp, but as soon as Brighid McFall had gasped out the news of Jeremy's arrest and told Kathie that he wanted to see her urgently she and her mother turned around and returned to Rathconard immediately.

'But surely you'll come to the fire to have a drink of something before you go,' said Kathie.

'No, thank you very much,' said Brighid McFall. 'We've come this far with our lives but I'm not risking staying up here a moment longer than we have to. I've given you the boy's message. Now we'll away back – God and the devils who live up here willing.'

With that, the two women scuttled away down the slope, the younger woman clutching her mother's elbow, neither one of them daring to look back lest they saw they were being pursued.

The news of Jeremy's arrest was very upsetting. Kathie wondered whether the women had been in possession of the full facts concerning Jeremy's arrest, or whether it could have been connected with Eoin Feehan. She intended going to Rathconard that night to learn the truth.

Getting away from the mountain camp was an easy matter: by now the Kilmar men were quite used to Kathie spending lonely hours among the rocks on the ridge behind the camp. Her only worry was that she might meet Eoin Feehan along the way; he had left the camp some time before she made her move. But she met no one and had no difficulty finding her way down the mountain in the bright moonlight.

Once in the town, Kathie asked a pipe-smoking old lady, sitting on her doorstep, the way to the lock-up and was given the directions without so much as a curious glance. The old woman had seen Kathie arrive in Rathconard from the direction of the mountains and one did not ask questions of those who made their home there.

The lock-up was a small but strongly built stone building with a stout nail-studded door at the front and the two high barred windows overlooking a piece of waste ground at the rear. The faint light from a flickering candle showed dimly between the bars, and Kathie hesitated before knocking at the door. She intended telling the constable she was a relative of the young prisoner and hoped he would accept her explanation without asking too many questions. She knew too little about Jeremy to be questioned closely about his background.

She need not have worried: the constable was out patrolling the town. The lock-up was a cold gloomy place and the guardian of the law spent very little time there. After knocking a few times, Kathie moved to the back of the building and stood in the shadows beneath one of the barred windows.

'Jeremy?' she called softly and waited. When there was no reply she called more loudly. 'Jeremy, can you hear me?'

Still there was no sound from inside the lock-up.

Groping around on the rough ground, Kathie took up a handful of small stones and threw them up through the window. Some of them rattled against the metal bars, but most of them fell through into the cell inside.

Kathie thought she heard someone stir in the small building and threw a second handful of stones.

'Who is that out there?'

Jeremy's knuckles showed white against the dark of the window as he gripped the bars and pulled himself up to look out.

'It's me . . . Kathie. Can you talk?'

'Yes, there's nobody else in here. Come close to the window.'

Kathie stood pressed up against the stone building and in a low voice Jeremy told her of Eoin Feehan's meeting with the corporal and of their conversation.

'. . . he told Eoin Feehan to be sure he was not in the camp on the night of the next full moon. That must be when the soldiers are going to come up there for you. They are already in Rathconard, camped just to the north of the town. I heard the constable talking about it today to one of the townsmen. You must move away from there.'

Kathie nodded her agreement in the darkness. 'The soldiers will not take any of us by surprise. They will have a wasted climb.'

'The corporal said something else . . . about it not looking too good for Eoin Feehan if it was known that he had told the soldiers to kill his own brother.'

Kathie drew in a sharp breath. 'You are sure of that? That he ordered the death of his own brother?'

'Quite sure.'

'Then Liam was right. Sean Feehan told the soldiers nothing. But for Eoin to do a thing like that . . . it . . . it's unbelievable.'

Jeremy was silent, and Kathie realised she had said nothing about the young orphan's own plight.

Reaching up, she grasped the hand that was clenched about one of the bars. 'You have done everything that Nathan asked of you, Jeremy . . . and done it well. You will have saved the lives of the Kilmar men. Nathan will be proud of you. But what can we do to help you in return?'

Jeremy allowed Kathie to hold his hand for a few moments, then he withdrew it from the bar.

'You don't have to worry about me. I didn't steal very much. I'll probably be whipped and then they will let me go.'

'Will it help if I get Liam, or Nathan, to come to court to speak for you?'

'Nathan mustn't come,' Jeremy said quickly. 'He's already been in trouble in County Wicklow. And what could Liam say? That when we first met I tried to help my friends to rob you? No, I'll be all right. I bet they don't even make me cry out when they whip me.'

Kathie's heart went out to the boy. He could be no more than eleven years of age, yet he was facing up to the prospect of his punishment like a man – and a brave man at that. It was as well she did not know the truth – that Jeremy would undoubtedly be transported. She had heard many horrific stories of the brutality and depravity to be found on the transports to Australia.

'Go to Kilmar, to Nathan, when they release you, Jeremy.

In the meantime, is there anything I can bring for you? Anything at all?'

'No, I don't need anything. . . .'

For the first time Kathie detected something of the eleven-year-old boy in his voice.

'Just tell Nathan I'm sorry for getting into this trouble.'

'I'll tell him much more than that, Jeremy. You've done a man's job for us. God bless you.'

The only sound was the faint rustle of straw as Jeremy threw himself down on to his simple bedding. Kathie had gone before the sob escaped past the knuckled fist he had pushed into his mouth.

Jeremy had given Kathie much to think about. He had confirmed her fears about Eoin Feehan, but the question now was what action should she and the others take to deal with him? He would deny everything, of course, and the Kilmar men would need more proof than the word of a young boy who was a self-confessed thief. There would no doubt be witnesses at the inn who had seen Eoin Feehan and the corporal talking together, but the fishermen were wanted men. They could hardly walk into Rathconard and begin asking questions.

The proof would come on the night of the full moon, of course, with an attack on the mountain camp, but that might be too late. Kathie wondered how many soldiers would be involved in the attack. Jeremy had said the soldiers were camped to the north of the town. Having come this far it would be foolish not to learn something more about them.

Kathie walked quickly through the streets of the small town, her way lighted by the house windows she passed, but once clear of the town it became more difficult to see her way. The night sky was clouding over, the moon slipping from cloud to cloud.

Then Kathie saw a fire in the distance and she quickened her step confidently – it was too far away for caution just yet.

She had hardly gone ten yards along the road when something moved in the shadows beside her. Kathie stopped and took a step backward, but before she knew what was happening strong hands gripped her from behind and held her fast.

The moon scurried across a gap in the overcast sky and she saw the red uniform jackets of soldiers. At first, Kathie thought she had been stopped by sentries, put out to guard the soldiers' camp against sudden attack. Then one of her captors ran his hands none too gently over her body from neck to waist and she smelled the reek of cheap whiskey on his breath.

'It's a woman all right,' said the soldier in hoarse excitement. 'And a young one by the feel of her.'

'What does she look like?'

'Who cares?' said a third voice. 'We'll not be waking and looking at her face in the morning.'

There was laughter from more than three men, and when the moon half-showed itself again Kathie saw there were at least six soldiers, including the one who held her, but she saw only two faces she would recognise again. One of them had the gold stripes of a corporal gleaming on his sleeve.

'She's a fine-looking girl,' said a young voice. 'Really pretty.'

'Then remember it for when it's your turn,' retorted another soldier, provoking another outburst of crude laughter.

'Quick! Get her over here, off the road.'

Kathie was pushed and dragged through the darkness, her legs scratched by briers, her dress catching in the undergrowth.

Once, the soldier holding her slipped and she was able to pull an arm free from his grip. She fought hard to escape, using her feet and her free hand, but then another soldier seized her free hand and she was dragged, still struggling, between two of them.

'This is far enough. We won't be heard by anyone on the road. I claim the privilege of rank. I'm going first. The rest of you can sort it out between you.'

The rough bark of a tree scratched Kathie's arms and then her breasts as she was bent over the trunk of a felled tree, one of the soldiers holding both her wrists and pulling from the far side. As she struggled to break free he put a foot against the tree and stretched her body out toward him.

Then her dress was lifted from behind and pulled clumsily over her head. Before she could cry out the rough hands of the corporal gripped her and she felt a cruel tearing pain inside her.

Biting back the cry that leaped to her throat, Kathie stopped struggling. She lay across the log, her body a silent rigid protest at the humiliation it was suffering, moving only to the sheer weight of the soldier who took her as though he were a dog and she a bitch.

The soldier began grunting and the sound reminded Kathie of a mating she had once witnessed between a boar and a sow in northern Ireland. The sow had tried to escape over a low wall to an adjoining sty, and the boar had taken her as her body straddled the wall.

Kathie almost smiled at the thought, so totally divorced was her mind from what was happening to her body. No, it could not be her body. This must be happening to someone else, not to her. She was witnessing it in some strange vivid nightmare.

She felt the soldier move away, but another took his place immediately. This one was more violent. His hands explored and hurt. But still Kathie made no sound, and the body that was not hers did not react to him.

By the time the third soldier took her, the laughter and excitement about her had died away. The men hardly spoke. When they did, it was in brief whispers, as though they were afraid of something they did not understand.

It was the young inexperienced soldier who put their thoughts into words.

'Why is she so silent?' he whispered. 'Why isn't she shouting, or crying – or struggling?'

'It's not natural,' mumbled the third soldier as he walked back to his silent companions. 'She's lying there like a corpse. I've never known any woman to be like this before.'

'I'll get a reaction from her.'

The fourth soldier put down the whiskey-jug and stumbled as he went to the fallen tree, unfastening his trousers.

Kathie was not prepared for him, and this time she did give a gasp of pain that was quickly stifled.

'Ah! I thought that would make you jump a bit. Now you'll know you're alive, me beauty.'

But the feeling of detachment had returned, and though Kathie bit her lower lip and the blood tasted salt in her mouth she never made another sound.

The fifth man bothered her no more than the second or third, and by now her mind belonged to her no more than did her abused body. She was no more than a part of the fallen tree that chafed and grazed the front of her body. She had no human thoughts or feelings.

The last man to take her was more gentle than any of the

others had been. He alone almost brought her body to life and stirred feelings that the others had all but destroyed. His clothing against her body felt different, too, more coarse than the uniform of the others.

Then it was the turn of the young soldier to take her, but he could not bring himself to perform the act.

'No,' he muttered. 'It's not right. We shouldn't have done this. No good will come from it.'

'Shut up! You're not man enough to take her and that's all there is to it. Stop trying to find excuses. What's done is done. You were a party to it the same as the rest of us, remember that. Now, anyone else?'

No one moved.

'What will we do with her now?' asked one of the soldiers.

'Why, can you think of something new?'

The reply brought a nervous laugh, and the soldiers became a party of drunken friends once more as the whiskey-jug passed among them.

'We'll leave her be. She won't recognise us again. It's not as though we met face to face, is it now?'

Their drunken humour restored, the soldiers crashed away through the undergrowth and, after an initial hesitation, the youngest soldier followed them.

Kathie lay motionless across the trunk of the tree until heavy drops of rain began to fall on her back, spattering noisily against the branches about her. She felt ill and exhausted but, pushing herself away from the rough bark, she straightened the dress about her bruised body.

Although still detached from the things that had happened to her, her mind was functioning well enough now. She was in full command of her senses and knew exactly what she had to do.

Ignoring the rain, she set off for the mountain refuge, walking with fierce determination through the grass and heather and scratching gorse.

Below the camp of the Kilmar men was a stream with a small waterfall and a pool that was deep enough for swimming. With the sudden heavy shower it was deeper than usual, water cascading off the slab of water-smooth rock above the pool. Stripping off her clothes, Kathie lowered herself into the icy water and swam to the waterfall. Standing up in the tumbling water, she allowed it to wash down over her, cleansing away the evils of the night. Doing the same for her mind would not be quite such a simple matter. That would require more than water.

When she began to feel the cold, Kathie swam back to the edge of the pool and climbed out, slipping her rain-sodden dress on over her head.

The camp was in darkness, the rain having washed away the last traces of last night's fire. Kathie did not go to her own sod-roofed dug-out, but pushed aside the heavy wet blanket guarding Dermot's cabin.

'Is that you, Kathie?'

'Yes.'

'I've been listening for you. When it started raining I went looking for you on the ridge. You weren't there. Where have you been?'

'That doesn't matter just now. I want to talk to you first.'

She heard his weight shift on the heather bed as he reached out for the candle that stood in a niche cut into the earth wall.

'No! No lights. I would rather speak to you in the darkness.'

'All right.' Dermot shifted his position again. 'It must be important if it can only be said in the dark and you need to come to me at this time of the night.'

When she did not reply immediately, Dermot said, 'Something is the matter, Kathie. What is it?'

'Do you remember the night Liam was here? What you said to me after he and my father had gone?'

'Yes. I asked you to marry me.'

She could sense his increased interest, even in the impenetrable darkness of the dug-out cabin.

'Why . . . ?'

'Is it still what you want?'

'Of course.'

'Then my answer is "Yes". But it must be soon, while we are still living up here in the mountains. Find a priest who will marry us quickly, Dermot.'

'I know one who will do it right away. But what has made you suddenly so sure this is what you want? And what about Liam . . . ?'

'I am not here to talk about Liam. I came here to talk about us. You and me.'

'Then I will arrange a wedding before you change your mind. Let's wake the others and tell them now. They have had little to celebrate since we came here—'

'No, there will be time enough for celebrating tomorrow. Tonight is for us. I want to stay here with you, Dermot.'

'Stay here? You mean . . . sleep with me?'

'Yes.'

Suddenly Kathie began shivering uncontrollably. Her teeth chattered together and her body shook so violently she could not control it. Dermot was thoroughly alarmed and reached out to hold her.

'Kathie, what is it?' He felt her wet dress. 'Why, you are soaked through. Get out of these clothes before you catch your death of cold. Put this blanket about you while I go to your cabin and get you something dry.'

'Not now, Dermot.'

Kathie pulled the wet dress off over her head and dropped it to the floor, but her violent shivering continued.

'Just hold me, Dermot. Hold me tight . . . please.'

Dermot drew her on to the bed, covering her naked body with the blanket and holding her to him. In a while, her shudders grew less violent and her mouth sought his in a hard demanding kiss.

Minutes later they were making love in a frenzy of passion that in some strange confused way made Kathie feel she was avenging her body for the degradation it had suffered.

Only when the storm had passed and Dermot was deep in an exhausted sleep beside her did Kathie's mind allow her to think about the things that had been done to her. But it was not self-pity that kept sleep away. Her whole being screamed out for revenge. Eventually, she did slip into a fitful sleep, only to wake herself crying out loud – calling for Liam.

The cry did not wake Dermot, but someone heard – and understood. In the cabin he shared with some of the Kilmar men, Eoin Feehan heard Kathie's call and he broke out in a cold sweat. He was glad he would not have to spend many more nights in the Wicklow mountains. If Kathie ever learned that he was one of the men drinking with Corporal Garrett and his soldiers near the fallen tree outside Rathconard, he would never live to enjoy the memory of what he had done that night.

Chapter Twenty-Five

Dermot McCabe and Kathie Donaghue were married on 17 May in the year 1846, the ceremony taking place in the decaying chapel of a ruined monastery, high in a Wicklow mountain valley. As it was a Sunday, the priest who conducted the service could not make his way from his own village until after his evening ceremonies were over. The sun had already disappeared beyond the peaks when the priest closed his prayer-book and pronounced them man and wife.

The priest impressed upon them the importance of the step they had just taken but said nothing else that was not in the book he held in his hands. There was little he could say. He knew nothing of their lives before this day and was too experienced in the ways of his countrymen to ask questions. When a man arrived for his wedding ceremony carrying a musket, accompanied by similarly equipped guests, one did not prolong the ceremony a moment longer than was absolutely necessary.

Not that the priest feared the men of the Wicklow mountains; they were as much his parishioners as the residents of the village where he had his church. He encouraged them to come to him for confession and had made this ruined chapel their own, a halfway house between the civilisation of the village and the remote and lawless refuge of the mountains.

The priest's success could be measured by the number of unmarked grassy mounds laid out in an untidy row behind the chapel. Here were buried men who lived their earthly lives outside the law of man, brought here after death in the hope of a better life beyond the grave.

This was the first wedding the priest had conducted in the chapel, and after he had shaken the hands of the newly-weds and wished them well he watched them walk away, surrounded by their armed friends. It was an inauspicious beginning. Although the priest had asked no questions, news travelled far in Ireland and he knew who they were and the village in County Wexford from whence they came. He would send news of the wedding to the Kilmar priest; it might ease the burden borne by the girl's parents. There was nothing else he could do for them.

The wedding itself was unusual enough, but Kathie planned a far more dramatic honeymoon. There would be a full moon the next night and Kathie was preparing a surprise for the soldiers. She had no doubt that an attack would take place. During the last few days Eoin Feehan had become increasingly surly, withdrawing himself from his companions more than ever. Even the excitement of the wedding failed to shake him out of his strange mood; if anything, it made him worse. More than once, Kathie caught him looking at her with an intense unreadable look on his face.

She told Dermot nothing of the impending attack until their wedding night. It was an incredible revelation for a bride to make to her husband, even in such unusual circumstances, and at first Dermot would not believe her. Not until she told him of Liam's suspicions did he begin to take her seriously.

'Why haven't you told me of this before?' he demanded. 'We could have got the truth from Eoin.'

'How? He would have denied every word and the others would have believed him. It has been hard enough convincing you. Besides, if the others had known they would have given something away to him by a look or a careless word. That isn't what we want.'

'But the others must be told. We have got to leave this place immediately.'

'Not until tonight. Eoin has not been to Rathconard for three nights, but I'll wager he goes tonight – and early. He'll need to tell the soldiers that we suspect nothing and will be here when they attack. As soon as he leaves we will tell the others. It will give us plenty of time to do what I have in mind.'

'And Eoin? Is he to get away?'

'Eoin Feehan will get away with nothing. When the soldiers arrive here to a warm welcome they will be sure he has played them false. That, and the news we send back to Kilmar of Eoin's part in his brother's death, will ensure that he will have nowhere in the whole of Ireland where he will be safe.'

'You have thought all this out very carefully, Kathie.' There was something in this that puzzled Dermot.

'Yes, I have. *Very* carefully. That's my way.'

'I know. For that reason I can't understand why you came to such a sudden decision to marry me.'

When Kathie made no reply, Dermot said, 'I suppose that had nothing to do with Eoin Feehan?'

'Of course not. Nothing at all.'

She said it so vehemently that Dermot was satisfied. It was not until later that Kathie herself realised that responsibility for everything that had happened could be attributed to Eoin Feehan. It was certain he had given the names of the Kilmar men to the soldiers. Had it not been for him they would not be in the mountains now. Then, had Jeremy not been keeping watch on him he would not have been arrested, and Kathie would not have gone to Rathconard. Eoin Feehan had a great deal to answer for.

The next evening went exactly as Kathie had predicted. After a day during which Eoin Feehan's nerves threatened to overcome him, he announced his intention of going to Rathconard, 'for a drink'. It was said in such a belligerent manner that everyone looked at him in surprise. His freedom to go to Rathconard was resented, but not one of the Kilmar men argued with him. His statement of intention made, Eoin Feehan wasted no time in carrying it out.

As soon as the turncoat was out of sight, Dermot called the others together and told them what Kathie had learned in Rathconard. At first they were as sceptical as Dermot himself had been, but as the story unfolded and they realised there must be some truth in what was being said they wanted to go after Eoin Feehan and bring him back.

'No,' said Dermot. 'There is a better way.' He explained Kathie's plan and, although the men would have preferred a swifter and more positive justice, they agreed that Eoin Feehan was unlikely to go unpunished for his treachery.

The soldiers would not attack until well after dark, and there was much to be done before then. Each man now had his own musket and it was loaded and primed, all available powder and musket-balls being divided equally between them. Kathie took over the weapon left behind by Eoin Feehan. She intended playing a full part in the forthcoming events of the night.

As the sun sank below the western horizon, the Kilmar men built up the camp-fires carefully before casually slipping away, ostensibly to their dug-out cabins. In fact they gathered their weapons and, making their way to the ridge behind the camp, took up concealed positions among the tumbled rocks there.

The moon was late rising and by the time it appeared above a dark bank of cloud on the eastern sky-line the fires in the camp were burning low and causing Kathie some concern. She was relying on the fires to show up the soldiers when they crept up on what they believed to be an unsuspecting group of outlaws.

'Are you quite sure they are coming tonight?' whispered one of the waiting fishermen. 'Perhaps there has been a change of plan that we know nothing about.'

'Keep quiet – and listen,' hissed Kathie. 'I thought I heard something then.'

She had hardly finished talking when something moved between the ridge and the dying fires. Suddenly, as they watched, the whole area around the dug-out cabins was alive with red-uniformed soldiers and the Kilmar outlaws were given a horrifying illustration of the fate planned for them.

While a few men lit previously prepared pitch torches from the fires, other soldiers ran to the dug-out cabins and, throwing back the blankets hanging in the doorways, discharged their muskets into the darkness inside. Seconds later the blazing torches were thrown in and the soldiers drew back, kneeling just beyond the firelight, muskets ready to shoot down the Kilmar outlaws as they fled from the blazing cabins.

It did not take many minutes for the soldiers to realise that their plan had misfired and the camp was empty. They gathered uncertainly about the burning cabins, leaning on their long muskets and making weak jokes. They were disappointed and felt foolish. After preparing themselves, mentally and physically, for a fierce battle the result had come as a tremendous anti-climax.

The soldiers relaxed too soon. As the dry wooden frames of the cabin roofs collapsed, sparks and flames rose high in the air, clearly illuminating those who stood about them.

'Now is the time to shoot!' Kathie whispered to Dermot. 'Give the order.'

As she spoke she raised her own musket and peered along the long barrel at the soldiers. Dermot hesitated too long, and Kathie knew that if she did not take the initiative the opportunity would be lost. She squeezed the trigger, and with a deafening report a musket-ball hummed away from the ridge, leaving behind a dense cloud of acrid black smoke.

The musket-ball did not find a target, but the sound of the shot startled the soldiers and before they recovered from the sudden shock the other Kilmar men opened fire to some effect. The soldiers fled from the firelight, leaving two of their number lying on the ground behind them.

Kathie and the Kilmar fishermen loaded their muskets frantically in the darkness and began firing at anything that moved or looked as though it might move. It was not long before the soldiers began returning the shots and the battle became a ragged and haphazard affair, both sides firing at powder-flashes and scoring no hits.

Soon it became apparent that the soldiers were working their way around the ridge in an attempt to get behind the Kilmar outlaws and drive them down to the firelight. Before their plan could succeed, the Kilmar men and Kathie quitted the ridge and made their getaway, passing close to the camp, but keeping its fires between themselves and the soldiers.

As they passed by, one of the wounded soldiers rose to his knees to call to them, believing them to be his colleagues. The flames from one of the burning cabins were reflected in the gold stripes on his arm and Kathie stopped in sudden shocked recognition as she saw his face. This was one of the soldiers who had raped her.

A wave of ice-cold hatred flooded over her and, raising her musket, she shot Corporal Garrett dead at point-blank range, the burning powder from her gun setting fire to the breast of the blood-red uniform coat.

The Kilmar men were horrified, and Dermot opened his mouth to say something to her, but a look at his new wife's expression was sufficient to make him shut it again quickly. A moment later a volley of shots rang out from a number of soldiers who had gained the ridge, and the outlaws hurriedly moved away from the camp and were soon lost in the darkness of the upland moor.

Kathie's murder of the wounded corporal had been witnessed by the first of the soldiers to reach the ridge. Five of them knew the reason for her action, but that night a legend was born of the ruthless girl who led a band of outlaws in the Wicklow mountains and gave no quarter to her enemies.

The Kilmar men met up with Eoin Feehan the next morning. He had not been in Rathconard when the soldiers returned from their abortive sortie into the Wicklow mountains. Tortured by thoughts of what was happening to his late companions, he had wandered through the mountains and heard the shooting from a distance. When Kathie and the Kilmar men found him he was trying to pluck up the courage to return to the camp and the scene of carnage he expected to find there.

At first, he pleaded ignorance of the events of the night, claiming he had been on his way back to the camp from Rathconard when he heard the sound of shooting and saw the camp in flames. He had, he swore, been wandering through the mountains all night, not knowing what to do.

Not until one of the Kilmar men had knocked Eoin Feehan to the ground for the second time did he cease to protest his innocence. He sat with his back against a rock, his limbs shaking, wiping blood from a split lip, certain he was about to be killed.

'You are a poor liar – and even less of a man,' said Kathie, trying hard to control the hatred she felt for Eoin Feehan. 'We knew all about the soldiers' plans, and your part in them. We were expecting you to leave the camp last night, and when you had gone we set an ambush for the soldiers. Some of them were killed. They believe you led them into a trap, Eoin.'

Eoin Feehan ran his tongue over his swollen bloody lip. 'I don't care what happened to the soldiers. They mean nothing to me.'

'I doubt whether such a lack of interest is mutual. I am sure they would love to have you in their hands.'

Eoin Feehan looked around the circle of unsympathetic faces wondering whether they intended turning him over to the soldiers. He did not know that Corporal Garrett was dead and he could only think of what his fate would be if the callous corporal had him in his clutches. He knew he would never live to be brought to trial. The perspiration of fear broke out on his forehead.

'I had to do what they asked,' he blurted out. 'They gave me no choice.'

Kathie was glad he had finally admitted his guilt. There were still some of the Kilmar fishermen who were not sure.

'How about ordering them to kill your brother, young Sean? Did you have no choice about that, either?'

'That . . . that was a mistake.'

Eoin Feehan broke down and began crying, and the Kilmar men looked at him in disgust.

'The soldiers tricked me. I didn't know they had Sean. He was the one who told them who you were. I said nothing.'

'That is not what I heard,' said Kathie. 'And it isn't the story that will be going back to Kilmar. If the soldiers don't get you, your father will.'

Realisation of what she had said came slowly to Eoin Feehan. 'You . . . you aren't going to kill me?'

Dermot answered his question with a shrug of his shoulders. 'Why should we? You'll have little enough to live for and no place where you'll be safe. Someone else will kill you soon enough.'

'Then I can go?' Eoin Feehan rose to his feet hesitantly.

'Not before you've told us what regiment the soldiers who attacked the camp belong to.' It would be a regiment to be avoided in the future, but Kathie had her own reason for wanting to know.

Eoin Feehan hesitated only briefly. He would gain nothing by pretending he did not know.

'The forty-eighth Regiment of Foot. They are in camp at Rathconard – that's all I know about them.'

'All right. Go now, before we change our minds.'

Eoin Feehan began to walk away, his eyes upon the ground, reluctant to look at his late companions.

He would have been well advised to avert his eyes until he was clear of them all, but as he passed Kathie he could not resist looking up into her face. It was only a brief glance but it was enough for Kathie. She saw contempt there and it brought back the memory of her nightmare experience in the darkness outside Rathconard. At that moment she realised that Eoin Feehan knew what the soldiers had done to her.

'Stop!'

At her shout Eoin Feehan froze and his muscles tensed in anticipation of the bullet he was sure would follow.

'Turn around.'

He turned with fear on his face to stare down the barrel of the musket held in Kathie's hands. He saw her finger tighten on the trigger and he stood before her, paralysed by fear.

Not until the very moment of firing did Kathie swing the barrel of the gun downward.

The musket-ball shattered Eoin Feehan's kneecap, and his screams were something Dermot would always remember.

'Kathie! Why . . . ?'

'To help him remember what he has done to us and what he did to his own brother. For the remainder of his life Eoin Feehan will never be able to take a single step without remembering.'

Kathie stepped over the writhing traitor without looking down at him, ignoring his screams for help.

As he and the other Kilmar fishermen followed her in silence, Dermot wondered how he could reconcile what he had just witnessed with the warm and loving girl who came to him so readily on their wedding night. One was so far removed from the other that he could hardly believe it was the same person. Dermot realised he did not know his wife at all.

Chapter Twenty-Six

With Tommy Donaghue standing in the bow of the boat ready to jump on to the quay steps, Liam brought the boat in under sail. It had been a good day's fishing. Tommy Donaghue's skill had improved with the weather. He was now a passable fisherman, if a poor sailor.

At the quayside, Norah McCabe helped them unload the baskets of fish and carry them up to the quay. Things were easier now for the Kilmar fishermen. With the opening of more soup kitchens inland and the need for the cottiers to tend their next season's potato crop there were fewer of them begging around the fishing village.

'If we continue to bring in catches of this size, we'll need to buy a bigger boat,' said Liam good-humouredly.

'It's certain I'll have to make more than one trip a week to Gorey,' agreed Tommy Donaghue. 'You'll need to take on one of the village boys to help you, Liam.'

Both Liam and his mother thought of Dermot, who should have been here with them, sharing in the work and the good fortune of the season. There was silence until Tommy Donaghue said, 'Here comes Father Clery. It isn't often he is to be seen down here at this time of the day. I wonder what he wants.'

The little priest threaded his way between the nets and baskets on the quay, pausing here and there to speak to the women gutting fish. His comments invariably drew a smile, but there was little humour in his glance when he looked down at the McCabes and their helper.

The look was wasted on Tommy Donaghue.

'Good evening, Father. If you're looking for a fine piece of fish for tomorrow's dinner, then you've come to the right boat. We've got the best catch in Kilmar today. Isn't that right, Liam?'

'I haven't come for fish, Tommy. I am here to give you some news. For good, or bad, it affects every one of you.'

'You've heard something from the mountains?' Norah McCabe looked anxiously up at the priest.

'I have.'

Father Clery made his way carefully down the wet stone steps and seated himself on the gunwale of Liam's boat, riding high against the bottom step.

'I have had a letter from the priest of a parish which takes in a large area of the Wicklow mountains. He tells me there was a battle there recently between a band of outlaws and the Army. Rumour has it the outlaws were led by a woman.'

'Led by a woman . . . Kathie?'

'Was anyone hurt? Did he say . . . ?' Norah McCabe was frightened of the answer, but the question had to be asked.

'The only men hurt were soldiers. It seems two of them were killed – one of them shot by the woman in cold blood. The priest says the woman and the men with her are from Kilmar.'

'How does he know that? Did he hear it from the soldiers?'

'No.' Father Clery took off his hat and wiped his brow with his forearm. 'He married the girl to one of the men only a day before the battle with the soldiers.'

'My Kathie married? Without the blessing of her own father? I don't believe it. It can't be true. Not Kathie.' Tommy Donaghue was stunned by the news.

'Who did she marry?' Liam asked the question but he already knew the answer.

'She married Dermot.'

Norah McCabe looked at Liam, but not by so much as the twitch of an eyelid did he reveal anything of his feelings.

'Why? Why?' she whispered.

'Only Kathie can give us the answer to that.' Liam picked up the long rope attached to a folded fishing-net and began to coil it carefully as he tried to think what could have happened to cause Kathie to marry Dermot so suddenly.

'Well. . . . She couldn't have chosen a better man,' babbled Tommy Donaghue. 'I'm happy for her – for them both. . . . But I wish they had gone about it differently.'

Norah McCabe had not taken her eyes from the face of her elder son, but when he spoke again it was not about the wedding.

'Did this priest know anything more of the battle? What action are the soldiers taking? Are they still in the mountains?'

'I don't know. Oh! There was one other thing. The day

after the battle someone made his way to a farm-house with an injured knee. The farmer said it was caused by a bullet, but the man did not give a name and a day or two later the farmer gave him a ride into Wicklow. He said he was heading north.'

'I wonder who that could have been?'

'I don't know. I'll send a letter to the priest at Wicklow, if you like. He might have some more news.'

'Don't bother.' Liam finished coiling the rope and threw it in the boat. 'Give me the name of this priest in the mountains and I'll go and see him myself.'

'Is that wise?' Father Clery frowned. 'If the soldiers are scouring the mountains in a vengeful mood, you could walk straight into trouble.'

'Someone has to go there to find out what is happening; it's no good waiting here for rumours. I'll see if Nathan Brock will come with me. Between us we should be able to avoid the soldiers.'

'I'll come with you, too,' said Tommy Donaghue, but he spoke without enthusiasm. 'After all, I am as concerned as you.'

'I'm sure you are, Tommy, but you will be more help to everyone here. Nathan and I will travel faster without you. I'll get one or two of the village lads to give you a hand with the fishing. I'll leave you and Mother to clean up now.'

'You are not leaving right away?' Norah McCabe was torn between wanting to know more about Dermot and fear for the safety of Liam.

'The sooner we learn the truth about all this the better.'

'I'll walk up to the village with you,' said Father Clery, and Liam nodded.

'Liam!'

He turned to his mother, and her eyes held his.

'This is not what either of us wanted, or the way it should have happened. But Dermot is your brother – and my son. Give him my love and say I look forward to the day when he brings his wife home to Kilmar. Tell him that, Liam.'

Liam nodded without comment and turned away.

On the way from the quay Father Clery told Liam what he knew of the mountain priest and where he could be found. Then he repeated his warning about the soldiers.

'They do not take lightly the killing of their own, Liam.

They will be searching with a bitter hatred of the Irish in their hearts – and they won't be looking to find any innocent man up there in the mountains. Keep well clear of them.'

'I'm not anxious to meet up with the soldiers,' said Liam. 'I'll stay out of their way.'

'Then may the Lord travel with you, my son.'

Liam found a bored Nathan Brock supervising no more than half a dozen men who were deepening the foundation trenches where Lady Caroline's house would one day stand. There had been a delay in the delivery of the stone blocks needed in the construction of the house, and work was at a virtual standstill.

When Liam informed Nathan Brock of the reason for his visit he was eager to go to the Wicklow mountains with him.

'But Lady Caroline will need to agree to let me go,' he said. 'She has been more than good to me and my family and I can't just walk out on her.'

Liam agreed, somewhat reluctantly, to talk to Caroline, and on the way to the house he told Nathan Brock everything that Father Clery had known.

'If Dermot and the others got the better of the soldiers in a fight, it sounds as though they must have led them into a trap. It could be that your suspicions of Eoin Feehan were right. Jeremy must have learned something and warned Kathie. Was there any news of the boy?'

'None, but I didn't ask, and I doubt if Father Clery would have thought of mentioning him, even had he known something.'

'It matters little; Kathie will know.'

When Liam made no reply, Nathan Brock looked at him sharply.

'You're not going to the Wicklow mountains to settle any personal feud, Liam?'

'Personal feud . . . ? I don't understand.'

'I always thought there might be something between you and Kathie, that if ever she came into the McCabe family it would be as Mrs *Liam* McCabe.'

'There was never anything between us. She was free to make her own choice – and I wouldn't fight my own brother over a girl who is his rightful wife.'

'I am pleased to hear it, Liam. We'll have troubles enough

without making any more for ourselves— Ah! There is Lady Caroline. I hope she is feeling better today.'

'Better? Why, has she been ill?' Liam spoke sharply, his eyes on the distant Caroline. She had been riding and was now walking her horse slowly towards the stables away from them.

'She works much too hard. Half the day she spends in the soup kitchen in Gorey; then she is involved with the new fever hospital they are building at Courtown – with her money. Yet, for all that, she is a lonely woman.'

'Sir Richard Dudley is in Dublin. Has he not been here?'

'Once only, and from what the servants told Shelagh he might as well have stayed away. He and Lady Caroline quarrelled most of the time. After being here for two days he left in a fury.'

'Why were they quarrelling?'

If Nathan Brock wondered why Liam was so interested in Lady Caroline's relationship with her husband, he made no comment. 'I understand she refused to join Sir Richard in Dublin. He said his career is suffering because his wife is not there to act as a hostess for him. Lady Caroline told him she considers starving cottiers to be more important than social etiquette. She suggested that Sir Richard set an example by ceasing to entertain and by donating the money to famine relief.'

Liam smiled; he could imagine the baronet's indignation when the suggestion was put to him.

'Sir Richard Dudley would not approve of that. He does not care for the Irish.'

'I sometimes wonder whether God himself cares,' commented Nathan Brock. 'By giving us famine, fever and the English he has made life in this green island of ours all but impossible. But it looks as though Lady Caroline has seen us.'

Caroline had turned her horse and was bringing it toward them at a trot. Pulling to a halt, she jumped to the ground before either man could offer assistance. Smiling at Liam she said, 'Well, this is a most unexpected surprise. Have you come to see Nathan – or to visit me?'

'Both of you.'

Liam gave her brief details of the fight between the Kilmar outlaws and the soldiers and said he wanted Nathan Brock to go with him to the mountains.

Caroline frowned. 'This battle has already taken place a long way from here. You cannot possibly do anything to help now. Do you think it is either sensible or necessary to become involved?'

Nathan Brock had taken the bridle of Caroline's horse and he deemed it wiser to allow Liam to argue his own case. Saying he would take the horse to the stables, he walked away with the animal, leaving Liam and Caroline together.

'You have far too much to lose by becoming involved in an act of rebellion, Liam.'

'I have nothing more to lose than a career as a coastal fisherman. It is far more important that I find Dermot. There are many young men in Kilmar who would willingly give up a boring life to follow Dermot and the others if they were fed enough romantic rumour.'

'You will not always be a fisherman if Eugene Brennan has his way, Liam.'

'He has said nothing to me. I haven't seen him since he left for Dublin – to see Sir Richard.'

A pained expression crossed Caroline's face at mention of her husband. 'I am sorry, Liam. I thought Eugene had already spoken to you. I should have said nothing.'

'Said nothing about what, Caroline? You are talking in riddles.'

Having said so much, Caroline could hardly refuse to say more – and she wanted to dissuade Liam from going to the Wicklow mountains.

'Eugene told me he would like to see you take a seat in Parliament. As an Irish MP you could one day take his place as leader of the All-Ireland Association.'

The statement took Liam completely by surprise.

'An MP? But I am just an ordinary fisherman.' He had dreamed of following in Eugene Brennan's footsteps, but that had been a lover's dream and had nothing to do with reality. 'As for taking over the All-Ireland Association, I am not even a member!'

Caroline smiled at his confusion. 'Eugene will have taken that into consideration, I am sure.'

'Was this Eugene's own idea . . . or yours?'

Caroline returned his look defiantly. 'It was Eugene's idea.'

It was quite true. She had merely told the old MP that Liam was wasted as a fisherman in Kilmar.

'I can hardly believe it . . . but there will be time enough to think of such things in the future. Right now I have more urgent matters on my mind. For my mother's sake I must find out what Dermot is doing. He is a hot-headed young fool, but he is her son, and my own brother.'

'Are you sure it is Dermot you are concerned for, Liam? What about this girl who nursed him back to health . . . I believe her name is Kathie? Nathan Brock told me you were very close to each other before she went away.'

'She and my brother were married the day before the fight with the soldiers,' said Liam quietly. 'So it would seem she was closer to him.'

'I am sorry, Liam. I did not know.'

She was not sorry. She was happier than she had been at any time since she prised the information about Kathie from the reluctant Nathan Brock and it showed in the way she smiled at him when he returned from handing the horse over to a stable-hand.

'Has it been decided? Am I to go with Liam?'

Caroline nodded. 'Yes, and I want you to take care of him, Nathan. Keep him out of trouble. He will be an important man one day. Now you had better go and let Shelagh know what you will be doing while I have some food prepared for you both to take with you. There will be little to be found along the way.'

Chapter Twenty-Seven

Lying in the bushes beneath a wooded ridge in the Wicklow mountains, Liam and Nathan Brock watched the soldiers searching the slope on the far side of the valley. They were out in considerable force with a long line of scarlet-coated infantrymen beating their way through the gorse and fern and ahead of them more than twenty blue-uniformed hussars, mounted on fine horses, probing the secrets of the undergrowth with drawn swords. Above the slow-moving troops a full company of riflemen armed with the latest-model percussion rifles commanded every vantage-point, ready to shoot any Irishman flushed out by the military 'beaters'.

Liam was alarmed at the scale of the search, but Nathan Brock reassured him.

'What we are seeing is probably the whole of the search party,' he said. 'I've seen it all before in these mountains. It is an opportunity for the English to exercise their soldiers and they use as many as they can find. They will search the open country over and over again for weeks, then they will go away and all the fugitives will come out of the forests where they have been hiding.'

'Why don't the soldiers go into the forests?' To Liam it seemed the obvious thing to do.

Nathan Brock chuckled. 'If they did that, they would lose the advantage of numbers and be picked off one by one, like apples from a tree. Oh no, Liam. You won't get soldiers looking for Irish rebels in a forest. They learned a hard lesson many years ago, and learned it well. For that reason we'll be safe from them while we stay in among the trees, and sooner or later we will meet up with Dermot and the others.'

Proof that Nathan Brock knew what he was talking about came on their second day in the forest. Two ragged men, armed with crude pikes of green wood tipped with rusty iron, stepped from the bushes ahead of them and barred their way, demanding to know their business.

'What is that to do with you?' asked Liam. 'If your intention is to rob us, then you are wasting your time. We have little money – although there is some food that is yours for the asking.'

'We'll have the food,' said one of the ragged pikemen. 'But we still want to know your business.'

'We are looking for someone,' said Nathan Brock. 'For Dermot McCabe. Do you know him?'

The two men were busy cramming food in their mouths, but both nodded. Swallowing hard and choking on a crust of pie, one said, 'We are his men. Have you come to join him, too?'

'You are his men? You are not from Kilmar. Who are you?'

The other man brought the point of his pike up close to Liam's face threateningly. 'We are the ones who ask questions. Who are *you*?'

'You are talking to Dermot McCabe's brother,' said Nathan Brock hastily. 'I am a friend. We have come from County Wexford to see him.'

'He don't look much like Dermot McCabe,' said the pikeman, eyeing Liam suspiciously. 'How do I know you're telling the truth?'

'It's easy enough to prove,' replied Liam. 'Take me to Dermot, if you know where he is.'

'All right,' agreed the pikeman grudgingly. 'But you'd better be who you say you are. We know what to do with spies.'

Tucking the remainder of the food from Liam's pack inside his dirty shirt, he said to his companion, 'You lead the way. I'll follow on behind and keep an eye on these two.'

The less aggressive of the two pikemen led the way along a path that ran through the undergrowth beneath tall forest trees that kept out the sun.

'What is all this talk of spies?' Nathan Brock asked Liam.

'For the answer to that we will have to wait until we meet up with Dermot. I have given up trying to guess what he is doing. Nothing makes sense any more.'

After about half a mile the leading man turned from the path and began pushing his way through the undergrowth. The other men followed him and soon the trees became farther apart as the undergrowth thinned.

When the sound of a waterfall became loud, the group was challenged by two more men, and one of these carried a musket.

Liam and Nathan Brock were subjected to the same suspicious scrutiny as before, the holder of the musket commenting that they appeared too well dressed to belong to the brotherhood of the Wicklow mountains. He allowed them to pass after warning their escorts to guard them well.

'Dermot must have gathered an army of men about him,' commented Nathan Brock as they were prodded on their way.

'An army made up of all the footpads and thieves in these hills by the look of those we've seen,' said Liam.

Further conversation was made impossible for a while as the path narrowed between huge mossed boulders. A few minutes later the path ended abruptly in a large clearing beside a stream tumbling down from the peaks above in a series of waterfalls. Here, Dermot had his camp. It was a sprawling shambles with shelters of every shape and size, made up from branches, fern, grasses and turfs. It was a thoroughly disorganised camp, and the smell rising from it indicated it was also an unwholesome one.

Their captors now began to shout for them to hurry up and the more aggressive of the two emphasised his words with his pike, catching Nathan Brock off balance and knocking him to one knee.

The pikeman repeated his blow, calling upon the ex-prizefighter to get up.

Nathan Brock rose slowly and turned to face the other man. 'If you touch me with that thing again, I will take it from you and break it over your head.'

The pikeman blustered, going red in the face, but Liam was more concerned with his silent companion. He had not seen what had happened. All he knew was that Nathan Brock was adopting a threatening attitude toward his companion. He drew back the pike, about to thrust it at Nathan Brock's back when Liam hurriedly stepped between the two men.

'Liam! What are you doing here?'

The shout came from Dermot as, pushing aside a crowd of men, he hurried toward them. The pike of the man facing Liam was lowered and the dangerous moment was over.

'And Nathan, too!' Dermot threw his arms about his brother and pounded him on the back gleefully. 'Have you both come to join the army?'

When Liam failed to respond with the same enthusiasm,

Dermot stood back at arm's length and scrutinised his brother's face. 'There's nothing wrong? Mother is all right?'

'Yes, mother is well. She's worried about you, of course. We've heard so many rumours.'

Dermot snorted. 'Rumours! No doubt they've been spread by the soldiers to confuse our supporters and prevent the uprising they know is coming.'

Seeing the two pikemen still standing uncertainly by, Dermot called, 'What are you doing here? Shouldn't you be on guard somewhere?'

'We brought these two in. We found them in the woods.'

'Found them? Didn't they tell you who they were?' Dermot slipped an arm about Liam's shoulders. 'This is my brother.'

'I know, but—'

'No "buts". It only needed one of you to show them the way here. The other should have stayed on guard. The whole English Army could have come through the forest while you have been wasting your time here. Get back to your posts and stay there until you are relieved.'

As the men went away, grumbling, Dermot turned back to his brother and Nathan Brock. 'I am surrounded by fools, but I'll make an army of them and we'll take Ireland back from the English when I'm ready.'

'With what? Sticks and stones?' Liam was looking at a ragged miscellany of men who were undergoing some form of training in marching manoeuvres. Their ages ranged from fifteen to sixty and they were 'armed' with pointed sticks, two of the younger boys also carrying slings and bags containing stone missiles.

'We've got a few muskets.' Dermot frowned at Liam's criticism. 'We'll take more from the soldiers as we beat them in battle.'

'Dermot, be sensible!'

Liam stopped before they came within hearing-distance of the men about the cooking-fires in the centre of the clearing.

'Not three miles from here we saw soldiers searching the hillside for you. They had infantry, cavalrymen and riflemen – yet they were just one small search-party. They have thousands more to call upon, yet that one search-party could wipe out you and every man here.'

'That's just what the soldiers thought they were going to do when they raided our camp,' replied Dermot scornfully. 'But we beat them, just as we will beat all the others. Men are flocking to join us from all over Ireland. When we march the whole country will rise and join us.'

Liam knew that by the end of the summer the whole of the cottier population would be too involved in harvesting potatoes to be interested in anything else and most of Dermot's 'army' would have gone back to the land. He decided to say nothing of this to Dermot; it was not what his brother wanted to hear. Time would pass on Liam's message for him.

'We heard about the fight with the soldiers. We also received news that you and Kathie were wed.'

Dermot gave Liam a quick uncertain glance, once more the younger brother, not certain he had Liam's approval.

'It was never meant to be a secret. We were married the day before the raid. It was Kathie's own idea.'

'Where is she now?'

Dermot looked about the clearing. 'She was here a few minutes ago. I expect she's gone to get cleaned up. We don't have many visitors here.' He grinned. 'Nobody who matters, that is.'

Kilmar men were coming to greet Liam and Nathan Brock now, eager for news of their families. While they talked a fight broke out at the edge of the clearing, and as men moved in that direction Dermot sent two of the fishermen to the scene to restore order.

'How does Kathie cope with the ruffians you have in your camp now?' Liam asked his brother.

'You need have no fear for Kathie; she can look after herself as well as any man.'

Proudly, Dermot told Liam and Nathan Brock of the soldier she had killed, and how she had shot Eoin Feehan in the knee.

Liam shared none of Dermot's pride. It was difficult to believe these actions had been carried out by the girl he had last spoken to on the ridge above the mountain camp. But nothing up here made sense any more. This place . . . Dermot . . . Kathie.

'Ah! Here is Kathie now.'

It had taken a great deal of will-power for Kathie to come here to greet Liam. She had seen him and Nathan Brock enter the clearing, and her first reaction had been one of panic. She had wanted to run and hide. Instead, she had run to the make-shift shelter she shared with Dermot and tidied herself as best she could while she composed herself for the meeting she accepted as inevitable.

'Hello, Liam. Nathan.'

It came out as barely more than a whisper, but Liam was too shocked by Kathie's appearance to take notice. Her efforts at improving her appearance had met with little success. True, her beautiful long hair was pulled neatly back behind her ears, but her clothes were dirty and there was a new air of wildness about her. It showed in her eyes and the gaunt lines of her face.

Aware that he was staring at her, Liam did his best to gather his thoughts together.

'How are you, Kathie?' He gripped her by the upper arms and kissed her on the cheek. 'Welcome to the McCabe family.'

Colour flooded to Kathie's drawn face. 'Thank you, Liam.' She was close to tears.

There was a loud roar from the crowd about the two fighting men and one of the Kilmar fishermen called for Dermot. Excusing himself with the remark that he was the only man capable of maintaining control over his followers, Dermot strode to the scene of the conflict. After a cheery wave at Kathie, Nathan Brock went with him.

'You keep a rough camp here,' said Liam to Kathie.

'The men need to be rough if they are to do what lies ahead.'

'What lies ahead for you and Dermot, Kathie?'

'I don't know and it doesn't matter much, as long as we kill soldiers. English soldiers.'

'Is that what all this is about – killing soldiers?'

'That will do for a start. Kill enough of them and they will leave Ireland. Then we can turn to other things.'

Dermot had almost reached the crowd of shouting men when the fight between the two men erupted into a battle as friends joined in on both sides.

'Is this to be the foundation of your new Ireland, Kathie?' Liam nodded toward the brawling men.

'These and the others who will join us when we are ready to march.'

'That is Dermot's dream. You don't really believe it can come true. You told me so yourself, remember?'

When Kathie did not answer, Liam said, 'Is this all you want from life, Kathie? Living in a twilight dream, surrounded by the dregs of the land?'

'It's what Dermot wants.'

'That isn't what I asked.'

Kathie turned to look directly at Liam. 'I am Dermot's wife now, Liam. Whatever he wants is what I want.'

'What happened to you back there, Kathie? What has made you like this?'

'Nothing happened. . . .' Her voice faltered. 'Nothing happened,' she repeated.

Liam would have questioned her further but Nathan Brock was returning and so he said nothing, giving her time to regain her composure.

Nathan Brock could see that both Liam and Kathie were upset, but the reason for it was none of his business.

'If Dermot can teach this rabble to fight the English as well as they fight each other, he will have a formidable army, but as they are Irishmen I doubt if he'll ever succeed.'

Nathan Brock smiled at Kathie. 'Young Jeremy must have done his task well. I was hoping I might see him here and persuade him to return with me, but I expect he was in a hurry to get to Dublin and make his fortune.'

Kathie immediately forgot her own troubles. 'Oh! I thought you must know. He was arrested for theft in Rathconard. They held him in the lock-up and I went to see him the night . . . a few nights before the fight with the soldiers. There was nothing I could do about it. I'm sorry, Nathan.'

Nathan Brock was filled with concern for the boy. 'What has happened to him since? Is he still in Rathconard?'

'I don't know, but there is no need to be too concerned for him, Nathan. Jeremy told me himself he would probably get away with a flogging. He'll soon get over that. He told me to tell you he still intends becoming a champion prizefighter one day.'

'Not in this country, he won't. Jeremy has been in trouble with the law before and he has no chance of it being overlooked. He will carry the lashmarks with him to the grave.'

'What does that mean?' asked Liam.

'It means he will be transported for at least seven years.'

'Is there anything that can be done for him?' Kathie felt guilty for not thinking about the boy before. She had been trying to forget everything that had happened on that night, and could not think about Jeremy without remembering.

'That depends on whether or not the trial has already been held. We'll need to go to Rathconard to find out.'

Nathan Brock made a frustrated gesture. 'I'll need your help, Liam. I daren't show myself there or I will end up in prison myself.'

'Then we must get down there right away.'

'But you have only just arrived,' protested Kathie. 'Will you return here after you have been to Rathconard?'

'Will I be able to persuade you and Dermot to come home to Kilmar with us?'

'No, Liam. It is too late for that.'

'Then there is little sense in returning. I came to check on the rumours we heard in Kilmar. I have seen for myself that you and Dermot are well. I would be happier if I left you both in better company, but I doubt whether your "army" will stay long enough for Dermot to do anything foolish.'

When Dermot heard the two men were leaving he added his protests to Kathie's, but he was secretly relieved. His older brother had an uncomfortable habit of applying common-sense rules to Dermot's ideas. He had also seen Kathie and Liam talking when he had been called away to discipline his men. Even from that distance he could see that Kathie was close to tears. No, he was not sorry that Liam would not be staying.

'At least you will be able to tell the men of Kilmar that their sons are leading the army of Ireland,' said Dermot as he said his farewells to Liam. 'They will be officers, every one of them.'

'And don't forget to tell them about Eoin Feehan,' said one of the Kilmar fishermen. 'Make sure they know how he had his own brother killed.'

'How about you, Kathie? Do you have any message for your father?'

'Tell him I am well . . . and happy. I pray for him – tell him that, too.'

'I hope Kathie prays for Ireland at the same time,' commented Nathan Brock as they walked away through the forest. 'She will need to if Dermot's army ever goes on the march. There can seldom have been such a gathering of villains and cut-throats outside of Dublin Jail.'

'I wish Kathie and Dermot were out of the whole business. No good can come from it at all.'

The two friends arrived at Rathconard early in the evening. The army encampment was much larger now and would need to expand even farther to accommodate the militiamen from Belfast who had arrived that afternoon to help in the search for Dermot and his men. For them it would be an uneasy camp. Dismissed by the English soldiers as 'Irishmen', they were hated by the local population for their Protestant background and their brutal record in putting down earlier uprisings.

Nathan Brock waited on the slopes above the town, well clear of both townsmen and soldiers, while Liam made his way to the small lock-up behind the church in Rathconard. He spent his time observing the activity within the military encampment. With the exception of the cavalry whose horses and tents were tethered in neat lines, the camp was a shambles. The militia appeared to have no tents at all and were preparing to spend the night in the open.

But, confusion and disorganisation apart, Nathan Brock estimated the Army must have gathered at least seven hundred men at Rathconard. Dermot had about one hundred poorly armed men up in the mountains. He hoped Dermot would not be in too much of a hurry to force a battle between the two ill-matched forces.

Liam returned from Rathconard at dusk with grim news of Nathan's young friend.

'The trial is already ended. It took place in Dublin two days ago.'

'And the sentence . . . ?'

'Transportation . . . for life.'

Nathan Brock expelled air noisily through his teeth. 'That's fierce. Who told you? Could there be any mistake?'

'None. The constable told me himself. He gave evidence at the trial and was more than happy to talk about it. He said the judge called Jeremy an incorrigible thief and told him he regretted that misguided reform prevented him from passing the death sentence on him.'

'A judge of Assize said that to an orphan boy of eleven? Is that what the law is about?'

Nathan Brock was angrier than Liam had ever seen him. 'There was no one to speak up for Jeremy, of course? No one to tell the court how he has had to steal in order to live? Damn the judge and his law. God, Liam! When is someone going to do something for the people of our country? Will there ever be a time when our children don't have to steal and our women don't have to beg in order to stay alive?'

Liam knew that, because he had asked Jeremy to stay behind, Nathan Brock felt responsible for Jeremy's present desperate situation and he tried to give him some comfort.

'You can't blame yourself, Nathan. The boy has been running with thieves all his life. He knew no other way.'

'There is little hope of teaching him different now. He'll learn many things on the transport to Australia, but honesty and decency won't be among them.'

Nathan Brock ceased his angry pacing. 'Did the constable know when Jeremy was being transported?'

'Not for a week or two. Until then he is being held in Kilmainham Jail, in Dublin.'

'Then I'm for Dublin to see him. Are you with me, Liam?'

'Of course, and if Eugene Brennan is in Dublin we'll ask his advice on how best to help the boy.'

Chapter Twenty-Eight

The walk to Dublin took Liam and Nathan Brock two days and they were almost too late. A transport had unexpectedly put into Dublin Bay to take on board all prisoners bound for the colonies. Those held in Kilmainham Jail were already being manacled with heavy chains, and at first the jailer told Nathan Brock it would not be possible to see Jeremy. When a half-sovereign changed hands, the jailer's attitude softened and he said he would have Jeremy brought to them.

They heard the clanking of the heavy chains long before Jeremy shuffled into the barred room, manacled hand and foot.

The boy's eyes filled with tears when he saw Nathan Brock.

'I wish you hadn't come here, Nathan,' he said. 'I didn't want for you to see me like this.'

This was a different lad from the cheeky youngster with a ready smile who had helped Nathan Brock to search for his family. Jeremy looked unhealthy and dejected. Prison was not a good place for a young boy.

'We couldn't allow you to sail away to a new life in Australia without coming to wish you luck,' said Nathan Brock softly. 'Are they treating you well enough, Jeremy?'

'I'm all right,' Jeremy mumbled, not trusting himself to look at the big man.

'Everyone from the Wicklow mountains send their thanks,' said Liam when he was sure the jailer who had escorted the boy was out of hearing. 'The soldiers carried out their attack but caught nobody.'

'Is Kathie all right?' For the first time since he had been brought to the room, Jeremy lost his apathy. 'She wasn't hurt bad?'

Liam was puzzled. 'No. As I said, they were ready for the soldiers. No one was hurt.'

'I don't mean then. I'm talking about the night Kathie came down to see me. The constable arrested a man for being drunk and threw him in the cell with me. When he sobered up in the morning he told me he had been drinking on his own just outside the town when he saw some soldiers drag a woman off into the bushes. There was another man with them who wasn't a soldier and they all had her. Afterwards they went away and this drunk thought they'd killed her, but then she got up and went away toward the mountains. It was Kathie. I know it was.'

'So that's it,' Liam whispered. Now so many things became clear. He went cold when he thought about Kathie's agony of mind at being raped. Her life had been a hard one and she owned nothing but her pride – and her body. Liam had often heard Tommy Donaghue say that Kathie's proudest boast was that, even if she was able to offer her future husband nothing else, she would give him a body that no other man had known. When the soldiers had taken that from her they had taken everything.

Liam wondered about the other man with the soldiers. Could it have been Eoin Feehan? He remembered the early incident on the quay at Kilmar. But he dismissed the thought. It was too easy to see Eoin Feehan's hand in every evil deed. Whoever it was, he and the soldiers had tapped a source of hatred that might well consume a great many lives before it ran its course.

'Is she all right?' Jeremy was looking at him anxiously.

'Yes, she's all right. She has someone to look after her now. She married my brother.'

Liam wished he could believe his own words. Kathie was a strong character; she would lead the Kilmar group, through Dermot, and her decisions were bound to be coloured by her hatred of English soldiers. They would not always be wise ones.

But Liam's reply satisfied Jeremy, and the boy managed a weak smile. 'I'm glad. She was good to me and I've been worrying about her.'

'How have you been keeping? Are the other prisoners looking after you?' asked Nathan Brock.

'They're all right,' Jeremy answered with a nonchalant lift of his thin shoulders.

'Is there anything you need? Anything we can get for you?'

Nathan Brock asked the questions quickly as he heard voices coming closer along the corridor outside, but before Jeremy could answer the jailer came in the room.

'That's as much time as you can have. The prisoners have to be taken out to the transport now.'

'Take care, Jeremy. Get word to me if you can. And keep out of trouble.'

Jeremy nodded, blinking rapidly and not trusting himself to speak. He turned to go, the heavy chains dragging on the stone floor. Suddenly he turned back again, almost falling as the chains took him off balance. Nathan Brock caught him, and the next moment Jeremy was sobbing against his shoulder.

A lump rose in Liam's throat, and even the jailer was moved to sympathy. He waited until the sobbing had died away to a shuddering fight for breath before he spoke again.

'It's time the boy was going, sir. They are all waiting for him.'

Nathan Brock nodded and, squeezing Jeremy's shoulders painfully, he held him at arm's length and said huskily, 'Take care of yourself, boy – and practise that right hook I showed you. One day you'll be the champion of Australia.'

Snuffling noisily, Jeremy rubbed his nose vigorously with the sleeve of his coarse shirt. 'I . . . I'll never be as . . . as good as you, Nathan. . . .'

The jailer touched Jeremy's arm and he turned away as the jailer turned to Nathan Brock.

'He'll be all right, sir. Don't you worry. These transports aren't nearly as bad as they were a few years ago.'

Not until he and Liam were outside the jail did Nathan Brock trust himself to speak, and then he said fiercely, 'Things can have changed as much as they like; it will still be hell on that ship for a young boy . . . but there is absolutely nothing I can do about it.'

The plight of Jeremy had made a profound impression upon Liam and he thought about it as they walked away from the high grey walls.

'We'll go to see Eugene Brennan now. If he will write a letter to the captain of the transport, I have five guineas to go with it. That should ensure the voyage to Australia will be as comfortable for Jeremy as it can be in the circumstances.'

'Then let's not delay,' said Nathan Brock. 'If Eugene will write a note, I will hire a boat and get out to the transport if I have to row halfway to Australia to catch her.'

Fortunately, Eugene Brennan was at home and he agreed to write a note to the captain of the transport, even though he was busy preparing to leave for London within an hour. He headed the note 'The House of Commons' and requested that

Jeremy be provided with all the privileges it was possible to give a prisoner and, in view of the boy's age, he asked the captain to keep him away from the 'ruffianly inmates' of the convict ship.

When the MP had signed the letter he handed it to Nathan Brock with the comment, 'I trust for the boy's sake that the captain is an Irishman and not a politically minded Englishman. There are those who would do me no favours, even though my request is backed by good gold.'

'I'll make some enquiries before handing the letter over,' promised Nathan Brock. 'Now I must hurry before the boat sails.'

'Nathan Brock is a good man to have as a friend,' said Eugene Brennan when the ex-prizefighter had hurried away.

'He thinks a lot of the boy – and so should every man and woman in Kilmar. Without his aid my brother and his friends would be dead now. I wish there was more we might do to help him. It is not right that a boy of eleven years of age should be transported for life, Eugene. There must be other ways of dealing with him – of helping him.'

'My boy, if you are bent on judicial reform, then you'll need to be in Parliament in order to achieve anything.'

'You've been there enough years, Eugene. Why haven't you done something?'

'If I were to try to right all the wrongs in this land, I would need to have more years than Methuselah. As it is, I am almost seventy years of age and lack the fire for new causes. You are young enough to fight for Ireland and couple it with any other crusade you wish. Do it, Liam. Come to Parliament and help me in my last years and I promise you at least forty votes for any bill on penal reform you care to introduce.'

Liam felt the stirrings of excitement within him. Was it really as easy as this to change the laws of the land? Could he, an ordinary fisherman, be elected to Parliament by the people of Ireland and influence the destiny of his own country? He remembered how long Eugene Brennan had been unsuccessfully campaigning for an end to Ireland's strangling union with England and knew changes did not come so easily. Nevertheless, Eugene Brennan had achieved much for his people. There was much that he, too, might do.

'Do you really think I could become a Member of Parliament, Eugene?'

The wily old politician knew he had won this particular battle. The idea had been put in Liam's mind some time before. Now he had dangled a bait before the fisherman and it had been taken without a fight.

'First you will need to join the All-Ireland Association. I can enrol you here and now if you wish. Then you will have to come to a few meetings with me when I return to Ireland. Perhaps you can give a short talk – about the effects of the famine in your own area, if you like. You've done that before. Then we will put your name forward as a candidate when an Irish parliamentary seat falls vacant. At the moment there are two such vacancies, both on the west coast. Can I count on you standing for us when a by-election is called?'

Liam made a pretence of thinking about the matter for a minute or two, but he had made up his mind soon after learning from Caroline that Eugene Brennan wanted him in Parliament.

'Yes, I'll stand for Parliament, but I will need time to arrange for my boat to be fished in Kilmar.' Liam grinned, excited at the thought of the changes in his life such a step would bring. 'My mother will need to be convinced that I'm doing the right thing, but you have my word, Eugene.'

'Splendid! Absolutely splendid!'

Eugene Brennan shook Liam's hand vigorously. 'I knew you would agree once you had thought about it. We should really have a drink to celebrate this occasion, but if I don't rush I will miss the boat to Liverpool and a chance to vote against Peel's latest Irish Bill. He's trying to put the whole of Ireland under martial law. If he can be defeated, it will mean a Whig government and one more sympathetic to our people. These are exciting times in Parliament, Liam. Hurry and settle your affairs in Kilmar and then return to me here. I have need of you. Our relief works are going well but I am still receiving almost daily reports of starving cottiers – especially from the west coast. I need someone to check on the truth of them. It would be a good opportunity for you to learn something about your future constituents.'

Eugene Brennan shook Liam's hand yet again. 'You don't know how happy you've made me. For many years now I have been haunted by the thought that when I die the All-Ireland Association and all it stands for will die with me. Now I feel my life's work will live on. Bless you, my boy. We'll win freedom for Ireland yet. I won't see it, but I hope that you or your children will.'

Liam allowed himself to be enrolled as a member of the All-Ireland Association and for another half an hour listened to Eugene Brennan's chatter about his hopes and fears for the future, as they rode to the docks.

There were rumours, the MP said, that many of the new season's potatoes were already diseased when they went into the ground. If this proved to be true, it meant that much of this year's crop would also be lost. It boded ill, even though Liam was able to report that the growing crops he had seen between the Wicklow mountains and Dublin looked green and healthy.

The MP was the last passenger to embark, and the ship's captain paced the deck impatiently while he and his luggage came up the gangway. Seconds later the gangway was pulled away and the mooring-ropes unlooped from the iron bollards on the quayside. Thrashing the water between ship and shore to a frenzy with its heavy paddle-wheels, the steamer moved slowly away. Before it was out of hailing distance, Eugene Brennan called to Liam that he would be writing from London.

While he awaited Nathan Brock's return from his trip to the departing transport, Liam thought much about the changes that being an MP would make to him. They were not all to his liking. As a fisherman he had always been his own man. As an MP he would be answerable to the men who voted for him. He wondered whether he might be able to do anything to help Dermot and the Kilmar fishermen exiled to the Wicklow mountains. Perhaps arrange an amnesty for them?

He thought, too, of Caroline. What would she say? He had no doubt she would be delighted.

He was still thinking about the matter when Nathan Brock returned, well pleased as a result of his trip to the Australia-bound transport.

'The captain is a sporting man,' he reported. 'He recognised me. It seems he has seen me fight twice, once in the port of Liverpool, the other time in London. I told him I had been teaching Jeremy to fight and he said he would have him brought from the hold and set to work where he could keep an eye open for him.'

'Well done, Nathan. I wish our journey to the mountains had been as successful. It's time we returned to Kilmar – and I have some good news to tell you along the way.'

In London, Sir Richard Dudley was dining with Sir Robert Peel, a meeting arranged between the two men by a mutual friend. Inevitably, in view of Sir Richard Dudley's Treasury duties in Ireland, the talk turned to that country and its troubles.

'Ireland has its problems,' admitted Sir Robert Peel. 'But they differ very little from those I had to attend to when I was Chief Secretary for that wretched country. If we could somehow damp down Eugene Brennan and his All-Ireland Association, the happenings there might drop out of the news. The man is the bane of my life. Offer him your right hand and he'll want your left. Give him your left and he'll ask for the right.'

This was exactly the opening for which Sir Richard Dudley had been waiting. Leaning across the table, he said, 'What if I offered to cut off *both* Mr Brennan's hands for you – metaphorically speaking, of course?'

England's Prime Minister was interested, but wary.

'Perhaps you would care to explain yourself more fully?'

'Would it be to your advantage if he were to be discredited in the eyes of his countrymen and of his association?'

'It would, but heroes of Eugene Brennan's stature are difficult to topple.'

'Not if I were able to prove his dishonesty beyond doubt.'

'Dishonesty? Eugene Brennan? Never! The man is a thorough nuisance but he is painfully honest.'

'Your generosity to a political opponent does you great credit, Sir Robert, but what if his dishonesty were to be proven in a court of law?'

'My dear Sir Richard, if you were able to prove such a thing, you could request your own government department and I would give it to you. The pressure would be off me and the Irish problem would regain its proper perspective. I would be able to govern the country without hindrance once more. But, I repeat, I very much doubt whether you will ever be able to prove anything against the honourable Irish member.'

'We shall see. We shall see.'

Sir Richard Dudley settled back in his chair, fondling the brandy-glass he held in his hands. He had received the promise of advancement he had been seeking. Eugene Brennan had done nothing to bring the fisherman to court as Sir Richard had requested. Very well. They would both be involved in the scandal that was about to break.

Chapter Twenty-Nine

On his way to Kilmar, Liam called at Inch House with Nathan Brock to tell Caroline of his meeting with Eugene Brennan. He had known she would be pleased to hear he intended standing for Parliament, but her impetuous delight took him by surprise. With a sudden surge of enthusiasm, she flung herself at Liam and hugged him excitedly.

'Oh, Liam! I am so pleased for you. I really am.'

Over her shoulder, Liam could see Nathan Brock's eyebrows raised in surprise. Extricating himself from her embrace as gently as he was able, he found it impossible not to smile at her pleasure.

'I doubt whether my mother will be quite so happy with my news.'

'Of course she will, Liam. When she has had time to think about it she will be the proudest woman in County Wexford. But before you go home we must celebrate this news.'

She pulled the bell-cord hanging by the beautiful fireplace. When the butler appeared she asked him to bring a bottle of her brother's best champagne from the cellars.

Later, when Nathan Brock was walking with Liam as far as the lodge gate, the ex-prizefighter said, 'Lady Caroline is very fond of you, Liam.'

'She takes a great deal of interest in the welfare of all the folk hereabouts.'

'That is not what I am saying, and you know it well. What there might be between you is none of my business—'

Nathan held up a big right hand to silence Liam's protest. 'I am only saying that if I can see it, then so can others, and it will bring you trouble.'

Nathan Brock looked at Liam honestly and squarely.

'I speak as a friend, Liam. You have travelled far along a road that few of us even set foot upon. Don't throw everything away for an indiscretion.'

Liam gave much thought to Nathan Brock's words along the road to Kilmar. He knew that his friend spoke the truth. Lady Caroline was a lovely and very lonely woman and she was becoming less and less discreet about her feelings for Liam. Any scandal would damage her reputation as surely as it would Liam's.

Yet Liam found her attentions flattering. More than that, he *wanted* her to show that she cared for him.

He wished he could analyse his own feelings for her with equal honesty. He knew he should look back at their relationship in London with shame, but he felt no shame when he thought about their nights together, only a deep hunger and painful memories.

He knew he should try to forget her. She had a husband and he was being constantly reminded that her background was far removed from his own, but there was something in Liam that refused to face all the facts. Lady Caroline herself would laughingly refer to it as a typical example of Irish stubbornness. Perhaps it was; but it was not stubbornness that brought uninvited thoughts of her to him when sleep was slow in coming.

Liam arrived home as his mother was preparing for bed, and she greeted his return with great relief. Hurriedly dressing, she prepared a meal, knowing there would be little sleep tonight. As the meal was cooking she questioned him closely about Dermot and Kathie. He was able to give her most of the answers she wanted, and then the families of the other exiled Kilmar men began to arrive, begging for news. Within half an hour the whole village was awake and Liam's every word was relayed from house to house.

Soon the little McCabe cottage was so crowded that it was becoming difficult to move. Liam repeated his story three times for the benefit of late-comers, then he announced he would call a meeting of the All-Ireland Association for the following evening and there tell the villagers everything he and Nathan Brock had learned in the Wicklow mountains.

Gradually, the villagers drifted away to their own homes. Then Liam saw Tomas Feehan standing in the doorway, talking to one of the fishermen.

'Tomas, I would like a word with you when the others have gone.'

Tomas Feehan frowned. He had never been on the best of terms with the McCabes and he made no secret of his view that Dermot McCabe was responsible for the abortive raid in which Sean had been killed. Only the thought that Liam must have something to tell him about Eoin kept him in the room. He stood to one side, tight-lipped and morose, as the chattering women of Kilmar and their menfolk made their way from the cottage.

As the last of them went out through the door, Father Clery came in looking decidedly ruffled.

'Why is it I am always the last to be told of what is going on in my own village?' he grumbled. 'There I am, all prepared for bed, when I suddenly realise that I can't hear myself pray for the prattle of women outside. When I come out of the house and ask what is going on, I am told, "Liam McCabe is home and will be addressing a meeting of the Association tomorrow night." Tell me, is there something I ought to know?'

A couple of women, slow to leave and anxious not to miss anything of importance that might be said, hung back in the doorway. Ushering them out, Liam closed the door behind them before answering.

'Yes, there is, and I'm glad you've come, Father. I have something to tell to Tomas that he is not going to want to hear.'

Tomas Feehan lost his indifference immediately. 'What is it? Is it Eoin? You're not trying to tell me that I've lost my other son?'

'He's alive, Tomas, but don't give thanks for that until you've heard what I have to say.'

Norah McCabe could see by Liam's manner that he had something serious to say to Tomas Feehan and Father Clery. She still had many questions to ask about Dermot, but she had learned he was well; everything else would keep until the morning. After telling Liam that the kettle was on the fire and an ounce of tea in the cupboard, she went to bed.

Liam had not yet told his mother of his talk with Eugene Brennan, but that, too, would wait until the morning.

Hesitantly at first, Liam told the two men the story of the raid on the mountain hideout and of its consequences. Then he told Tomas Feehan what Jeremy had learned of Eoin Feehan's part in the death of his younger brother.

'I don't believe it!' burst out the burly fisherman before Liam had finished talking. 'You have only that boy's word for what was said. By his own admission he is a thief who knows no decent way of life.'

'He had no reason to lie, Tomas,' said Liam quietly. 'And

Eoin himself admitted he was the cause of Sean's death. True, he said he did not know it was his own brother when he told the soldiers to kill him.'

'It's not true! It can't be true!' Tomas Feehan whispered, more to himself than to the others.

'It gives me no pleasure to tell you,' said Liam. 'But the facts are there to see, Tomas. Eoin was taken by the soldiers. He bought his freedom with the life of Sean and the name of every Kilmar man who took part in the raid on the grain-wagons.'

Tomas Feehan's face showed the struggle taking place within him for control of his feelings, and his hands alternately clenched and opened as he thought his own terrible thoughts.

'Where is Eoin now?'

'I don't know.' Liam told the distraught fisherman what had been done to his son, but he did not tell him it was Kathie who had fired the crippling shot.

Tomas Feehan stood up suddenly and looked at Liam fiercely. 'They should have killed him. Why did they allow him to live?'

'Don't say such a thing, Tomas.' Father Clery put a hand on the burly fisherman's arm. 'Whatever you are thinking now, don't wish ill upon your own son.'

'From this moment I have no son. I never want to see or hear of Eoin again and I thank God his mother never lived to see this day. To know that this is what we worked so hard for, struggling to build a future for two sons. Determined they wouldn't be tied to the life of a curragh fisherman for all of their days.'

Unchecked tears were streaming down the face of the tough fisherman as he turned to the priest.

'You've known me since I was a boy, Father. What have I done in my life to deserve the punishment God is giving me now?'

'If I understood the good Lord well enough to answer that, I would be more than a simple parish priest, Tomas. I can only offer you my help, and my prayers. I will pray for Eoin, too, as he goes through life with his own mark of Cain upon him.'

'Pray that he never returns to Kilmar,' said Tomas Feehan with frightening venom. 'For if he does I will have to kill him, and I doubt if the Lord will forgive me for that.'

With these terrible words, Tomas Feehan turned and

stumbled blindly from the McCabe house, ignoring Father Clery's call.

When the priest would have followed the distraught fisherman, Liam stopped him.

'Tomas Feehan will need to be alone for a while. There will be time enough to talk to him later.'

Father Clery shook his head sadly, 'You are right. I hate to see anyone with so much pain locked inside him, but Tomas is an independent man. He wouldn't thank me for chasing after him. Perhaps you ought to be telling me what else you learned while you were in the mountains.'

Liam repeated his story for the fourth time and also told Father Clery of his meeting with Eugene Brennan and their plans for the future. When he ended, the little priest could hardly contain his excitement. He clasped Liam's hand and pumped it with both his own.

'That's wonderful news, Liam. News that has brightened a terrible year. I am so proud of you that I could burst into tears. To think that a boy I taught in my own school should end up in Parliament in London! It makes up for all the frustrated years spent uselessly trying to cram a modicum of learning into the heads of children who are working just as hard to push it out again. Did Eugene say when he would be putting you up as a candidate?'

'He said he would let me know soon enough, but right now I would like your advice on how much to tell tomorrow night's meeting about everything that has happened.'

The two men talked together far into the night. Upstairs in her room, Norah McCabe listened to the drone of their voices and speculated on what they were saying. She had heard Tomas Feehan leave hurriedly and knew that something of importance was happening. Silently she prayed that, whatever it might be, it would not take a second son from her.

The next morning Liam told his mother of his agreement with Eugene Brennan. The news was so startling and exciting that it did not matter that Liam would have to spend long periods away from his home.

'Are you sure this is what you want?' she asked him for the third time as he ate his breakfast.

'I'm fairly sure,' he repeated patiently. 'If ever I become tired of the grand life, I can always come back here to you and our boat. In the meantime there will be no shortage of men willing to work it for us. I will arrange all that before I leave.'

'I know you will, Liam.'

Norah McCabe was quiet for a long time, and then she said, 'I want you to know I am proud of you, Liam. Your father would have been, too, God rest his soul; but it's a strange world to be living in. Here am I with one son away in the mountains fighting for Ireland and my other son about to go away to London to do the same thing, but in the Parliament. Work hard at it when you get there, Liam, for you've got to be showing Dermot and the others that your way is the right way.'

A few evenings after the meeting of the All-Ireland Association, Liam's boat bumped against the stone of the Kilmar quay and as he stepped ashore with the rope to moor the boat a small boy jumped down the steps to meet him, breathless with the importance of his mission.

'Mrs McCabe says will you come home right away. There's a fine lady with a carriage waiting to meet you,' he added.

'It sounds as though Lady Caroline is here to see me,' said Liam to Tommy Donaghue. 'She might have a message from Eugene Brennan about the by-election. Look after things here for me.'

'Haven't I been doing that for weeks? Ah well! With you moving up in society I suppose I had better be getting used to it. Away with you now; there's more to life than gutting fish with a silly old man for company.'

Caroline had a message from Eugene Brennan, but it was not the one Liam had been expecting.

'Liam, you have got to go away from here,' she said, as soon as he walked into the cottage. 'I have had word from Eugene. He has been arrested in London and charged with stealing money collected for the famine relief fund.'

Before Liam could recover from the shock of her incredible news, she said, 'You are to be arrested, too. Constables are on their way here from London to take you back with them.'

'But that is ridiculous. I've done nothing wrong.'

'I know you haven't. It is a plot to discredit Eugene; but that will not prevent you from being arrested and carried to London. You must leave Kilmar and go into hiding until the constables have gone. You can come to Inch House and stay there, if you wish.'

'No.' While she had been talking, Liam's thoughts were racing ahead of her words, assessing their implications, and now he reached a decision. 'I am not running. There will not be two members of this family outside the law. I am innocent and nobody can prove otherwise. This must be some stupid mistake. I will stay in Kilmar until the constables arrive and try to persuade them of my innocence. If I fail, I will go to London with them and prove it there.'

'That is foolish, Liam.' Caroline was so distraught that Norah McCabe looked from Liam to her sharply. 'We know you have done nothing wrong, but proving it may not be quite so straightforward. More than one innocent man has been wrongfully convicted. Go into hiding until Eugene Brennan has won his case in court. He may well establish your innocence at the same time.'

'I am grateful to you for coming here, Caroline, but I am not having it said I ran from justice. I am not afraid of standing trial.'

'If you refuse to help yourself, then your friends will have to do it for you. I intend leaving for London today. By the time you are brought there I will have arranged for the best lawyer in London to take your case.'

So genuine was Caroline's concern for Liam that it took away much of the sting of her news for him and he smiled warmly at her. 'Eugene is as good a lawyer as you will find anywhere. I am sure he has already organised our defence. You must not involve yourself, Caroline.'

'Eugene is an old man. He makes mistakes. One of them is to believe that all men are as honourable as he is himself. I will go to London and do whatever I think is necessary. I will send Nathan here to help with your fishing business while you are away.'

Norah McCabe followed Caroline outside. She had been watching the younger woman carefully during the time she had been in the McCabe cottage and was very concerned about what she had seen. As Caroline was about to step into her carriage, Norah McCabe asked, 'Will Liam be kept in prison while he is in London?'

'No, I will stand bail for him.'

'That's very kind of you.'

Norah McCabe hesitated before asking the question that had been bothering her. 'Why are you taking such an interest in my son?'

Caroline paused, with one foot on the carriage step. Slowly she set it back on the ground and turned to face Liam's mother.

'Your son and I are friends, Mrs McCabe. I am happy to be in a position to help him.'

Norah McCabe studied the other woman's face. There was certainly concern in the wide-spaced eyes of this beautiful woman; but her unhappiness was also there for any observant woman to see, and Norah McCabe could guess at its reason.

'No, there is more than friendship between you. I knew something had happened to Liam when he returned from London, but I had too much on my mind to pry into the truth of it then. I should have made it my business to find out. You are a married woman, Lady Caroline, living in a world of carriages and servants. This "friendship" you talk about can bring nothing but trouble to Liam.'

'Liam is an Irishman, Mrs McCabe. Trouble is his heritage. Soon he will be entering Parliament and seeing much more of this "world" you say I live in. It could well become his world, too, if he wishes. I *can* help him, Mrs McCabe. I *will* help him. I will also do my best to ensure he is not hurt. I fully understand your anxiety for him, but please trust me. We are both concerned for his well-being.'

Confirmation that her suspicions had been well founded left Norah McCabe with a tight knot of unhappiness inside her. 'You and I are interested in Liam's well-being for very different reasons,' she said. 'I am thinking of his future happiness.'

'Then we need never quarrel, Mrs McCabe. Liam's happiness is very important to me, too.'

Eugene Brennan had sent a swift messenger to Caroline. It was not until three days later that two detectives from London arrived at Kilmar in a shabby coach, accompanied by three nervous constables from Dublin.

The senior detective confirmed that he was talking to the right party and politely asked if he might enter the McCabe cottage, taking off his hat as he greeted Norah McCabe. While he and his colleague were in the cottage, the Irish constables crowded in the doorway, nervously eyeing the silent but hostile fishermen who quickly gathered in the narrow street outside.

In the kitchen, the detective took a stiff-papered document from an inside pocket of his long coat.

'Liam McCabe,' he said loudly, 'I have a warrant here ordering me to arrest you and produce you at Bow Street Court, in London, to answer to a charge of embezzling monies received by you for the famine relief fund set up by one Eugene Brennan.'

'I never saw any money. As far as I am aware it was only promised at the meetings I addressed and was paid direct into the fund later.'

'I will record that reply, sir, but nothing you say alters the fact that I must take you back to London with me. You may bring a few comforts, but I will be obliged if you put these handcuffs on without making any fuss.'

'If you want no trouble, then you'll put those handcuffs away again.'

Norah McCabe stood in the centre of the room and wagged a finger vigorously at the detective.

'My son has already told you he saw no money that didn't belong to him. He is no thief. Had he wanted to run away he could have done it three days ago when we were told you were on your way. It was his own idea to wait here and go to London to prove his innocence – though God only knows why; there's little enough justice to be found there for an Irishman. Having made his own decision, there is no need to secure him. If you hope to leave here without finding more trouble than you can handle, you will accept the truth of that. There are many men in Kilmar angered enough already by what you are doing. Put those things on Liam's wrists and you'll be lucky to leave here alive.'

The constables in the doorway exchanged fearful glances. They had not wanted to come to Kilmar without an escort of militiamen. The fishing communities had a reputation for protecting their own.

The senior detective tucked the handcuffs through the belt of his trousers, from whence they had come.

'I'm obliged to you, ma'am. My duties are always easier when there is goodwill and understanding all round. I hope your son is able to prove his innocence and return home to you quickly.'

The detective meant every word. He had been a detective for enough years to recognise an honest man when he met one. But he also knew that in Liam's case honesty might not be enough to secure an acquittal. The order to arrest this fisherman had come from a much higher authority than was usual in such cases.

Chapter Thirty

London in June 1846 was suffocatingly hot, and in the unventilated cells beneath the police station at Great Scotland Yard Liam spent an uncomfortable and sleepless forty-eight hours. He was questioned by the detectives for most of the daylight hours and it developed into a frustrating and repetitious ritual. Liam's answers never differed. He knew nothing of the finances of the famine fund. He had taken no money. He had been given no money. He had been brought to London to talk of the horrors he had seen, and he had talked. There was nothing more he could say.

Then Eugene Brennan came to the police station and arranged for Liam to be bailed out of police custody. Liam had never been so happy to be looking up at the clouds of an approaching summer storm. It seemed that all London was waiting for rain. In the carriage on the way from the police station Eugene Brennan constantly mopped his brow with a damp limp handkerchief, and as they talked Liam looked out through the open carriage windows at the sullen faces of the too-hot Londoners walking along their narrow airless streets.

The two men talked about the trial. Eugene said they would appear before a magistrate toward the end of the week and could expect to go before a judge at the London Sessions before the month was out.

'We are privileged prisoners, Liam,' said the old politician. 'It is not unknown for common criminals like ourselves to languish in prison for longer than a year awaiting a trial. We are being hurried before the court with an eagerness that is almost indecent.'

Eugene Brennan chuckled, and Liam looked at him in astonishment.

'It amuses you that we are to be tried for a crime about which we know nothing?'

Eugene Brennan stopped chuckling and looked at Liam seriously. 'No, my boy, it doesn't amuse me. It pains me greatly, but it will hurt others more, you can be sure of that. Before this trial is over those behind it will be wishing they had never heard of Liam McCabe and Eugene Brennan and the famine relief fund.'

'Those behind it?' echoed Liam. 'Do you mean this is a deliberate attempt to discredit us – or you?'

'That is exactly what I mean – but ask me no more questions. We are innocent. You know it and so do I. By the time this trial is over, all Britain will be aware of it, too.'

'That may be so, but it will put an end to my chance of becoming a Member of Parliament.'

'Put an end to—? Good heavens, Liam, this court case will put you straight into the House of Commons. There will not be a voting Irishman – or an Englishman, come to that – who won't know the name of Liam McCabe.'

Liam wished he had the confidence of his companion. He was very worried about the outcome of the trial. The two days he had spent in police custody had demoralised him. He was a man who cherished his freedom and loved the outdoors. Locked in a tiny cell with no natural light coming in, and being totally dependent upon others for every necessity of life, was an alien and terrifying experience for him. Like many other strong and active men, Liam hated to rely upon others for anything.

The carriage turned into a narrow cobbled alley and speech became impossible for a while as teeth were clenched against the violent movement of the vehicle. After a hundred yards of this bone-juddering motion, the alley opened out upon a crowded dingy square and the carriage stopped outside one of the shabby terraced houses.

'Here we are,' said Eugene Brennan with relief. 'This is my home. You will be staying here while you are in London. It may not be as grand as your last lodgings, but it's comfortable. You'll need to carry your own bag inside. I employ only one servant and she will do nothing but the cooking and cleaning. Go on in; there's a friend waiting to greet you. I'll follow in a minute or two, when I have settled up with the driver.'

Liam knew who the 'friend' was the moment he stepped inside the gloomy hall. Caroline's perfume was as distinctive as its wearer.

Caroline was sitting in the small lounge reading a book but she jumped to her feet and rushed to embrace Liam when he entered the room. He felt ridiculously pleased to see her again and held her to him, grinning like a half-wit until she eventually pushed him away. Taking both his hands in hers, she looked up at him.

'My poor Liam, you look so tired. Was it terrible in your cell?'

Liam doubted whether he was as tired as she. Strain and tension shared a place on her face and her skin had an unhealthy pallor.

In Ireland he had deliberately kept her at a distance, her husband a dark shadow between them, but he cared for her very much and was concerned for her health.

Sensing a subtle change in his attitude toward her, Caroline put a hand up to his face, but at that moment the street-door slammed shut and Eugene Brennan called to them from the hall. When he entered the room they were standing with a respectable distance between them.

Caroline gave the old politician a greeting only marginally less affectionate than the welcome she had given to Liam. She kissed him on the cheek as she hugged him to her, and Eugene Brennan beamed happily.

'I knew you would rescue Liam, Eugene, but you were only just in time. I arranged with your housekeeper to have dinner ready for half-past six. I guessed Liam would be ravenous after two days in that horrible place. We hardly have time for a drink before dinner will be ready.'

She smiled at Liam. 'Save a drink for me. I must go to the kitchen to see what is happening.'

When she had left the room, Eugene Brennan poured out three generous measures of whiskey and handed one to Liam.

'Lady Caroline is a very special kind of woman. A little too independent and self-willed for my taste, but an exceptional girl for all that.'

'She is all those things.' Liam was embarrassed at discussing Caroline under Eugene Brennan's unwavering gaze, and the MP nodded knowingly.

'She is very fond of you, Liam – but you don't need an old man like me to tell you that. You know all about it yourself.'

Eugene Brennan neither expected nor wanted a reply, but he had a word of warning to add to his observation.

'Be discreet in your friendship with Lady Caroline, Liam. A court-case is not likely to damage your parliamentary career –

certainly not one held in an English court. Win it and you will have gained yourself a hundred votes in Ireland, but get involved with a married woman and you will lose a thousand. You can't afford to do that at this end of your career. Leave it until you are my age. By then you will be happy to give away a thousand votes, just to have folk think such a thing of you.'

Eugene Brennan chuckled, but Liam knew that he had just been given a serious warning. He accepted it without comment and asked the politician why he had no wife. It was an unthinking question and one Liam immediately regretted asking.

Eugene Brennan carried his drink to the window and gazed out at the shabby square, where the first heavy drops of rain were beginning to fall.

'I once had a wife, Liam. We were married after being childhood sweethearts for as long as I could remember. We lived in Wexford Town in those days, although I spent much of my time in Dublin and my wife would come with me. Then, in ninety-eight, she was pregnant and could no longer travel with me. That is how we came to be parted when the "glorious" rebellion broke out. In Wexford my wife witnessed the fighting and the atrocities committed by both sides. She herself was not physically hurt, but the sight of such wanton slaughter made her ill. She lost the baby only a month before it was due to be born. She never recovered from that blow, Liam. She wanted a child so much. She just wasted away and two years later she died. There was nothing I could do to help her. I was still younger than you are now, Liam, and I was a widower.'

Eugene Brennan took a drink, half-emptying his glass.

'I am seventy years of age, Liam, but I remember her as though all this happened only yesterday. I remember how the corners of her eyes crinkled when she smiled, and how sweet her hair smelled when we were caught in the rain and sheltered beneath a tree. The strange thing is, I can never remember her tears, but I know there were a great many.'

The long-threatened storm had broken now and thunder grumbled above the rain-washed slates of London.

'Somehow I never found the time to marry again. I suppose it could be said I married Ireland.' Eugene Brennan shrugged his shoulders. 'I could have done worse.'

Downing the remainder of his drink, Eugene Brennan

turned to look at Liam as a sibilant flash of lightning fragmented the sky behind him, followed by a crashing peal of thunder. When it rolled away, Eugene Brennan said, 'Now you understand why I am opposed to any form of violent action. Such a course is usually advocated by those with the least knowledge of its effects. War and rebellion are not all glory and green flags. They cause death and suffering and misery. Our victory will be a much greater one if it can be achieved without adding to the burden that Ireland already carries.'

Some of the vitality drained from Eugene Brennan, and as he stood staring morosely down at the empty glass he twirled in his fingers his shoulders sagged wearily.

'No doubt my young opponents within the Association would be able to use what I have just told you to their own advantage. They would say I am getting old and allowing a personal tragedy of many years ago to cloud my judgement. Perhaps they are right. There are many times now when I want to give up what I am doing. To return to Wexford Town and walk with the past until I am a part of it myself.'

'I am sorry, Eugene.' Apologies seemed totally inadequate. 'I didn't know about your wife.'

'Few people do,' shrugged the old politician. 'And fewer would really care if they did.'

He smiled sadly. 'Ah well! There's nothing like an old Irishman for enjoying the sorrows of the past – but my nose is telling me something of the joys of the present. I think that delicious smell means dinner is ready, my boy.'

The magistrate's hearing was a mere formality. The magistrate expressed his view that Liam and Eugene Brennan had a case to answer and he committed them for trial at the London Sessions.

During the days that followed, Liam was taken to the House of Commons to meet some of Eugene Brennan's fellow-Irish MPs. They were polite enough but, in spite of Eugene's assurances, Liam suspected, did not regard the charges against the veteran politician lightly and were concerned lest they were thought to be involved.

Caroline was a constant visitor to the accused politician's house and, although Eugene Brennan rarely left Liam and

Caroline alone together, they regained much of the warmth that had been missing from their relationship for a long time.

Occasionally, the three of them would go out for a carriage ride, enjoying the view from Hampstead Heath, or sampling the pleasures of a fair at London Fields. One evening they took a box at the theatre to see a new comedy. But most of the time they remained in Eugene Brennan's small house, playing cards and talking.

Eventually the day of the trial arrived, and it proved to be grey, wet and unseasonably chilly.

'I hope this is not an omen,' said Liam, shivering with cold and nervous anticipation, as he and Eugene Brennan left the house.

'It will be a grey day for someone,' grated the old MP as he climbed stiffly into the carriage. 'But I don't think it will be us.'

Settling himself in his seat, he leaned forward, both hands resting on the silver handle of his walking-stick.

'Don't worry about a thing, Liam. I will be conducting our case. You have only to answer my questions clearly and honestly. Remember, when you give a speech in Parliament very few people outside the House are interested in what you have to say. Speak from the dock in a criminal court and the public hang on your every word. There is no place like it for promoting a good cause, or putting forward a political point of view. We must make the most of our opportunity.'

Eugene Brennan chuckled happily, and an incredulous Liam realised that the politician was actually enjoying the thought of appearing in court. He wished he could share his pleasure, but the charges against them were far too serious.

Liam's apprehension increased when they arrived at the forbidding court-building and surrendered to their bail. As Eugene Brennan was conducting their defence, he was permitted to remain in the court-room. Liam was taken down a narrow stone staircase and lodged in the dungeons below the building. He shared a communal cell with a dozen other prisoners who had been brought there from London's prisons and who carried with them an unhealthy prison smell. The offences they had committed ranged from pickpocketing to murder. One of the accused murderers was unquestionably insane. The poor demented man was secured hand and foot with heavy chains and threshed about on the floor in a frenzied passion, screaming obscenities at creatures only he could see.

It came as a relief when Liam's name was called and he was led from the cell to the court-room above.

The large high-ceilinged room was packed with men and women who were by no means hostile to the two men on trial. When Eugene Brennan joined Liam briefly in the spike-rimmed dock there was an outbreak of cheering from the public gallery. The stern-faced judge silenced them by banging on the bench before him with a wooden gavel. When he could make himself heard, he left the members of the public in no doubt about the action he would take should they repeat the outburst.

Liam and Eugene Brennan were jointly charged with embezzling money from the Irish famine relief fund and using it for their own purposes. After the charges had been read and the two men in the dock had declared forcefully that they were not guilty, Eugene Brennan was allowed to leave the dock and the prosecution opened their case.

Prosecuting counsel told the court that this was a case where two men, one being in a position of high responsibility, had preyed on the emotions of kind-hearted people. They had persuaded the gullible to part with their money and then creamed off part of it for their own use. It was, prosecuting counsel stated, a felony of the most despicable kind. The money had been collected to help the starving thousands in Ireland and was donated largely as a result of an appeal by Liam McCabe. The two accused men knew that every shilling they took from the fund represented the difference between life and death for some sick and starving child.

'. . . And what did they do with this money?' Prosecuting counsel withdrew a hand from inside his black gown and wagged a finger at the twelve jurymen. 'Did they use it to settle some pressing debt or unavoidable expense incurred during their travels to help their suffering countrymen? No. Much of it went to purchase extravagant clothes for Liam McCabe.'

The barrister turned to look at Liam, who was dressed in his best suit for this occasion. 'Liam McCabe is probably wearing some of those clothes here, before you. I see he has on a suit that I would not be ashamed to wear, that any fashionable man of London would be proud to own. Yet Liam McCabe is not a fashionable man of London. Neither is he a barrister. This well-dressed young man standing before you is a poor fisherman from County Wexford in impoverished Ireland. A land where people are dying for want of a few pence with which to buy food.'

The barrister jabbed an accusing finger at Liam. 'Yet this "poor" fisherman comes to London and buys clothing to the value of sixty-five guineas with the cottiers' money.'

There was a gasp from the public gallery and prosecuting counsel was quick to force home the impact his words had made.

'Yes, I will repeat that sum. Sixty-five guineas to buy clothes for a fisherman.'

The barrister turned to the jury once more. 'When you are hearing evidence that may confuse you, or if doubts arise in your minds, I would like you to reflect on this fact. Where could a poor fisherman obtain such a sum of money – unless it be from a deliberately mismanaged fund of money, collected from gullible and misled donors. Now I will call my first witness.'

Liam had listened to the prosecution's opening speech with dismay. He had no idea of the cost of the clothes bought for him from Eugene Brennan's tailor, but he had no reason to doubt the sum quoted. What was even more damning was that the MP himself had told Liam that the money for the clothing had come from donated money. Eugene Brennan had called them 'a justifiable expense'. When Liam looked across the court-room, the white-haired MP was leaning back in his chair with apparent unconcern. When he caught Liam's anxious glance he smiled reassuringly. Liam wished he could share Eugene's confidence. He did not see how the prosecution case could possibly be shaken.

The first witness was a man to whom Liam vaguely remembered being introduced at one of the meetings he had addressed. His name, he told the court, was Ephraim Butt, and he was a junior Treasury official. He had somehow managed to obtain a list of the persons present at that first meeting, together with details of their contributions to the famine relief fund. The total amount was £2300. Butt gave his evidence nervously, his tongue constantly flicking out to moisten dried lips, and his eyes never once looked toward Eugene Brennan or Liam.

'Did you become suspicious that not all of this money would find its way to the fund for which it was intended?'

The prosecution did not ask why Butt's suspicions should have been aroused.

'I did.'

'And did you take certain action as a result?'

'Yes. I obtained a statement of the amount of money paid to the famine relief fund as a result of this meeting.'

'Will you please tell this court how much this most deserving cause actually received?'

'One thousand seven hundred and twenty pounds.'

'Thus revealing a discrepancy of five hundred and eighty pounds. Thank you, Mr Butt.'

Eugene Brennan rose to his feet slowly, almost lazily, and smiled amicably at the witness.

'Hello, Ephraim – I am sorry, Mr Butt – we are not drinking together at the club now, are we?'

Ephraim Butt squirmed uncomfortably.

'You were concerned that the money you donated to the fund might be misused?'

'Yes.'

'Will you tell this court how much money you gave to this – "most deserving cause", I believe was the phrase used by my learned friend.'

There was a pause before Butt replied, in a low voice, 'Two pounds.'

'I'm sorry, Mr Butt. Will you speak up, please?'

'Two pounds.'

There was a snigger in the public gallery which was quickly stifled when the judge looked in that direction.

'You were so concerned about your two pounds that you made extensive enquiries into the manner in which the fund was administered?'

'I felt it was my duty.'

'Very commendable, Mr Butt, and I trust you made a thorough investigation. You did, of course, realise that the two thousand three hundred pounds that has been referred to was money that was *promised* to the fund. No doubt you checked whether it was actually *received*?'

Ephraim Butt looked genuinely shocked. 'The promises were made by gentlemen, Mr Brennan. I have no doubt at all that their promises were kept.'

'I find such faith in my fellow-men quite touching, Mr Butt, but I regret to inform you that most of the persons at that meeting were parliamentarians – a breed notorious for unkept promises. I will say no more on that subject, but will merely call your attention to a single name on this list. J. Hart, Esquire. He promised one hundred pounds, did he not?'

'Yes.' Ephraim Butt looked uneasy.

'You are aware that Mr Hart was taken ill and died on his way home from the meeting? He was therefore unable to honour his promised donation.'

'I learned about it later. I did not know at the time I began my enquiries.'

'Ah yes, your enquiries. Did you start them immediately after the meeting?'

'No.'

'No, indeed you did not.' A strong Irish brogue had crept into Eugene Brennan's voice. 'Will you tell this court when you started to make your enquiries – and upon whose instructions?'

'I started them about six weeks ago – but nobody told me to do it.'

'Perhaps "instructed" is the wrong word. "Suggested" might have been more suitable. Never mind. One last question, Mr Butt. You are in the Treasury Department. Will you tell me the name of the head of your particular section?'

Ephraim licked his dry lips and looked quickly about the court, as though worried his department was represented there.

'Come, Mr Butt. Your section head, please?'

'Sir Richard Dudley.'

Liam's mouth dropped open in surprise. He hardly heard Eugene Brennan inform the judge that he had no further questions for this witness. Liam now had an inkling of the direction Eugene Brennan's questioning was taking. Yet many things remained unexplained. He could understand why Sir Richard Dudley should wish to see him in trouble, but why Eugene Brennan? Was this part of the political hatchetry of which the MP had spoken?

The next witness had been at a later meeting. His story

differed very little from that already told by Ephraim Butt. He, too, produced documentary evidence to show that the amount actually paid into the famine relief fund was less than that promised. This time the discrepancy was £400.

Once again Eugene Brennan's questioning was almost casual until he asked the witness about his employment at the time he attended the meeting.

'I was in the Commissariat.'

'And now?'

'The Treasury Department.'

'At a greatly increased salary, I believe.'

The witness nodded.

'Will you tell this court who arranged your promotion to this new post?'

'Sir Richard Dudley.'

There was a stir of interest in the court. Nobody yet knew the significance of Eugene Brennan's questioning, but he had drawn the baronet's name from both witnesses. The judge and jury would remember the name of Sir Richard Dudley.

The next witness was the tailor who had made Liam's clothes. His evidence was terse. Yes, he had made clothes to the value of sixty-five guineas for Liam. Yes, he had been paid. Mr Brennan had given him a letter drawn on Messrs Lubbock & Company's bank for the full amount.

To Liam's surprise, Eugene Brennan declined the opportunity to question the tailor at this stage. Instead, he requested that he might recall the witness at a later stage in the trial. The judge grumbled that it was not good legal procedure, but he acceded to Eugene's request.

The last witness for the prosecution was the detective who had arrested both Eugene Brennan and Liam. He gave evidence of arrest and told the court he had charged both men with the offence for which they were now standing trial.

It was now Eugene Brennan's turn to take the stage and in his opening speech he showed some of the fire and power that had made him one of the most powerful forces in Irish politics for half a century.

The charges brought against himself and Liam, he said, were both false and malicious. He promised to supply absolute proof of their innocence. He went on to assert that the charges were political in their inception and had been pursued by persons in authority who had no love of either Ireland or the Irish. He told of his own long record of public service and years as an MP. Then he spoke of Liam. Far from being no more than a 'simple fisherman', he told the court, Liam was a man of some standing in his own community. Giving the truth a certain amount of elasticity, Eugene Brennan told the court that Liam owned a substantial fishing boat, had established trade with inland markets – using his own transport – and was currently employing a number of men to fish for him.

Finally, Eugene Brennan informed the court that in Liam they were looking at a future Member of Parliament, and a man who would leave this court without a blemish on his character. Then Eugene called Liam to the witness-box.

When Liam had taken the oath, Eugene Brennan asked him to repeat what he had told his audiences when he was speaking on behalf of the famine relief fund.

The prosecution immediately objected that such evidence was irrelevant, aimed only at gaining the sympathy of the jury. The judge called upon the politician to explain himself.

'My Lord,' said Eugene Brennan, 'I and my young friend are on trial for felonies of such a serious nature that both our lives will be ruined by a wrongful conviction. I have no intention of allowing that to happen. Liam McCabe is a humanitarian, dedicated to helping his fellow-Irishmen. I want him to tell this court of the horrors he has seen among the cottiers of Ireland. Then they will realise that only the Devil incarnate would divert money from these poor creatures – and Liam McCabe is not such a person.'

With some misgivings, the judge indicated that Liam might give his evidence. The fisherman told his story to a hushed and horrified court and when he ended there was a stunned silence before an angry roar burst from the throats of the Irish men and women in the public gallery. It was minutes before the court officials were able to re-establish order and allow Eugene Brennan to continue his defence.

He resumed his questioning of Liam without comment, well aware that the court's sympathy was his.

'Mr McCabe. . . .' The formality sounded strange to Liam. 'Mr McCabe, did you at any time handle any money collected for the famine relief fund?'

'No, I never saw any money.'

'Were you even aware of how much money was raised by your efforts?'

'No . . . only an approximate amount.'

'Thank you. I have no further questions.'

Now it was the prosecution's turn once more and counsel questioned Liam anew about the money taken at the meetings, but Liam was able to tell him no more than he had already told Eugene Brennan.

Then prosecuting counsel came to what he believed would be one of the most damning pieces of evidence against Liam. The question of his clothes.

Again, Liam was less than helpful, yet scrupulously honest. He told his questioner he did not know the source of the money used to purchase his clothes.

Prosecuting counsel made as much as he could from this fact.

'Come now, Mr McCabe. Are you telling this court you accepted clothing to the value of sixty-five guineas without enquiring who would pay for them?'

'No, Mr Brennan paid for them.'

'Oh? From his own pocket?'

'No. He said money was specially donated for such purposes.'

'Really, Mr McCabe?' The words were weighted with heavy sarcasm. 'And of course you believed him?'

'Yes, Mr Brennan is an honest man.'

Liam saw Eugene Brennan smiling as prosecuting counsel snapped, 'That, Mr McCabe, is for the jury to decide. I doubt if they will prove as gullible as you would have them believe you are.'

At this stage the judge announced that the court would adjourn for lunch. Liam was returned to the cells beneath the court, but this time he was given a cell to himself and he ate a meal ordered for him by Eugene Brennan. It was spoiled only by the foul smell of the unsavoury food served to prisoners in the nearby communal cage.

Eugene Brennan came down to the cells later in the lunch adjournment, and Liam asked him how long he thought the trial would last.

'Oh, we'll bring it to a close soon after we go back into the court this afternoon,' was the confident reply.

'You'll *bring* it to a close?' queried Liam.

'That's what I said, my boy. Enough has been said to interest the newspapers and give a big boost both to the Association and your future career. All that remains is for me to produce the evidence that will clear our names and then we will go home and celebrate.'

'I wish I shared your confidence, Eugene. There were a lot of questions raised in court to which I have no answers.'

'Of course there were. Had you known all the answers you would have blurted them out to the court and spoiled my surprise.' Eugene Brennan clapped a hand on Liam's shoulder. 'Don't worry about a thing. While you are waiting for the case to start again, decide what you will order for your meal tonight.'

The cell door was locked after Eugene had gone, and Liam was left pondering over what had been said until the hearing resumed at two-thirty.

The sky over London was dark and overcast, and gas-lamps were burning around the walls of the court-room. The heat from these and from the perspiring bodies packed tightly in the public gallery made the room unbearably hot.

The judge looked hotter than anyone in his heavy wig and gown, and Eugene Brennan thought this might be a very good moment to announce that he intended bringing the proceedings to a close.

The judge looked at the MP suspiciously. 'Will you please tell the court exactly how you intend to do that, Mr Brennan?'

'Certainly, my lord. Much has been made of the alleged unbusinesslike manner in which the famine relief fund has been administered. I would like to set the record straight by presenting to this court certified receipts for all monies received by the fund, together with the names of all donors and the amounts they gave. I also have a separate list of amounts promised but not received.'

He produced a sheaf of documents and handed them up to the judge.

'Mr Brennan, am I to understand you have been in possession of these documents the whole time? If so, perhaps you will explain why they were not produced before? Had you done so, I very much doubt whether this case would ever have reached this court.'

'Quite true, my lord, but that would have meant there would always be rumours circulating . . . damaging rumours . . . concerning this matter. It was necessary for the case to come to this court and for Mr McCabe and myself to be fully exonerated by someone as distinguished as yourself.'

'And, no doubt, gain a great deal of political publicity into the bargain,' retorted the judge. 'Do you have anything else to say, Mr Brennan?'

'Yes, my lord. There is the matter of the clothing purchased for my young friend. I would like to recall the tailor.'

The judge mopped his brow and sighed. 'Very well, Mr Brennan, if you must. But please keep your questioning brief. I will have no more time-wasting in my court.'

As the tailor entered the witness-box he smiled at Eugene Brennan, and Liam knew that, prosecution witness or not, the tailor was on their side. He and Eugene had no doubt already discussed the case at some length.

The tailor began by confirming that Liam's clothes had cost sixty-five guineas and that the account had been settled.

'But of course, Mr Brennan, you have always been a man who settled your accounts promptly. If everyone settled as quickly as you, there wouldn't be so many tailors going out of business in London.'

Eugene Brennan acknowledged the tailor's compliment. 'You have told us you were paid by means of a letter drawn on Messrs Lubbock's bank. Was the signature on the letter mine?'

'No, Mr Brennan. It was not.'

'As far as you are aware, does the person who signed that letter have anything to do with the famine relief fund?'

'Why, I would doubt it very much, Mr Brennan.'

'Then I have no further questions, my lord,' Eugene Brennan said to the judge.

'But I have!' The angry prosecuting counsel pointed at the tailor. 'This witness deliberately misled me. I demand to know whose signature was on that bank letter.'

The tailor stayed silent and Eugene Brennan said, 'It has nothing to do with the case. You need not answer.'

'Mr Brennan, that is for me to decide.' The judge rapped on the bench in front of him and looked sternly at the tailor. 'You will answer counsel's question or go to prison yourself.'

'There is no need. I signed that letter. I paid for the clothing.'

The voice came from the back of the court-room, and as the

court erupted into excited sound Liam leaped to his feet and turned to look at the speaker.

There was a timid knock on the mahogany office door and Sir Richard Dudley called, 'Come in,' without loking up from his writing to see who it was.

The door opened and Ephraim Butt entered the room. He stood before the large square desk shifting his weight from foot to foot and mouthing noiselessly, as though rehearsing what he would say.

Sir Richard Dudley put down his pen with a sigh and looked up at his visitor. His frown changed instantly to a welcoming smile.

'Butt, my good chap! Well, what news do you have for me? What sentences were passed upon them?'

Ephraim looked unhappier than ever and when he spoke he stuttered over his words. 'They weren't. . . . I mean . . . they were found "not guilty". They got off.'

'Not guilty!' Sir Richard Dudley sprang to his feet angrily, and Butt took a pace backward as though he feared the baronet was about to spring at him.

'I told you to obtain irrefutable evidence. What happened?'

'Eugene Brennan produced certified documents to account for every penny he had ever received for his fund.'

'Damn! I never thought the old fool would be so cautious. But what about the fisherman – his clothes? He could never have afforded them. The money must have come from the fund.'

Ephraim Butt seemed to be having trouble breathing.

'Well, where did the money come from? You must know. Speak up, man.'

'Lady Caroline,' the unhappy man stuttered. 'Your wife stood up and told the court she bought them for him.'

Chapter Thirty-One

On Thursday, 25 June 1846, the government of Sir Robert Peel fell, defeated on the second reading of the Irish Coercion Bill.

On the same day, the Corn Law Amendment Bill, cause of so much resentment among the members of his own party, finally passed through the House of Lords.

Sir Robert Peel's defeat had been assured once he had brought about the relaxation of the Corn Laws protecting the land-owners from foreign competition. It mattered not at all that he had been forced into this course of action by the desperate situation in Ireland.

When Peel had been Chief Secretary for Ireland, he had been in the habit of drinking the Protestant Orangeman's toast to the glorious memory of William III. Now Ireland had wreaked a wry revenge and caused the downfall of a brilliant, albeit an occasionally misguided, prime minister.

Eugene Brennan had remained in London to vote against Peel on the crucial issue, while Liam began his journey home to Kilmar – with Caroline.

It had been necessary to keep the fact that they were travelling together a secret from the MP, but he was far too involved in plotting Peel's downfall to think of much else.

They were not travelling on the railway, to Liverpool. Instead, they were making a four-day journey in a cross-country coach to Holyhead and taking the much shorter sea route from there.

Their first day's journey was along good roads, and the coach rolled into the yard of a Rugby inn for the night stop with three hours of daylight remaining. The dinner was good English beef helped down with a fine claret, and for the first time since the trial began Liam felt himself relaxing. In spite of Eugene Brennan's constant assurances, there had been times when Liam doubted the wily old politician's ability to secure their acquittal. He should have known better, he admitted to himself. He did not doubt now that he would one day become a Member of Parliament, but it would be a very long time before he acquired Eugene Brennan's craftiness and guile.

'Can I share your thought, or is it a secret?'

Caroline watched his smile with much pleasure.

Liam told Caroline what he had been thinking, and she agreed with his opinion of the Irish MP.

'Eugene is an old fox. He has kept his place during some very difficult years. But he behaved with such confidence throughout this trial that I had the feeling he had been prepared for it even before his arrest. I think Richard must have said something to alert him when they met in Dublin.'

The mention of Caroline's husband took much of Liam's pleasure from him. She saw his change of expression and knew the reason.

Pushing back her chair, Caroline looked around the crowded dining-room. 'Do you think we might go out for a walk, Liam? It is terribly hot and stuffy in here.'

Outside the inn, she took a deep breath of air. 'This is much better. Look at that beautiful sunset, Liam.'

A bank of heavy grey cloud hung above the horizon like a thick dull curtain, but beneath it a full red sun balanced on the distant landscape, sending long shadows across the countryside.

'Isn't that beautiful, Liam? I am glad we came by coach. Had we travelled by train we should no doubt be spending the night in Birmingham, the most dismal town in the land.'

She took his hand as they turned along a path that followed the infant River Avon along part of its way. 'I wanted us to travel by coach, together. It will give us time to walk, like this . . . and to talk. We need to talk, Liam. To make a decision about the future. I . . . I have been very unhappy without you.'

Liam stopped and pulled her to face him.

'You know why I have not spent more time with you. You have a husband. That is not something I can easily forget.'

'Liam, please listen to me. I have already told you that Richard and I go our own ways. After what he tried to do to you I will have nothing more to do with him. He has never done anything like that before; but, then, I have never before met a man who meant as much to me as you do.'

'Have there been many other men, Caroline?'

She did not turn her head away, or avert her eyes. 'No man

has ever possessed me as you have, Liam. You take me into another world. I probably should not tell you, but I am not good at hiding my feelings for you. I am sure Eugene knows . . . and your mother guessed. No doubt Richard did, too, and became jealous of you.'

Liam gave a disbelieving laugh. 'Sir Richard Dudley jealous of me – a fisherman?'

'Yes, Liam. You have something he has never had – and cannot buy. My love.'

'Yet he has something I want more than anything in the world – but can never have. You for a wife.'

'Liam.' She came to him and he held her close.

'Tonight we will forget the rest of the world,' he said fiercely. 'Sir Richard, Eugene Brennan – and discretion. We will enjoy being together in a place where we are not known and where no one cares who we are or what we do.'

'Yes, let's do that, Liam . . . please.' She snuggled against him happily.

'But first I think we should hurry back to the inn. The sun has gone and, unless I am mistaken, there is rain in the air.'

They reached the inn, breathless, as the skies opened and rain drenched the darkened streets of Rugby. Laughing at their own undignified flight from the rain, they made their way upstairs and along the deep-shadowed corridor to Caroline's room. Closing the door behind him, Liam stood with his back to it. As Caroline turned, he reached out for her, not trusting himself to speak.

When the dawn cast indistinct shadows into the room, Liam still lay with his arms about her. Not until there was continuous noise and bustle from the inn kitchen and the rattle of harness and the early-morning blowing of horses in the yard did he leave and go to his own room to prepare for the coming day's journey.

That morning a loud and talkative passenger who introduced himself to one and all as Jacob Burke joined the coach. He was, he told Liam, a salesman, travelling to Ireland to discuss with the government the supply of alternative foodstuffs to prevent a recurrence of the 'shortages' of the last year.

'They've grown too dependent upon the potato, y'know,' he declared in a strong North Country accent. 'Get them used to eating greens and bread and things like that and they'll be much better off. Before you know it they'll find they quite enjoy other food. Can't be good for 'em, all those potatoes.'

When Liam asked quietly where the Irish cottier was going to find the money for alternative foods, the salesman declared airily, 'Oh, they'll find the money readily enough when they have to. Folks do in England, y'know. The first thing they think of when you try to sell them something is "I can't afford it". But then you sit down and work out the cost for them. Show them how by cutting down on one thing they can afford something else. That's what selling is all about. Educating the people to do what's best for them and taking no notice of what they say in the first place. I don't suppose the Irish are any different from the rest of us. They just need educating, that's all.'

Liam wondered how the salesman would set about educating a family with no income, but he said nothing. Instead, he pretended to sleep, very aware that Caroline was sitting beside him, each bump and pot-hole in the road jolting her body against his. He thought pleasurably about the two nights they would spend at inns before reaching Holyhead and wished they could have taken an even longer route. He felt an overwhelming childish urge to hold her hand, but when he opened his eyes to see if the gesture would be noticed he saw Jacob Burke watching Caroline between half-closed eyelids.

That evening, with the coachman heralding their approach well in advance with blasts from his horn, they stopped at an inn close to Shrewsbury. A short while after they had disembarked a post-rider on a well-lathered horse clattered into the inn yard to change horses and bring news of Sir Robert Peel's defeat in Parliament. The news was shouted from yard to inn, and Liam ran from his own room to tell Caroline. They hugged each other in delight. In common with most other Irish men and women of the day, they held Sir Robert Peel responsible for most of their troubles. Under a Whig government they felt sure things would rapidly improve.

An hour later, Liam and Caroline went down to dinner and found the busy dining-room still buzzing with the news. Shrewsbury was at the centre of a rich farming area, and Peel's action in removing the protection of the Corn Law had caused bitter resentment here. The farming community expected the Whigs to re-impose import restrictions on corn. They, like the

Irish, had high hopes of the new government – hopes that would remain unrealised for six years while Lord John Russell led his party along a path that would all but destroy Ireland.

Liam thought of returning to London to be on hand if Eugene Brennan needed him, but Caroline persuaded him that he should continue his journey. It would be a week or two before the Whigs could form a working government, and Liam ought to be in Ireland settling his affairs and preparing for the by-election that would take him into Parliament.

When they finished their meal they decided to take a walk to sample the delights of the local countryside. It was a warm evening, but the low dark clouds threatened a shower, and Liam went to Lady Caroline's room for her cloak, leaving her waiting for him in the dining-room.

He was longer than he intended to be, having encountered a talkative chambermaid in the room. When he re-entered the dining-room he was surprised to see another man seated at the table facing Caroline. His back was toward the door, and not until Liam drew nearer did he realise it was the traveller from the coach. One look at Caroline was enough for Liam to see that she was not enjoying Jacob Burke's company. As he reached the table the reason became apparent. The salesman was drunk.

The man's arm was waving to emphasise some drunken point of view, and a glass he had brought with him went crashing to the floor.

'I'm sorry I have been so long,' said Liam, ignoring the salesman. 'Shall we go?'

As Caroline rose from her chair, Jacob Burke clumsily lurched to his feet in front of Liam.

'Who are you? You go and find your own woman. I saw this one first.'

'I think the best thing you could do is to go and lie down,' said Liam firmly. 'Carry on drinking and you'll land yourself in trouble before the night is over.'

'I'll go and lie down when I like – and with who I like,' said Jacob Burke stupidly. 'And I've got first claim on this lady.'

As Jacob Burke looked toward Caroline, Liam signalled for her to walk around the table to put herself behind him. As she turned, the drunken man leaned across and gripped her arm, sending condiments and sauces scattering in all directions.

Liam immediately took a hold on Jacob Burke's collar and heaved him backward, breaking his hold on Caroline's arm. But Jacob Burke was a heavily built man who had been involved in brawls before. Twisting in Liam's grip, he straightened up with fists flailing. One of them grazed the side of Liam's face, but before Jacob Burke could follow up his advantage Liam brought his fist up in a short uppercut that landed flush on the heavier man's chin. Jacob Burke was raised to his toes for a brief second before collapsing on the floor.

Short as the fight had been, it set diners at nearby tables scurrying hastily to safety, and one elderly woman was screaming hysterically when the landlord rushed in, closely followed by a big leather-aproned cellarman.

They advanced upon Liam menacingly until one of the customers called, ''Tis all right now, Tom. The man on the floor was being a nuisance to the lady. This gentleman settled his hash for him.'

'Is that what happened?' The landlord seemed reluctant to accept the explanation and looked accusingly at Liam.

'Yes, I returned to the table to find this man pestering Lady Caroline. When we made to go he tried to stop her. I would say you had allowed him to drink one too many, landlord.'

The landlord's attitude had changed immediately Liam mentioned Lady Caroline and it was to her he now spoke.

'Begging your pardon, m'lady, but you'll be Lady Dudley?'

Caroline nodded.

'Ah! I have a letter for you, m'lady. It was brought here by the post-rider to catch you before you completed your journey. I'll fetch it for you directly.' Turning to his potman, he said, 'Sam, drag this drunkard out of here. I'm sorry you've been troubled, m'lady. And I'm obliged to you, sir.' The landlord raised a hand in salute to Liam.

As the potman dragged the unconscious salesman past them, he added, 'When he comes to I'll inform him who it was he insulted and then I'll pitch him out on the street.'

'He is travelling on the coach with us,' said Liam. 'It could be embarrassing tomorrow. . . .'

'Don't you worry yourself, sir. I'll see the coachman about that. You won't have him with you tomorrow, and if he makes a nuisance of himself again he'll be lucky if he gets a place on a coach this week. Now I'll fetch your letter, m'lady.'

Caroline waited until he brought the letter to her and then told Liam that she no longer felt like taking a walk. She was concerned with the slight graze the salesman's knuckles had left on the side of Liam's face and insisted on taking Liam up to her room and washing away the blood.

When she was satisfied, she took Liam's face between her hands and kissed him gently.

'You are a reckless fool, Liam. Don't you realise the scandal it would cause if details of this evening's incident ever became known? The newspapers would pay handsomely for such information. Can you imagine the headlines? "Prospective MP in brawl over married mistress." My God, Liam, it is as well this happened here and not in London.'

'Are you telling me I should have done nothing? That I should have allowed that drunken oaf to insult and manhandle you?'

'No, my darling.' Caroline hugged him to her. She had hurt his feelings. He was a little boy who had washed his face by himself for the first time only to be scolded for using too much soap. 'It was very exciting to have a man willing to fight for me. It has never happened before. I am only saying that as an MP you will have to learn to use words instead of your fists.'

Even as she said it, Caroline remembered something she had said to Norah McCabe about her elder son. "He is an Irishman; trouble is his heritage." She feared that statement might always be true for Liam. He had an honest directness and lack of guile that would always bring him into a headlong clash with trouble that some other men might walk round.

'I'll learn to use words when I have to,' said Liam. 'And, talking of words, who would be sending you a letter? I thought no one knew you were returning home along this route,'

'I told only a close friend. It must be from her. She is probably giving me the news of Peel's defeat. London will be talking of nothing else.'

But the letter was not about the defeat of the Tory Prime Minister. Caroline broke open the sealed envelope as she was talking to Liam and now, as she read, her expression became one of consternation.

Looking up from the letter, she said, 'It is about Richard. Peel dismissed him from his Treasury post shortly before his government's defeat. He has been transferred to the staff of the Commissariat in Dublin.'

Liam and Caroline looked at each other in dismay. This was a catastrophe. In times of famine the Commissariat was responsible for the distribution of food supplies to the starving population – and Sir Richard Dudley had nothing but contempt for the Irish people. He would hardly go to great lengths to save them from starvation.

'This is a final stroke of genius on the part of Peel,' said Liam unreasonably. 'Had he wanted to take his revenge on Ireland for bringing his government down he could have made no finer appointment.'

'We can only pray there will be no famine this year,' agreed Caroline.

'Perhaps the new Whig government will offer him another post.'

'I doubt that. Richard has always been Peel's man. He would have lost his Treasury post as soon as the Whigs took office, anyway. The Commissariat in Ireland is enough of a demotion for the Whigs to allow him to stay there.'

She looked at Liam unhappily. News of Sir Richard had reminded them of what they would soon be returning to face, in Ireland.

For that one night, at least, the problems awaiting them in the future affected them less than the summer storm rumbling noisily along the Welsh border country. As it turned out, the storm was on their side. Moving westward to the Irish Sea it raged for four more days, making a passage to Dublin impossible. After a night spent in a tiny inn high in the Welsh hills, they had another three nights together in Holyhead, waiting for the weather to break.

On the last night, Liam correctly read the weather signs and told Caroline that they would be able to make the crossing the next day.

The thought of returning to lead their own separate lives once more cast a pall of gloom over this last night together. Not until the grey pre-dawn was upon the hills did their love break through the misery surrounding them. Then Caroline came to Liam with a fierce desperation that left him gasping and her sobbing.

'Liam ... Liam, promise me something.'

At this moment he would have promised her anything and he told her so.

'Liam, whatever happens, don't stop seeing me, or loving me. I will be there whenever you want me and I will come to you anywhere. You can love me in a field if there is nowhere else, but never stop wanting me, Liam. Never . . . never . . . never. . . .'

Chapter Thirty-Two

Kathie was pregnant. She had tried to ignore the symptoms for some time, but now she was certain. Yet she managed to keep her secret from Dermot in spite of constant nausea and fierce bouts of sickness. Her husband had enough problems without having fatherhood thrust upon him.

Men were drifting away from Ireland's great new army in ever increasing numbers, disillusioned with the life they were leading and with Dermot's leadership. There had been a couple of indecisive skirmishes with the militia, but then Dermot had struck at a small outlying military post. Too late he discovered it was defended by regular troops. It was a costly mistake, and the Irishmen returned to the mountains having suffered a heavy defeat.

Now only about thirty men remained with him, and Dermot knew that when it was time to lift the new potato crop he would be left with only the Kilmar fishermen.

Yet, even with such reduced numbers, finding enough food was becoming increasingly difficult. They had lost the goodwill of the upland farmers by constant raids on their crops, and there were few animals left to hunt about the camp. The outlaws were forced to forage much farther afield – and often the men did not return from such forays.

The news of Peel's fall from power had reached those who remained and filled them with a sense of vague excitement. For weeks they waited for something to happen. What that 'something' would be, nobody knew, but they did not doubt it would be to their advantage.

For a while men who had been living only for the day began to talk openly of the future. They believed a Whig government would prove more sympathetic to their cause than the Tories. They anticipated more freedom for Ireland to manage her own affairs. A few even spoke of a general amnesty for the outlaws of the Wicklow mountains.

Dermot did not share their optimism. Aware of his waning authority within the group, he growled at the men and snapped irritably at Kathie. Pregnant as she was, she tried to make allowances for his moods, but it was becoming increasingly difficult. Dermot no longer shared his thoughts with her. He left her alone for long periods, and sometimes she saw him watching her as she worked about the camp. The looks made her feel uncomfortable without knowing the reason why.

Then, early one morning, when Kathie thought Dermot and the others in the camp were still asleep, she made her way out of the camp to the stream that ran nearby and there she was violently sick. This morning was worse than usual and the retching left her kneeling, moaning and gasping, by the water's edge. When a shadow fell across the water in front of her. Kathie looked up in alarm and saw Dermot standing over her.

'You are pregnant?' It was more of an accusation than a question.

Kathie nodded unhappily. She would have preferred to give him the news at a time and place of her choosing. Now, when she hardly possessed the strength to rise to her feet, was not the right occasion.

'How long have you known?'

'Scarcely more than a week.'

'Are you sure you haven't known for some months?'

Kathie looked up at him, not understanding.

'How could it be? We've only been married a couple of months—'

She stopped. The expression she had seen on his face so often of late was there now.

'I think you already knew about the baby when you married me. Am I right?'

The blood drained from Kathie's already pale face and her dark eyes widened. 'What are you saying, Dermot? Do you believe—?'

He ignored her anguish. 'Whose child is it?'

'It is yours, Dermot.'

She tried to drive away all thoughts of the soldiers who had taken her by force, but suddenly the sheer horror of that night returned to her and for a few seconds she trembled uncontrollably.

'Is it Liam's child?'

The trembling suddenly ceased and colour rushed back into

Kathie's face. She looked at her husband in disbelief. 'You believe I would marry you when I was carrying your own brother's child?'

'I'm not a fool, Kathie. I knew you never loved me when you married me. It has always been Liam for you, from the first time you saw him on Kilmar quay. Ever since the night you came to me and told me you would marry me, I have wondered why. I have been waiting for you to tell me you were carrying a baby. I knew it would have to be that.'

Kathie was on the verge of telling Dermot of her rape by the soldiers, but she held back. Dermot would not believe her; he would think she was saying it to protect Liam.

'Why did you marry me, Dermot?'

'Because I love you.'

'You love me – yet you think this of me?'

When Dermot made no answer, Kathie said, 'Would you believe me if I swore before God that Liam and I have never been lovers?'

'No!' Dermot stood over her, his anger held tightly in clenched fists. 'I saw the way you looked at him when he last came to the camp. It sickened me.'

'Dermot, I am carrying a child and it will be your child. It will be a son, Dermot McCabe. Will you acknowledge it as your own?'

'No, by God, I'll not. I've given it my name so it won't grow up being called the Donaghue bastard. I'll give it nothing else.'

Dermot choked on his words and turned away to stumble blindly through the undergrowth toward the camp.

'Dermot . . . Dermot, please!'

He did not come back to her. Did not even turn.

The other outlaws realised that Dermot and Kathie had quarrelled and they made no comment when she did not appear at breakfast-time. They maintained their silence when she did not cook a noonday meal for them, but when she was still missing in the late evening the Kilmar men could keep silent no longer. By this time Dermot, too, was alarmed. Admitting there had been words between them, he set out with the others to scour the forest for his missing wife. They searched until the darkness drove them back to the camp, every man hoping that some of the others might have found her. But Kathie had gone.

Liam was out fishing with the two young men who would work the boat in his absence when Tommy Donaghue came down from the hill to break the news to Norah McCabe that Kathie had returned to Kilmar.

'Why, that's wonderful news,' exclaimed Norah in delight. Untying her heavy salting-apron, she said, 'I'll away up the hill to see her right away. Does she look well? I hope she's home to stay now and that her husband will soon be following her.'

'I wouldn't be knowing about that,' confessed Tommy Donaghue. 'She's said little to me. I would be obliged if you would speak to her, Norah. There's a strangeness in her that I don't understand. I ask her something but I'm not sure she is hearing me. Then she looks at me, yet through me, as though I am not there. Go up the hill to her, Norah. She may be better for you.'

When Norah McCabe entered the cabin on the hill and saw her daughter-in-law she was shocked beyond belief. Kathie was wild-eyed and tangled-haired, her dress tattered and dirty. She returned the older woman's kiss without warmth and there was a stiffness in her embrace far removed from the loving girl who had left Kilmar to go to the mountains and tend Norah McCabe's younger son. The change alarmed her.

'What is the matter, Kathie? Will Dermot be coming home soon – or has something happened to him? Is that why you are here?'

'Dermot is well.' Kathie spoke like a woman unused to talking. 'He has his own things to do in the mountains, but he is all right.'

The sudden tight fear left Norah McCabe. But there was undoubtedly something wrong. Kathie was as taut as one of her father's fiddle strings. Norah McCabe began to talk of other things, unimportant happenings in the village.

Gradually, Kathie relaxed, until quite suddenly, as though she had at that moment made up her mind, she said, 'I've come back to Kilmar because I'm having a baby.'

Norah McCabe's natural urge was to hug her son's wife, to congratulate Kathie and say how delighted she was, but she held back. Kathie had thrown the news out almost as a challenge. Something was wrong, but only Kathie knew what it was, and she would say nothing until the time was right.

'That is wonderful news, Kathie. How did Dermot take it when you told him?'

'He wasn't pleased – but he will be when I present him with a son who looks just like him.'

'Of course he'll be pleased – and I'm sure he will be just as happy if it is a daughter. By then I hope he will be out of those mountains and back here, where he belongs.'

Norah McCabe repeated her words to Liam when he returned that evening. He nodded his head in agreement, but said nothing. Too much had happened this summer to hold out any hope of Dermot's return. Every killing, every robbery and unsolved theft within fifty miles of the Wicklow mountains had been blamed upon Dermot and his diminishing army. The time was coming when none of the band would dare set foot outside the mountains.

'I'll go up to see Kathie before it gets too dark,' he said, finishing his meal. 'I won't stay long; I expect she's tired.'

Liam wondered what had happened to force Kathie from the mountains this early in her pregnancy. Although no mention had been made of her name on any 'wanted' posters, she had become more notorious than any of the other outlaws. There was not an Irishman who had not heard of the woman who supposedly led the outlaw band in the Wicklow mountains, killing soldiers and militiamen on sight. It was rumoured that she had personally killed at least a hundred men. Such was the stuff of Irish legend.

Passing the ale-house, Liam could hear Tommy Donaghue's fiddle leading the boisterous singing. He was celebrating his daughter's return in the only way he knew.

The Donaghue cabin was in darkness and, believing that Kathie might be sleeping, he pushed the door open quietly. He could not see her immediately and began closing the door again, thinking to call again the next day. Then Kathie's voice called, 'Come in, Liam. I've been expecting you.'

Pushing the door open wide, Liam saw her slumped in a chair beside the small window.

'Why are you sitting here alone in the dark? What sort of a

homecoming is this? Here, let me put a light to these candles—'

'No, Liam!'

Her cry stopped him as he was reaching down a candle from the shelf by the door.

'There's still enough light from outside. Leave it for now.'

The fact that her face was no more than a pale smudge in the room belied her words, but Liam pulled up a stool from the table and sat down to face her in the near-darkness.

'I've heard about the baby. Congratulations!'

'It has given me no reason for celebration so far. It caused a quarrel between me and Dermot; that's why I left the mountains.'

'Quarrels are soon forgotten, but you'll be better off having a baby here in the village with women to look after you. We'll get a message to Dermot and everything will be all right between you soon enough, you'll see.'

'It is far more serious than that, Liam. Dermot thinks you are the father of the child I am carrying.'

The shock of her words brought Liam to his feet.

'He thinks what . . . ? Holy Mother! You didn't leave him before you'd put that right? He doesn't still believe it?'

Liam's concern was for his brother. Dermot was a reckless man, inclined to do things without sufficient thought. With such an evil belief tormenting his mind he was likely to do something stupid enough to get himself killed.

'I told him he was the father of the baby. I could not do more. He said many things to me that would have been better left unsaid, Liam.'

'Kathie, does Dermot know what the soldiers did to you?'

There was a long silence in the cabin broken only by Kathie's laboured breathing as she fought to regain control of herself.

'How did you find out?'

'From Jeremy. He learned that the soldiers had raped a girl. From what was said he realised it must have been you. Does Dermot know?'

'No. I couldn't tell him. I couldn't tell anyone.'

The next question hung between them, unspoken. Then Kathie said, 'The baby *is* Dermot's, Liam.' Her voice trembled as she added, 'If I thought otherwise, I would kill myself. Who else knows what the soldiers did to me?'

'Only Nathan. He will say nothing.'

Kathie nodded, grateful for the darkness that hid the tears flowing silently down her face.

'When you came to the forest you asked me what had happened to change me, Liam. Now you know.'

'But you married Dermot without telling him?'

'I didn't need to tell him, Liam. You can see that, surely? There was never anything between us until . . . until after that night with the soldiers. I went to Dermot and he took me as I was. I couldn't have told him about . . . about anything. Had you been there it might have been different. I think I would have been able to say something to you. I wish you had been there, Liam.'

Her voice broke and a sob racked her body.

'The soldiers should have killed me afterwards, Liam. At the time I wished to God they had.'

In the darkness Liam dropped to his knees before her and held her to him.

'Hush, Kathie. Don't think about it any more. It's all over and done with now.'

'If only it was.' Kathie clung to him. 'I killed one of them, Liam. I saw his face on the mountain after the soldiers attacked us. He'd been wounded, but he pushed himself up to look at me and I recognised him. I shot him, Liam. As he looked at me, I shot him.'

She shuddered, and Liam gripped her more tightly.

'I see that face often, Liam. I have nightmares. I wake up screaming at him to go away and leave me alone. I'm frightened, Liam. Frightened of nights . . . of having the baby . . . of what is to come.'

Kathie took Liam's hand and held it to her face.

'Help me, Liam. Please help me.'

Chapter Thirty-Three

Eugene Brennan returned to Kilmar in August full of energy and enthusiasm. A by-election had been called in County Kerry in south-west Ireland, one of the poorest parts of the land, and Liam's name had been put forward as a candidate. It was, Eugene assured Liam, a fishing area and in Liam the people would see a man able to recognise many of their problems.

'When is this election to be?' asked Liam. He was flabbergasted when Eugene Brennan informed him that voting day was only a week ahead. Before then Liam would have to go to Kerry, carry out his campaigning and – hopefully – be elected. It was a daunting thought, but Eugene Brennan brushed the problems aside in a characteristic manner.

'The All-Ireland Association is particularly strong there,' he assured Liam. 'They will be doing most of your campaigning for you and telling the voters whom they should elect. All you need do is show your face here and there and let the people have a look at you. Then in a week's time you'll go round thanking them all before you leave to take your place in the House of Commons.'

The day passed in a fever of activity. Norah McCabe was going to use Liam's departure as an excuse to persuade Kathie to come to live in the McCabe house, to 'keep her company'. Kathie was better than she had been when she first returned to Kilmar, but it would be a very long time before she was able to lay the ghosts that haunted her.

On the way to County Kerry, Eugene Brennan insisted upon calling at Inch House to visit Lady Caroline. Liam had been there more than once since their return from England, but his heart still beat faster at the thought of seeing her again. He felt sure the astute old politician would see his agitation.

If he did, Eugene Brennan said nothing of it and he beamed happily when Caroline greeted him as a very dear friend.

'I am sure Liam will be a credit to you in the House,' she said when Eugene Brennan told her where he and Liam were going. 'But your need for support will not be as great now Lord John Russell is Prime Minister?'

Eugene Brennan's face lost much of its humour.

'You would think so,' he said, with much bitterness in his voice. 'Had it not been for the help of the Irish MPs, Peel would still be Prime Minister and John Russell no more than the Duke of Bedford's political brother, but now he will do nothing to help us – or anyone else. Lord John Russell is afraid of being thought controversial before he calls an election next year. We must hope he is returned with a small majority and needs the support of the Irish MPs. If he has no need of us, I fear we might as well have Peel back in office.'

'I am afraid Ireland will have need of Lord John Russell's support long before then,' said Caroline. 'Nathan tells me there are definite signs that the blight is in the potato again this year. If it is serious, the Government will have to move quickly. Another potato famine would be disastrous for the cottiers.'

'Heaven forbid it should happen,' said Eugene Brennan fervently. 'If there is another famine, Archbishop MacHale should ask the Almighty why such a devout nation as ours should also be the most accursed.'

Soon afterwards, Eugene Brennan announced he was taking a walk to look at the house being built for Lady Caroline, before he resumed his journey, but he declined her offer to accompany him.

When he had gone, Caroline came to Liam and kissed him passionately.

'It is most obliging of Eugene to leave us alone. Do you think he has accepted our situation?'

Liam shook his head. 'I am afraid not. Eugene has left us together because he expects me to tell you we must stop seeing each other now.'

'Is that what you are going to tell me, Liam?'

'No. A couple of months ago I might have been able to consider it, but not now. I could not stop seeing you even if I wanted to – and I don't.'

'I am so glad, Liam. I will be discreet, I promise you. Everything will be all right, I know it will. We will be able to meet in London. I have the address of a friend to give to you. Go to see her; she will know of rooms or even a small house that you can rent. We will be able to meet there.'

'It will be hardly worth taking accommodation. Eugene says Parliament will be rising soon until early next year. I will hardly spend any time in London.'

'Never mind. Take the name of my friend and go to see her. It will give her more time to find somewhere for you.'

'And you? Will you continue to live in your own house?'

'No, that is Richard's house. I, too, must find somewhere else – but I see Eugene returning. Is there anything I may do for you – or your mother – while you are away?'

Liam thought of all the family problems that had arisen out of Kathie's return.

'I would be obliged if you could spare Nathan to go to find my brother and tell him that Kathie has returned to Kilmar.'

'Kathie is your brother's wife?'

'Yes. She is expecting a child and returned to Kilmar after an argument with Dermot. She did not tell him she was leaving.'

'Of course Nathan may go – and I will visit Kilmar to see that all is well with her. Perhaps she might like to come here with me. I would be happy with the company.'

Liam hoped Kathie would not be wearing the dirty rags in which she had returned home when Caroline called. He had no time to think of any further considerations because at that moment Eugene Brennan returned to the room and announced that it was time they left for County Kerry.

The road to County Kerry proved to Liam and Eugene Brennan that Ireland was indeed God's accursed land. They passed through some of the finest potato country in the whole of Ireland. But, instead of lush dark-green potato haulms, they saw nothing for mile upon blighted mile but black foliage lying limp and withered upon the rain-sodden ground.

The potato disease was upon the land again, and this year it brought with it the promise of starvation and death to half of Ireland's people.

Although Liam and Eugene were not aware of the full extent of the disease, they were witnessing a catastrophe that would change for all time the Ireland they had always known. Because of the coming famine, Irish emigrants would flee to every country of the world, taking with them such a hatred of England and the English that it would survive for generations to come.

In County Kerry, the failure of the potato crop was the major talking-point at all of Liam's election meetings. Questions on what he proposed doing about it came at him from every side.

Liam could say only that he would use every means possible to make Lord Russell's government aware of the grim situation, and demand that the Prime Minister take immediate action to send food to Ireland.

It was exactly the same answer as the one given by his opponent. But Liam was a man of the people, sponsored by their own association. The other candidate was a land-owner, with a record of recent cottier evictions.

On polling day, Liam received three times as many votes as his rival and was declared to be the people's duly elected representative to Parliament.

Liam and Eugene Brennan spent a wild evening at a celebration party thrown for them in a small village at Dingle Bay. Later, in the peace of his room, Liam looked out of the window for a long time, watching the moonlight sparkle on the dark waters of the bay – and thinking.

He turned back into the room a much sobered man as realisation of the responsibility he had taken upon himself came home fully to him.

Liam carried the oil-lamp to the dressing-table mirror and looking back at him saw the serious face of a young man. A fisherman with little experience of life, unskilled in the art of politics and with only the learning he had gained at the hands of a parish priest. Yet he must now fight for the rights of the people who had elected him, and the millions of fellow-Irishmen who did not have a vote.

However insignificant his contribution might prove to be when the sum worth of his life was taken into consideration, Liam now had a part in the destiny of his people.

It was a formidable task for a twenty-eight-year-old.

Chapter Thirty-Four

Liam's initial taste of parliamentary life was as brief as he had anticipated. After receiving the congratulations of those Irish MPs who, only weeks before, had avoided him as a possible embarrassment, Liam took the oath of allegiance and Eugene Brennan led him to a seat on the crossbenches.

Lord John Russell adjourned Parliament on 28 August, but Liam found the few days before this eventful, and at times even rowdy.

The noisiest session came when, after weeks of side-stepping the issue, the diminutive Whig leader stood up and gravely announced to the House that he had received word from Ireland that the potato crop had failed for the second year in succession. This time it was feared that the failure was total.

'However,' added the Prime Minister, as the Irish MPs recovered from their stunned astonishment, 'various public works are being carried out by my government and I am quite confident we will be able to contain the problem.'

Immediately, there were cries of opposition from non-Irish MPs.

'What about the hungry Scots?'

'And the Welsh?'

'Everyone is hungry. Let the Irish look after their own.'

The Irish MPs erupted in howls of anger, and words such as 'laggard' and 'hypocrite' were hurled at Lord John Russell.

Liam found himself shouting as loudly as his fellows, but his anger was not directed solely at the Prime Minister. He was shocked at the reaction to Lord John Russell's announcement by the other members of the House of Commons. They were indignant with the minimal relief measures that had been announced because the English, Welsh and Scots were 'hungry'. Not starving to death, as were the Irish, but 'hungry'. Their attitude gave Liam his first intimation of the low regard in which his fellow-countrymen were held. An unfamiliar emotion welled up inside Liam and he found himself hating these people as he had never hated before.

Guided by Eugene Brennan, Liam tried to have the plight

of his less fortunate countrymen discussed at greater length. He had seen the results of famine at first hand and knew how much more needed to be done.

It was a bitter and frustrating experience and he was blocked at every turn. Within the House of Commons there was always 'more pressing business' for the House to deal with. Outside, Lord John Russell and his Ministers were too busy organising the new administration to give him their time.

Finally, in sheer desperation, Liam broke away from Eugene Brennan's guiding influence and sent a personal note to the Home Secretary, demanding to know what action was being taken to help the Irish cottier. To Liam's surprise, he received a reply by return, granting him an immediate interview with Charles Trevelyan, the Assistant Secretary who was Permanent Head of the Treasury Department and responsible for Irish relief measures.

It was well after normal working-hours when Liam arrived at Downing Street and was shown into the Treasury building through a small private door.

Charles Trevelyan was seated behind an enormous desk that was piled high with papers and letters and the cluttered miscellany of a very busy office. The 'in' tray overflowed with a vast number of unopened letters, mute evidence of Trevelyan's proud boast that he maintained personal control of every aspect of the current Irish 'problem'. He stubbornly refused to acknowledge that the vast complexity of the situation was too much for one man to handle.

The senior Treasury official was a much younger man than Liam had expected and, in spite of the huge volume of work before him and the enormity of his task, he was relaxed and courteous, exuding a practised air of efficiency.

Charles Trevelyan was also an ambitious man. He saw the famine in Ireland as a unique opportunity to further his career as an administrator and, he hoped, bring a peerage to his ancient Cornish family.

Firmly shaking Liam by the hand, he said, 'I am pleased to make your acquaintance, Mr McCabe. I have heard much of you. I believe you were once a fisherman.'

The administrator made the occupation sound like a prison sentence.

'I am still a fisherman, Mr Trevelyan. I am also a Member

of Parliament – an Irish Member of Parliament – and that is why I am here. We have a famine in Ireland, a very serious one, and I want to know what is being done for those people who are without food of any kind.'

As always happened when he felt very emotional about something, Liam's Irish accent thickened. In contrast, Charles Trevelyan's sonorous voice emphasised his superior education and displayed his love of the English language.

'You may rest assured that we have the matter in hand, Mr McCabe. As you must know, this is not the first occasion on which the potato crop has failed in your country. We in the Treasury have experience of many such failures. There is no immediate urgency; it will be some weeks before dependence upon the new season's crop becomes absolute.'

Liam looked at Trevelyan incredulously. 'You are talking about a famine following a normal season. Doesn't your department know that last year's crop failed, too? The cottiers have nothing to eat *today*. They can't wait until you *think* it is time to do something about them. They will starve long before then.'

'Sheer conjecture, Mr McCabe. As I have already told you, we are fully aware of Ireland's shortage of food. Exaggerating the facts will help no one.'

Trevelyan's smile was still in evidence, although he was furious with this fisherman who had the temerity to come to his office to question his ability and judgement.

But Trevelyan's anger was as nothing compared to Liam's own.

'I don't think you have any idea of the seriousness of the potato failure. All your fine words will not fill a single belly. I want to know – I *demand* to know – what is being done about feeding the cottiers.'

'I will do whatever I feel is necessary – when the time comes. I am being kept fully informed of the situation by Commissariat officers who are on the spot.'

'During my tours of cottier settlements I have never met with one of your Commissariat officers. I think they must sit in warm and comfortable offices thinking up new excuses for doing nothing. I suggest you travel to Ireland and assess the situation for yourself, Mr Trevelyan. It cannot fail to shock you, as it shocked me. The tragedies I have witnessed during this last year will haunt me for all the days of my life – and this during only a partial potato failure. This year even Lord John Russell admits there is a *total* crop failure. That is all the information needed, Mr Trevelyan. You should be acting now to avoid total disaster. Give the order for your inspectors to throw open the Commissariat depots and issue grain to the cottiers.'

Had Liam only known, he had touched upon the subject that lay at the root of Trevelyan's apparent unwillingness to issue food to the cottiers. There was no grain in the Commissariat depots.

Alarmed at the amount of money spent by the previous government on Irish famine relief, Trevelyan had repeatedly turned down urgent requests by the Commissariat inspectors for their depots to be restocked before the winter. Now every one of them was as empty as Mother Hubbard's cupboard. Finally, Charles Trevelyan had been forced to admit to himself that he had been guilty of a grave error of judgement and he had made desperate overtures to mercantile houses and corn factors for maize grain, but he had acted too late. There was a world shortage. Cargoes arriving in England were being sold at a price far beyond anything contemplated by the niggardly keeper of the Treasury's purse.

'I have no intention of opening the Commissariat depots; it should prove unnecessary. Ireland is producing ample grain to feed its own people.'

'All Ireland's grain will leave the country as fast as it is harvested.'

Trevelyan shrugged and spread his hands in feigned exasperation. 'If the Irish will not look after their own, what can you expect me to do, Mr McCabe?'

'The Irish are your own, too,' Liam retorted. 'They were made so by the Act of Union. Give us back a government of our own and we will not have to come to England begging for the right to live. We would throw out those English landlords who, in the name of profit, call for English troops to guard their corn on the way to the ships, to prevent it from being stolen by starving cottiers.'

'I suggest you save your political speeches for the House of Commons, Mr McCabe,' Charles Trevelyan said angrily. 'I am an administrator, not a politician. I repeat, I will take whatever measures I deem necessary – when the time arrives.'

'People will die feeding on your promises, Trevelyan. They

have nothing else. If you have not yet taken relief measures, then it is already too late.'

Liam rose to his feet and glared angrily at the Assistant Secretary for some moments. Then his shoulders sagged and much of his anger left him.

'I did not come here to quarrel with you, Mr Trevelyan, but to try to persuade you to help people who are dying of starvation. They are not mere figures on a report. Every one of them is made of flesh and blood. They hate and they love, laugh and cry – just like you and I. They enjoy eating and drinking, and they feel hunger. By God, but they feel hunger. For a year they have had little else to go to bed with. All I am asking is that you spend money on food to keep them alive until they are able to feed themselves once again. Do that, Mr Trevelyan, and a prayer will go up for you from every church in Ireland.'

Charles Trevelyan gave Liam a benign smile. 'I appreciate the reason for your concern, Mr McCabe. Indeed, it does you great credit. Not all elected Members of Parliament are as concerned about their constituents as yourself.'

Rising, Trevelyan took a bottle of Port wine from a cupboard. 'Will you have a drink with me?'

When Liam declined, Charles Trevelyan poured a careful half-glass and set it upon the desk before seating himself once more.

'I am not inhuman, Mr McCabe. My department has a certain unenviable reputation, but I can assure you that the Treasury is staffed by ordinary caring people.'

'I am aware of that. I am also aware that in common with other humans, you are – "fallible" is a word I remember from my schooling days. You can make an error of judgement. I sincerely believe you will make the biggest error of your life if you do not send help to Ireland immediately.'

'You will be pleased to know that something has already been done,' Charles Trevelyan beamed. 'Only yesterday I gave instructions for a fifty-thousand-pound loan to be made available to the Public Works Department for various approved schemes. Naturally, I shall expect your own Irish landlords to be equally generous. . . .'

The Assistant Secretary's benevolent smile disappeared and his voice faltered as he saw the disbelief on Liam's face.

'You have made available *fifty thousand pounds* to save a nation from starving to death? *Fifty thousand pounds?*'

The words came out in a whisper. 'I have been reading the proud parliamentary record of the fight to abolish slavery. I read that the sum of twenty million pounds was granted to free the negro slaves of the West Indies. Are the Irish so much less than negro slaves, to England?'

Before Trevelyan could reply, Liam said, 'I am sorry I have wasted your time, Mr Trevelyan – and you mine. My place is not here among men who have such little understanding for my people. I must go to Ireland where I can do something useful to help them. If it means going outside the law – your law – to do it, then so be it. Your ways are not our ways.'

'Come now, Mr McCabe. There is no need for such melodrama. I have already pledged my support for your cause.'

Charles Trevelyan was alarmed at Liam's comparison of the Irish problem with the aid given to the West Indies. If he were to repeat his words often enough, someone in the Government might have a twinge of conscience and suggest that a much greater sum of money be allocated to Irish famine relief. Charles Trevelyan knew there were few honours to be won by a Treasury administrator who spent the country's money in Ireland.

'When you return to your country contact the new Commissariat Inspector for Western Ireland. I am sure you will find him most helpful.'

Liam was at the door before the full impact of Charles Trevelyan's words struck him.

'This new Commissariat Inspector. Who is he?'

'Sir Richard Dudley. Do you know him?'

'I know him. May God save Ireland. She will have no help from the Commissariat.'

Chapter Thirty-Five

As Liam had predicted, there was to be no period of preparation for Ireland's latest disaster. The stranglehold of hunger was already upon the land, and the cottiers fought a desperate battle for survival.

For a while they ate anything that grew in the fields and hedgerows – Nettles, acorns, blackberries, bitter wild damson, and finally grass. Boiled in water until it was reduced to a stringy unpalatable mass, it was fed to protesting and gagging children when their mothers had nothing else to offer them.

But even such a diverse bill of fare as this was not inexhaustible in the cold and wet autumn of 1846, and while Liam was on a storm-tossed ferry boat on the Irish Sea the men from his new constituency were marching upon Castlemaine harbour, where a grain-ship was being loaded.

News of the advancing mob reached the captain of the vessel and he hastily slipped the ship's moorings and headed out into Dingle Bay, leaving behind on the jetty many laden wagons. Before they could be hauled away and hidden from view, the crowd was upon them. By now it numbered five hundred strong and the cottier men surrounded the luckless wagoners, demanding grain for themselves and the families they had left behind. They were not violent, appealing rather to the generosity of the wagoners.

But then the resident magistrate appeared on the scene, having given a fast horseman time to reach the Army in nearby Tralee.

The magistrate called upon the hungry cottiers to be silent. When he was sure he had their full attention he read out the Riot Act to them, demanding that they disperse, 'in the name of the Queen'.

Far from dispersing, the cottiers became angry that no one would heed their plea for food. They resumed their demands on the wagoners, this time accompanying them with threats. One wagoner, bolder than his fellows, used his whip on a man who climbed on to the shaft of his wagon, knocking him to the ground. Immediately, the mob erupted in fierce anger. The wagon belonging to the man who had wielded the whip was turned on its side and two others with it. The excited cottiers began scooping up corn to take home with them, carrying it in anything that would hold grain, most men tightening their belts and stuffing it inside their shirts, ignoring the sharp seeds that scratched a way down to freedom inside their tight trouser-legs.

Then, at the height of this late and illegal harvest, a full company of the 1st Dragoon Guards galloped into Castlemaine, their gold-plumed helmets reflecting the sun. At an order from their commanding officer, the horsemen halted to form a long line before advancing slowly toward the edge of the crowd of cottiers.

Some of the younger cottiers, over-confident after their easy victory over the unarmed wagoners, began stoning the Dragoons with cobbles ripped up from the jetty. Immediately, the horse guards retreated, followed by the jeers and derisive cries of the rioting cottiers.

But the soldiers did not move far away. When they were out of range of the heavy stones that bounced about the feet of their horses they were ordered to draw and load their carbines.

The sight of the weapons had an instant sobering effect on the majority of the cottiers. The stone-throwing ceased and an unnatural silence fell upon the five hundred or so men crowded about the overturned wagons.

The Dragoons officer called out another order, and with their carbines carried before them the long line of soldiers advanced toward the crowd.

The cottiers fell back, trying to keep a respectable distance between themselves and the silent menacing horse guards.

The slow-moving Dragoons would have driven the cottiers from the quay without incident had not one of the foolhardy young cottiers suddenly run from the crowd with a heavy rounded stone in his hand.

He ran to within fifteen paces of the leading horseman and, drawing back his arm, threw the stone with unusual skill. The Dragoons officer flung up an arm to protect his face but he was too late. The stone glanced off the peak of his helmet and struck him on the cheekbone. Swaying in his saddle, the officer barked out an order and the Dragoons brought the carbines to their shoulders and fired independently.

The stone-throwing cottier, running toward the shelter of the crowd, executed a grotesque flailing somersault and was dead before he hit the ground. But he did not die alone. Five other cottier men slumped to the ground about him as the suddenly terrified crowd broke and ran in every direction, half a dozen of them staggering or limping with a lead ball from a trooper's carbine lodged in their bodies.

The Dragoon Guards reloaded immediately after their first volley, but they had no need to fire again. The brief riot was over and their officer's broken cheekbone the only injury suffered by the soldiers.

But their rout at the hands of the soldiers had done nothing to ease the hunger of the cottiers. The following day they returned to Castlemaine harbour, hoping for a greater degree of success. They found the Army waiting for them. Now there was a full squadron of Dragoon Guards, drawn up behind two companies of the 47th Infantry, marched in overnight from Tralee.

The sight of more than five hundred armed and disciplined men guarding the loading-quay would have unnerved braver men than the hungry and undernourished cottiers. Daring to do no more than mutter their frustration, they withdrew to the edge of the town to jeer and shout angrily as heavily guarded wagons were brought in from the surrounding countryside loaded with corn for export to England.

There was little else for the cottiers to do and so they returned to Castlemaine day after day. Their numbers quickly grew to more than two thousand as other cottiers and their families hopefully followed the laden wagons for miles along the bumpy country lanes. They pounced on grain that fell to the ground through cracks in the wood planking – or was surreptitiously thrown down for them by a sympathetic wagoner carting the corn for his landlord.

This was the scene that greeted Liam when he rode into Castlemaine a few days later. He first went to speak to the Infantry Colonel who had been sent to take charge of the Army in Castlemaine. Liam found the senior officer courteous and understanding of the cottiers' problems. But he had been sent to the town with orders to provide protection for the men loading grain and he intended carrying out those orders. If the cottiers attempted to interfere with the wagoners, or the ship, his men would fire on them – be they men, women or children.

When Liam pleaded to be allowed to talk to the wagoners in an attempt to persuade them to turn some of their loads over to the cottiers, the Colonel replied, 'I suggest you talk to the Commissariat Inspector first. He has been here for two days and may already have made an arrangement along the lines you suggest.'

'The Commissariat Inspector is, of course, Sir Richard Dudley?'

'Yes. You know him? Then perhaps he will be able to help you. You will find him lodging at the house of the resident magistrate.'

Liam nodded his acknowledgement of the information and turned away, all hope sinking within him. He knew he would have to speak to the baronet before the day was over but, putting the moment off, he went instead to talk to the cottiers waiting outside the town.

A few of the men recognised him from his brief election tour and within minutes he was surrounded by dozens of shouting, gesticulating cottiers, each eager to put his own point of view.

When Liam eventually managed to silence them, he said, 'All this talk is doing no more good than trying to stare out the soldiers in the town. They will load the grain and you will only grow hungrier. How desperately do you need the food?'

It was the wrong question to put to them; everyone wanted to tell him the answer.

This time, when he quietened the shouts to a grumbling angry murmur he picked upon a ragged and insignificant little man.

'Do you have a family?'

'I do that, sir. A wife and eight children – and not a lumper potato or a handful of meal between the lot of them for four days.'

'How far is your home?'

'Just the other side of that hill, sir.' He pointed to a low swelling on the ground less than a mile away.

'Take me there and let me see them for myself.'

Liam and the little man set off, followed by most of the two-thousand-strong crowd. It became a less than grand tour of inspection of cottier homes and families. As Liam came to a junction in the worn and winding footpath, someone would step forward and insist that he deviate from his route and visit yet another cottier hovel.

In every one of them Liam saw the same pathetic scenes he had witnessed the previous year around Kilmar.

When he had seen enough, he turned his steps toward Castlemaine once again. This time he was filled with a grim determination. The cottiers needed food – and food they would have.

He arrived at the home of the resident magistrate to find Sir Richard Dudley at dinner with his host. There was a third person at the table, and Liam was taken aback to see Jacob Burke, the salesman he had knocked to the ground in the Shrewsbury inn!

But Liam's surprise turned to anger when he saw the rich fare on the table before them. There was food such as few cottiers had ever seen, or ever would see. They would die of hunger, unaware that such food as this existed.

When the magistrate stood up, dabbing his mouth with a starched napkin and making hasty introductions, Liam cut him short.

'I have already met your guests,' he said, inclining his head briefly in Sir Richard Dudley's direction and ignoring Jacob Burke. 'I am here about the cottiers.'

'Ah yes!' The magistrate laid the napkin on the table and pushed his still-laden plate from him. 'A most unfortunate incident, but we will have no more trouble from them. I called in the Army and they now have everything under control. Another day or two and the grain-ship will sail. Then the cottiers will return to their homes.'

'I am not interested in how you maintain law and order,' retorted Liam. 'I want to know what arrangements have been made to feed the cottiers and their families?'

'That is hardly my responsibility . . . ,' began the magistrate. but Liam ignored him and addressed the baronet.

'You are the Commissariat Inspector, Sir Richard. Have you come to Castlemaine to open a depot? How soon can we expect it to be supplying the cottiers?'

'I am here to do no such thing,' declared Sir Richard Dudley indignantly. 'I am on a tour of the west coast of Ireland to assess the situation for myself – and I will do nothing while a mob of good-for-nothing peasants terrorises the countryside.

Give in to them and they will rise throughout the length and breadth of the country.'

'Ignore them and they certainly will,' replied Liam. 'These men and their families are starving. They need food desperately.'

'Then they must *buy* grain,' said the baronet airily. 'That is what the people of England are having to do.'

'What do you suggest they use for money?' asked Liam. 'Cottiers give their landlords work in return for a plot of land in which to grow their potatoes. They don't earn money – and, if they did, a week's wages would not buy enough corn to feed a man's family for one day. Most of them know that from harsh experience; they have pledged their decent clothes, and even their bedding, to buy food.'

'Be that as it may, it is not the Commissariat's intention to open a depot in Castlemaine – or anywhere else in this part of County Kerry. I have seen what I came to see and will be leaving as soon as the grain-ship is ready to sail with us.'

'It could hardly be more appropriate.' said Liam bitterly. 'A Commissariat Inspector travelling on a ship taking grain from Ireland, leaving the people to starve. Before you go perhaps you'll ask the magistrate to take you on a tour of the cottier holdings, hereabouts – that's if you have the stomach for such an experience. See how they are faring. I doubt if it will change your attitude toward them, but I guarantee you'll remember the pot-bellied rickety children every time you sit before a full plate.'

A nervous movement from Jacob Burke caught Liam's eye and he turned toward him. The salesman froze with a spoon halfway to his mouth.

'I thought you were coming to Ireland to assess the needs of the Commissariat? I doubt if it is coincidence that you are in Castlemaine at the same time as a grain-boat, but the price of Irish barley is too high for Trevelyan's purse. You are buying for English merchants?'

After a false start, Jacob Burke's voice came out strained. 'I am a trader. I buy what people want, and sell to the best market.'

'I have no doubt the profit is higher if you carry on your trading when travelling at the Treasury's expense,' commented Liam. 'You keep good company, Sir Richard.'

Before the Commissariat Inspector could reply, Liam had

gone from the room. There was much to be done before nightfall. Liam was determined the grain-ship would leave Castlemaine harbour with space in her holds. He went to the local branch of the All-Ireland Association, to persuade them to purchase as many wagonloads of grain as their funds would allow.

He could not hope to save the lives of everyone doomed by the failure of the potato crop, but he would buy a few more weeks of life for the cottiers of Castlemaine.

'Damned upstart!' fumed Sir Richard Dudley, when Liam had gone from the room. 'A few years ago a gentleman was a gentleman, and a fisherman was a fisherman. Every man knew his place and the world was a damned sight better for it. Put a fisherman in a gentleman's clothes and he begins to think he is as good as his betters. As for electing him to Parliament . . . ! What on earth were the people of County Kerry thinking about?'

The magistrate had been quick to call out the Army when the cottiers had marched on Castlemaine, but he was an Irishman. He was unhappy at the plight of his countrymen and resented the baronet's callous disregard for them. He said, 'Eugene Brennan's association calls the tune in this part of the country – as in many others. Your work will be easier if you can get along with them, Sir Richard.'

The baronet snorted and reached for his brandy glass. 'Eugene Brennan's association and Ireland deserve one another. I only wish I had been posted to a more civilised country.' He glared over the glass at Jacob Burke. 'McCabe seemed to know you. Where have you met before?'

Jacob Burke was reluctant to give an answer. He had told Sir Richard Dudley of his meeting with Lady Caroline on the journey to Holyhead, but had made no mention of the incident at Shrewsbury – or of Liam McCabe. He licked his lips and looked at the magistrate, reluctant to say anything with another in the room.

'Well? Speak up, man. Where did you meet McCabe?'

'On the coach to Holyhead.'

Sir Richard Dudley lowered his glass and frowned hard at Jacob Burke. 'Travelling on the same coach as my wife?'

Jacob Burke gave another quick glance at the magistrate before answering.

'He appeared to be escorting her. They dined together at Shrewsbury.'

Sir Richard Dudley's face turned scarlet and as the anger built up inside him Jacob Burke feared he would burst a blood vessel.

'Damn it! I will put up with that man's cheek no longer. By the time I have finished with him he will do nothing more ambitious than launch a curragh for the remainder of his life. Why did you not tell me of this before today?'

'I . . . I thought you must know. I didn't dream that he and your wife were . . . I mean . . . I thought you had asked him to take care of her.'

'Ask McCabe? I would not ask an Irishman for anything.'

'If you gentlemen will excuse me.'

The embarrassed magistrate pushed back his chair from the table and stood up. With a shallow, stiff bow to the baronet, he turned and left the room. He had no wish to learn of the indiscretions of County Kerry's newest MP and Sir Richard Dudley's wife. He had already decided he did not like the Commissariat Inspector.

Sir Richard Dudley hardly noticed the exit of his host.

'McCabe should not be sitting in Parliament. The man is a scoundrel. A – a – blackguard!'

'He might well be something far worse,' said Jacob Burke, anxious to make amends for his earlier omission. 'He is probably a traitor, too.'

'Eh?' The statement was enough to startle the baronet out of his own dark thoughts. 'What are you talking about?'

'I'm talking about Liam McCabe, Member of Parliament. He's probably guilty of treason. His brother certainly is . . . and of murder, too.'

'Stop talking in blasted riddles, man. What are you trying to say?'

'Liam McCabe's brother is a wanted man. He attacked some soldiers escorting grain-wagons and stole the wagons. He fled to the Wicklow mountains with his gang and has gathered an army of criminals about him. They terrorise the countryside and are responsible for the deaths of scores of soldiers and innocent people. Liam McCabe must be involved with them. I am told he goes to visit his brother frequently. I mean, how would he know exactly where to find them if he didn't know what was going on? The Army have been looking for them all year without success.'

'Where did you hear this talk?' Jacob Burke had Sir Richard Dudley's full attention now.

'From the potman at the inn where I stay in Dublin. He knows the McCabe brothers. He was a fisherman himself until an injury to his knee forced him to give up the life. I don't suppose it would do McCabe any good if that story were to get about.'

'On the contrary, Liam McCabe would become a hero in the eyes of his countrymen – but this potman, is he a friend of McCabe?'

'There was little friendship in the remarks he passed to me. I would say he hates Liam McCabe. He's probably jealous of his success—'

'I am not interested in your speculation,' snapped the baronet. 'When we return to Dublin bring this potman to me. I want to know exactly how much truth there is in what he says. Now, where is that magistrate? My glass is empty.'

Chapter Thirty-Six

Liam found the return ride to Kilmar from County Kerry even more depressing than before. For mile upon mile of carefully ridged land the potato haulms lay limp and black. Where the tubers had already been dug, the stench of diseased and rotting potatoes hung like death on the air and the tens of miles of sheer desolation frightened Liam.

He wondered whether anything could possibly help the cottiers now. He had done what he could for the families in the hills about Castlemaine, convincing the All-Ireland Association that they would never again be able to hold up their heads in the land if they allowed people to die while they still had funds. But one man could not save everyone.

The resident magistrate at Castlemaine had sold the last few wagonloads of his corn to the Association at a reasonable price and had persuaded other local land-owners to do the same by convincing them that it was good insurance. They lived in the area and would still be there when the English soldiers had returned to their barracks in Tralee.

Association money was also being provided for another scheme to provide food during the long hungry months ahead. Local fishing was so poorly organised it could not properly be called an industry. The prevailing wind along the Kerry coast was westerly. It brought long Atlantic rollers crashing against the high cliffs and surging inside the wide bays of this exposed coast. Even on the finest days it was often impossible for the light-framed curraghs to venture outside a few sheltered inlets. Liam had told the Association of the advantage of wooden boats, capable of going out in all but the roughest weather, and the members had agreed to purchase two such boats. Liam had promised to return to teach the local fishermen how to handle them.

While he was at Castlemaine, the scheme had seemed ambitious and progressive. Now, seeing again the alarming extent of the potato blight, Liam became thoroughly depressed. Only a full-scale programme by the English Government could stave off a total disaster.

His depression did not lift until he rode up to Inch House. To his surprise, Kathie came running down the path to meet him. She was living with Nathan Brock and his family, but this was a different Kathie from the dirty and ragged girl he had last seen in the cabin on the hill above Kilmar. Her long hair hung down her back, shining and clean, and she looked a picture of health, the plain woollen dress she wore revealing only a trace of pregnant thickness about her waist.

She greeted him warmly, and as he disentangled himself from her uninhibited hug he saw Caroline watching them from the main doorway of Inch House.

Caroline's manner toward Liam was far from warm. She greeted him only because not to have done so would have attracted comment.

Liam was puzzled; he was not aware that he had done anything to upset her. As soon as he could, he sent Kathie to find Nathan and tell the ex-prizefighter he would like to see him before leaving.

Inside the house, Liam turned to speak to Caroline, but she had a question for him, first.

'Why did you not tell me that Kathie is in love with you?'

Liam was about to laugh at the preposterous statement, but then he looked at Caroline's face. She was in no mood for humour.

'This is absolute nonsense! Kathie is married to my brother.'

Caroline stared at Liam for a few moments before saying quietly, 'And I am married to Sir Richard Dudley.'

Liam could think of no immediate answer to such a blunt statement, but as he floundered Caroline came to him. Putting her arms about him she clung to him in an agony of self-reproach.

'I am sorry, Liam. I should have known better. . . . I *did* know better. . . . But I have never been so jealous in all my life.'

She kissed him, and as her body pressed against his he wanted her so desperately it was a physical pain. For a while they kissed wildly, but then she pushed him away.

'Kathie will return in a few minutes, my Liam. I must regain my composure before then.'

She looked at him and, in direct contradiction of what she

herself had just said, she threw herself at him and kissed him again.

'Oh Liam! My darling, I have missed you so much.'

She took him by the hand and led him to an armchair. When he was seated, she said, 'I have been so unhappy, Liam. Since Kathie came to the house she has done little but talk about you – no, it is all right. I made it my business to learn exactly what there had been between you, but seeing you together when you arrived made me utterly unreasonable.'

Caroline perched herself on the arm of his chair. 'Poor Kathie has been through a great deal and she is deeply disturbed about something. Shelagh Brock tells me Kathie has dreadful nightmares and wakes screaming.'

Liam thought he knew of the things that were troubling Kathie, but now was not the time to tell Caroline about them. He had other things to say before his brother's wife returned. Quickly, he told Caroline of his meeting with Sir Richard Dudley and his salesman companion.

'No doubt Sir Richard is supplementing his Commissariat salary by becoming involved in corn buying,' he said. 'I don't know a great deal about trading, but with such a desperate shortage of food everywhere the price of grain must be going up daily. Anyone who has a shipload for sale could make a small fortune.'

Caroline nodded. 'And Richard will consider it no more than his due. His salary with the Commissariat will be less than he was receiving at the Treasury. He will be most anxious to make up the difference. However, it is unforunate that you and he have already fallen out about famine relief. Richard can be very stubborn. He may well refuse to open new depots in your area.'

'I think that decision has already been made for him. My belief is that Trevelyan will delay the opening of Commissariat depots for as long as possible in order to save Treasury money.'

'I cannot believe that any man who is in possession of the true facts would even consider such a thing,' declared Caroline, but she said it without conviction. Unless Trevelyan acted very soon there could be little doubt that his tardiness was deliberate policy.

Further discussion was ended when Kathie returned with

Nathan Brock and Liam questioned his friend about his journey to the Wicklow mountains.

Nathan Brock shook his head apologetically. 'I was unable to find Dermot. I asked everyone I met with there, but if any man knew where he was he was not telling me.'

Liam waited for the other man to say more, but all Nathan Brock would say was that he had left word here and there that Kathie was safe and well. Then Caroline broached the subject of the current famine. They discussed it at some length and it was decided they would do much as they had the previous year. If Nathan Brock went out and found the cottiers, Liam would donate all the fish surplus to his immediate requirements. Caroline intended increasing the work force on the estate immediately, supplying as much food as was possible. She would also contact famine relief organisations in England and obtain their help. Even Kathie promised to help wherever she could, for as long as her forthcoming child would allow.

It was dusk before Liam left for Kilmar, and Nathan Brock walked part of the way with him. When they were clear of the house, the big man said to Liam, 'I am worried at the news I heard in the mountains concerning Dermot and his men.'

'You said no one would tell you anything.'

'I didn't want to speak in front of Kathie, but I heard far more than I liked. Dermot is no longer a hero, Liam. Leastwise, not to the law-abiding folk who live in the Wicklow mountains. They are calling him and his men thieves and murderers.'

'I am not surprised. The description fits most of the men who were with him when we last saw him. The rumours will soon die away.'

'I am not so sure. I spoke to a farmer who swore it was Dermot's men who killed his son when he tried to prevent them stealing stock. The sanctuary of the mountains depends upon the silence of those who live there. I doubt if they will remain silent to protect Dermot.'

'What can be done? Dermot should be warned.'

'*You* can do nothing. *I* will try to think of some way to bring Dermot out of the mountains. There are many other matters needing your attention. When you reach Kilmar go to see Father Clery. I have never seen him so worried. Last week a dead child was left on his doorstep and on Sunday morning he found a woman lying dead in his church. He needs help.'

'Has Eugene been to Kilmar while I have been away?'

'No. He is in London, and I heard that he has been ill.'

Nathan Brock saw Liam's immediate concern, and added quickly, 'I don't think there is anything to worry about now – but Father Clery will be able to tell you more.'

At the lodge gate Nathan Brock said he would return home, and Liam thanked him once more for his attempt to locate Dermot.

'When I have more time we will go looking for him together.'

'You would be well advised to stay clear of the Wicklow mountains. It will do you little good in England if it becomes known your brother is a fugitive.'

'We will argue about it some other time, Nathan. I will be coming to Inch House to see you again soon.'

'To see *me*, Liam?' Nathan Brock did not expect a reply, but he believed there were some things that needed to be said. 'Lady Caroline is a remarkable woman. Indeed, I have never known another like her, but she belongs to a noble family, her brother is a great land-owner . . . and she is married to Sir Richard Dudley. Be careful, Liam. You are not your own man any longer. You have become an inspiration to every young hopeful in Ireland. An example of what each one of them might become. You have shown them it is not necessary for a man to own land in order to represent the people. The whole country is watching you. Don't let them down, Liam.'

Liam arrived in Kilmar late enough to expect to have to wake his mother, but there were lights showing in the windows of most of the cottages and much activity was centred on the church.

When Liam entered the building it looked more like a poorly equipped hospital than the house of God. It was a frightening scene. At least a hundred cottiers were accommodated in the nave of the church, most of them women and children. All of them were in an advanced state of malnutrition. Children lay four or five beneath a single blanket, from which protruded fleshless legs resembling twigs from a long-fallen oak-tree. Above the blanket their eyes looked out on the world about them with a disconcerting hopelessness.

Liam found Norah McCabe kneeling beside a boy who might have been any age between seven and fourteen. With his head cupped in her hand she fed him fish soup that trickled out again from the corners of his mouth as he worked desperately hard at swallowing.

Norah McCabe acknowledged the arrival of her son with a nod of her head. A smile would have been out of place in the midst of so much suffering, and there was no time for words as the boy began choking on the soup.

Father Clery laboured into the church, carrying a fresh cauldron of soup and perspiring from the heat of the fire over which it had been boiling. Liam took the vessel from him and carried it to a trestle table beside which some of the walking cottier skeletons waited patiently. The whole church was filled with the smell of fish soup – and of cottiers.

'Thank you, Liam.' Father Clery took out a handkerchief and dabbed it over his face and inside his frayed clerical collar. 'It is good to see you, but I wish God had sent a miracle along with you. We are going to need one.'

'What is happening? Where have all these cottiers come from?'

'It was an eviction, not a couple of miles from here. Their potatoes failed, they had no rent, so the landlord had the soldiers turn them off the land. Then he pulled their houses down. They did not go far away, sleeping in the ditches, praying and waiting for the landlord to allow them back. He didn't, of course, not even when they began dying. Then Tommy Donaghue came across some of them on his way back from Gorey market and told me. We've spent the whole day bringing them here, but I doubt if we have found them all. We will need to go out again tomorrow.'

An emaciated woman lying on the church floor nearby began to have convulsions, and Liam went to her aid. Kneeling beside her he lifted her head and shoulders, shocked at the lack of weight in her body. A convulsive twitch dislodged the rag shawl from about her shoulders, and he saw she wore nothing else above the waist, her flat breasts lying on her ribs, as empty as used parchment envelopes. Father Clery hurried to Liam's side with a mug filled with water. He managed to spill some in the woman's mouth, and her convulsions slowly subsided.

Liam lay the woman gently back on the floor, not knowing whether her eyelids were closing because she was exhausted, or whether she was dying.

Father Clery had no such doubts. 'She's gone, I'm afraid. We'll lose a great many more before this famine is over. Unless something more permanent is done for them soon we'll merely be giving them enough strength to face death all over again. What are they doing in London, Liam? When are they going to send us help?'

'They have no intention of sending aid.' Liam told Father Clery of his meeting with Charles Trevelyan. '. . . So we must do what we can, ourselves, however little it may be.'

'We can't hope to keep the cottiers alive without help from England. There must be at least two million of them. By God, but this is murder on a grand scale.'

'Then pray for your miracle, Father. Nothing else will save them. Meanwhile, all the fishing boats must be out from dawn to dusk, whatever the weather. We are going to need every scrap of food that can be obtained. I'll ride around to speak to local land-owners and ask them to forgo this year's rents. Perhaps they will donate some of their harvest, too, but I won't be able to see them all. My constituents in County Kerry are no better off, and I must do the same for them. We need Eugene back here. People listen to him.'

'Eugene Brennan is an old man, Liam, worn out by a lifetime of fighting. He is tired and has been ill. I have a couple of his letters in my house. I will show them to you. They were not written by the man we have known in the past. It saddens me to say it, but I think this latest disaster will be the death of Eugene Brennan. It might have been different if Peel were still in office. Eugene had grown used to fighting him. When Lord John Russell came to power, Eugene thought his fighting days were over. He had helped the Whigs for many years and he expected them to show some gratitude. Now they are proving that Ireland means less to them than it did to Peel. Their indifference is breaking Eugene's heart. He believes he has come to the end of his road and can help Ireland no more.'

'Then the sooner he is back where he belongs, the better,' said Liam firmly. 'His people have need of him.'

Chapter Thirty-Seven

The grain-ship on which Sir Richard Dudley was a passenger put into Dublin after a long and rough passage from Castlemaine harbour. For four days and nights it had battled against adverse winds and rough seas. The baronet was not a good sailor and suffered greatly, but he had work to do and was in his office the morning after his arrival. His sickness was over, but a brandy-induced headache boded ill for anyone who crossed him during the day.

It fell to Jacob Burke to be the first man to put Sir Richard Dudley's temper to the test. He came to the office to inform the baronet that Eoin Feehan had refused to see him.

Jacob Burke cringed before the fury of the ill-humoured Commissariat Inspector. When his wrath had subsided, Sir Richard Dudley ordered a carriage and, with the sulking salesman seated opposite him, rode through the streets of Dublin to the Drum Inn, a tavern standing in the shadow of the Four Courts.

When Jacob Burke introduced Sir Richard Dudley, the landlord was sufficiently impressed to put a small private room beside the bar at the baronet's disposal and send his potman from the cellar.

When Eoin Feehan limped into the room, Sir Richard Dudley wasted no time on niceties. Keeping the red-haired potman standing before him, he asked what he knew of Dermot McCabe.

Eoin Feehan cast a baleful glance toward Jacob Burke. 'I know nothing. Anyone who says different is a liar.'

Sir Richard Dudley sighed; this was going to be more tiresome than he had thought.

'No doubt I would gain little by asking you what you know of the Wicklow mountains?'

'I know nothing,' Eoin Feehan repeated, glaring at Jacob Burke.

'H'm! I see. Leave us alone, if you please, Mr Burke.'

When the surprised salesman looked at Sir Richard Dudley for confirmation of his instruction, the baronet shouted, 'You heard me. Get out! And stay outside until I tell you I want you again.'

Jacob Burke knocked over a chair in his haste to escape from the room, and the baronet drummed his fingers on the table before him as the flustered salesman righted the chair and apologised for his clumsiness. The moment the door-latch had dropped behind him, Sir Richard Dudley turned his bad-tempered glance upon Eoin Feehan.

'You have a bad limp. How did you come by it?'

'I hurt it in a fishing accident.'

'Would you like me to call a surgeon and prove that the injury was caused by a musket-ball – no doubt from a soldier's gun?'

'The shot came from a Kilmar gun – for helping soldiers,' said Eoin Feehan, throwing away his pretence.

Sir Richard Dudley shrugged casually. 'A surgeon can prove only that a wound has been caused by a musket-ball, not from whence it came. I doubt whether you would convince a jury with your story.'

'You can't frighten me. I've done nothing wrong.'

Eoin Feehan turned as if he was about to leave the room.

'We will see about that. In the meantime I advise you not to try to leave Dublin. A limping man will not travel far with every soldier in Ireland looking for him.'

Eoin Feehan limped back to where the baronet sat looking speculatively up at him.

'Why are you threatening me? I have done nothing to harm you.'

'Neither have you agreed to help me.' Sir Richard Dudley knew he had won his game of bluff. Eoin Feehan would do what was required of him. 'Sit down and listen to me. I know you were with Dermot McCabe's rebels in the Wicklow mountains. I also think I know *why* you were there, but that is of little consequence. What matters is that Dermot McCabe must be captured and brought to justice. He is one of the Queen's enemies and a danger to all law-abiding people. For those reasons alone it is your duty to help me in any way you can. Do you understand me?'

Eoin Feehan's lips had become suddenly unnaturally dry and he ran his tongue over them nervously. 'I can't go back to the Wicklow mountains. Dermot and the others will kill me on sight.'

'There will be no danger for you. Show English soldiers where the rebels are most likely to be hiding and they will do the fighting. When they take your friends prisoner identify Dermot McCabe and your part is done. On your return you will learn that I am a generous man to those who serve me well.'

It sounded so easy when the rich easy-living baronet spoke of the task he required Eoin Feehan to perform for him. But Sir Richard Dudley had never been obliged to spend days and nights among the Wicklow mountains searching for a band of desperate men, every one of whom hated him enough to take a risk to kill him. Eoin Feehan shuddered at the thought, but he had no choice in the matter.

'Good man! I knew you would see sense in the end. Now, go and find Mr Burke and tell him to bring some drinks in here for all of us. We will drink to the success of our venture – but you must keep your silence about what has been said here today. If McCabe and his men are not to be found in the mountains, I will blame the failure on you.'

Eoin Feehan left the private room at the Drum Inn knowing that whatever happened in the Wicklow mountains he was going to be the loser. He contemplated disregarding the baronet's warning and leaving Dublin. But, as Sir Richard Dudley had reminded him, he would not get far before the soldiers caught up with him.

Not until later that night, in his straw bed above the stable, did Eoin Feehan remember the look on Kathie McCabe's face as she put the musket-ball in his knee-cap. He wondered whether it might not be better to risk Sir Richard Dudley's anger rather than chance meeting with her again.

Eoin Feehan was called upon to accompany the soldiers in November. He protested that the decision to go into the Wicklow mountains now was madness. The weather had turned bitterly cold and it was beginning to snow intermittently, the small icy flakes blown in from the north-east by a moaning wind. A continuous frost had frozen the ground solid, and in the rough terrain of the Wicklow mountains a man was liable to slip and break his ankle if he took a single careless step.

Brevet-Major Gordon of the 72nd Highlanders privately agreed with Eoin Feehan. He had been ordered to undertake the operation with one company of his own regiment and a company of militiamen brought south from County Armagh. It gave him two hundred and fifty men in all. This was a much smaller force than the one envisaged by Sir Richard Dudley but, as the Commander-in-Chief had maliciously pointed out, it was the baronet himself who had reduced military expenditure in Ireland. A large-scale operation against a handful of wanted men was difficult to justify. However, the Commander-in-Chief had recently received a plea through a family connection for Brevet-Major Gordon to be confirmed in his rank. Promotion was slow in any peace-time army, but a successful campaign in the Wicklow mountains would enable the promotion to be made without any undue comment.

Because of his bad limp, Eoin Feehan was allowed to ride on one of the provision-wagons bringing up the rear of the small column. Huddled inside a borrowed army greatcoat, he cursed himself for a fool for ever discussing the McCabes with Jacob Burke.

The Wicklow mountains began hardly more than an hour's ride from Dublin, but it would be a full day before the column reached the area where Eoin Feehan believed they might find Dermot McCabe and the men from Kilmar.

As the exposed road began to rise through the mountains, the weather deteriorated still further. The wind tore out the canvas flap on the wagon where Eoin sat, causing it to flap and crackle noisily. Ahead of the wagon the soldiers marched in increasingly ragged formation, those in the rear slipping and sliding in the snow pressed tight by the feet of their companions.

The Armagh men, in particular, were resentful of being forced to come out on this 'fool's errand', as they already referred to the expedition. When the column halted for a midday meal, Eoin Feehan learned, to his consternation, that the militiamen blamed him for the operation.

It was useless for him to argue that he was an unwilling participant. He was an outsider, the odd man out in the column. Without him the militiamen knew they would not be here; therefore it must be his fault. Besides, he was a Catholic, and they were Protestant to a man.

Eoin Feehan finished his meal alone, scorned by the professional soldiers and resented by the Irishmen from the north.

Farther on in the mountains, the snow on the road had drifted to a depth of two feet in some places, but the military column succeeded in reaching Rathconard by nightfall on the second day. Here the regular soldiers were accommodated in the half-empty barracks, whilst the grumbling militamen made a cold and draughty camp under canvas at the edge of the town.

To Eoin Feehan's great relief, he was found lodgings at an inn. That night he stumbled to bed with his body warmed by whiskey and the tap-room fire, thoughts of the morrow driven from his mind by the heady fumes.

Early the next morning the soldiers set off to climb the slopes behind Rathconard. It had stopped snowing but cloud clung to the mountains like a wet grey cloak and the wind buffeted the climbing soldiers, hurling tiny needles of frozen snow at their faces.

It was difficult to recognise snow-covered landmarks in the mist, but Eoin Feehan was able to locate the camp used by the Kilmar men to ambush the soldiers who had tried to take them. From here he was able to lead Brevet-Major Gordon and his men to the first of the alternative camp-sites chosen by the Kilmar men during the time Eoin Feehan was with them.

The way lay along the mountain ridge. The snow was deeper here, muffling the sound of the two hundred and fifty soldiers who floundered along with an icy wind in their faces.

Eoin Feehan was limping along ahead of the column with Brevet-Major Gordon and one of his lieutenants, when a sound that might have been a voice was carried to them on the wind from the grey mist ahead. The commanding officer stopped and raised his hand high as a signal for his men to halt, and the lieutenant ran back among them, urging the men to silence.

With so many men straggling along the length of the ridge it was some minutes before any order could be brought to the column. Then, in the silence, the sound they had heard before was repeated. It was a man's voice, shouting.

The captains of the two columns came forward and were given their orders. The soldiers were to load their weapons and advance, one company on either side of the ridge. Brevet-Major Gordon repeated the instructions he had been given when he was briefed for this command. They wanted prisoners. There was to be no shooting unless he gave the order.

The captains hurried back to their men, weapons were cocked and primed, and Eoin Feehan was told to remain well to the rear of the two companies. There was no place for him in the forthcoming attack.

Minutes later the soldiers and militia filed past on either side of Eoin Feehan, the experienced Highlanders quietly confident of their abilities, the Armagh militiamen nervously eager.

Soon Eoin Feehan was standing alone and he shivered, more from apprehension than as a result of the cold. For long, long minutes there was only the booming voice of the wind across the mountains to listen to – then a wild hullabaloo broke loose somewhere in the mist. Eoin Feehan's head came out of his overcoat much as though he were a tortoise emerging from its shell. The uproar continued and then he heard the flat crack of a musket-shot. After a long nerve-racking silence, the babble of voices swelled on the wind.

Eoin Feehan suddenly felt alone and very vulnerable. Sliding down the slope to the tracks left by one of the companies of soldiers, he hurried toward the noise ahead.

It was not long before the colour of uniforms showed through the blanket of cloud, and then Eoin Feehan was among the soldiers. He pushed his way through them until he reached a trampled clearing around which stood a few miserable sod huts with sagging roofs. Before the huts were two groups of ragged shivering cottiers. Women and wide-eyed frightened children in one group, men in the other.

Between the two, Brevet-Major Gordon kneeled in the snow beside a cottier woman. She had been shot through the lungs. Her thin shawl-covered bosom rose and fell as though she were panting, but when she coughed noisily the snow about her became spattered with blood for a yard around.

It would only be a matter of seconds before she died. Brevet-Major Gordon rose to his feet and turned angrily on a pale-faced young militiaman standing between two tall Highlanders.

'You young fool! If you can't handle a musket, you should not be in the militia. It might just as easily have been one of my soldiers you killed.

'Keep him under guard until we return to Dublin,' he said to the regular soldiers. 'He will answer for this.'

To Eoin Feehan, the officer waved an arm in the direction of the angrily sullen cottier men. 'Do you recognise any of them?'

'I have never seen any one of them before.'

'That is what I thought. We have stumbled upon a group of peasants. Weren't you aware they were living here?'

'I doubt if they have been here for long. They were probably evicted and came here for shelter.'

'Shelter? There is little of that to be found up here.' The Highland officer sniffed scornfully. 'That trigger-happy young militiaman probably did the girl a favour. Another few days and she would have starved to death with the others. However, although that girl is too far gone to be helped, her death will give the others a chance to survive. We will have a cold camp before moving off and these people will be left with enough food to last them at least a week. It will be taken from the militiamen – is that understood, Lieutenant?'

'Leave food for cottiers . . . ?' The lieutenant had been in Ireland for a long time and had nothing but scorn for these ignorant and dirty peasants.

'That is what I said – and do not stint on the quantity. I will inspect it before we leave.' To Eoin Feehan, the Brevet-Major said, 'How far is it to the next camp-site?'

'About two or three hours from here, but it should be easier walking. It lies in a valley, among trees.'

Brevet-Major Gordon replied with a non-committal grunt. His expedition had got away to a bad start. The death of a cottier was not important, but it had shown up the lack of experience and discipline of the militiamen. This was no parade-ground, where discipline, at least, could be improved.

Here in the Wicklow mountains, battling with a difficult terrain and atrocious weather, the militia would rapidly become increasingly disgruntled and unruly. He contemplated returning to Rathconard until the weather changed, but he would make no decision before the two companies arrived at the next place where the outlaws might be found.

This time, fortune was with Brevet-Major Gordon. Following the course of a wide valley, he and his men came out of the cloud less than half a mile from their destination. It was more sheltered here, and from a small copse of trees ahead a thin plume of smoke rose a hundred feet toward the sky before being blasted away by the wind that hurtled across the higher slopes of the surrounding mountains.

Gordon would not allow himself to become excited. In all probability this was no more than another group of homeless cottiers, but he took no chances and withdrew his command back to the shelter of the low-hanging cloud. Here he detached half his Highlanders and sent them to work their way through the broken rocks of the mountainside to take up a position behind the copse.

The militiamen were also split and to them fell the task of preventing any escape on either side of the suspected outlaw camp.

The half-company of the Highland Regiment disappeared in the mist and did not reappear until they made their way swiftly and silently into position across the far end of the valley. Not so the Armagh Militia. Straggling along the mountain slopes they were as often below the cloud as within it, and Brevet-Major Gordon fumed at their disregard for elementary caution. But they gained their positions with no sign of activity from the vicinity of the copse, and the Scots officer became more convinced than ever that it was occupied by cottiers.

When his own half-company emerged in an extended line from the mist, it was the signal for the other soldiers to close in.

They succeeded in completely surrounding the small copse before there was a splutter of shots from among the trees and two militiamen fell wounded. Without hesitation, the remainder of the militiamen threw up their muskets and returned the fire. Their musket-balls hummed angrily through the trees and sent leafless twigs spinning to the ground.

Brevet-Major Gordon raged at the indiscipline of the men from Armagh and despatched a sergeant and half a dozen Highlanders to each half-company of the militia to hold them in check. His orders were to take prisoners, and only his own soldiers could be relied upon to achieve such an objective.

Four more shots were fired at the soldiers as they advanced, then Brevet-Major Gordon drew his sword and ordered his soldiers to fix bayonets.

A few minutes later four figures stumbled from the copse. Weaponless, they waved their arms to signify surrender.

Brevet-Major Gordon's luck was greater than he realised.

The Kilmar men had moved to the valley only that morning, driven down by snow and gale-force winds from a mountain-top camp unknown to Eoin Feehan.

But the soldiers had captured only half the band. The others had gone to purchase food from a remote farm-house farther down the valley. It was a departure from their usual practice of stealing what they wanted, but the outlaws were desperately short of ammunition. The defenders of the copse had been left with only eight musket-balls and a tiny amount of black powder between them. When these had been used they had little alternative but to surrender.

The four men were secured and brought before Brevet-Major Gordon while his men searched the camp.

'Are these some of the wanted men?'

Eoin Feehan nodded, avoiding the eyes of the Kilmar men. He named Dermot McCabe and three former fishermen.

The officer tried not to show his elation. The operation had been a success after all. He had captured the leader of the band, the man who had boasted he would lead a new Irish uprising. Seeing the frail young man clad in cheap and inadequate clothing standing before him proved something of an anti-climax.

'So you are Dermot McCabe, the rebel? Forgive me if I say I find you less than formidable.'

Dermot looked at the officer defiantly. 'Tell that to the two men who lie bleeding.'

Brevet-Major Gordon smiled. 'They will be displaying their scars to friends long after your body is cut down from the gallows, McCabe. But what has happened to the remainder of your men? Not long ago rumour had it that your followers were numbered in hundreds.'

Dermot bit back the retort that more men were coming and said, 'It's as well for you that there are only four of us here. Any more and you would have been obliged to go back to your barracks for a few hundred more soldiers.'

'I admire your spirit, McCabe, but I regret it will not save your life. You will hang for sure.' Turning away, he ordered the lieutenant to place a strong guard on the outlaws. He did not intend losing them now.

Before the four men were taken away, the officer dismissed them from his mind and called to Eoin Feehan.

'You have carried out your task well, Mr Feehan. As soon as we arrive in Rathconard I will arrange transport for your return to Dublin. You will be back in your nice warm potman's job at the Drum Inn by this time tomorrow, I have no doubt.'

As Dermot McCabe was led away by the none-too-gentle Highlanders, he committed the address uttered by the officer to memory. He was not a dead man yet, and Eoin Feehan had much for which he might one day have to answer.

Chapter Thirty-Eight

When the iron-studded door of the Rathconard lock-up slammed shut behind Dermot McCabe and the Kilmar exiles, their future looked both bleak and brief. But there was as little hope for many of their countrymen – and for them the winter of extermination had begun early.

Those with determination – and the means – fled from Ireland, some crossing the Irish Channel to England to seek work – but there was no welcome for them there.

The English workers bitterly resented the arrival of men willing to take work at near-starvation wages, undermining the efforts of the newly formed 'workers' unions' to obtain better working conditions.

Others emigrated even farther afield, to America, only to learn that here, too, they were unwanted. America was hungry for men with skills, to build up a fast-growing nation. The cottier knew only how to cultivate potatoes.

In a firm bid to keep the unwanted immigrants out, the American Government raised the price of cross-Atlantic passages, but it made little difference. Unscrupulous captains and ship-owners crammed the cottiers together in unsuitable – and frequently unseaworthy – vessels, to land them at some remote cove on the extensive American coast.

Meanwhile, those left behind managed as best they could.

Liam's constituency in County Kerry was one of the main potato-growing areas, and the people here suffered greatly. The two wooden fishing boats purchased by the All-Ireland Association put to sea from Castlemaine harbour in most weathers and worked on a non-profitmaking basis, but the catches the fishermen brought in were hopelessly inadequate for the needs of the cottiers.

Liam wrote numerous letters and submitted tedious and repetitious reports to the Treasury concerning the consequences of their callous policy before he received a reply. A brief businesslike note from Charles Trevelyan informed Liam that Sir Richard Dudley had been instructed to open a depot in Castlemaine for the supply of corn and meal to the victims of the potato famine. It was a victory, but a hollow one. The depot was established, but no corn or meal was forthcoming to fill the empty building.

During the early months of winter Liam managed to visit Kilmar and the great house at Inch on a couple of occasions, but it was difficult to be alone with Caroline. Kathie seemed to have no suspicion that he and the baronet's wife were lovers and she stayed with them, telling Liam all the gossip from Kilmar and the latest rumours from the Wicklow mountains. She left them alone only when they began to talk 'London business' as she called any discussion about Parliament or about government aid for Ireland.

Not until Liam arrived very late and unexpected on one occasion was he able to spend a night alone with Caroline.

He rose before dawn and, as he dressed, Caroline stretched contentedly on the bed.

'It has been far too long since you last stayed with me, Liam. I need you more often than for one single night every few months.'

'I need you, too. Sometimes, after riding about the country surrounded by misery and despair, I feel I must get away from it all and come to you. Then I ride into another cottier settlement and know I must go on. For now we must both be content with occasional nights like this.'

Caroline reached out and took his hand. She, too, was working desperately hard, and every day was becoming harder to face. But this morning her weariness was that of a woman who has been making love, and she was happy.

She kissed Liam's hand and held it to her face. 'Oh, Liam, my love. What is to become of us?'

'We will continue as we are, meeting when we can and hoping for a miracle to happen – for us and for Ireland.'

Liam ran a hand wearily through his unruly hair. 'I sometimes think I might as well be sitting in a fairy ring, asking the little folk for their help, as sitting in Parliament.'

'Poor Liam – but you must not take everything to heart so or it will break you completely.'

She pushed herself up on one elbow, allowing the bedclothes to slide unchecked from her body. 'But now let me give you some good news. My friend in London has found a small house for you. It is owned by one of Lord Palmerston's relatives and he has been appointed to a post in the Cape Colonies. You will love it, Liam. If you wish, I will pay the first year's rent for you.'

'That won't be necessary.'

The statement sounded more abrupt than Liam intended, but he still found it difficult to accept that Caroline was so wealthy that she could make such an offer unhesitatingly.

'I'm sorry, Caroline. I don't mean to sound ungrateful, but the County Kerry All-Ireland Association has guaranteed to pay for any accommodation I decide to take in London.'

'Good.' She was aware of his sensitive pride and did not pursue the matter. 'When will you next be in London?'

'In January. The next parliamentary session begins on the nineteenth of the month. I will arrange to be there a few days early.'

'Then I will come to London and be with you for at least a week – longer, if you wish.'

Liam did not reply immediately; he was thinking ahead, to ways of allaying Eugene Brennan's suspicions.

Caroline knew the reason for his delay in replying and said crossly, 'Oh, Liam! Damn your parliamentary reputation!'

She was immediately sorry for her outburst of temper. 'I did not mean that. I will be so discreet that not even my closest friend will know where I am – but please show some enthusiasm for the idea.'

He smiled and kissed her.

'I will more than match your enthusiasm when we are together in London. We will damn my parliamentary reputation together. But now I must leave you, or there will be no reputation to lose.

'Will I see you again before you leave for London?'

'Yes.' He thought of the cottiers he would meet before their next meeting. 'Fever and the state of Her Majesty's roads permitting.'

Chapter Thirty-Nine

The three free men of Dermot's band of outlaws arrived in Kilmar on the first day of December. On their way back to the camp in the mountains with half a dozen chickens, they had heard the sound of their companions expending the last of the musket-balls. They hid in some bushes well off the track while the soldiers and Eoin Feehan passed by with their prisoners. Then they followed them to Rathconard where they saw Dermot and the others bundled into the lock-up.

With their numbers depleted so dramatically, and without a leader, they could not face a return to the mountain wastes. They were cold, poorly clad and totally dispirited. They decided to leave the mountains behind them and return to the almost forgotten comforts of a real home in less hostile surroundings.

They were in poor shape when they reached their own village, and the older men who were not of their families viewed them with tight-lipped disapproval. They had gone against the policies of the All-Ireland Association and were now paying the price of rebellion.

Those of the old men who had witnessed the revolutionary bloodshed fifty years before hoped fervently that the young outlaws would soon go away again. They would bring trouble in the form of soldiers back to the village once more, and the punishment for harbouring the fugitives would be harsh.

The young men would tell the worried Norah McCabe nothing more than that her youngest son had been captured by the soldiers. They had come to the house seeking Liam, but when they were told he was somewhere on the long road between Kilmar and County Kerry they said they would go and find Father Clery instead.

'You'd best be keeping him out of this,' said Norah McCabe. 'He has more than enough troubles for an old man, priest or no priest. Besides, he's out of the village somewhere, attending to the needs of the cottiers. Away to your homes, the lot of you. Be your mothers' sons again for a few hours. I'll go to the big house at Inch and fetch Nathan Brock. He'll know what to do.'

Nathan Brock agreed to come immediately. 'Just wait here a few minutes,' he said. 'I'll get out the gig to take you back to Kilmar.'

'You'll do no such thing,' said Norah McCabe indignantly. 'My legs were good enough to carry me here. They'll take me back again.'

'I'm sure they would,' said Nathan Brock. 'But, although Lady Caroline is in Dublin, she would never forgive me if I allowed you to walk back to Kilmar – and here comes Kathie. She'll want to come, to learn more about Dermot. She is in no condition to walk.'

Almost eight months with child, Kathie was having an uncomfortable pregnancy and now she hurried heavily toward them, concern on her face.

'What is the matter?' she asked Norah McCabe. 'Is something wrong with Liam – or Dermot?'

'Dermot has been taken by the soldiers. Three of the lads who went off with him are back in the village, but they will tell me nothing more.'

'They will tell me.'

'That's what I thought you would say,' said Nathan Brock. 'I'll get out the gig.'

The young men from the Wicklow mountains gathered in the McCabe house in front of Nathan Brock. At first they were reluctant to tell their story with Norah McCabe and Kathie present, but eventually it came out and, as the speaker ended, Kathie erupted in a characteristic manner.

'You saw Dermot being taken to Rathconard lock-up and all you did was to put your tails between your legs and scamper back to Kilmar? I would have been too ashamed of myself to show my face had it been me.'

'There was nothing we could do,' said one of the men, stung to anger by Kathie's remark. 'Things have changed since you left us – and not for the better. Not one of us had a gun; we had left ours with Dermot and the others. Would you expect us to go against more than two hundred soldiers with nothing but our fists?'

'I would expect you to think of something to do other than run away,' retorted Kathie scathingly. 'As it is, we've already wasted more than enough time talking here.'

She looked at Nathan Brock. 'Will you come to Rathconard with us, Nathan?'

'You can't go to Rathconard in your condition,' cried Norah McCabe before Nathan Brock could answer. 'What on earth are you thinking of?'

'I am thinking of getting Dermot and the others from that lock-up – and my condition is not going to stop me. There are cottier women on the roads who are farther on in their time than me, *and* they have a lot less flesh on their bones.'

Kathie looked at the men who had brought the news of Dermot's capture. 'Do we all go to Rathconard, or are you going to leave things to Nathan and me?'

'We'll come with you, but we'll need to rest first. We've been on the move since yesterday.'

'That makes sense,' said Nathan Brock before Kathie could argue. 'And we can't enter Rathconard in daylight. We'll leave here at first light tomorrow. I'll bring the gig for Kathie. Now, you men go and get some rest. We've a busy time ahead of us.'

Norah McCabe began to protest once more about Kathie's condition. 'It's not right . . . it's downright dangerous. What do you think you can do to help Dermot? I'm sure he would rather you stayed here where you will be safe—'

Nathan Brock interrupted before Norah McCabe could say more. 'We'll have need of Kathie, Mrs McCabe. We haven't a weapon between us – and, if we had, we couldn't hope to shoot it out with two hundred soldiers. We'll need to use trickery if we are to rescue Dermot and the others. I have an idea how it might be done – but we need Kathie.'

It was an uneventful journey to Rathconard. The weather remained cloudy and blustery, but the snow had cleared from all but the most sheltered hollows.

Outside Rathconard they drew off the road and waited for darkness, the Kilmar men shivering in anticipation of what was to come.

Nathan Brock would not allow them to move until the lingering dusk had become black night, and then they separated to enter the small town, with Nathan Brock and Kathie in the gig.

They had chosen a good night to make their rescue attempt. Brevet-Major Gordon and his company of Scots infantrymen had that day left on a forced march to put down a riot by the hungry people of Wicklow Town. Responsibility for the prisoners was now in the hands of the less-experienced Armagh Militia.

The gig passed the inn where young Jeremy had been apprehended by the constable and through the windows Nathan Brock could see the bright red uniforms of the militia officers. They were in good voice and with a few of their NCOs they had the inn to themselves. Local men did not care to listen to the songs of the Orange Lodges and had wisely transferred their custom elsewhere. To the men of Rathconard the Armagh Militia were not fellow-Irishmen. They had more of the ways of an occupying army.

Nathan Brock stopped the gig short of the lock-up and, after a few whispered words to Kathie, handed the reins of the horse to one of the Kilmar men, waiting in the shadows.

He slipped away into the darkness and when he returned Kathie saw the white of his smile.

'It couldn't be better. The lock-up is only large enough to hold four guards, and I have just seen two of them go off to the camp for a meal. Now, you know what you have to do?'

Kathie nodded.

'Good girl! Get them to open the door then move out of the way quickly. We will do the rest.'

They approached the lock-up together, but as Kathie walked boldly to the stout door Nathan Brock stepped aside into the shadows.

Kathie banged on the door, waited a few seconds and banged again. A small panel, no more than a few inches square, opened in the door at eye-level and a militiaman looked out.

'Who is it? What do you want?'

'I'm from the tavern. One of your officers has sent me to deliver a jug of ale to you – and heavy it is, too. He should have sent the potman.'

'You won't have to carry it for very much longer, my love,' chuckled the militiaman. 'I'll relieve you of it right away – and I'm telling you, the jug will be a lot lighter before you set foot in the tavern again.'

There was the sound of heavy bolts being drawn as, still chattering, the militiaman swung open the door. Kathie stepped back quickly, and in an instant Nathan Brock had his shoulder to the door. It crashed open, bowling over the militiaman and sending him sprawling to the ground in the small guard-space. Leaping over him while he lay dazed, the big man reached the second militiaman before he had time to reach for one of the muskets leaning against the wall.

Nathan Brock's fist hit him on the side of the jaw, and the militiaman dropped senseless to the floor. Behind him, the other part-time soldier was being beaten into insensibility with less skill but equal enthusiasm by two of the Kilmar men.

In the steel-barred cell, the prisoners raised a cheer, only to be quickly silenced by Nathan Brock.

'Time enough for cheering when you are free. Where is the key to the cell kept?'

There was a moment's stunned silence, then Dermot said, 'The constable carries it with him. He's on patrol in the town.'

'Damn!' This was wasting more time than Nathan Brock would have wished. Turning to one of the men with him, he said, 'There is a rope under the seat of the gig. Get it tied to the window bars at the back and let the pony pull them out.'

Turning back to the prisoners, he said, 'When the window bars go I want you to climb through as quickly as you can and make your way to the road south of the town. We will all meet up there and head back to Kilmar.'

At that moment Dermot saw Kathie standing in the lock-up doorway.

'Kathie! What are you doing here?' His eyes went from her face to her distended stomach and filled with tears. 'Why did you come . . . ?'

His arms came out between the bars as she moved across the lock-up to him.

'Hush now, everything is going to be all right. You'll be out of here in no time at all.'

'I'm sorry, Kathie. I'm sorry. God! But I've missed you. I'll make it all up to you – I swear I will.'

'There's a whole lifetime ahead of us to talk about whatever we will.'

Behind Dermot there was a creaking as the rope about the bars took the strain. Then, with a tumbling of cob and stone, the barred window, complete with frame, crashed to the ground outside the lock-up, leaving a ragged-edged hole.

This time Nathan Brock could not stifle the cheer raised by

the Kilmar men as they dived for the window to be the first one through to freedom.

Dermot had looked round at the window when the bars had gone but now he swung back to Kathie and his gaze went past her and filled with fear.

The two missing militiamen had returned from their meal.

Nathan Brock was quick enough to take a grip on the first militiaman's musket and twist it from his grip before he could pull the trigger, but there was nobody close enough to tackle his companion. The second Armagh militiaman threw his musket to his shoulder, then he hesitated momentarily, uncertain of his target.

It was now that Kathie acted. She was barely a yard from the muzzle of the wavering musket and, reaching out, she grasped the gun, trying to force it up toward the ceiling.

Dermot saw the danger she was in and shouted for one of the free Kilmar men to go to her aid, but before help could arrive the gun went off with the muzzle only inches from Kathie's face. She staggered back, crashed against the corner of a small table and fell heavily to the floor.

Too late one of the Kilmar fishermen came through the door and felled the militiaman with a heavy piece of timber. By this time Nathan Brock had disposed of his opponent and he dragged Kathie clear as Dermot scrambled through the window of the cell and reappeared seconds later at the doorway.

'The musket-ball seems to have missed her,' said Nathan Brock. 'But she has bad powder burns on her face and must have hit her head on something when she went down. Help me to get her out to the gig. We have to get away from here quickly. That shot won't have passed unnoticed.'

They carried Kathie between them to the gig, Nathan Brock calling for the other Kilmar men to run away quickly. Lifting Kathie up on to the seat, he climbed up beside her. With Dermot supporting her on the other side he flicked the reins and soon had the pony moving off, away from the partly demolished lock-up.

They were turning from a side-street on to the long main road that split Rathconard from north to south when a voice called upon them to stop. Moments later they were surrounded by militiamen.

Nathan Brock knew that if they once caught a glimpse of Dermot's face the game would be up with three of them.

'Out of the way!' he roared. 'I've a woman here about to give birth to a child. If me and her husband don't get her to a doctor quickly, she'll have the baby right here on the street.'

A door opened nearby as a man came out to find out what was happening. Just enough light was released from the house for the soldiers nearest to the gig to see that Kathie was indeed very pregnant. She lay back on Dermot's shoulder, her head effectively hiding his face, seemingly fainting with pain.

'Let them through,' called a corporal of the militia. 'It's a woman in labour. Let them through.'

'Bless you, sir,' called Nathan Brock, cracking the reins over the back of the pony as he drove the gig past the obliging soldiers and along the street to the edge of town.

But Nathan Brock's lie turned out to be prophetic. When the gig and the accompanying men were little more than a mile from Rathconard, and the Kilmar men were already congratulating each other on the success of their escape, Kathie began to regain consciousness.

At first, Dermot thought her groans were caused by the pain from the blow she had received. Holding her to him, he stroked her powder-burned forehead and reassured her that they would soon be home in Kilmar.

Kathie's groans ceased for a few minutes as she clung to her husband, but then she pulled away from him, her body writhed in agony and she screamed for him to help her.

Nathan Brock pulled the gig to a halt, thoroughly alarmed.

'The baby . . . it's coming!' Kathie hissed between closed teeth. 'It's hurting like the Devil. . . . Aah! It's hurting me. . . .'

'What can we do? She can't have it here.' Dermot looked up at Nathan Brock as though he could provide some miraculous answer.

'Then pray that we make it to Kilmar in time,' said Nathan Brock grimly. 'We'll take the gig on ahead of the others and make the best time we can, but I wish there was less cloud about. I can hardly see the road.'

Nathan Brock whipped the pony to a trot and strained his eyes into the darkness. When the moon put in an appearance he urged the pony to a near-gallop. Then, as suddenly as it had appeared, the moon slid behind a cloud, plunging the countryside into darkness. Before Nathan Brock could haul the pony to a halt, the gig left the road, skidded – and overturned.

Fortunately, the ground beside the road was covered with wiry heather and no one was hurt. But it took them some minutes to right the gig and set off again.

By far the worst part of the journey was listening to Kathie's screams and not being able to do anything to help her. Dermot did his best to comfort her as she clung to him between spasms, but once the pain caught her there was nothing to be done.

After one such agonising bout, she said, 'I'm frightened, Dermot. Not for myself, but for your son. He is much too early.'

Then the pain attacked her again, and for some minutes Dermot fought to hold her in the seat of the frail carriage.

When the spasm passed, Kathie whispered, 'If only it wasn't so dark, Dermot. If I could see, it wouldn't seem so bad.'

Dermot looked up quickly. Nathan Brock had heard her words and he returned Dermot's apprehensive look. The moon was between clouds and the countryside was clearly visible for half a mile about them.

They were still five miles from Kilmar when the late dawn broke and they drove into the fishing village at a gallop. By now Kathie's cries were almost continuous, the birth of her child seemingly imminent.

One other thing was equally certain. The blast from the musket at such close range had seriously injured her eyes.

Kathie was blind.

Nathan Brock brought the pony and gig to a halt in the narrow street outside the McCabe cottage and, while the lathered animal threw its head and trembled in the traces, Nathan Brock lifted Kathie from the seat as Norah McCabe rushed out and threw her arms about her son, overjoyed to have him with her once more. Then Kathie screamed and Norah McCabe saw what was happening on the far side of the gig.

The situation needed no explanation. In the darkness of the ride the two men had only Kathie's screams to tell them of her agony. Now, in the morning light, it could be seen that the dress she wore was soaked in her own blood.

'Bring her inside quickly,' said Norah McCabe. To an open-mouthed young girl onlooker she snapped, 'Now you've seen enough to give you nightmares hurry away and call Bridie O'Keefe. Get her here as quickly as she can come. Do you hear me? Run as fast as your feet will take you.'

Kathie's screams quickly brought other women on the scene from nearby houses, and before long the McCabe house was as busy as the fish-quay on an evening tide.

When a weary Nathan Brock left to return the lathered pony and the gig to Inch House, Norah McCabe turned her son out of the house.

'It's a long way from the homecoming I had planned for you, Dermot. But it's best that you are away from the happenings in this house today.'

'But where shall I go . . . ?' None of his companions had yet returned and, dressed in his rags, Dermot felt a stranger in his home village.

'Go to the church. Fall on your knees and pray for your wife.'

Bridie O'Keefe had come through the door unnoticed as Kathie's screaming reached a new crescendo.

'While you're about it you had better put in a word for me. If the girl who came to fetch me told the truth, then it will need more than the skill in these old hands to right the wrong that's been done to the poor girl upstairs. Away with you, now. This is woman's work. It's no place for a man.'

Dermot turned to go from the house, but Bridie O'Keefe called him back.

'Dermot McCabe! Pray for yourself most of all. There's a darkness about you that is the Devil's making – and he'll tempt you sorely today.'

Norah McCabe listened in dismay, looking from the old crone to her son. She knew better than to scoff at Bridie O'Keefe's premonitions. If she said she had seen the Devil's darkness, then it was here, in this house, now. . . .

'I'll pray for all of us, Bridie. Do your best for Kathie . . . and the child.'

On his way to the small village church, Dermot met Tommy Donaghue hurrying toward the cottage. Unshaven and stupid with sleep, the old fiddler had been called from his bed by one of the village women. Grasping Dermot's hand in both of his, he muttered, 'It's great to see you back in Kilmar again. But

Kathie? How is she . . . ? The woman said the baby had started.'

'She's not at all well, Tommy. You'd best go along to see her – if Bridie will let you in the house.'

Dermot was embarrassed by the warmth of Tommy Donaghue's greeting. He blamed himself for all that had happened to Kathie. He had caused everything. It was for him she had left Kilmar in the first place. She had suffered every kind of hardship with him in the mountains, and then when she most needed him he had let her down and forced her to leave the mountains.

Last night, during the nightmare journey from Rathconard, Nathan Brock had taken the opportunity to tell Dermot of the attack upon Kathie by the soldiers and their unknown companion. To Dermot it explained away all of Kathie's uncharacteristic behaviour in the beginning. He wished she had been able to tell him herself. He would not have blamed her; nothing that had happened had been her fault. If only she had told him. But he realised he had not made it easy for her to talk of such a thing to him. He had been obsessed with the relationship he suspected between Kathie and his own brother.

Dermot was deeply ashamed of himself. Bridie O'Keefe was right: the Devil kept him company and fed his jealousy. Yet, in spite of the way he had behaved toward her, Kathie had insisted on coming to Rathconard to help him to escape. Risking her life and the life of the child she bore, for him. He had much to pray for.

But Dermot never got as far as the inside of the church. He was met outside the porch by Father Clery. When the old priest had been given a summary of the night's events, he insisted that Dermot come back to his house and tell him everything. Along the way they were joined by a disgruntled Tommy Donaghue. Bridie O'Keefe had refused to allow him inside the house.

Sharing the priest's frugal breakfast, Dermot told the two men of the hard times he had endured during the last few months and how his dreams of raising an Irish army had crumbled about him. It seemed that, this morning, Dermot McCabe was seeing things clearly for the first time.

Later, the Kilmar outlaws straggled into the village to receive an emotional welcome from their families, but in every case their first question was about Kathie.

There was little that Dermot or anyone else could tell them. Although Dermot and Nathan Brock had feared the baby might arrive during their drive to Kilmar, it had still not been born by nightfall, although Kathie was in constant labour.

Norah McCabe was worried. Bridie O'Keefe had not been able to stop the bleeding, or bring the baby into the world, and Kathie was now very weak. Her blindness was also upsetting her, and when Dermot and Tommy Donaghue were allowed to see her for a few minutes she wept for the whole time.

Liam arrived from County Kerry while the two men were with Kathie and, after a brief explanation, his mother took him straight to the room. His presence only seemed to make Kathie worse, and when she clung to him, sobbing, Liam felt embarrassed for Dermot. But when Bridie O'Keefe ushered all the men from the room and they were downstairs Dermot embraced his brother with all the affection of earlier days.

'I've been a fool, Liam,' he said. 'But I'll make it up to Kathie. Nathan told me.' He said no more as Tommy Donaghue was within hearing.

'You have both been through a bad time, Dermot, but it is nearly over now. Soon you and Kathie – and your child – will be able to go off to a happy new life together.'

'Where?' asked Dermot with a gesture of hopelessness. 'I'll be a wanted man as long as I live.'

'Not in America.'

'America?' Dermot looked at his brother as though he had suggested he should go to the moon.

'Yes, you, Kathie and all the men who were in the mountains with you. There will be no difficulty in arranging the passages, and you'll find so many Irishmen already there that it will be just like home. Everyone who can raise the passage money is going to America. It will be a great opportunity for you, Dermot. You think about it.'

'Whatever it is you have to think about, then, you had better do it somewhere else,' said Norah McCabe, pushing past them to the kitchen. If it had not been for the poor girl in the bed upstairs, she would have been bursting with pleasure at having her two sons together in the house. 'We are too busy to be moving you from room to room all the time. Go down to the ale-house. I expect you'll find the others there tonight.'

'All right.' Liam looked at his tired and distraught brother. A few whiskeys would do him good. 'But you'll call us if anything happens upstairs?'

'Of course. Now, away with all of you.'

Liam, Dermot and Tommy Donaghue walked through the village, stopping more than once to answer questions about Kathie.

The inn was buzzing with the excitement of the returned young men, but here, too, there was much concern for Kathie. However, when it was established that there was no change in her condition, the conversations once more centred on the men from the mountains. Everyone was fully aware that their unexpected reunion could not last. They were wanted men, and it would not be long before the soldiers came to Kilmar looking for them. But, for that very reason, there was a determination to make this one evening as memorable as possible.

There was one man who took no part in the homecoming celebrations. Tomas Feehan came into the ale-house later in the evening and stopped short when he saw Dermot and the others. In the sudden hush that greeted his arrival, he turned on his heel and left again without a word to anyone.

The landlord of the inn suggested that Tommy Donaghue fetch his fiddle and give them all a tune but, as Kathie's father stood up to leave, a messenger arrived from the McCabe cottage, asking the three men to return as quickly as possible.

The long and difficult birth was almost over, but the men were obliged to wait downstairs with no news for a further half-hour. Then, from the bedroom immediately above them they heard the sound of an infant's first weak protest against the world. It was not repeated, but the single sound was enough for Dermot. He bounded up the stairs and into the room where half a dozen women surrounded the still figure on the bed. Another woman stood to one side, holding the baby.

But it was to Kathie that Dermot went. She lay upon the bed breathing weakly, her eyes closed.

Dermot dropped to his knees beside the bed and took one of her hands in his. It was ice cold. He looked up at his mother and fear took hold of him when she turned her head away.

'Dermot?' Kathie's voice came as a faint whisper as her sightless eyes opened to search the darkness.

'It's all right. I'm here.'

'It's a boy, isn't it?'

Dermot looked up and one of the women inclined her head wordlessly.

'Yes, it's a boy, Kathie.'

'I told you. . . . I said it would be . . . a boy.'

The faint change of expression on her face could only have been a smile.

'Who does he look like, Dermot?'

The woman holding the baby was in the shadows on the far side of the room. When Dermot beckoned to her she hesitated and looked first at Norah McCabe. Not until she received a nod did the woman bring the tiny bundle to the bedside and hold it down for Dermot to look at the baby.

'Who does he look like?' Kathie repeated.

'He's the image of me, Kathie.'

This time there was no mistaking the smile on the face of the exhausted girl.

'I told you. I told you, Dermot. . . . He is your son . . . your child.'

Norah McCabe moved forward, signalling for Dermot to move away from the bedside, but as he tried to remove his hand from Kathie's she stirred.

'Let me have him, Dermot. Our son . . . let me hold him.'

The fisherwoman laid the baby gently down in the cradle of Kathie's arm as Dermot stood up and backed away from the bed.

He blundered blindly from the room, passing Tommy Donaghue and Liam outside the door without a word. In the kitchen he slumped in a chair and covered his face with his hands. He heard Tommy Donaghue's noisy grief pass by the door and was staring vacantly at the dancing yellow flames of the fire when his mother came quietly into the room and rested a hand on the shoulder of her younger son.

'She's gone, Dermot. It was a terribly hard childbirth and she had lost a lot of blood.'

Norah McCabe clenched her son's shoulder savagely. 'What you did upstairs was the kindest thing you will ever do in your life, Dermot. It made me proud to be your mother.'

Dermot said nothing, and Norah McCabe touched his unkempt black hair. She felt the need to hug her son to her and comfort him, but Dermot stood up abruptly and strode to the window to look out at the window-lit darkness that was Kilmar.

'Kathie was a good girl. She deserved more from life.'

He was silent for a long time and then, in a carefully controlled voice, he asked, 'What will happen to the baby now?'

'He's a weakling, Dermot, and is having great difficulty with his breathing. Bridie says he will be with Kathie before the morning.'

'Then God has some mercy. . . .' Choking on the words, Dermot ran to the door and, flinging it open, fled from the house.

Kathie's baby died with the day that dawned as red as the hair on its own head.

As red as the hair of a Feehan.

Chapter Forty

Bearing the name of Dermot McCabe, the baby was buried with its mother in Kilmar churchyard, surrounded by generations of McCabes.

Caroline returned from Dublin in time to attend the funeral. Disdaining a carriage, she rode to Kilmar. Afterwards, she asked Liam to return to Inch House with her. Liam now had his own riding-horse and, collecting it from the stable behind the ale-house, he rode with her along the road that curved around the side of Kilmar hill, away from the sea.

Along the way they talked of the rescue of Dermot and his friends from the lock-up at Rathconard. Caroline told Liam that the military authorities in Dublin were furious at the way the Armagh Militia had bungled their duties.

'Soldiers will certainly be sent to search Kilmar. Your brother and those who were with him must leave as soon as something can be arranged. I will provide any money they may need.'

'Giving money to wanted men is not the same as helping cottiers. You will keep out of this, Caroline.'

'Nonsense! I will help because it is in everyone's best interest to get Dermot and the others out of the way. A public trial of Irishmen, accused of rebelling against the Queen, would be the worst thing that could happen. The cottiers need help and sympathy from the English. They will lose both if Dermot and his friends are captured.'

Liam's look at Caroline acknowledged her clear thinking. 'You would make a fine wife for a politician, Caroline.'

'But a poor mistress, I fear. We have been out of sight of Kilmar for minutes now, and I have not kissed you.'

Liam reined his horse alongside hers and they kissed hungrily until one of the horses tossed its head impatiently and almost unseated them both.

Caroline laughed breathlessly. 'You have started something that will need to be satisfied before this day is out, Liam McCabe.'

They rode side by side in silence for a while; then Liam

said, 'I am hoping to persuade Dermot and the others to go to America. They should be safe enough if they set off from a south-coast port. After this business with Kathie and the baby it will be a good thing for Dermot to get right away from Ireland.'

'Poor Kathie. She had neither the man nor the baby she wanted – and I suspect that precious little else came her way during her lifetime. But you are right, Liam. America would be a splendid place to make a new start. It is a country with unlimited opportunities. More than a man might find here at this moment, with fresh troops arriving from England every day. Dublin has the look of a town under siege, and they say the Lord-Lieutenant has told Lord John Russell he expects a cottier uprising at any time.'

Liam snorted. 'There is no strength in them for rebellion. Did you see Sir Richard while you were there?'

'Yes.' There was a hint of sadness in her voice and Liam moved closer to her so that their knees were touching. 'He apologised for all that had happened in the past. Then he asked me to return to him.'

'And what was your reply?' Liam asked softly.

'I said I would not live with him in Dublin or anywhere else. I told him we no longer have anything to give to each other.'

'Did that make him angry?'

'No, not at first.' Liam could see that Caroline was upset. 'He was just . . . terribly hurt. I was not prepared for that. He broke down and pleaded with me to return to him. It made me remember the many nice things he had done for me in the past. How kind he could sometimes be. . . .'

Liam took her hand, and she gave him a wry smile.

'Then he told me tongues were wagging in Dublin because I never attended any of the official functions with him. He *demanded* that I return. When I still refused, he said he knew what was going on between you and me. He promised to humble me and have me ostracised by society on both sides of the Irish Sea. He also threatened to see that you were thrown out of Parliament. He was angry when he said it, but he was serious, for all that.'

'I don't doubt it. If someone were to take you from me, I would be equally serious in my dealings with them.'

'No one could take me from you, Liam. Not now – or ever.'

Her husky-voiced assertion roused a hunger in his body that matched her own. There was no need for words. When Liam turned his horse off the road on to a track leading to a low heather-covered hill, she turned with him. Stopping beside a small copse of low trees, he helped her down and her arms went about his neck and refused to release him. There, in deep heather, on a cold December afternoon she came to him and they made love with total abandonment.

Afterwards, as they lay together watching the slate-grey clouds race each other across the dull sky, Caroline whispered, 'I told you once that you could take me in a field, if you needed me. I am glad you remembered.'

Liam's arms tightened around her. 'Many men and women are forced to make love in fields and ditches because they have no homes of their own.'

Even at such a time as this, Liam found it impossible to forget the plight of his countrymen. Caroline bit back a sharp comment, and smiled instead. 'One day, Liam McCabe, I am going to take you to a remote island where you will have nothing to think about but you and me – and making love.'

'I'm sorry, Caroline. . . . I. . . .'

She laid a finger across his lips and then rose on one elbow to look down at him.

'Shh! You need never apologise to me. I know you have a great deal on your mind. But I wish I knew what will become of us. If only I could look into the future. . . .'

Now Liam sat up. 'Future? What future is there for anyone while death and misery walk so openly through the land?' Fiercely he said, 'I love you, Caroline. For myself I want nothing more than to be with you, night and day. I have great happiness in my love for you – but I can never forget there are cottiers who know nothing of happiness. Even when they make love they are surrounded by hungry children whose birthright is . . . hopelessness. For the moment I can think of no future but helping them. It will be enough if I can keep *some* of them alive to see better times. To learn there is more to life than a constant fight to feed their bellies.'

The fire died within Liam as suddenly as it had flared into life. 'I wish things could be different for us, Caroline. Perhaps one day they will . . . but not yet.'

To Liam's surprise, when he looked at her, Caroline seemed unbelievably happy.

'Liam, you have just told me for the very first time that you love me. I love you, too, much more than I ever believed I would love anyone. I will ask no more from life until Ireland has become a happier land.'

She kissed him and then stood up. 'Come, it will not help if I am the cause of your catching pneumonia. We will gallop on to Inch House and I will fill you with my brother's best brandy.'

'Your brother . . . will he be returning to Ireland soon?'

Caroline snorted. 'Not until there is no danger of him contracting fever. He is terrified of sickness. I had a letter from him before I went to Dublin. He says he will probably remain on the Continent for the rest of this winter.'

'He is wise to be concerned. Black fever is raging in the hills and remote areas. It is only a matter of time before it affects the villages once more.'

Liam helped Caroline to mount her horse. 'I wish Eugene were here to help. I feel the need of his strength and logic. More than once lately I have found myself wondering whether it makes any sense to appeal to charity to help the cottiers; whether it might not be better to take what the cottiers need from those who have more than they require.'

'This is not the time for violence, Liam. Our people are weak and dispirited – and England has more soldiers in Ireland than the country has seen for very many years.'

'And every one of them eating food that should be filling cottier bellies.' As they reached the road, Liam turned his horse alongside hers and shook his head sadly. 'It is madness, Caroline. People are dying for want of food, and instead of sending us corn the English send soldiers.'

'Then you must raise the question in Parliament, Liam.'

'I would as soon stay in Ireland. At least I can *see* I am doing some good here.'

'You can do much in London. I will be there to ensure you meet some of the right people.' She saw the lift of his eyebrow. 'You need have no fear of gossip; I have to be in London. Richard is selling our house there and I need to remove a few things.'

'Does his decision to sell have anything to do with you and me?'

'No,' she lied. 'He says he no longer has need of such a large house – but isn't it pleasing? It gives me a wonderful excuse to be in London.'

They passed a straggling family of ragged cottiers. Dejection showed in the narrow bowed shoulders of the man and the twig-like frailty of the children's limbs. Not a sound came from any of them as they trudged along in hopeless silence. The two youngest children, both girls, walked hand in hand behind the others. One of them raised big dull eyes to look at Liam and Caroline as they drew level and the look cut into Caroline like a knife.

For a few moments she said nothing, then wheeling her horse she rode back and pulled the beast to a halt in front of the cottier man. He looked up at her as startled as a man woken from a dream.

'Where are you going?' she called down to him.

'I . . . nowhere, ma'am. We're just looking for a place to sleep. I'll make sure the children stay on the road. We won't go into any fields—'

Caroline cut through the man's abject promises.

'Are you looking for work?'

The cottier looked at her in disbelief. Then, squaring his shoulders, he said, 'That I am, ma'am. If you've anything that needs to be done, you won't find a stronger man anywhere. Anything, I'll do it well. . . . I promise you.'

'Then make your way to Inch House. You'll find it a couple of miles along this road. Ask for Nathan Brock and tell him Lady Caroline says he is to give you work. He'll find you a cabin, too.'

'God bless you, m'lady. You won't regret this kindness. Bless you.'

'You can't give work to every starving cottier you see,' said Liam as they resumed their ride to Inch House.

'I know.' The dark eyes in the small pinched face were still haunting Caroline. 'But only a few minutes ago we were talking of the happy times we would have in London next month. Where do you think that family would have been by then, Liam?'

Liam looked over his shoulder at the cottier man who was

gathering his children together and urging them forward with renewed hope and purpose.

'Most of them would have been dead,' he replied honestly.

'Yes, and those two little girls would have been the first to die,' said Caroline in an unsteady voice. 'I just saved myself from having one more unforgettable nightmare.'

Chapter Forty-One

The wanted Kilmar men agreed to go to America, but Liam and Dermot had a few days together before they left the village. During that time they regained much of the close comradeship of earlier years. They went out fishing, enjoying the experience that was no longer a part of either of their lives. They talked of their mother, of the boat – and of the future.

The evening before Dermot was due to leave the two brothers walked together to the quay to watch the boats coming in. It had been a good fishing day, and the Kilmar men who now worked the McCabe boat for them proudly showed off their catch. It would feed them all and still show a handsome profit. From the quay, Liam and Dermot walked along the sand to where the nets were laid out to dry between upturned curraghs.

Dermot had been more than usually silent today, but Liam thought he understood the reason. Dermot would take a long time to recover from Kathie's death. He held himself largely to blame and could not forgive himself for making her so unhappy during the months of her pregnancy. Dermot suddenly shivered, and Liam said, 'You are cold. We had better go home now.'

'Cold? No, Liam. The last couple of months in those mountains taught me what it is to be cold. I learned many other things, too, things I would rather forget. Sometimes I would lie awake remembering how I used to grumble to you about fishing for a living. Yet I would have given half my life to be able to come back here with a chance to start all over again.'

'I can believe you. I, too, lie awake sometimes wishing I could forget all I know and return to the old days and the life of a fisherman. It was a good life, in spite of its many hardships.'

'It could be a good life again, Liam. For you, me – and mother.'

'How? We have both gone too far along our own roads. We couldn't return to Kilmar and start again as though nothing had ever happened to us.'

'Maybe not in Kilmar . . . but we could do it in America.

Come there with me, Liam. You and Mother. Sell the boat and the gear and we'll all go off together. There's fishing to be done there – you've told me so yourself. We could all start a new life with another boat. What do you say?'

Dermot had put forward an argument that was tempting in many ways: to sail away from the poverty of Ireland and take up the old and familiar way of life in a new country. Caroline could come, too. She would become part of the new beginning.

Then sense broke in upon Liam's daydreams. Caroline was no fisherman's wife. Besides, there was too much to be done here, too many lives at stake.

'For a moment you tempted me, Dermot, but my life is no longer so simple that I can throw everything up for a sudden whim. I must stay here, but I'll give you enough to get off to a good start. You'll be able to buy a boat and help the others.'

'I'll take no more than my passage money and enough to feed me for a month.' Dermot had desperately wanted Liam to agree to go to America with him. He had made his own secret decision about the future – and it did not include a passage to America. Only Liam's agreement to go there as a family would have made him change his mind. Now he knew what he had to do.

Liam argued that the money he wanted to give to Dermot came from the recent year's profits and was rightly Dermot's, but the younger brother was adamant.

'I don't need it. Give it to Mother.'

Finally Liam gave in to him. 'All right. But if you are ever in need you have only to write and I will send money to you.'

'Thank you, Liam, but I will be needing nothing.'

There was something in the way Dermot said the words that worried Liam, but he could read nothing from his brother's expression and he could draw him out no more.

The following morning the whole village turned out to give the emigrants a noisy and emotional send-off. Norah McCabe managed to stay cheerful until her waving son disappeared from sight with the others; then, without a word, she returned to the cottage and remained in her bedroom for a full hour. Dermot had gone from her and she knew she would never see her younger son again. It was more than mother's instinct. The dark silence had descended upon Dermot before he left, and Norah McCabe remembered Bridie O'Keefe's warning. It was the Devil's darkness, and she knew it would destroy her son.

Not until they reached the main Dublin-to-Waterford road did Dermot announce that he was leaving the others. He gave them no reason for his decision and, when they protested, he said only that he needed to speak to someone before he left Ireland. He promised he would do his best to catch up with them before their boat sailed for America. Then he turned his back upon them and set off along the road to Dublin.

Ireland's capital city was a frightening place for a Kilmar fisherman, and in its busy streets Dermot found himself thoroughly bewildered. Only a few miles away Irish families were dying of starvation, yet here was food in plenty. From behind stalls piled high with a variety of produce, vendors vied with each other to call attention to the quality of the food they were offering for sale. Neither was there a shortage of buyers. Servant girls and city housewives walked away from the market-places with baskets piled high with food. People here had money to spend on food – and some to spare for the silks and fripperies of city fashion.

There was another lesson here for Dermot. For months he had hidden in the Wicklow mountains, kept alive by his wits, and dreaming of revolution. He had convinced himself that the whole country lived with the same dream; but now he saw people smiling at the English soldiers. Shopkeepers joked with them. They drank in the taverns and walked the streets with laughing Irish girls clinging to their arms.

It was the final bitter blow for Dermot. For the first time he was forced to admit to himself that he had been living in a make-believe world. There would be no uprising, no revolution. Had Dermot marched upon Dublin at the head of a thousand men there would have been no support for them here. They would have stood alone against the might of England. Ireland was not ready for a rebellion.

It was a depressing revelation. Dermot thrust his hands deeper into his pockets, and the cold wind stung his eyes to tears. Everything he had done had been in vain. The first, disastrous, attack upon the wagons; the months spent fighting; avoiding the soldiers in the mountains; Kathie's death . . . the baby.

Even the final act he was about to play out would achieve

nothing. But he owed it to Kathie. He would never be able to live with himself until he had paid the debt.

He arrived at the Drum Inn at an hour when the men of Dublin were ending their daily work and seeking the warmth of tavern and ale-house. Before pushing open the door, Dermot put a hand to his belt where he carried a razor-edged gutting-knife.

Inside the well-appointed tavern, Dermot saw a potman collecting empty tankards and glasses from crowded tables – but this man was not Eoin Feehan. The thought came to him that the Kilmar turncoat might have left the Drum Inn and moved elsewhere. Dermot's stomach contracted with the prospect of this final failure.

Pushing his way through the crowded inn, he almost bowled over two barristers from the nearby courts. Ignoring their protests, Dermot made his way through the first bar-room, heading for a door that led to another.

He reached the door and was about to put a hand upon the latch when it was opened from the other side. Dermot stood back as the door swung open – and there, standing before him, with a tray of empty glasses in one hand, was Eoin Feehan.

The expression on the red-headed ex-Kilmar fisherman's face went from astonishment, through disbelief, to fear.

Dermot was the first to recover and suddenly he was quite calm and certain of himself.

'I can see you were not expecting me, Eoin.'

Eoin Feehan's lips had suddenly become very dry and he looked at Dermot apprehensively.

'I came here especially to see you, Eoin. To bring you the latest news from Kilmar. I thought you should know about Kathie. She is dead, Eoin.'

'Kathie . . . dead? I don't understand. . . . Why come to tell me?'

Two men pushed through the door behind Eoin Feehan, and Dermot tensed, expecting the other man to make some attempt to escape. But Eoin Feehan knew he would not get far and he stayed where he was, believing Dermot would do nothing in the presence of so many witnesses.

'Kathie died in childbirth – after being involved in a fight at Rathconard. You remember Rathconard, Eoin? You should; you have done much there – you and the soldiers.'

Eoin Feehan licked his lips again as his glance touched every part of the room without meeting Dermot's eyes. 'I don't know what you are talking about.'

'I think you do, Eoin. You more than anyone else know what happened to Kathie when she went to Rathconard that first time. You know why her baby was born with red hair – just as though it were a bastard Feehan.'

Another customer pushed through the door, passing between them. This time Eoin Feehan did not hesitate. Dropping the tray of glasses with a crash that turned every head in the two bars, he ran.

The man in the doorway impeded Dermot, and Eoin Feehan might have made good his escape had he not been handicapped by his leg, crippled by a shot from Kathie's musket. Halfway across the bar-room he swung the leg awkwardly and his toe caught the outstretched foot of a customer. He sprawled on the floor and before he could rise Dermot was on him. The gutting-knife rose in the air and plunged deep into Eoin Feehan's side.

There was a horrified hush in the Drum Inn as the customers saw the blood-stained knife plunged again and again into Eoin Feehan's body. Then the horror changed to anger. Dermot was pounced on and beaten to the ground, his arm twisted painfully behind his back and the knife kicked away across the stone-flagged floor.

Dermot made no move to defend himself, but before he was beaten unconscious he saw that he had succeeded in what he had come to Dublin to do. Eoin Feehan was breathing blood, his mouth open wide in a vain attempt to suck in air. He would be dead within minutes. Kathie's death had been avenged.

On a crisp, clean, January day, Liam was a passenger on the Wexford-to-Dublin mail coach. He was travelling to London for the new session of Parliament. As the coach neared the centre of Dublin it was forced to slow down before coming to a reluctant halt as thousands of people swarmed about it, on their way out of the city. The vast majority were on foot, although there was a fair sprinkling of gigs and coaches, and even a few lumbering farm-wagons crammed with people. They were in a merry and excited mood.

Liam was anxious not to miss the boat to Liverpool. Leaning out of the coach window, he called up to the coachman on his high seat, enquiring whether they had arrived in Dublin on a fair-day.

'No, sir,' replied the coachman as he flicked the reins over the backs of his four horses, seeking to gain a yard or two against the flood of excited people. 'There's been a public hanging today.'

'It must have been a well-known felon to attract a crowd of this size,' Liam commented as the lead horses shied and threw up their heads in protest at the people milling so closely about them.

'Why, bless you, no, sir. It doesn't have to be anyone special. Hangings are very popular here in Dublin. Folks will travel from miles around to see a man dance the Kilmainham jig, though I never could see why, myself. The sight of a man dangling by his neck from the end of a rope does little to excite me. There was nothing in this hanging of particular interest. No one knew the poor fellow – and never will now. He killed a potman in a fight at the Drum Inn, just around the corner from here. He never said a word after he was arrested and refused to give his name to anyone – even the judge who sentenced him to death. Came from a good family and didn't want them shamed, I've no doubt. Only a young fellow, too, so I heard. There will be a poor woman somewhere wondering what happened to her son, may the good Lord forgive him.'

'May she never learn the truth,' said Liam, but his mind was already moving ahead. To London, Eugene Brennan and the new session of Parliament.

As he drew his head back inside the coach the crowd began to thin, and with a crack of his whip the coachman urged his horses forward.

Chapter Forty-Two

Liam was very pleased with the little house in Hertford Street, obtained for him by Lady Caroline's friend. It was furnished with good taste, and the owner was not wealthy enough to have achieved a standard of luxury that might have made Liam feel uncomfortable.

Liam was able to walk to the House of Commons on all but the wettest of winter days, and before the new session began he went there often to meet with the other Irish MPs. Gradually a campaign was plotted to force the English Government to take immediate action in Ireland. Only the MPs from Dublin and Belfast and a couple of the larger Irish towns would not lend their support. They represented a few men who were making a fortune from the Irish troubles. They had bought corn and flour when prices were little more than reasonable. Now there was such a demand that no asking-price was too ridiculous. If the Government stepped in with famine relief, it would send these prices tumbling.

The one notable absentee from all these meetings was Eugene Brennan. None of the MPs had seen him and, although Liam went to Eugene's house on three occasions, there was no answer to his repeated knocking.

When Eugene Brennan did not arrive for the opening session of Parliament, Liam became really worried. It was not like the MP to be absent at such a critical time, but when the session began Liam had other problems to think about. The clamour from the Irish benches could not be ignored, even by a prime minister who was as little moved by the plight of the Irish as Lord John Russell.

The leader of the Whig Party refused to be stampeded into what he termed 'precipitous action'.

'This government is well aware of the problems facing Ireland,' he declared arrogantly. 'All such steps as I consider to be necessary are being taken. Soup kitchens are to be established—'

This declaration brought cheers from the Irish MPs, but they were quickly checked when Lord John Russell refused to answer questions about payment for setting up the kitchens and could not give details of how food was to be obtained from which to make soup.

Then the Prime Minister caused an uproar when he disclosed that the government-sponsored public works scheme was to end. This programme, inefficient and frustrating though it had proved to be, gave a tiny income to many Irishmen, providing the difference between a man having a hungry family and one that starved to death.

There was not an Irish Member of Parliament that day who did not have to face up to the stark fact that under Lord John Russell's administration 1847 would be an even more terrible year than the previous one had been. At least Sir Robert Peel had *tried* to do something, albeit half-heartedly. Lord John Russell was bringing an air of unreality to the desperate situation. He promised relief measures that had not yet reached the planning stage whilst at the same time withdrawing one of the few measures to offer any real benefit to the cottiers.

While angry accusations and counter-accusations were being hurled back and forth across the floor of the House of Commons, one of the Irish MPs came to where Liam was sitting and leaned down to speak in his ear. It was a few minutes before Liam was able to hear above the din. When he could, he sprang to his feet and hurried from the chamber. He had been told that Eugene Brennan was outside.

The antechamber was a large room with high windows and great areas of shadow. At first, Liam could not see the old MP and thought he must have left. He was about to hurry to the door when he saw Eugene Brennan sitting on the edge of a seat in the deepest shadow of a corner of the room.

But this was not the dynamic politician who had become a legend in his own time. The man seated with his hands clasped between his knees was no more than a shell of the man he had once been. Even his voice when he replied to Liam's greeting had changed. It was totally lacking in strength, and Liam was shocked beyond words.

'Eugene, where have you been? I have been looking all over London for you.'

'I was at home once when you called. I didn't want company. I . . . I. . . .' The old man's voice faded and his eyes looked at things far beyond the walls of the Parliament building.

'Are you all right, Eugene? Would you like me to take you home?'

'Home, Liam? Where is home? It was Ireland once, but I dare not return there – again.'

Liam had to put his head close to Eugene Brennan's lips to hear his words.

'I've been to Ireland, Liam. I went there to see things with my own eyes and was so ashamed that I had no wish to see anyone I knew. The situation has become an open-ended tragedy, Liam. For fifty years I have served Ireland, and believed I was gaining a more hopeful future for her people. This time I saw exactly what I had given them. Starvation and fever – that is what my policy has given to them, Liam. Death and suffering. Can you believe that a man who wanted to avoid bloodshed could lead them to this?'

'Eugene! None of what is happening there is your fault. Without you things would have been much worse—'

'Worse, Liam? Is that possible?'

The suffering in the old man's eyes went too deep for words to ease.

'I came back to England determined to make Russell and his Ministers do something. They wouldn't see me. Worse, Russell had me physically removed from his office. Thrown out. After fifty years of serving my country I was thrown out into the street and there was nothing I could do. Failure comes harder to an old man, Liam. To realise that I had achieved nothing in all those years came hardest of all. All I have done is to bring Ireland to her knees. May God and her people forgive me.'

'Stay here, Eugene. I'll call a cab and take you home, to your house.'

'You'll do no such thing!' Eugene Brennan raised his head to look at Liam. 'I came here to speak to the House and I won't leave until it's done. Here, help me up.'

'Are you sure . . . ?' But the old MP was already struggling to his feet, and Liam assisted him.

Eugene Brennan leaned heavily on Liam as they crossed the floor of the anteroom, but when they reached the door of the debating-chamber and an usher held it open before them Eugene Brennan shook off Liam's hand and walked in ahead of his apprehensive colleague.

One of the Irish MPs was on his feet, trying to make his voice heard above the shouts and catcalls of Lord Russell's Whigs, when suddenly all noise died away. The surprised MP looked around for the reason and when he saw Eugene Brennan he promptly sat down.

The veteran MP was unsteady on his feet but he made his way slowly to his usual seat as his fellow-Members of Parliament made way for him. But Eugene Brennan did not sit down. Instead, he addressed himself to the Speaker of the House and in an uncharacteristically querulous voice said, 'Mr Speaker, do I have your permission to address the House?'

The Speaker hesitated. Many MPs had put down questions on the Irish famine issue and time was already overtaking his planned programme.

'As this will almost certainly be the last occasion on which I address this House I crave your indulgence, Mr Speaker.'

The Speaker was a senior Member of Parliament who had known Eugene Brennan for a great many years. He had observed the old Irishman's unsteady progress through the chamber and, like Liam, he was shocked by the change he saw in the veteran Irish MP's appearance. Without further hesitation, he said, 'The honourable member for Wexford has the floor.'

'Thank you.'

Eugene Brennan reached out to grasp the back of the bench-seat in front of him, and there was not a man in the chamber who did not see how much his hands shook.

In a voice that was tantalisingly low, yet full of emotion, Eugene Brennan began to speak.

'As representative of my constituents and the people of Ireland I have spoken in this House on very many occasions, and on many subjects. But it has never been my misfortune to have to tell you what must be said today. These old eyes of mine have gone beyond weeping. Now it is my heart that is bleeding for my country. Gentlemen, Ireland is dying! At this very moment, as I stand here before you pleading for your goodwill and understanding, my country, on its knees for so long, is lying down to die. I am not here to put the blame on anyone. If it helps, I will take the responsibility upon my own shoulders. I have failed my country as surely as any man ever did. In her darkest hour I am unable to persuade the men who govern her to send Ireland a single bag of corn.'

There was an uncomfortable fidgeting among government ministers on the benches across the chamber.

'I have tried. . . . God knows, but I have tried. . . .'

Eugene Brennan's voice faltered, and Liam feared he would slide away into a dream, as he had in the antechamber, but after a few moments Eugene Brennan spoke again. His voice had lost its forcefulness, but his words might have been made more memorable by the loss.

'I am used to watching people die. I was a young man when my country rose in bloody rebellion against England. I spoke against that rebellion. I have never ceased to speak against rebellion. Now I am left wondering whether I have done my country a disservice.'

There were a few angry murmurs from the government benches, but Eugene Brennan had not finished yet.

'Had Ireland risen against England she would have lost many of her young men. She would have lost the fight as surely as she did once before. But the English are generous in victory and your generosity would at least have saved the women and children. Now, I fear they are beyond salvation.'

Eugene Brennan squared his shoulders and looked from one end of the large chamber to the other so slowly that there was not an MP in the House who who did not believe that he was personally included in the look.

'I will not be bothering this House again with the troubles of my constituents, or questioning the competency of Ministers of the Crown. I have devoted a lifetime to politics and the time has come for me to place my sword into younger, more able hands.'

The shoulders sagged again and Eugene Brennan looked and sounded very tired.

'There was a time when I would have looked upon my small achievements with pride . . . but no longer. Set against this one great failure, they crumble to insignificance. I leave this House shamed and ashamed. But I cannot go without one final plea. Gentlemen, in God's name, save my people.'

The old politician turned to go, and Liam saw the tears streaming down his face. Liam stood and took Eugene Brennan's elbow and, as they reached the gangway, another Irish MP took his other arm.

Then, as they slowly walked from the chamber, the House of Commons, led by Eugene Brennan's long-time opponent, Sir Robert Peel, paid the veteran MP a last mark of respect. One by one they rose to their feet until only Lord John Russell and his Ministers remained seated.

Outside the chamber, Liam sat Eugene Brennan down and sent an usher to call a cab. Eugene Brennan blew his nose loudly before saying to Liam, 'After all my years in the House of Commons, I have to cry and make a fool of myself on my last day.'

'You were magnificent! And there is no reason why this should be your last day. You are still the MP for Wexford – and I can see no man ever voting you out.'

'They must, Liam. I am not up to this work any more. I am too old – and far too tired. There is nothing more tiring than failure.'

'We'll have no more such talk,' declared Liam firmly. 'You'll come back to my house and we will have a drink together. You'll feel better with a glass or two of good Irish whiskey inside you. I bought a bottle in Dublin, especially for you.'

There was a surprise for both men waiting at the house in Hertford Street. Caroline was there. She was full of concern when Liam told her the old politician had not been well. She fussed around him and, in spite of his protests, Eugene Brennan was delighted by her concern.

Later that evening, after they had eaten and were seated before a crackling fire, each nursing a large glass of whiskey, Eugene Brennan felt relaxed enough to tell them more of the events that had caused him to make his decision to retire from politics.

The politician admitted that his biggest mistake had been to support the Whigs against Peel's Tories.

'I was wrong to expect the Whigs to show their gratitude. The word has no place in Lord John Russell's vocabulary. I served my purpose and now he is in power. His philosophy is that the winner takes all – and owes thanks to no man. I am too old to pick up the stones of the house that has tumbled about my ears and build it again. There must be a way of persuading our Prime Minister to do something for Ireland, but a younger man must take on the task.'

'Have you ever discussed the famine with Lord John Russell?' asked Caroline.

'Oh yes. He gave me a few minutes of his time before I last went to Ireland,' affirmed the old man. 'I took with me some of the letters I had received. Desperate letters. Pathetic letters. . . .'

The old man's voice trailed away as it had on a number of earlier occasions, and Liam and Caroline exchanged anxious glances.

'What did he say?' Caroline prompted gently.

'Uh? I beg your pardon?'

'What did Lord John Russell say when you showed him the letters?'

'Oh, he said an Order in Council had been issued. It directed the churches throughout the land to use the Dearth and Famine prayer in their services. A prayer – ha! "Behold, we beseech thee, the afflictions of thy people and grant that the scarcity and death which we do now most justly suffer for our iniquity, may through Thy goodness be mercifully turned into cheapness and plenty." '

Eugene Brennan quoted the prayer as Liam and Caroline looked at each other again in consternation. Was the old man's reason going?

But Eugene Brennan was unaware of their thoughts.

'Cheapness and plenty,' he repeated. 'By the merest stroke of a pen Lord John Russell could have become as God himself to the Irish people. He could have imported corn and sold it at a price that every man and woman could afford. Instead, he passes the whole problem to the Almighty. "Here you are, God. Here is a problem. I could solve it myself, but I would rather you did it for me. After all, God, they are your people, too." '

Eugene Brennan looked up suddenly and caught the worried expressions on the faces of his two companions. He smiled. 'I can see I have been talking for far too long. I thank you both for this most pleasant evening. I have enjoyed it more than any other I can remember for a very long time.'

He struggled up from the chair before Liam could offer him any help.

'Now I will return home. Will you call a cab for me, Liam?'

'Of course – and I will come with you. Then tomorrow you must come here again. I will call for you at your house.'

'No, Liam. I am going away from London. I have a nephew in the French court. He has long wanted me to pay him a visit. I leave tomorrow. I understand he will be taking me to the south of France before returning to Paris. I shall be away for some months. I will be thinking of you and Ireland, Liam. Work through the Association and place no reliance upon the Government. That is the only advice I have to offer you.'

Liam left the house to find a cab plying for hire. It took him some minutes; then the two Irishmen shook hands warmly and Eugene Brennan left.

Liam and Caroline went into the house together and the moment the door closed behind them they embraced with the fervour of lovers who had been parted for too long.

As they walked hand in hand to the lounge, Liam said, 'I am surprised that Eugene made no comment about your presence here.'

'He did, while you were out looking for a cab.' Caroline smiled. 'He said what a pity it is that we are not free to marry. He thinks we make a lovely couple.'

Liam remained in London for three weeks. It was a busy time. Caroline arranged a number of famine-relief meetings at which Liam and a number of other Irish MPs spoke.

The support for their cause at this informal level was overwhelming, but two weeks after her arrival Caroline had to return to Ireland to organise similar soup kitchens to those she had set up the previous year. Liam missed her greatly, but Europe was in the grip of the harshest winter experienced for many years and there were those who needed her more.

Meanwhile, in London, the Irish MPs held many meetings at which they compared the letters received from their various constituencies. The most desperate came from the remote areas of western Ireland where rumours of cannibalism were rife.

Liam thought the time had come for him to tackle officialdom, in the form of Charles Trevelyan, once more. He went to the Treasury and, after making some enquiries, a clerk in an outer office informed Liam that Mr Trevelyan was unable to see him. Liam promptly sat down and announced his intention of remaining where he was until the Treasury official *did* see him.

The flustered clerk scuttled back and forth between Trevelyan's office and his own until he finally informed Liam that Mr Trevelyan was now available.

Liam's reception was icy. Charles Trevelyan did not rise from his desk, neither did he proffer his hand. Nevertheless, Liam did his best to put the latest situation in Ireland to him.

Trevelyan listened impatiently for some minutes before interrupting Liam in mid-sentence.

'I would prefer you to be brief, Mr McCabe. I am a very busy man.'

'Busy with what? There is more to famine relief than paper-work, Mr Trevelyan.'

'And there is more to my work than you see here,' Trevelyan snapped.

'Tell that to the people of Ireland. They have seen no results of your work – unless you count death, disease and misery.'

'Famine is a visitation of the Lord, Mr McCabe. I suggest you and your people pray to Him.'

It appeared that Lord John Russell was not alone in passing on his responsibilities to a higher authority. Further angry exchanges did nothing to help anyone, and after Trevelyan said he had nothing to add to his earlier statements Liam left. He had achieved nothing.

He reported his failure to the London meeting of Irish MPs and it was the final blow that split the rock of the All-Ireland Association wide open. There had always been a faction within the Association dissatisfied with the progress being made toward Irish self-determination. They favoured direct action. Violent action. They had always grumbled at the lack of progress, but until now Eugene Brennan's wide experience and natural guile had held them in check, making use of their restlessness and energy for the Association's purposes.

But Eugene Brennan was no longer with them and at the final meeting in London they walked out, never to return. Within days they had formed their own militant society which they knew would attract many of the younger members of the All-Ireland Association. They planned action to achieve their ends. For them, the time for talking was over.

Although Liam spoke as strongly as he was able in favour of patience, he could not disagree with them and he returned to Hertford Street with his heart as heavy as the snow-laden skies above London. He wished that Caroline was there to help him make sense of the confusion in his mind.

He had begun to wonder where his own future lay. He realised he was no more than a second-class MP, a member of no recognised political party. The Irish MPs had no real power in the House of Commons. They were playing a game, clinging to the coat-tails of those who really ruled their country. Enduring scorn and insult, waiting for a weak government to come to power in order that they might bargain for a few minor concessions for Ireland in return for their support.

There was to be a general election in the summer, but Lord John Russell was assured of a sweeping victory and would need no additional support.

It was not Liam's idea of how Ireland should be governed, or of how he should be occupying his time. He felt he could do more real good in Ireland, and so Liam returned home.

Chapter Forty-Three

Strong westerly winds in February 1847 made for a rough crossing of the Irish Sea, but they also brought a thaw to the snow-piled roads of Ireland. Upon his arrival in Dublin, Liam immediately took horse to County Kerry. During the few months he had been their MP, Liam had made a number of friends there. Among the most surprising was Harvey Gorman, the magistrate who had acted as host to Sir Richard Dudley during the Commissariat Inspector's only visit to the west of Ireland.

Liam made the magistrate's house his first stop in Castlemaine and expressed his surprise at seeing no one on the streets of the town.

The magistrate nodded grimly. 'It is the famine fever, Liam. It puts an unnatural fear into the most rational of men. It has hit Castlemaine and the areas around here badly. Last week more than thirty new cases were reported here in town. In the country nobody bothers to count any more.'

'What about food? Are the wooden boats bought by the Association still bringing in fish?'

'The fishermen are doing their best, but they understand little about sails and rowing a boat is hard work for a man who knows all his catch will go to others at the end of the day. When the boats come in the cottiers descend upon them like starving herring gulls. As often as not they make off with everything, leaving none for salting. I don't know where things are going to end, Liam. Our world here has become insane.'

'Where are the boats now?'

'They have been taken to Ventry, farther along the bay. It's closer to the Blasket Islands; that is where the fish are to be caught.'

'I think I will go along to see how they are getting on there,' said Liam, stretching his aching limbs.

'It will wait until tomorrow,' said Harvey Gorman. 'You've had a long ride in bad weather. You need a good meal and a warming drink inside you right now.'

Liam needed little persuading; the strain of his long journey from London was beginning to tell on him, and he allowed himself to be ushered into a warm dining-room.

Over a meal, Liam asked whether Sir Richard Dudley had made another visit to Castlemaine to put grain into his empty depot.

'Sir Richard Dudley has not set foot in the west of Ireland since you last saw him here,' declared the magistrate. 'And the Commissariat depot is as empty as the day it was built.'

'Then I fear I must seek out Sir Richard when I am next in Dublin. It is not a meeting which will give me any pleasure.'

'Be careful in your dealings with him, Liam. Sir Richard Dudley has no love for you.'

When pressed for an explanation of his words, the magistrate showed considerable embarrassment. His knowledge of the baronet's feelings toward Liam had been obtained by eavesdropping on the conversation between the Commissariat Inspector and his salesman travelling companion.

Eventually, Harvey Gorman told Liam everything he had overheard, and Liam listened in silence. Now he knew why the soldiers had been sent out in strength, in atrocious weather, to seek out a handful of outlaws. It also explained why Eoin Feehan had been with them.

Then Liam thought of something that filled him with sudden horror. The magistrate had referred to Eoin Feehan as 'a potman from Dublin'. Liam remembered what the coachman on the Wexford-to-Dublin mail-coach had told him when they were held up by the crowds coming away from the hanging. He had said the hanged man had killed a potman and then refused to give his name to anyone, preferring an anonymous death to disgrace for his family.

If ever a man had just cause to kill, it was Dermot – and his victim would have been Eoin Feehan, a potman in a Dublin inn. Liam would know little peace of mind until news reached Kilmar that Dermot and the others had arrived in America. Liam doubted whether such news would ever come. He believed that the unknown man who had been hanged in Dublin was his own brother.

Liam heard little else that the magistrate had to tell him, and later, as he lay in bed, he thought about the baronet who had twice attempted to discredit him. There must be much hate in Sir Richard Dudley's heart – or much love for Caroline.

Early the next morning, Liam set off for Ventry. A weak far-off sun was doing its best to bring some warmth to the land, but the strong westerly wind was still blowing, and Liam expected to find the fishermen and their boats idle in the small fishing harbour.

To his surprise, because the wind from the sea was even stronger here, he learned that the two wooden fishing boats were out. The news was given to him by one of a hundred ragged cottiers, huddled together for warmth behind a low wall which kept off much of the wind. The cottier's clothing was totally inadequate for such weather, yet Liam knew that a wagonload of good warm coats and dresses had been sent to them by one of Lady Caroline's charities less than a month before. When Liam questioned them he learned that every item of clothing had been pledged as soon as it was received. He could not be angry with them. The money they received had been used to buy food – a more important commodity than warm clothes. A baby could be cuddled to put some warmth back in its tiny body. If it starved, nothing could restore life itself.

Some of the cottiers recognised Liam and they quickly crowded about him, demanding to know what was being done for them. Others, in the belief that the movement toward this warmly clad stranger meant food, or money, pressed forward with the others, pleading their extreme hunger and begging loudly. They startled his horse, and when the prancing animal had cleared a space about him Liam asked one of the cottiers if he knew the whereabouts of the fishermen.

Wordlessly the cottier pointed farther westward, beyond the towering cliffs of Slea Head, and Liam frowned. Out there were the Blasket Islands and beyond them the wide expanse of the Atlantic Ocean. It was not a good place to be on a windy day like today. Even here, in the lee of the hill, the wind was strong enough to stagger a weakened cottier.

Quick to realise that Liam was not distributing food or money, the cottiers hurried back to the shelter of the wall and Liam kneed his horse away from them.

He followed a track that curved around the base of the hill, close to the edge of the high cliffs. Once clear of the protection of the hill, the strength of the cold wind drew tears from his eyes and occasionally a wild gust caused his horse to throw back its head and snort in frightened protest.

At the top of a steep path that wound down the cliffside to a narrow strip of sand, Liam pulled his horse to a halt and scanned the rough waters anxiously. To his relief he soon saw one of the wooden fishing boats bucking the waves halfway between Great Blasket Island and the mainland, heading shoreward. There were four men rowing and one at the helm, and the boat was making good headway toward the calmer waters of Dingle Bay.

Liam looked for the second boat and at first could see nothing, but then, as he scanned the wind-blown waters, he saw it nose tentatively out into the open sea from the lee of a small island. As the boat drew clear Liam saw the boat had a net out and he silently cursed the men on board for fools. An attempt to fish in open waters in such a wind was suicidal.

It seemed the men on the fishing boat realised the danger they were in and they all began to heave on the net in an attempt to bring it into the boat as quickly as possible.

They were too slow and already too far from the shelter of the island. A long wave, roaring in from the Atlantic, bore down upon the boat and carried it onward. The net was well filled with fish; acting as a badly positioned sea-anchor, it dragged the boat sideways-on to the running sea. The boat slid over the crest of the giant wave and tilted to one side with a suddenness that threw three of the five unprepared fishermen into the water.

The two remaining men realised their own danger too late, and Liam could see them sawing frantically at the ropes holding the net to the boat. They succeeded in their desperate efforts as the next wave struck the fishing boat. The boat seemed to be actually swallowed up by the wave and for almost a minute it disappeared from Liam's view. When he saw it again it was floating upside down, with no trace of its former occupants.

By now the first fishing boat was almost level with Liam, and sliding from his horse he hurried as fast as he dared down the treacherous cliff path, shouting and waving to attract the attention of the fishermen. It was a few minutes before any of them saw him and then the man holding the tiller did no more than raise a hand in a desultory greeting.

Liam redoubled his efforts, gesticulating wildly, and futilely shouting against the noise of wind and sea.

As Liam reached the narrow beach, one of the oarsman recognised him and called to the helmsman. The fishing boat turned to nose in toward the shore, and a few minutes later Liam plunged knee-deep into the shallow water and clambered over the side of the tossing boat as it bottomed on the shingle.

Pointing out toward the Blasket Islands, Liam shouted news of what he had seen to the others. 'I'll take the tiller,' he bawled at the helmsman. 'You get for'ard and keep a look out when we get close to the islands.'

One of the fishermen began to protest that they were tired and could not possibly row back to the islands. Liam cut his words short.

'There is no time for argument. Get out of the boat and push us off.'

To the helmsman he said, 'Take his place and we'll be on our way.'

The reluctant fisherman jumped out of the boat, pushed it clear of the beach – and then swung himself inboard again. In answer to Liam's questioning look, he growled, 'I changed my mind.'

'Good man.' Liam knew that the man was not frightened, but genuinely tired. 'Get for'ard and be prepared to hold us off the rocks if we get in too close.'

It was a rough pull against the combined opposition of sea and wind, but by steering wide of his eventual destination Liam was able to put the bulk of Great Blasket Island between the wind and the boat, making things a little easier for the straining oarsmen.

When they drew close to the upturned fishing boat, the man in the bow called excitedly to Liam that there was a man clinging to it. The news put new vigour into the oarsmen, and they gasped noisily as they heaved back on the oars. Soon Liam was manoeuvring the boat skilfully alongside the man in the sea. He had held tenaciously to his grip on the upturned boat, against the pull of the sea and the effort of each successive wave to dislodge him.

The two boats bumped together, gently at first, then with a

frightening crash as the man in the bow, assisted by one of the oarsmen, took a grip on the half-drowned survivor and pulled him, gasping, into the boat.

He lay in the bottom of the boat among tangled ropes and dead fish, grey-faced and fighting for breath as Liam steered the boat around in a wide circle. The rescued man had won his battle with death with only minutes to spare. Numbed with the cold, his mind had already begun to call on his protesting body to give up the hopeless fight. Only an inborn stubbornness had kept his fingers hooked on to the upturned keel.

Liam intended returning to the other boat and towing it back to the mainland. Its loss would be a disaster to both the fishing and cottier communities. As he circled around the upturned craft, waiting for a calmer moment before going in closer, the fisherman in the bow began shouting and pointing towards a small rocky islet, perilously close by.

Liam stood up to take a closer look and saw the outstretched body of a man lying face downward on a tiny shingle beach.

Liam thought the man must be dead, but then as the tide ran up the beach about him his arms and legs moved in an instinctive attempt to crawl away from the advancing water. There was no place for him to go. Another arm's length away the fragment of beach ended in a sheer wall of burnished black stone.

Once again the fishermen strained at their oars as Liam headed for a gap in the rocks scarcely wider than the boat. He successfully guided the fishing boat through, but one of the weary fishermen was slow in raising his oar clear of the rocks and the stout oar was snapped off as easily as though it were no more than a piece of kindling wood.

Minutes later, with the second rescued fisherman lying alongside his companion in the bottom of the boat, Liam steered out into open water once again.

After searching unsuccessfully for the other three members of the upturned boat's crew, Liam took the fishing boat in tow and beached it on the lee side of Great Blasket Island. Here he was able to right the boat and put a man aboard to steer the craft during the tow back to the mainland.

It was a long hard pull across the Blasket Sound, and by the time Liam guided the boat into Ventry harbour the fishermen were on the verge of collapse – but they arrived to a hero's welcome.

Word of the disaster and rescue had gone around with uncanny speed, many of the Ventry fishermen actually witnessing the final stages of the rescue from Slea Head. Even the cottiers, who had long been given little cause for celebration, heaped their congratulations upon Liam.

Whatever Liam's political future might be, he had earned himself a reputation as a great seaman, and the story would grow with every telling in this corner of County Kerry.

Chapter Forty-Four

Liam remained at Ventry for a few days, instructing the fishermen on how best to use the sails of the wooden fishing boats. He was on the quayside on the third day when a troop of twenty blue-uniformed light dragoons rode into the village and headed straight for the harbour.

The soldiers had to pick their way through a huge crowd of cottiers, for it was a fine day and the hungry families knew Liam would be taking the boats out to fish when he had completed his period of instruction.

'Are the owners of these boats here?' The young dragoons officer waved a gauntlet-clad hand toward the two wooden fishing boats.

'They belong to the community,' replied Liam. 'Bought from the funds of the All-Ireland Association.' He felt uneasy in the presence of the soldiers; they were not in the habit of visiting a village with good news.

The officer recognised that he was not talking to a simple west-coast fisherman, and his voice lost some of its arrogance.

'I regret to inform you that I have orders to destroy all wooden boats along this part of the coast.'

'Destroy them?' Liam repeated in disbelief. It was like the nightmare of Kilmar all over again. 'You can't do such a thing. These people rely on them for the only food they can get. Destroy the boats and you starve fisherman and cottier alike. What nonsense is this?'

'I am sorry. It does seem hard . . . but I have my orders.'

'Orders from whom?' Liam demanded.

Instead of giving Liam a direct answer, the dragoons officer went into an explanation.

'A grain-ship standing well off the coast was recently raided by men in boats. Sir Richard Dudley says it must have been carried out by men using wooden boats as curraghs could never put out that far. As a result, I have been ordered to destroy all the wooden boats along this section of the coast.'

'Sir Richard Dudley knows no more of boats than he does of filling Commissariat depots,' Liam declared angrily. 'I have heard about this incident of piracy. It occurred fifty miles to the north of here and everyone on the west coast knows it was carried out by desperately hungry men – using curraghs.'

The dragoons officer was relatively inexperienced in leading men, but he came from a good yeoman family and he was not prepared to allow this man dressed as a fisherman to insult the titled Commissariat Inspector.

'You would seem to know more about the attack on the ship than you should. Who are you?'

'My name is McCabe and I am the Member of Parliament for this area. Furthermore, I and five of these fishermen risked our lives to save one of these boats from the sea only a few days ago. We'll not stand by and see you smash them now.'

The young officer was impressed by Liam's status. Although only an Irish MP, he had a seat in the House of Commons and helped to govern the land. He thought it would be wise to proceed with caution.

'Those are my instructions, sir. I am sorry.'

'You'll not lay a finger on these boats if you value the lives of your men. Try to carry out your orders and you will all be torn to pieces.'

The young officer looked at the sullen crowd surrounding them and hoped his nervousness was not apparent to anyone else.

'As a Member of Parliament and a responsible citizen it is your duty to prevent any disorder, sir.'

Liam shook his head. 'I could do nothing to prevent bloodshed if you went ahead with your folly. These people rely upon the boats for their very existence. Destroy them and they will die as surely as if you had run a sword through them. There are many here who would prefer to die as men rather than wait for starvation.'

An angry murmuring had begun in the crowd, which was at least five hundred strong, and as though to confirm Liam's words the women and children were pushed to the rear and the cottier men moved toward the dragoons.

As the officer eyed the crowd, Liam said, 'Unless you wish to be held responsible for the bloodiest incident to occur since the uprising you will go away and leave our boats alone.'

Liam could have felt sorry for the young officer's predicament had it not been for the purpose of his visit to Ventry.

'I will have to report this incident to my commanding officer, Mr McCabe. You are obstructing an officer of the Queen in the execution of his duty.'

'I, too, will be making a report – to the Prime Minister. Now, I suggest you leave while the cottiers are still peaceable. I have work to do – and hungry mouths to feed.'

The young dragoons officers still hesitated, but Liam had already turned away and was speaking to the fishermen.

'Get these boats into the water. We have fish to catch and few enough hours of daylight left to us.'

As the boats were being manhandled into the water, the soldiers rode away and Liam breathed a sigh of relief. He had been by no means certain that the young officer would see sense and leave. Returning to his commanding officer and reporting his failure would not be easy for him.

Before another week had gone by, Liam found himself in conflict with Sir Richard Dudley yet again. It was becoming increasingly obvious that the fishermen would not be able to bear the burden of supplying food to the thousands of cottiers who were flocking to the coast. Another source of food had to be found.

For some time, rumours had been circulating that the main Commissariat depot at Limerick, to the north, had been stocked with grain brought in by ship from England. It was said that when the order was given by Sir Richard Dudley this depot would despatch grain and meal to all the other depots on the west coast. So strong were the rumours that even Harvey Gorman, the magistrate, was convinced they were true. He gave Liam the names of two ships in which, it was said, grain had been brought in for the depot.

Armed with this information and faced with a rapidly deteriorating situation among the cottiers, Liam rode to Limerick and called upon the Depot Officer to throw open his gates to the cottiers.

The Depot Officer refused, saying that he was following Sir Richard Dudley's instructions.

'Damn Sir Richard Dudley!' Liam flared. 'People are dying, and I refuse to stand by and do nothing. Either you open your doors or I will have the cottiers do it for you.'

Liam took the arm of the reluctant Depot Officer and led

him to the window. Word had gone round of Liam's arrival, and a huge mob of cottiers was gathering outside, calling for the gates to be opened to them.

'Do you see that? Open the gates yourself and I will be able to control the cottiers. We will keep a record of the amount of meal issued and you will be paid by the All-Ireland Association. Force me to order them to break down the doors and there will be no holding that crowd. They are so hungry they would strip the depot within hours.'

Liam released his grip on the man's arm. 'Well, what is it to be?'

The Depot Officer knew he had little choice. 'I will fetch the keys.'

'Good!' said Liam jubilantly. 'I'll arrange for men to come in and help you with the issue. We will bring our own wagons and take meal and grain away for distribution. I want to get some food to the cottiers in the hills as quickly as possible; they are in a particularly bad way. Let me see, now. . . .' Liam made some rapid calculations. 'I will need about thirty tons for this first issue.'

The Depot Officer gulped in alarm. 'You can't take that much. . . .'

Liam rounded on the man angrily, but the junior Commissariat official added in a strangled voice, 'I only have a total of twelve tons in stock – and it is all last year's meal.'

'I don't believe you.'

'Come with me. I'll show you.'

Eagerly, the Depot Officer reached down a ring of keys from a nail in the wall of his office. His disclosure of the state of the depot stocks came as a great relief to him. He, too, had heard the rumours and the burden of his own knowledge weighed heavily on him. He had lived in fear of the day arriving when news of his actual stockholding became known. He felt sure that angry cottiers would smash down the doors and take what they could, while it was still there.

Liam walked around the almost empty depot and plunged his hand into one of the sacks of meal. Sniffing it suspiciously, he tasted some on the tip of his tongue. It was stale. Here, in one of the biggest Commissariat depots in all Ireland were twelve tons of stale meal to feed all the starving cottiers of west Ireland.

'Start unlocking those doors,' he said to the Depot Officer. 'Give away all your stock while it is still eatable. I am going straight to Dublin to see Sir Richard Dudley. I think it is time he and I had a talk.'

Chapter Forty-Five

If Liam had any doubts about the course of action he was taking, he would have lost them on his two-day ride to Dublin through the dying heart of Ireland.

Before he had covered half the distance, the sight of death had become so commonplace that when his horse shied at the body of a cottier lying across the road Liam did not waste time dismounting. He reined his horse around the withered corpse and continued on his way.

But Liam could never get used to seeing starving children. He wept to see so many tiny bodies wasted and distorted by hunger. Their deep-sunk, dark, hopeless eyes haunted him every mile of the journey. They never said anything to him, and he was glad, for there was nothing he could do for them. He was of the living. They already had one foot over the threshold of death.

Hunger had reached Dublin now. True, there were carriages filled with well-dressed happy people rumbling along the cobbled streets, and the shops displayed a wide variety of foods. But the price of foodstuff put it beyond the reach of many of the working men. Now they, too, knew something of the hunger felt by the cottiers.

Liam thought he would have to wait, perhaps for days, for an interview with Sir Richard Dudley, but within minutes of outlining his business to a stoop-shouldered clerk he was being ushered into a large and comfortable office.

Sir Richard Dudley stood across the room, his back to a crackling fire. He appeared smaller and more slightly built than ever before, and Liam had to remind himself that this thin-lipped man held the lives of a great many people in his hands.

'You have a damned impudence coming here to see me, McCabe. Your interference with the Army at Ventry could land you in jail – and probably will.'

'So could emptying your Limerick depot of meal,' retorted Liam. 'But it is done, and a few cottiers will live longer because of it.'

'You did what . . . ?'

Liam had travelled faster than the Depot Officer's letter, and the Commissariat Inspector knew nothing of this latest incident.

'I took all the near-mouldy meal from your depot and distributed it to the cottiers – for whom it was intended. Your man holds my receipt. The All-Ireland Association will pay more than a fair price for the full quantity.'

'You have gone too far this time, McCabe.' Sir Richard Dudley spluttered his anger at Liam. 'That was government property. You will not get away with this.'

'I put the meal to the use for which it was intended. Stale and weevilled though it was, it has pushed starvation a few days farther away for some. I doubt if you will have me arrested for doing something you should have ordered weeks ago. If you do, I will ensure a public enquiry is held into the reason for all the west-coast Commissariat depots being empty. You know as well as I that if the cottiers learn the true level of the stocks in your depots there will be rioting in every city and town throughout the land. There will not be a landlord's store left standing. No, Sir Richard, you will not run such a risk.'

'Don't be so cocksure, McCabe. The policy is Trevelyan's, not my own. I am paid to see it is carried out – to the letter.'

'That may well be so, Sir Richard, but would Charles Trevelyan admit that to a board of enquiry? I think not. He demands total loyalty from his paid men. I would ensure the board knew of your involvement in the trumped-up charges against Eugene Brennan and myself, and of your using your influence to send troops against my brother. I think the obvious conclusion would be that you allowed your personal feelings to affect your judgement. I am quite sure Charles Trevelyan would endorse such a finding.'

Sir Richard Dudley looked at Liam with a new and grudging respect. He conceded that he had seriously underestimated him. But he also believed Liam was bluffing.

'You would not dare give evidence against me to a board of enquiry. If you did, your own career as an MP would be over and every door in London would be closed against you.'

Liam smiled. He and Sir Richard Dudley lived totally different lives. Neither would ever understand the other.

'Being a Member of Parliament doesn't matter very much to me. I was happier as a fisherman. I became an MP only to help the cottiers. I believe I will be able to help them as much outside the House of Commons.'

Sir Richard Dudley saw that Liam was in earnest. Being an MP really was unimportant to him.

'Does Lady Caroline's reputation also mean so little to you.'

'It means a great deal – to both of us, albeit for rather different reasons. Let's stop playing games with each other, Sir Richard. You will not have me arrested, but even as we are talking people are dying. What are you going to do to help them?'

Sir Richard Dudley shrugged and moved from the fire to stand behind his desk. The light from the window was behind him now and Liam could not see his face so clearly.

'I can do nothing. Yes, the depots are empty and Charles Trevelyan is fully aware of the fact. My colleague who is responsible for the south-east depots was foolish enough to call Trevelyan's attention to the matter. He was told in no uncertain terms that it was none of his business and he was exceeding his duties. I have no intention of making a similar error.'

'Rather than risk a rebuke from Charles Trevelyan you will allow the cottiers to starve?' Liam looked at Sir Richard Dudley in disgust.

'The cottiers are born to poverty and exist in squalor. They live from day to day, with little thought of the morrow. Their standards are no higher than those of the animals with whom they share their homes. Are you asking me to put my career at risk for such people? The majority of them would be better dead. However, be that as it may, what are *you* prepared to do for your precious cottiers, McCabe?'

'Do you want me to list all the schemes I have begun—?'

'No,' Sir Richard Dudley interrupted. 'I asked what you are *prepared* to do. I even have a suggestion. If you agree, I might be able to persuade Charles Trevelyan to change his policy and send corn and meal to the depots here in Ireland.'

Liam became instantly suspicious. The baronet would do him no favours and he had just admitted he had no sympathy for the cottiers.

'What is your suggestion . . . and what part do you want me to play?'

'The part of an honourable man, McCabe. Stay away from my wife and still the wagging tongues.'

In any other circumstances Liam would have told Sir Richard Dudley to go to hell. He had long ago lost all feeling of guilt about cuckolding this man who had never been a husband in the full sense to Caroline.

But circumstances were far from normal. The lives of tens of thousands of cottiers were at stake. Their fate would be determined by the whims of this one man.

'You feel you could save lives . . . yet you impose conditions?' Liam fought desperately hard to control his temper and hide his contempt for the baronet. 'If you can obtain food for the cottiers, then for the love of God get it for them.'

'Ah, I am afraid you have misinterpreted my words, McCabe. I said I *might* be able to change Charles Trevelyan's policy – given sufficient incentive, of course.'

Sir Richard Dudley smiled mockingly at Liam. 'Now you are in a position to do something for your starving cottiers, McCabe. What a pity you will not be able to tell them of your decision. You could become the greatest hero since Brian Boru.'

The baronet had neatly passed responsibility for the fate of the cottiers to Liam. Not to see Caroline again was unthinkable. But if the alternative was to see thousands of cottiers die . . . ? Sir Richard Dudley had presented Liam with a *fait accompli*. There could be only one answer. Liam could not bring himself to admit it, here and now, but as he turned to go the baronet called to him.

'Don't take too long to reach a decision, McCabe. You know just how much time your precious cottiers have left to them.'

When Liam had left his office, Sir Richard Dudley rang for his clerk.

'Where is that report I wrote describing the situation of the west-coast cottiers?'

'On my desk, Sir Richard. I have copied it and it is now awaiting despatch to London.'

'Bring it here, to me. I am going to hold it back for a while. Instead, I want you to prepare a short dispatch to Trevelyan. Tell him things are serious – but not yet out of hand. When you have it ready bring it here for my signature.'

The clerk looked bewildered. 'But your report says it is most urgent that meal is obtained—'

'I know what is in my report. Do as you are told. Bring the report to me then write that note.'

Another letter also went to London that day.

Liam walked aimlessly through the streets of Dublin, his mind on his own troubles until he was accosted by a beggar-woman with two small and very dirty children clinging to her skirts.

The incident brought him to his senses. Returning to the room he had booked at an inn, he sat down and penned a long letter to Lord John Russell. In it Liam painted a vivid word-picture of the plight of the people of Ireland's western seaboard. Liam doubted whether the letter would serve any useful purpose, but it was a last desperate attempt to ward off the decision that had to be taken.

Chapter Forty-Six

Liam returned to Kilmar without first calling at Inch House. There would be time enough to see Caroline when his thoughts were in some semblance of order. He found the fishing village seething with excited gossip over the belated news that Eoin Feehan had been murdered.

It seemed Eoin Feehan had told another of the Drum Inn's potmen that he was from Kilmar. The recipient of the news was himself from Waterford and had called at Kilmar on his way home for a visit. He had delivered his grim news, assuring the interested fishermen that the hangman had settled Eoin Feehan's debt for him.

Norah McCabe was as full of the news as any other villager.

'There are those in Kilmar who say they could foresee such a violent end for Eoin Feehan from the time he was a small boy,' she said to Liam. 'There's no doubt he could make enemies wherever he was.'

Liam said very little in reply. He dreaded the day when Kilmar received its first letter from the young exiles in America. He was certain it would tell that Dermot was not there with them. Then the whole village would know who had killed Eoin Feehan – and who had been hanged for his murder.

Liam was relieved when his mother's chatter turned to other matters.

'We've had fever break out among the cottiers up on the hill again. A small child died and two others in the same family are still ill. But we have been lucky. I am told there are villages where there is hardly a soul who isn't racked with fever. I don't know what the country is coming to. Mind you, things would be a lot worse hereabouts if it wasn't for Lady Caroline.'

Liam jumped at the sudden mention of her name.

'Yes, to be sure. Tommy Donaghue says that poor girl is working herself into an early grave. Tending the sick, running a soup kitchen, and then dashing off to Dublin, London and such places to raise more money for relief work. Tommy says— ah! But you wouldn't be knowing. I let Tommy go off with the horse and cart to help Lady Caroline for most of the week.'

Norah saw Liam's surprised expression.

'Well, it takes Tommy's mind off Kathie, God rest her soul, and it makes some use of the horse. There's nothing else for it to be doing here. Nobody is catching enough fish to send to Gorey. There's enough to eat and a little over to salt – and that's the whole of it. If there is any to spare, it is given to Father Clery. He is trying to keep another soup kitchen going up on the hill. Besides, Lady Caroline keeps the horse fed and that saves us money.'

'I must go and see Lady Caroline while I am home,' said Liam casually.

'Of course you must go and see her.'

Norah McCabe made a lot of noise chopping a turnip for the cooking-pot.

'That girl deserves more from life than working herself to death for ungrateful cottiers. If every land-owner worked as hard as she does, there would be no hungry cottiers and Ireland would be a land flowing with milk and honey.'

Liam had never before heard his mother speak of Caroline with such enthusiasm. He had always believed she disapproved of his relationship with the Earl of Inch's sister. The thought brought his mind back to what he had to say to Caroline and he sat through the remainder of Norah McCabe's gossip wrapped in a morose silence.

Liam set off for Inch House the following morning, telling his mother he would not return to Kilmar but would journey on to Kerry.

Caroline's new house was nearing completion and, although much smaller than Inch House, it was still an ambitious project. Liam stopped to admire the house and chat to Nathan Brock, who was supervising a veritable army of workmen.

Nathan Brock greeted Liam warmly, but his delight was not only at seeing an old friend.

'Perhaps now you are here Lady Caroline will stop work for a while,' he said to Liam as they walked from room to room of the new house. 'She is doing far too much, Liam. Shelagh and I are worried about her. I sometimes feel the cottiers could do more to help themselves, but when I look about me here and see how hard they will work when given the opportunity I know their troubles are not of their own making. Ordinarily, this house would have taken twice the time to complete – even with a work force of this size. All the cottier needs is enough money to keep his family with full bellies and he is a happy man. You should see them in the evening, when Tommy Donaghue is up here with his old fiddle. They would dance all night if he could keep going.'

Nathan Brock gave Liam a lop-sided grin. 'But you don't want to stand here listening to me chatting about everything under the sun. Get on up to the big house and see Lady Caroline.'

A troubled Liam set off toward Inch House but he had not gone many paces when he swung around and called to his friend.

'Nathan, take care of Lady Caroline. Whatever happens in the future, take *special* care of her. She may need you.'

Liam said no more, but as he trudged away Nathan Brock looked after him with an unhappy frown, wondering what he meant. Liam was a good friend, but Nathan had come to love Caroline. He, more than anyone, knew how hard she worked – and how much she cared for Liam. He hoped the fisherman was not about to do anything to make her unhappy.

Caroline saw Liam approaching the house and ran down to open the door for him. He was shocked by her tired appearance, but when he mentioned it she shrugged off his words and as the door of her own sitting-room swung shut behind them she threw herself at him, almost knocking him off balance in her eagerness to hug him.

'Oh Liam! . . . My love! . . . You don't know how I have missed you. It seems a whole lifetime since I last saw you.'

Liam held her slim body close, enjoying the clean smell of her and the excitement that always ran through him when she was close. The thought came to him that this might be the last time he would hold her like this, but he put it from him and held her even tighter.

'You have been working much too hard,' he chided gently as he looked at her taut drawn face and the dark smudges beneath her tired eyes. His concern brought a pleased smile from her.

'We are *both* working too hard,' she agreed. 'But neither of us could do less.'

Taking his hand, she led him to the settee. 'When things

have returned to normal we will be able to rest. Until then there is far too much to do to think of ourselves.'

It would have been an ideal opening for Liam to tell her of Sir Richard's ultimatum, but he remained silent. He knew it was a cowardly thing to do, yet it was more than cowardice. Liam was a stubborn man and he had not fully accepted that there was no other course of action to take.

It was doubtful whether Caroline noticed his sudden silence. She was happy to have him with her again.

Caroline was not a woman to pass her problems on to others, but in recent weeks she had witnessed much misery and grief and Liam's arrival came as a great relief to her. To him she was able to pour out all her fears and anxieties.

Not until they were lying tangled in each other's arms in a darkened bedroom did the tension finally drain from Caroline's body – and then she wept openly.

Liam held her close and understood. He held her until she slept and then brushed the hair back from her tear-damp face and lay beside her.

She was still sleeping when he rose from her bed and dressed quietly, kissing her gently on the forehead before making his way from the house in the grey damp dawn.

He went away making excuses to himself for his lack of courage in not telling Caroline of her husband's ultimatum.

Liam rode to Castlemaine and there had to face a storm of anger about the latest government directive from London. Lord John Russell had implemented his decision to end the programme of public works in Ireland. There was to be no more road construction, ditch-digging, or wall-building at government expense.

Ironically, this decision coincided with a sharp drop in the price of maize meal, and had the public works programme continued many people would have been able to buy enough food for themselves.

Once again Liam wrote to Lord John Russell, complaining of the criminal folly of this latest move. At Liam's suggestion, letters were also sent by the Castlemaine magistrate and many of the county's land-owners.

Lord John Russell's reply was to rush through Parliament the Poor Law Extension Bill, ordering each impoverished parish to support its own paupers.

Liam could have broken down and wept with anger and frustration. The rate returns for the vast majority of parishes in County Kerry were non-existent. The lesser landlords were in almost as dire straits as their starving tenants. With no potatoes for two seasons they had received no rents and could contribute little toward supporting the cottiers. The large estates were better off because many of them grew corn, but these were owned by landlords who were resident in England. Quick to call in the Army to help in the collection of rents and the eviction of non-paying tenants, they managed to resist all efforts to force them to contribute toward the local rates.

Then, when it seemed that nothing more could be done, and contrary to all the English Prime Minister's declarations, an under-powered paddle-steamer limped in through the entrance of Castlemaine harbour and unloaded fifty tons of meal for the Commissariat depot. The captain of the steamer informed Liam he would be delivering a similar amount to every depot along the whole of the west coast.

As Liam had not been near Inch House for two months, he took the unexpected delivery to be an acknowledgement by Sir Richard Dudley of his own promise.

Unfortunately, the paddle-steamer had been constructed for river work and was not equipped to cope with the Atlantic swell found off Ireland's west coast. Twenty miles north of Castlemaine her uncertain engines faltered and died and the ship was swept on to the rocks of the Magharee Islands. The crew were taken off safely by the escorting naval frigate, but the ship and its cargo of meal were lost in the depths of the ocean.

This was the last grain-ship seen on the west coast of Ireland during all the years of famine.

Chapter Forty-Seven

Early in June 1847, Liam was in Tralee, watching as the residents of this fever-hit town erected a makeshift hospital, when he saw a tired splay-legged horse enter the town from Castlemaine road. The rider was kicking the ribs of the horse in an attempt to make the poor beast move faster. As the hard-working duo approached, Liam saw that the horse carried no saddle and its bridle was more suited to a cart-horse.

Then, as horse and rider came closer, Liam's amusement quickly changed to alarm. It was Tommy Donaghue, mounted on the horse that usually pulled a cart between Kilmar and Gorey.

Liam's first thought was that something must have happened to his mother. She could not write, and so he had heard nothing from her since leaving Kilmar three months before.

He shouted, but Tommy Donaghue would have ridden by without seeing him had Liam not run out and grabbed the horse's bridle.

'Tommy! It's me . . . Liam. What's the matter?'

For a few seconds Tommy Donaghue's legs continued to drum against the stationary horse's flanks, as though he had no control over them. Then he sagged over the horse's neck before sliding gratefully to the ground.

'Is it my mother, Tommy? Is she ill?'

'Your mother . . . ? No, Liam, it's not your mother. Just give me a minute to collect myself. I think the riding has bounced what little brain I own right out of me head.'

Liam tried to hide his impatience as the other man put both hands to his head and shook it gently from side to side.

'It's Lady Caroline,' he said eventually. 'She's got the fever. She must have caught it from the cottiers. It is a miracle she hasn't gone down with it long before now, as I told your mother. I was with Lady Caroline when she was taken ill. I carried her back to Inch House in the cart. By the time we got there she was in such a bad way she didn't know where she was.'

Tears suddenly sprang to Tommy Donaghue's eyes. 'She was

calling for you, Liam. She was so ill that she couldn't have given anyone her own name, but she was calling for you. It broke my heart to see her, Liam. I went to your mother and she said I should come for you right away.'

With tears streaming down his face, the old fiddler said, 'Go to her as quickly as you can, Liam, and I pray to heaven you won't be too late. She's a wonderful woman.'

Liam found lodgings for Tommy Donaghue in Tralee and was on his way to Inch House within the hour.

It was a hard two days' ride with no change of horse, and for long stretches of mountain road Liam walked beside the animal to give it the only rest it could expect during the daylight hours.

The journey was long enough to make Liam feel guilty for not giving Caroline a reason why he had not visited her for so long. He had taken the easy way out of his predicament, keeping to the letter of Sir Richard Dudley's ultimatum, without being forced to discuss it with her. True, Liam had not actually told Sir Richard Dudley he would not see Caroline again, but the baronet obviously thought he had Liam's tacit agreement.

Alone, on this ride, Liam was able to view the situation much more clearly than before. He doubted whether Sir Richard Dudley could really change the policy of the English Government to any great extent. There *had* been the delivery of meal by the paddle-steamer, but Liam believed it would probably have arrived without any effort on the part of the Commissariat Inspector.

As it happened, Liam was correct. The meal on the paddle-steamer had been loaded before he and the baronet had held their talk. Far from arranging the delivery, Sir Richard Dudley had kept it back, hoping to convince Liam when the time was right that he had the power to supply meal for the cottiers at will.

Liam thought long about his relationship with Caroline. Looked at logically, in the light of day, he had to accept that it held out no chance of ending happily. They came from different backgrounds. She had a great deal of money, he had very little —and she already had a husband. The situation was entirely without hope for the future.

But at night, lying on his back in the heather and listening to the lonely call of a solitary curlew, he looked up at a million stars and all the hopelessness fell away. He was left with only the clear and unwavering fact of his love for Caroline, and suddenly everything became possible once more.

Liam rode into the courtyard of Inch House soon after darkness had fallen. He was reeling in the saddle from fatigue, having pushed himself and the horse to the limit to arrive at the house that night.

The door was standing open, and Liam went inside and made his way upstairs before he met anyone. He had almost reached the top stair when the door of Caroline's room opened and a woman came out. It was his mother. Seeing Liam she ran to him and hugged him with great relief.

'Thank heaven you're here, Liam. I was beginning to think you would never arrive in time.'

'In time . . . ? Is she so ill?'

Norah McCabe nodded unhappily. 'Yes. I am afraid she is.'

'Can I see her now?'

'Not yet. She is in a coma. If – when she comes out of it Shelagh Brock will tell us. She is staying with her for now.'

It was apparent that Norah McCabe did not believe Caroline would recover, and Liam knew she must be very ill indeed, but it did not explain why his mother was here in Inch House.

'I came here after I had sent Tommy off to find you,' Norah McCabe said, in answer to Liam's question. 'As she was asking for my son I thought it was the least I could do, but it doesn't mean I approve of what is going on between you two. No, Liam, don't try to deny anything; I'm not a fool. I have known you for too many years not to know what you are up to now. It is wrong and nothing will ever make it right. She already has a husband. All right, so he is not a good man – I have heard all about that from Nathan and from Shelagh – but Lady Caroline took him for better or for worse and I don't like to think of a son of mine coming between a husband and his wife.'

Norah McCabe sniffed noisily. She had voiced her disapproval; now she showed her generosity.

'Be that as it may, I told Tommy where he might find you because I thought you could help to bring Lady Caroline back to good health again. A lady she may be, but she's a mere slip of a girl who has broken herself for the sake of others. Without her, relief work for the cottiers would have collapsed ages ago. It will for sure now. Nathan is out somewhere doing the best he can, but it won't be enough. That girl in there can bully, cajole, plead or demand – and if it is called for she can charm the skin off a toad, sure enough. There is no man alive who can do all that – not even Nathan Brock.'

They walked slowly together down the stairs and Norah McCabe said seriously, 'I think you ought to know that Sir Richard Dudley has been sent for. It was not my idea,' she hastened to explain. 'That cold fish of a butler told me he had sent for him before my arrival. He considered it "his duty". He would have sent for the Earl, too, but it seems he is abroad.'

Liam nodded wearily. It no longer mattered to him that there might be any angry confrontation with Caroline's husband. If she was going to die, then nothing mattered any more. She had caught a fever from the cottiers, and in his present tired state he blamed them for everything.

Caroline came out of her coma soon after midnight, when Norah McCabe was once more sitting with her. Liam was hurriedly summoned and he arrived bleary-eyed from sleep. His mother had told him that Caroline usually came out of her fever in the cool of the night, and he had been sitting in a chair in the big hall, waiting, when sleep overtook him.

Caroline was very ill and extremely weak, but there was no mistaking her joy when she recognised Liam in the dimly lit bedroom. Telling Liam to feed Caroline with some of the soup she had prepared, Norah McCabe tactfully left the room.

'It is . . . so good to see you again, my Liam. It has been so long . . . so very long.'

Liam leaned over her swollen face, and she recoiled in alarm. 'No, Liam . . . don't touch me. . . . The fever. . . .'

Ignoring her protests, Liam kissed her moist brow and brushed back the long fair hair from her face.

'I am sorry to be such a nuisance. . . .' Her fingers plucked at the bedclothes in her distress.

'You are not a nuisance, and I should have come to you before now. I wanted to. . . .'

She looked up into his face. 'Is that the truth, Liam? Did you really want to see me?'

'Of course.'

Her eyes closed, and he had to lean closer to her lips to hear her next words.

'I saw Richard when I was last in Dublin. He . . . told me . . . told me you had agreed not to see me. In return . . . he would not cause a scandal and have you . . . lose your seat in Parliament.'

'He lied,' said Liam angrily. 'I saw him, yes. But—' He stopped talking as he looked down at Caroline. Talking had exhausted her. She lay back on her pillow with eyes closed and lips parted, and her breathing was a shallow whisper against her lips.

'This isn't the time to tire you with talk. I am here, and here I will stay. Now you must try to take some of my mother's soup.'

Liam propped her up so that she lay back in his arm as he fed her with soup from the bowl. She took no more than half a dozen spoonfuls before her head dropped against his shoulder.

He laid her carefully down upon the pillow, smoothing the bedclothes about her, willing her to get well again.

He found his mother waiting outside the bedroom and told her that Caroline had held a conversation with him and taken a few spoonfuls of soup.

'She is very weak, but perhaps the fever has broken,' he said hopefully.

Norah McCabe shook her head. 'The fever has left her every night I have been here – but each time she is weaker than before.'

'There must be something else we can do,' said Liam. He knew there was not a doctor within forty miles, but. . . . 'Why don't you send for Bridie O'Keefe to come here? She would be able to do *something*.'

Norah McCabe looked away from her son's tortured face. 'Bridie O'Keefe was with me when I first came here to be with Lady Caroline.'

'Then why isn't she here now? What did she do?'

'She turned around and went straight back to Kilmar. She said that her business was with the living. She said there was no place for her here'

Chapter Forty-Eight

Sir Richard Dudley arrived at Inch House soon after noon the following day. He was hot and dusty and not in the best of humour. When he met Liam in the hallway of the great house his bad temper exploded in anger.

'What are you doing in this house? We had an agreement. I should have known better than to trust the word of a man who is so clearly not a gentleman.'

'You *assumed* we had an agreement,' corrected Liam. 'And, as I remember it, your part was to provide aid for the cottiers.'

'I said I would *try*,' retorted the angry baronet. 'I did my best. A grain-ship was sent to the west coast. It was not my fault that it sank.'

'Fifty tons were landed. Fifty tons to save the whole of the west coast from starvation. Is that how a gentleman keeps his word, Sir Richard? But now is not the time for such arguments. Caroline is lying upstairs very ill. She needs the attention of a doctor, urgently.'

'Then I will take her back to Dublin with me today.'

'She is not fit to be moved. The fever has not yet broken. A doctor will need to come here to treat her.'

'Fever?' Sir Richard Dudley's face suddenly drained of blood. 'I knew nothing of any fever. I was told only that Caroline was seriously ill.'

'She caught the famine fever from the cottiers. She lies in a coma for most of the day and it is becoming increasingly difficult to get her to take food.'

The mention of famine fever – typhus – put a cold and unreasonable terror in Sir Richard Dudley. His fear of the loathsome disease bordered upon hysteria. He had witnessed its effects during his travels abroad and now he cursed the man who had come to Dublin for not telling him the nature of her 'illness'. He had managed to keep clear of the disease in Dublin and he had no intention of being put at risk here, so far from medical care.

'I must return to Dublin,' he said abruptly. 'I will send an army surgeon to call upon Lady Caroline. No other doctor will undertake such a journey.'

'But you have not even visited her.'

'It would serve no useful purpose. If she is in a coma, she will not know me.'

It was not yet known how typhus was transmitted. It could be food, touch – or the germs might live in the air about sick persons. Sir Richard Dudley wanted only to get out of this house of sickness, but before he left he had a word of warning for Liam.

'You would be well advised to spend your time in County Kerry and stay away from this house. Lord John Russell has called an election for next month. You will need more than the friendship of an ageing politician to win the seat for you this time.'

With this warning, Sir Richard Dudley left Inch House, less than ten minutes after his arrival. The servants, who had just begun to unload his baggage, hurried to put it back on the carriage again.

Norah McCabe, bristling with indignation, accosted the baronet as he was about to step into his carriage after a brief and impatient walk in the gardens of the great house. She knew why he was leaving in such unseemly haste – she had known many others with a similar fear of the fever – but to leave without even seeing his wife was unthinkable.

'Are you leaving no message for your wife before you scurry back to Dublin? Am I to tell her that you came to this house and left only minutes later without asking to see her?'

Sir Richard Dudley looked with distaste at the tall gaunt-featured woman standing before him with her hands resting on her hips. The Earl of Inch ran a lax household here. As an Irish peer, the Earl could not be expected to maintain the same standards as his English counterparts, but to allow Liam McCabe and riff-raff like this woman free run of his house was inviting trouble.

'What I do is none of your concern. You may tell Lady Caroline that I will soon be returning to the Treasury Department to take up a senior post in Canada. I shall expect her to accompany me.'

Sir Richard Dudley spoke loudly, aware that Liam was listening. He then negotiated the high carriage-step with some difficulty and settled himself inside before ordering the coachman to drive off.

'Why, the mean-faced little greenbone! He is so full of puffed-up pride and his own importance that he never even asked how Lady Caroline was.'

Norah McCabe quivered with rage. 'If that's the way gentlemen behave, then I'm pleased I brought you up to be a fisherman.'

Liam was thoughtful as he watched the baronet's carriage depart along the long driveway from the house. Sir Richard Dudley's visit had been very brief, but he had imparted a great deal of information in that short time.

The news of the forthcoming election came as no great surprise to him. It had long been known that Lord John Russell would have to call one sometime during 1847. Of more interest was Sir Richard Dudley's warning that Liam might have difficulty keeping his parliamentary seat. It sounded as though the baronet had already begun a campaign to discredit Liam in County Kerry.

To Liam's own surprise, he realised he did not care. He had set a relief programme in motion that others would be able to see through and there were troubles enough here in County Wexford to occupy all his time. Had he spent more time nearer to home, Caroline might not be so close to death at this moment. For the moment, the most important thing in his life was to see her restored to health. Time enough then to worry about Sir Richard Dudley's threat to take his wife to Canada with him.

Fleetingly, Liam wondered how the baronet had found his way back into favour.

It was fortunate that Liam did not know. The appointment was Sir Richard Dudley's reward for rigidly enforcing Charles Trevelyan's harsh policy of not supplying food to the cottiers, however desperate their needs. The baronet was the only Commissariat Area Inspector to hold out against the suffering of the populace. His firm stand supported Trevelyan's stated belief that it was not necessary for the Government to provide an unending supply of food to the ungrateful Irish.

The Permanent Head of the Treasury chose to ignore the files of harrowing reports which told of the thousands of deaths directly attributable to his determination to withhold Treasury funds.

Liam remained at the great house that night, sitting in the room with his mother during her vigil at Caroline's bedside.

As she had on previous nights, Caroline came out of her coma soon after midnight, when lightning was flickering across the night sky and the wind rattled the casement windows of the room.

Tonight the period of lucidity was briefer than it had ever been before. Caroline opened her eyes, smiled weakly at Liam and reached for his hand. In a whisper she told him how happy she was that he was there with her, but before Norah McCabe was able to bring hot soup to the bedside Caroline had lapsed into unconsciousness once more.

'The poor little soul.' A tearful Norah McCabe stood with the unwanted dish in her hands. 'If she doesn't eat, I can't see her lasting another night.'

'I'll not allow her to die.' Tucking Caroline's hand beneath the bedclothes, Liam rose to his feet. 'I'm going to fetch Bridie O'Keefe. She'll come whether she wants to or not.'

Norah McCabe called to Liam from the window as he strode from the house, but he was deaf to everything but his own determination and the wind blew his mother's words back in her face.

In the darkened stables Liam had to awaken a stable-boy from his comfortable bed of straw in order to locate his horse. Ignoring the sleepy lad's grumbling, Liam made him hold a lantern while he saddled the animal before riding out into the night.

The storm was far out beyond the land. On the horizon jagged lightning noisily stitched sky to sea, and the wind blew strong and clean upon Liam's face as he rode toward Kilmar.

It was still a couple of hours short of dawn when Liam reached the village and began banging on Bridie O'Keefe's door. She was a heavy and determined sleeper, and the noise wakened her neighbours long before the old healer stirred. Twice Liam was obliged to explain his errand and only when the obliging neighbours pounded upon their bedroom walls and rattled the cottage windows with boat oars did Bridie O'Keefe fling back her bedclothes and stamp her way to the window to show her night-bonneted head to those outside.

'What are you making all that din for? I'm not deaf. Who is it who wants me in the dead of night?'

'It's me, Liam McCabe. I've just come from Inch House. I want you to come back there with me and do what you can for Lady Caroline.'

'You've woken me in the middle of the night for that? I've already been to see her. I told your mother there was nothing more to be done.'

'I believe there is,' shouted Liam doggedly, above the wind. 'If she could only be brought out of her fever for a while, she might gather enough strength to pull through.'

'Is that so? A doctor as well as a Member of Parliament are you now?'

'I am no doctor, Bridie, but I have seen it done – and anything is worth a try. I can't just wait around for her to die.'

'And why should you be the one to do the waiting, Liam McCabe? There are others who should be more concerned than yourself – and I doubt whether folks will be slow to say as much, behind your back.'

'Sir Richard Dudley was at the house yesterday. He is going to send an army surgeon from Dublin, but I fear he will be too late.'

The wind roared along the narrow street, distorting Liam's words and rattling the open window of the old lady's house. Reaching for the catch, she said, 'I've yet to meet the army surgeon who is fit to do more than gut a fish. All right, Liam McCabe, I'll come with you – but she will probably die anyway.'

It seemed an age before Bridie O'Keefe emerged from her house. She was wrapped in a large dark shawl and cursing the night and the wind. Refusing to mount Liam's horse, she walked beside it, taking frequent rests and wheezing all the time, as noisy as a County Waterford beam-engine. When they were still a mile from the great house, the threatened storm caught up with them. Even now the old lady refused to ride, and by the time they reached the house they were both soaked through.

Bridie O'Keefe went directly to Caroline's bedroom, and as Norah McCabe clucked about her, wielding a large towel, the old woman told Liam to go about his business and leave her to the task of bringing down Lady Caroline's fever.

An hour later the storm had moved on and Liam rode off in search of Nathan Brock, who was somewhere in the cottier settlements. Liam felt the need of someone with whom he could talk, and Nathan Brock was a good listener.

Liam failed to find his friend, but he did not return to Inch House until late evening. Although the wind and rain had returned, the windows of Caroline's bedroom were flung wide open.

When Liam entered the room he saw that the fire had been extinguished and Caroline lay on a bed from which all the linen had been removed.

An army surgeon was also there. He had been sent from a regiment Sir Richard Dudley had met with along the Dublin road. The surgeon was a very senior officer, having begun his army service with the Duke of Wellington's forces on the hillside of Mont St Jean – later to be known as the battlefield of Waterloo. But his seniority counted for nothing to Bridie O'Keefe. He pinned his hopes of the patient's recovery on forcing draughts of laudanum down Lady Caroline's throat and advocated a blood-letting. Bridie O'Keefe refused to allow him to touch *her* patient. She informed him in no uncertain terms that Lady Caroline could afford to lose none of her blood. As for medicine, when the time came for it to be taken it would be a herbal mixture, made up by Bridie herself. She told the army surgeon that the most useful thing he could do was to take hold of one side of the bed and, with Liam on the other side, move it closer to the open window.

The two men carried out Bridie O'Keefe's orders with only a modicum of protest from the army surgeon.

All that night and until well into the following day the old lady battled to save Caroline's life, while the surgeon remained as little more than a frustrated bystander. Liam stayed in the bedroom for as long as Bridie O'Keefe would allow, but on the second day his mother persuaded him to go to bed in Nathan Brock's cottage.

Liam woke after a long sleep to find the cottage empty and ominously quiet. Looking out of the window he saw that the sun was beginning to set over the western hills, but there were no signs of activity in the vicinity of the great house. Fearing the worst, Liam quickly dressed and hurried there.

As he approached he saw, with dread, that the windows of Caroline's room were now closed and only a solitary light burned inside. Taking the stairs two at a time, Liam pushed through a crowd of servants outside the bedroom door and entered the room. Caroline was propped up against the pillows of her bed! She was dark-eyed, but able to smile at him. Liam could hardly believe the change he saw in her. He looked at Bridie O'Keefe, and the old lady nodded her head.

'She's over the fever now.'

'God bless you, Bridie.' Liam strode across the room and kissed the wrinkled cheek of the surprised woman.

'I think He already has,' commented the army surgeon. 'I have seen a miracle performed here. When I first came into this room and saw Lady Caroline I believed I was looking at a dead woman. I realised that anything I might do would be merely a face-saving routine. I knew of no way to bring her back to health.'

He looked at Bridie and smiled ruefully. 'I wish Mrs O'Keefe would tell me what herbs she used here. If I could cure the fever in the Dublin barracks, I would be assured of becoming Surgeon-General of the Queen's Army.'

'All the herbs in the world wouldn't help if it wasn't to be. Life or death is not decided by anyone on this earth.'

Bridie O'Keefe met Liam's eyes and she lowered her voice so that it would not carry to the bed. 'Death took her by the hand and nothing has been done in this room to break his grip. He will walk with her wherever she goes. Remember that, Liam McCabe. Now I'll be going home.'

The old healer walked from the room without a look back at the woman she had cured and, trying not to let Caroline see how deeply he had been disturbed by Bridie O'Keefe's words, Liam went to the bedside and took her hand.

The army surgeon looked perplexed. He was used to a fairly ordered life, and here his world had been turned upside down, his medical knowledge scorned and his presence unwanted. He had been humbled by a dirty old woman who would have been burned as a witch not many years ago, and in the sick room of a baronet's wife people seemed to come and go as they wished. However, he had come here at the urgent request of Sir Richard Dudley. He would at least have the satisfaction of returning to his regiment and sending word to the baronet of his wife's recovery.

Looking across the room to where Liam and Caroline were talking happily together, the army surgeon thought it would be wise to tell Sir Richard Dudley no more than that.

Chapter Forty-Nine

Caroline's strength was slow in returning to her, and Liam remained at Inch House for two weeks. He spent most evenings reading to her in her room, but during the day he went out with Nathan Brock with food for the cottiers. They had to search for them now because the famine-hit families were behaving like sick animals, seeking out-of-the-way places where they might die in peace.

Then, one day, Liam returned to Kilmar and went out in his boat with the two men who were working it for him. It was a relief to leave the land behind and spend a day with the clean salt-scented wind blowing in his face, losing his troubles in hard physical labour.

But even here Liam was unable to stop his mind from working. It was apparent that the Kilmar fishing fleet was working well below its full capabilities. The boats were remaining too close to the shore, not bothering to go into deep water where the shoals were larger.

It did not take Liam long to discover the reason for this lack of enthusiasm. It was the story of the Kerry fishermen all over again. The Kilmar men resented risking their lives for the sake of the cottiers. The peasants from inland had become a permanent and unwanted burden on them.

It was a difficult situation, and one that Liam felt might best be resolved by Father Clery.

The old parish priest listened patiently as Liam talked and nodded his head in agreement when Liam asserted that it was essential for the fishermen to catch all the fish they could.

'I know a way to make them catch as much as their boats will hold,' he said. 'I will ask a few of them to come with me when I visit the cottiers' cabins. They are good men. Once they see the pitiful state of the women and children out there nothing will hold them back. They will go fishing in fair weather or foul – and row halfway to America, if need be. Talking of good men, have you heard anything of Eugene lately?'

'Not a word. You'll be needing him here before the election.'

'No. Oh, there will be some who won't be happy if he doesn't show himself, but we will put him up as our candidate and he will be voted in with no opposition. Eugene has devoted his life to us. If he never sets foot in Ireland again, he will still be our Member of Parliament on the day he takes his last breath of God's good air.'

'I wish County Kerry had the same confidence in their MP,' said Liam ruefully. 'I received this letter yesterday.'

He handed an envelope to the parish priest, who put on a pair of spectacles with badly twisted frames and began to read. Pausing occasionally to frown, or go over a particular line more than once, he slowly turned the pages.

The letter was from the secretary of the Castlemaine All-Ireland Association and told Liam of a split in the ranks of the Association. A militant group intended putting up its own candidate for the forthcoming election. So, too, did the land-owners, resentful of Liam's efforts on the cottiers' behalf. The letter went on to tell Liam of the damaging rumour being spread about of his involvement with a married woman. Finally, it ended with a plea for Liam to persuade Eugene Brennan to return to Ireland and give the All-Ireland Association the leadership it so desperately needed.

'What are you going to do about this, Liam?'

'I must go to County Kerry and see if there is anything I can do to help them.'

'What about the Association? Will you take over the leader-ship . . . as Eugene intended?'

'I couldn't, even if I were so inclined. Just as County Wexford will never have another Member of Parliament as long as Eugene lives, so the All-Ireland Association will never follow another man. Besides, Father, I think it will be better for the Association if I remain in the background of their affairs for a while.'

'H'm. Perhaps you are right, Liam. I will keep an open mind until you are ready to bring your problems to me yourself – and make it soon, for everyone's sake.'

Liam gave a non-committal reply and stood up to leave the preacher's house.

'How is Lady Caroline's health now?'

'She is fit enough to leave the house and sit in the sun for a while each day, but I fear her recovery is going to be a slow business. However, my mother will be returning to Kilmar this week and she would not be leaving Inch House unless Lady Caroline was well on the mend.'

At Castlemaine, Liam went first to the house of Harvey Gorman to learn what had been happening in County Kerry during his absence. Within minutes, news of Liam's arrival had reached the secretary of the All-Ireland Association and he joined them.

Both the magistrate and the Association secretary told Liam that this election campaign was like no other they had known. There were few speeches, no grand meetings with free food and drinks. The land-owners' candidate had provided one such repast, but even the most ardent of supporters baulked at enjoying his lavish hospitality, surrounded as they were by such a shortage of food. The candidate did not repeat the occasion.

But there was little enthusiasm for campaigning; no one seemed to care very much. Whoever was elected would be able to do nothing to improve the situation in Ireland, so there seemed little sense in voting.

The two men agreed that the rumours circulating about Liam had cost him much of his expected support. The majority of the men who had voted for him in the by-election were staid middle-class Catholics – the very men to be most offended by any indiscretion. Liam would always be something of a hero to the cottiers and the fishermen, but they held very few votes.

The secretary of the All-Ireland Association was a very worried man. The Association was disintegrating about him. Its membership was halved, its funds gone to feed the cottiers – and now it seemed it would lose its MP.

Liam agreed to tour the area in a bid to gain votes and perhaps bring more donations into the Association's funds. But money could hardly be expected from the majority of their members. They were finding it hard enough to live on what little they had.

As Liam had anticipated, his last-minute campaign was a waste of time. Indoor meetings were reasonably well attended, but the outdoor meetings which had once drawn huge crowds were attended only by the cottiers. The reason was not political; it was self-preservation. Fever was raging everywhere, and the cottiers were blamed for its spread. No one would risk mingling with them at a meeting. It was better to stay at home, with doors and windows shut tight to keep the fever outside.

For the same reason a great many voters stayed home on election day. A tight-lipped Liam toured the polling-booths but saw few of his supporters. Most of the activity came from the land-owners, who ushered their committed voters back and forth in a determined effort to have their candidate elected to Parliament.

Long before the votes were counted, the result was a foregone conclusion. The land-owners' man won the seat but, much to Liam's surprise, he learned there had only been thirty-three votes between the two of them. The militant ex-Association candidate came a poor third.

Liam was disappointed only because he was left with the feeling he had let down his friends in County Kerry. For himself, he felt nothing but great relief. Now he could return to Kilmar, to his boat and a life he enjoyed. He would be his own man once again, not forced to divide his time between Kilmar, County Kerry and London. He would continue to help the cottiers because he was aware of their continuing need, but it would be practical help, taking much of the burden from Caroline.

At Inch House, Liam found Caroline seated on the lawn in front of her own new house, enjoying the July sunshine. Her joy at seeing Liam quickly gave way to distress when she learned he was no longer an MP. She knew his defeat was due in no small measure to their relationship and Liam's concern for her. Liam tried to explain that it did not matter, but he knew she did not believe him.

She still looked very ill, and Liam told her she needed to get right away from Ireland for a while. To go somewhere far from the constant parade of begging cottiers who came to her house, reminding her of the things she felt she should be doing.

Caroline hesitated before she replied. She knew Liam was right, but was reluctant to admit it, even to herself.

'I have had a letter from my brother. He has taken a house in Paris and would like me to join him there.'

Liam looked at her thin pale face. 'You will go, of course.'

'It is so far from you, Liam. I don't *want* to go.'

She was close to tears, her trembling lip betraying her weakened state.

'I will be close to you in thought every minute of the day, but I think you must go if you are to recover as quickly as possible. Besides, it will take you well away from Sir Richard. By the time you are well enough to return here he should be on his way to Canada.'

'But this house, Liam – there are still so many things to be done.'

'Leave everything to Nathan.'

'I seem to have been doing that ever since he first came here. Since my illness he has been running the whole of the Inch Estate.'

'Then you have nothing to fear – but where is he now? I would like to speak to him before I leave.'

'You are not going so soon? I have been looking forward to having you with me for so long and you have only just arrived.'

Liam took her hand in both of his own. 'I have to get used to being a fisherman again, Caroline, and this is fishing weather.'

He kissed her gently, afraid of the frailty of her. 'I will be here often to see you, and if you are strong enough you must come to Kilmar before you leave for France. My mother would love to fuss over you, and the sea air will put the colour back in your cheeks. Get yourself really fit and I will even take you out in a boat and make a fisherwoman of you.'

When one of the servants came to help Caroline back to her room, Liam went in search of Nathan Brock.

As Caroline had said, Nathan Brock was managing not only her lands, but those belonging to the Earl of Inch as well. Liam found him marking out the line of a new boundary wall. Stretching for more than a mile, it would keep a large gang of cottiers in work for many weeks.

As they walked back to the house together, Nathan Brock commiserated with Liam over the loss of his seat in Parliament, but welcomed the news that Liam would soon be fishing again. He offered to purchase as much fish as Liam could spare, to feed the cottiers now working at Inch House. Nathan Brock was also delighted with the news that Caroline would be going to France for a period of convalescence.

'She is getting better, Liam, but not as fast as she should. She still spends far too much time worrying about the things she feels she should be doing. I fear that if she is not soon taken away from here she will have a relapse – and things would be very different in these parts without her influence.'

'Yes,' agreed Liam quietly. 'She means a great deal to all of us.'

Liam found village life little changed. At first, the fishermen showed him a certain deference, but after they had heard him cursing the vagaries of the sea as vehemently as the best of them as he worked elbow deep in guts and fish-scales he became one of them once more. Soon they were following his boat into deeper waters and bringing home the largest catches Kilmar men could remember.

Liam managed to visit Inch House, where arrangements were going ahead for Caroline's visit to France, two or three times every week. She was still reluctant to leave Liam and her new house, but had agreed to leave Ireland in September, before the damp winds of winter arrived. Her health was improving but at such a painfully slow rate that Liam was more worried than he dared tell anyone.

Late in August, Liam returned from Inch House to Kilmar to find Father Clery waiting for him with a letter from Eugene Brennan.

The priest had written to the MP to tell him of his re-election to Parliament and to say that his salary was assured by his constituents. But the priest had urged his friend to return to Ireland, if only for a short visit, to put new heart into his supporters and rally the flagging spirits of the members of the All-Ireland Association.

When Liam asked what news the old politician had sent, Father Clery handed the letter to Liam without comment.

Liam read the untidy scrawl with great difficulty, and the words made little sense when deciphered. Irrelevant political doctrine vied for space with details of Eugene's little French cottage, obtained for him in Paris by his nephew, but the letter said nothing intelligible.

Liam handed the letter back to Father Clery, saddened by the insight it gave into Eugene Brennan's present state of mind.

'He is an old, old man, Father.'

'True, Liam, and this country owes a debt to Eugene Brennan that can never be repaid. History will prove him right in so many things that have not always been understood by his people – but I have men and women in my parish who need more than a page in history.'

The old priest sighed. During his many years in Kilmar he had been given more than enough of life's problems to solve and they had not lessened with his own advancing years. Eugene Brennan had always been a stout staff for him to lean upon in the past. Now he, too, had become a burden.

'In my own letter to Eugene I told him he had no need to attend the House of Commons. I did not want him to feel he had to do anything before he was ready – but there has never been a time when County Wexford needed a spokesman in Parliament more than it does today. If I knew that Eugene was being well cared for in France and that he would never return to politics, I would arrange for a new MP to be elected in his place – but how can I be sure? I have a duty to my people, but I would resign from the Church before I would break that old friend's heart.'

Liam had been thinking seriously as Father Clery talked, and now he arrived at a quick decision. 'I'll go to France to see Eugene.'

'You . . . ? To France . . . ?'

'Yes.' Liam felt a surge of excitement go through him at the decision he had just made. 'Lady Caroline is going to Paris to stay with her brother for the winter. I have been worried about her travelling alone in her condition; she is still far from strong. I will go with her and see Eugene when I reach Paris.'

Some of the enthusiasm faded from Father Clery's face.

'Ah! So you'll be going with Lady Caroline?'

'Pay her a visit, Father. You'll see for yourself that she should not travel alone for such a distance.'

Father Clery bit back his disapproval. He knew it would make no difference to Liam's decision. The old priest had long ago learned to accept the frailty of men without useless comment. When the right day came he would be able to help. He wanted Liam to feel he was always able to come to him.

'I don't doubt she is a sick woman, Liam. Take care of her on the journey, and give my blessing to Eugene.'

Chapter Fifty

Liam's news that he would be travelling with her to Paris made all the difference to Caroline. She prepared for the journey with all the enthusiasm of a convalescent child. It would be an exciting adventure – a shared adventure – and for a while the household at Inch House was happier than it had been for a very long time.

Caroline's own happiness lasted until the day they landed in France. Then realisation came that she must soon face a parting with Liam, perhaps for many months. She became quiet and more and more withdrawn as the wheels of the carriage they had hired ate up the miles to Paris.

When they came within sight of the bloody hillside of Crécy, where the Black Prince had won his knight's spurs five hundred years before, the thin veneer of good health crumbled away and Caroline collapsed. Thoroughly alarmed, Liam ordered the carriage to the nearest inn.

They found a small inn nestling in a copse of trees on the bank of the small River Maye. Nobody here spoke any English and Liam knew no French, but Caroline's illness cut through all language barriers. The proprietor of the inn took one look at her and had her brought inside, at the same time despatching one of his sons to fetch a doctor.

To Liam's great relief, the doctor spoke good English and Liam was able to explain the background to Caroline's collapse. Everything Liam said was translated by the doctor for the benefit of the innkeeper and his large family. The translation was received by them with much head-shaking and a wide variety of sympathetic noises.

The doctor then went to the room to which Caroline had been taken and gave her a thorough examination. When he returned downstairs, Liam was sharing a bottle of brandy with the innkeeper and his wife. The doctor's expression was so grave that Liam jumped to his feet in alarm.

'What is the matter? Is she worse . . . ?'

The doctor waved Liam back to his seat. 'She is no worse –

but that does not mean she is any better. You are the lady's husband?'

'No, a very close friend.'

If the reply surprised the doctor, he did not give any indication. 'I see. You are travelling far?'

'To Paris. Lady Caroline will be staying there with her brother.'

'*Lady* Caroline? But that is good. It means she will be able to afford the doctor I will send to see her there. He is a good man – the best doctor in France.'

'Is there something seriously wrong with her? I can't understand it; she has been improving steadily since she recovered from the fever.'

Even as he said the words, Liam remembered how worried he had been at her slow progress back to health.

'Outside, she is improving. Inside . . . who can say? I am but a country doctor. My friend in Paris is more knowledgeable than I. Perhaps he will be able to learn more. The lady is able to speak now. I think perhaps she would like to see you. I will return tomorrow and in the meantime will send a letter to Paris, to my friend.'

'How long will it be before she is able to continue her journey?'

The doctor shrugged. 'I think a week. But after today she will be able to leave her bed and may take short walks along the river bank. The sun and the air will be good for her.'

Greatly relieved, Liam thanked the doctor and went upstairs to see Caroline. She was propped up on her pillows, looking very tired but otherwise no worse than she had been before her collapse.

'Poor Liam,' she said as he fussed over her. 'I am a worry to you. But it was no more than a foolish faint. Tomorrow I will be well again.'

'Perhaps. But the doctor says we should stay here for a week before moving on.'

'Why, that is wonderful! A whole week together. It will be like a honeymoon.'

'No, the doctor also said your activities must be restricted to short walks along the river bank.'

Liam smiled at her happily. The news that they were to be

together for another week had done more to restore her to health than any medicine the doctor had given to her.

In spite of the worry of Caroline's illness, the week they spent at the inn became one of the happiest times either of them had known. Isolated from those about them by the difference in language, they were able to enjoy each other's company with few interruptions. The walk along the river bank became a regular feature of their stay at the little French inn, Caroline being able to walk a little farther each day.

On their last evening, they sat by the river, beneath the hanging branches of a green willow-tree, watching the sparkling colours of a pair of kingfishers. The birds were methodically quartering each stretch of the river, seeking food for a late brood of gaping-beaked nestlings.

'This has been a wonderful week, Liam. I wish it could last for ever.'

Seated on the grass, Caroline leaned back against Liam, who had both arms about her. He thought he had never before known her so relaxed and free from tension.

'Do we have to leave tomorrow?'

'I am afraid we must.' They both knew they could not stay any longer. 'Your brother will be worrying. He expected you a week ago. Besides, you have to see the doctor in Paris.'

'Why not allow the whole world to believe we have simply disappeared? Then we could stay here for the rest of our lives.'

His arms tightened about her as he said, 'I wonder how many lovers have said the same words?'

Tomorrow they would be returning to a world where they must act out a lie, but the memory of these few days would give them something to cherish for a very long time.

As Liam had predicted, the Earl of Inch was extremely worried about his sister and his relief at seeing her was quite evident – but he was puzzled by Liam's presence. However, when Caroline introduced Liam and explained he was an ex-MP, travelling to France to speak to Eugene Brennan, the Earl became quite affable.

'Ah yes! The father of Irish politics. Poor old chap. When did you last meet him?'

'Early this year, in London.'

'Then you must prepare yourself for a shock. Old age has caught up with Eugene Brennan since he came to France. He will never again draw a crowd of ten thousand to one of his meetings – but you will see the change for yourself. Will you be staying in Paris for long?'

'A day or two at the most.'

'No doubt we will meet again. Thank you for taking care of my sister, Mr McCabe.'

As Caroline went inside the house with her brother, surrounded by clucking servants, she waved to Liam, a sad uncertain gesture. He departed feeling he had left a part of himself behind in the Earl of Inch's Paris home.

The Earl's house was in the fashionable suburb of Neuilly. Eugene Brennan's home was far more modest and closer to the heart of Paris. Yet, in a quiet cul-de-sac, it was away from the noise and industry of the main thoroughfares of France's capital city.

A grey-haired expressionless housekeeper opened the door to Liam and led him through the house to a secluded walled garden bright with the flowers of late summer. Here Liam found Eugene Brennan kneeling beside a freshly dug bed of roses, a small trowel in his hand. A frail stooped figure, he stood up when Liam walked from the house. Frowning, he seemed annoyed at being disturbed and there was no recognition in his eyes.

'Hello, Eugene. It's me – Liam McCabe.'

Liam found himself talking gently, as though to a child.

'Ah yes. . . . Of course. . . .'

His expression held only puzzlement. 'Have you seen my roses? Look, are these not the most beautiful flowers you have ever seen?'

'They are very beautiful, Eugene.'

The old politician kneeled on the grass once more and resumed his digging about the base of a rose-bush. Liam squatted beside him.

'I have come from Ireland to talk to you, Eugene. To discuss your seat in Parliament with you. Father Clery asked me to—'

'Parliament, you say? I remember Parliament. I was there, you know. Member for County Wexford – that's in Ireland. But it was a long time ago. A long time. Now I am in France.'

Eugene Brennan made a vague gesture with his hands as though he was about to say something, but the gesture faded into nothing and he looked at the trowel in his hand for a long time before speaking again.

'Have you seen my new rose? It's a white one. My nephew brought it here. He's very good to me. A good boy. . . .'

The door of the little white-washed house closed quietly behind Liam and he walked to the waiting carriage deeply saddened by his meeting with the man who had been his friend and inspiration. What he had just seen was the total mental disintegration of one of Ireland's greatest sons. His only consolation was that Eugene Brennan was in exile. His friends and followers in Ireland would always be able to remember him as the great champion he had once been.

Next, Liam paid a call on Eugene Brennan's nephew. One of many Irishmen who occupied senior posts in the French Army, he was a military adviser to the ageing King Louis-Philippe. He told Liam that his uncle's mental state was a permanent condition. The nephew had called in the finest doctors in Paris, but there was nothing anyone could do for the old politician. He was an old man who had pushed his mind and body too hard in the past. The acid wit that had delighted his friends and infuriated his political enemies was gone for ever.

The nephew was understanding about the needs of the people of County Wexford. Indeed, he was both surprised and moved to learn that his uncle was still their Member of Parliament. He promised to have a letter of resignation drawn up and signed by Eugene Brennan, and assured Liam that the old MP would want for nothing for the remainder of his life. Finally, he asked Liam to thank all the politician's friends for their concern.

In such a way, far from the scenes of his many triumphs, the career of a great Irish politician came to an end. The seat Eugene Brennan had filled since the passing of the Emancipation Bill, allowing Catholics to sit in the House of Commons, would go to another. Liam thought that a successor would be hard to find. Few men would care to try to take the place of a national hero.

When Liam returned to the house of the Earl of Inch the next day, his welcome had none of the cordiality of the previous meeting. He was shown into a room, and when the Earl of Inch entered he glowered at Liam for long seconds before speaking.

'What are you doing here?'

'I told you yesterday I would be calling to see Caroline before I returned to Ireland.'

'Yesterday I did not realise who you were. You have a nerve coming here, McCabe, after all the rumours linking your name with that of my sister. Well, you can go back to Ireland without seeing her. A Kilmar fisherman can have nothing that needs to be said to Lady Caroline Dudley.'

Liam controlled his anger carefully. 'We have been friends for a very long time. I will be obliged if you will tell her I am here.'

'I'll do no such thing! And I'll not have you calling here again. I have no doubt this "friendship" of yours is the reason she has worked so hard for those wretched cottiers and seriously weakened her heart.'

'Weakened her heart? I don't believe you!'

'I don't care whether you believe me or not – but I'm damned if I will be called a liar by a fisherman. A doctor came to see her yesterday evening and he confirmed it beyond any doubt. Now, get out and return to Ireland, McCabe, and make no attempt to see Lady Caroline again.'

'I will go – after I have seen Caroline.' Liam's quiet reply hid the deep anxiety he felt for the Earl's sister.

'Then I'll have you thrown out – by the servants. You'll not speak to my sister in this house.'

'Would you rather Liam and I went to a tavern instead, Edward?'

Neither man had heard the door open as they argued with each other. Now Caroline stood in the doorway, pale but determined.

'You should be in your room, resting – and McCabe is about to leave.'

'He will go after I have said goodbye to him and given him messages for my own household in Ireland.'

Coolly ignoring her brother's angry glare, Caroline walked across the room to Liam. Taking his hand she rose on her toes and kissed him on the cheek.

'Liam, my dear. You look tired and in need of a drink. I

will have one brought for you. But now we have things to discuss. Edward, will you leave us for a while, please.'

Liam thought the Earl would choke.

'No, I'm damned if I will. This is my house, Caroline – and I have told this scoundrel to leave.'

'Edward! If you persist in this ridiculous behaviour, I will ask Liam to take me to a place where we *can* talk. I am not a child who can be ordered to bed for misbehaving, I am a grown woman – and I warn you, if I leave I will never again return to this house. Now, will you please leave us alone to talk for a while?'

Caroline had always been stronger-willed than her brother and she seemed to be in full command of the present situation. Only Liam was aware that her hand was clutching his tightly to prevent it from shaking uncontrollably.

At first it seemed to Liam that the Earl was going to stand his ground, but with a smothered oath he swung away toward the door. There, he paused to fling back a final warning.

'You are no longer a child, Caroline, but you are still my sister. I will not stand by and do nothing while a philandering adventurer makes a fool of you.'

With that, the Earl of Inch slammed the door shut behind him and a few moments later Liam heard him shouting in the hall for a horse to be brought to the door for him.

Caroline sagged against Liam in relief. 'Hold me, Liam. Hold me very, very tight.'

Liam took her in his arms and held her until the tension of the last few minutes left her and her trembling stopped.

'You must not excite yourself like this. Your heart. . . .'

'So Edward told you. You must not worry about it, Liam. I will be all right. I have been ill and it has been a strain on my heart, that is all. When I am stronger there will be nothing to worry about – but I do not want to talk about it. Tell me, how is Eugene?'

Liam told her of his meeting with the old man and of the talk with Eugene's nephew.

'Poor Eugene. I will visit him as soon as I am able. Perhaps he will remember me. But now County Wexford will have to elect a new Member of Parliament. Will you stand, Liam?'

'No.'

Soon after leaving Eugene Brennan's nephew, Liam realised

that he was the logical choice for the County Wexford seat and had thought about it until well into the night.

'Has your decision anything to do with me?'

'No. I have no wish to return to Parliament. I want to spend a few years building up Kilmar's fleet of fishing boats. When everyone owns a wooden boat there will be a great many more fish caught. In the long term that will benefit both Kilmar and the cottiers far more than I could as their MP.'

They talked about the decision until Liam saw that Caroline was looking tired. Then he announced that it was time for him to leave.

Caroline was tearfully reluctant to have him leave her, but she, too, knew it was time.

'You will write to me, Liam?'

'Of course – and I shall expect to hear from you often.'

'God, Liam! I am going to miss you. I need you with me so much.'

'Don't, Caroline.' Liam saw the trembling of her lip and held her to him. 'I will miss you, too, but I must go now.'

'I know.'

They heard footsteps outside and, as they drew apart, a servant came to the room to tell Caroline that the doctor had returned to see her.

As Liam left the house he could hear the doctor chiding Caroline for having left her room and calling for the servants to help her upstairs.

He wished he could have claimed the right to be told the truth about the nature of her present illness. But Liam had no rights. He had only a great and enduring love for another man's wife.

Chapter Fifty-One

Liam arrived back in Kilmar in October 1847, to a country preparing for its third long winter of famine and fear. The plight of the cottier had not improved – indeed, it had worsened. The people of England had by now become weary of hearing about the troubles of the Irish. The famine had lasted for so long that it had become a bore. There was little enthusiasm for private relief schemes and the English Government had its own financial worries. The destitute cottiers were now the responsibility of their own area poor-houses. It mattered little that the poor-houses themselves were bankrupt. A law had been passed. It was now up to the Irish to feed their own.

England, led by Lord John Russell, shut its ears to the cries of a starving people and turned its back upon Ireland.

In their desperation, the starving and sick people fought to leave their native land and start life anew in the brave new world beyond the Atlantic Ocean. They set sail in any ship that could stay afloat for long enough to limp clear of the harbours and bays around Ireland's coast. Lemming-like, many of them realised it would be a voyage to certain death. In that winter, when emigration was normally at a standstill, 100,000 men, women and children fled from their dying country. Of these, perhaps 60,000 survived to fill the cellars and shanty-towns of Boston and New York. The remainder were either lost at sea, or perished soon after their arrival in an unfamiliar and, as yet, unfriendly country.

But the boats that reached America returned carrying mail, and one day the letter that Liam had been dreading arrived in Kilmar. One of the young exiled Kilmar men wrote to his mother to tell of his progress in the new country – and to ask when Dermot McCabe would be coming to join them.

'What does it mean, Liam?' Norah McCabe was distressed and bewildered. 'If he did not go to America with them, then where is he now?'

'I don't know,' Liam lied. 'But you know Dermot. I expect he had some dream of his own to pursue. He is probably in

England right now, making a lot of money. One day he will return home in style and impress us all.'

Liam knew she did not believe him and there were many others in Kilmar who voiced their own opinions on the subject of Dermot's mysterious disappearance.

A few days after the letter arrived, Liam went down to the quay before dawn to prepare his boat for the day's fishing. He often came down here before the other fishermen had left their houses, welcoming the silence and the opportunity to be alone. But this morning someone was here before him. As he threw fishing tackle into the boat he smelled the aroma of burning tobacco.

Looking about him, Liam saw the faint glow of a clay pipe only a few yards away.

''Morning to you, Liam.' The voice of Tomas Feehan came to him from the darkness.

'Good morning, Tomas. You are up and about early. Are you fishing today?'

'I have little heart for fishing, these days. I have only myself to feed and I can do that well enough with a line from the rocks. I see no sense in making hard work of staying alive.'

When Liam made no reply, Tomas Feehan shook the spittle from the stem of his pipe, and said, 'It's a strange thing – Dermot not going to America with the others.'

Liam tensed, glad that the darkness hid his face from Tomas Feehan.

'I expect he had his own reasons, Tomas.'

'I am sure he had, and I would bet my boat that I know what they were.'

Tomas Feehan cleared his throat and spat over the edge of the quay. Liam waited until the tough old fisherman had returned the pipe to his mouth and sucked hard to set the burning tobacco crackling.

'The man who was hanged for killing Eoin. . . . I believe he refused to give his name to anyone before he died?' Tomas Feehan spoke around his pipe.

'So I hear.'

This was what Tomas Feehan had come to talk to him about. Liam wiped his hands on his rough trousers, preparing himself for whatever might come. The older fisherman was a strange moody man, known more for his violence than for his powers of speech.

'I respect him for it – whoever he was. It's a shameful thing for a family to have to live with. Having a son hanged for murder.'

The edge of the sky to the east was taking on a hint of red and a seagull greeted the first sign of the coming day with a raucous clatter that was quickly taken up by a dozen others.

Waiting until the noise died away, Tomas Feehan continued, 'Nothing could equal the shame and pain that Eoin has brought upon me. I should have killed him myself. I was going to. I swore I would when I learned that he had been responsible for the death of my young Sean. I made an oath to seek him out and kill him – and, God help me, I meant every word.'

The rough old man choked on his words and by now Liam could make out his shape as he sat huddled against a stone bollard.

'Yes, one day I would have met up with my son and would have had to kill him. I am not a religious man, Liam, but I doubt if God would have forgiven me for such a sin as that. So, you see, I owe a debt to the memory of this unknown young man who did the deed for me.'

The big fisherman stood up with his back to the dawn. 'We Feehans always repay whatever we owe, Liam. Be it good or bad it is paid back in kind. Now, I have held you up for long enough. Good luck to your day's fishing, Liam McCabe.'

Liam watched the big fisherman walk away along the jetty and wondered what he intended to do. He did not have long to wait. Within days a strong rumour swept Kilmar that the unknown man who had been hanged in Dublin for the murder of Eoin Feehan was himself a Feehan, sent to avenge Sean's death by Tomas.

It was a rumour that Tomas Feehan refused to either confirm or deny, and no man dared press him on the subject, but the fishermen of Kilmar went about their business satisfied that they had learned the answer to the Dublin mystery.

The subject of Eugene Brennan's resignation was less easily resolved. When the letter from France first arrived, the members of the All-Ireland Association refused to believe that Eugene Brennan really meant to resign. Liam attended a number of branch meetings and managed to convince them that the old politician really had come to the end of his parliamentary career. Liam told them that their MP was tired and ill, and that the doctors in France had ordered his retirement.

But, far from resolving the problems of the Association, the news broke it into a number of new factions. There were those who refused to acknowledge another leader, and who wanted no other Member of Parliament but Eugene Brennan. They were determined that he should remain their MP until the day he died, whether or not he ever again attended a sitting in the House of Commons. Others accepted the situation but wanted Liam to take Eugene Brennan's place in Parliament.

The younger men wanted neither Eugene Brennan nor any of his disciples. They were for a new militant initiative. They wanted a man who would be willing to use more than words against the English.

They echoed the mood of many of the country's young men, and their voice was beginning to be heard, even across the Irish Sea. More soldiers than ever before were sent from England in anticipation of the troubles that must surely come. Ireland became a fortress – but the guns were turned inward, upon herself.

The break-up of the Association in County Wexford worried Father Clery greatly, and he begged Liam to reconsider his decision not to stand for Parliament.

'The Association and the county need you, Liam. They must have someone they can trust. Someone who knows their problems.'

'You have such a man,' declared Liam. 'And you will find him not too many miles distant from here. I am talking about Nathan Brock.'

'Nathan? But he is – or was – a cottier.'

'Who better to understand their problems? Nathan will fight for them – and with more than his fists. If he were to rise to his feet in Parliament and talk about the plight of the cottiers, it would take more than Lord John Russell and his Whig Party to silence him.'

'You know, you could be right, Liam!' Father Clery became excited at the thought. 'I have heard Nathan speaking on the cottiers' behalf and he is very impressive. Very impressive indeed. But airing his views before an ignorant old priest and a crowd of fishermen is easy. Could he do the same before the men who hold Ireland's fate in their hands?'

'Given a worthy cause, Nathan Brock would not be overawed by the Devil himself,' said Liam. 'He knows he is as good a man as anyone who listens to him. You will find no worthier successor to Eugene, Father. He is respected by the older members of the Association and I feel sure the younger men will follow him, too. I can think of no other man capable of holding the Association together. Go and see him today, Father, and refuse to take "no" for an answer. The people need him.'

Chapter Fifty-Two

Nathan Brock was not easily convinced that he was the man County Wexford needed to have for its next Member of Parliament. Not until he had spent many evenings discussing the matter with Liam did he agree to put his name forward as a candidate.

The by-election was called for the last week in November but, long before then, Nathan Brock was assured of a seat in the House of Commons. Liam and Father Clery took the ex-prizefighter to many meetings of the All-Ireland Association, and it was evident that he was acceptable to all sides and needed no one to speak on his behalf. The few men in the county who disagreed with the Association's choice also realised that no other candidate stood a chance, and he was returned unopposed.

Nathan Brock had been concerned that he was letting down Caroline by accepting the nomination, but she sent him a letter, via Liam, assuring him that she was absolutely delighted with the people's choice and wishing she had been well enough to return to join him in his election campaign.

But before Nathan Brock went to London to take his seat and begin the new chapter in his life, an event occurred that was to have a momentous effect upon Liam's own future.

A blustery easterly wind, accompanied by cold stinging rain, had been blowing off the sea for days, making fishing impossible. The Kilmar fishermen, anxious to obtain a stock of fish to salt away for the approaching winter months, sat indoors listening to the rattling doors and windows and grumbling about the bad weather.

At sea, all those ships large enough to defy the elements steered well clear of land and either rode out the storm or used the wind to their advantage. A few foolhardy captains, hoping to clip a day or two from their voyages, took chances – and the toll of wrecks in that late autumn storm was unusually high.

It was midday on the fifth day of the storm when Liam, quietly writing to Caroline in a corner of the McCabe kitchen, was brought to his feet by the cries of a Kilmar boy running along the street outside.

'A ship in trouble! There's a ship in trouble just off the reef.'

Liam reached behind the door for his waterproof coat and shrugged it on.

'Wait a minute. I'll come with you.' Norah McCabe unfastened her apron and ran for her own coat.

All along the narrow street fishermen and their families ran from the houses and, with the wind and rain beating against their faces, made for the stone quay. It had been many years since a ship was last wrecked on this coast.

Liam could see the vessel as soon as he ran clear of the houses. It was large – very large. Launched as a five-masted transatlantic passenger-ship, she now limped northward on three, having lost two masts to a huge wave. From the foremast the shredded remains of a sail aimed a hundred tattered pennants toward the land.

For more than twenty minutes the crowd on the quay watched as the ship failed to make any headway on her course. Then, slowly and cumbersomely, the big sailing ship turned until its clean clipper bow pointed in the direction of Kilmar.

'She's going to try to make our harbour, here,' shouted Norah McCabe, rain streaming down her face.

'Her captain can't know about the reef,' said Liam. 'She'll go aground at any minute.'

At that moment a long wave raced down upon the ship and crashed hundreds of tons of water on to the wooden deck. The ship reeled beneath the blow, and above the noise of the storm Liam heard another sound. It was the roar of eager voices. Turning, Liam saw a huge crowd of cottiers, surging along the shore, beyond the village. There must have been at least a thousand of them.

'They've been following the ship for miles.' The information came from the boy who had brought the news of the ship to Kilmar. 'They are waiting for it to go aground. They won't have long to wait now.'

There was an angry murmur from the assembled fishermen. It had long been the tradition that the spoils of any wreck on this part of the coast belonged to them. They wrested a dangerous living from the sea and had a right to any bounties it thrust their way.

But Liam's mind was working in another direction. 'There are passengers on board that ship – women and children. If we don't do something to help them quickly, every one of them will perish on the reef.' Appealing to the fishermen, Liam said, 'I need six strong men to come with me out to that ship.'

'You can't take a boat out in this sea.' Norah McCabe was aghast. 'It would capsize before you were halfway to the reef.'

'A curragh might, not a wooden boat. Not our boat.'

Liam turned to go where his boat was pulled high up on the sand, and his mother clutched his arm. 'Liam, take care. It was in just a storm as this that I lost your father. You are all I have now.'

'Don't worry, Ma. We will be all right. Our boat will stand up to rougher seas than this one. You and the others be preparing food and blankets for those we bring safely to shore.'

There was no shortage of volunteers to crew Liam's boat. Strong young Kilmar fishermen ran to fetch their own oars from their curraghs before helping to push the heavy wooden fishing boat down the beach to the sea.

As Liam's craft hit the water Tomas Feehan was gathering another crew, and only minutes later his boat, too, was being manhandled down the sloping sand of the beach.

'I hardly expected to see a Feehan set out on a mission of mercy,' said one of Liam's oarsmen, as they pulled away from the shore.

'Tomas has as much regard for human life as any man,' replied Liam as he wiped salt spray from his lips.

'More likely he doesn't want you to pick up the cream of the spoils,' retorted another of the fishermen. Seconds later all talking ceased as they crashed through the breaking surf. Three times they pulled clear of the beach – and three times the sea threw them back again. At the fourth attempt Liam urged his crew to use every ounce of their strength. Straining on their oars, the Kilmar fishermen slowly pulled the boat clear of the surf and moved out into the angry sea.

Liam peered through the rain and spray and saw the ship swing broadside on to the reef and lurch over beneath the pounding waves.

'She's going over on the reef,' he shouted to the others 'Pull harder . . . together.'

The sea fought the fishermen every foot of the way. For the last fifty yards to the reef they battled through an ever-increasing accumulation of debris, spurred on by the screams that were now reaching them above the howling of the wind.

Battered by wind and waves, the ship was lying almost on its side but, miraculously, one of her lifeboats had been launched safely. It was hove to on the lee side of the sailing ship, and Liam saw the crew urging a middle-aged woman to jump from the impossibly angled deck into the sea.

As the hysterical woman clung desperately to a torn and twisted guard-rail, a wave surged beneath the ship, lifting it up and then throwing it back upon the reef with a juddering crash that splintered many of its oak timbers. The screaming woman was catapulted into the sea and swept past the ship's lifeboat as the sailors hastily pulled clear of the stricken vessel.

Liam steered his boat toward the woman, but when they were still yards away her flailing arms sank beneath a foam-capped wave and she disappeared from view.

Meanwhile, another wave had thrown the ship even farther across the reef and on to a smooth tooth of black rock which pierced the hull, splintering the massive timbers as though they were kindling. As the ship rose and fell to the movement of the sea, the rock worked away in the manner of a giant crowbar, enlarging the hole it had made and allowing the sea to flood inside.

The noise echoed through the doomed ship, and the passengers, who had been clinging to the false but familiar safety of cabins and state rooms, abandoned all hope of a miracle and fought their way to the acutely sloping deck.

Once there, the bravest among them plunged headlong into the sea and struck out for one of the three boats that now stood by to rescue them.

Some made it to safety, others were swept away and swallowed up by the hungry waves.

The more timid of the passengers clung to the sloping deck, and Liam brought his boat dangerously close to the ship to pluck them to safety. Then, only seconds after Liam's crew had pulled to safety, a long high wave roared in from seaward.

Crashing down upon the ship it drove the vessel across the reef and into deeper water where it immediately began to sink.

Now the last of the passengers leaped from the ship and the already overcrowded boats moved amongst them, pulling still more survivors inboard.

As Liam's boat moved toward a small group of passengers who were fighting each other for a life-saving grip on a spar from a shattered mast, Liam reached over the side and grasped the clothing of a man who was being swept helplessly past the boat. Helped by the swell of a wave, Liam lifted the man up to the gunwale in a single movement.

As the man lay balanced between the safety of the boat and certain death, he lifted his head to look up at the man who had pulled him from the sea – and Liam looked down into the fear-filled face of Sir Richard Dudley!

The ship to whose assistance Liam had come was the trans-atlantic passenger vessel *Atlantis*. On the England-to-Canada run, she was making one of the last voyages of the season to Quebec. Among her passengers was Sir Richard Dudley, *en route* to his new Treasury appointment in the North American colony.

The captain of *Atlantis* had put to sea from Liverpool against all advice, hoping to take advantage of the easterly gales and arrive at Quebec before the winter ice closed in upon the port.

Passing through St George's Channel on her way southward, *Atlantis* had encountered a storm of unprecedented ferocity and lost two of her masts. In desperation, the captain had put his ship about and sought the safety of an Irish harbour. He had been making for Dublin when *Atlantis* foundered on the Kilmar reef.

It seemed to Liam that he looked down at Caroline's husband for long minutes. In fact, it was a matter of seconds only. For his part, Sir Richard Dudley thought that Liam was about to throw him back into the sea. He did not protest, or plead with Liam for his life. He had given himself up for dead when *Atlantis* lost her two masts. Retiring to his cabin, he had quietly settled down to await the end, fortified by a bottle of good French brandy.

He was surprised that the ship lasted so long, and his bid for survival when *Atlantis* struck the Kilmar reef was instinctive rather than determined

Now, as he looked up at Liam, the man who more than any other had cause to wish him dead, he maintained the same strange calm and waited to feel the cold water close about him once more.

Abruptly, Liam tipped the baronet into the bottom of the boat and reached for the tiller as they bumped against the spar to which other survivors were clinging.

The fishermen hauled in the gasping passengers until the boat was dangerously overloaded; then Liam called for them to look to their oars and pull for the shore. There were still scores of passengers in the water pleading to be pulled to safety, but there could be little hope for them. The ship's lifeboat was already on its way shoreward, and Tomas Feehan's boat was as crowded as Liam's own. The luckier survivors would find flotsam to cling to and, hopefully, drift to the shore. The remainder would drown.

Atlantis had grounded on the reef slightly to the north of Kilmar, and to bring the boat in alongside the quay would have meant going across the running sea, a dangerous manoeuvre with such an overladen boat. Liam decided to beach close to the point from where he had set off.

The fishing boat soon overtook the crowded ship's lifeboat and led the way toward the shore. When he was less than a hundred yards from land, Liam saw the huge crowd of cottiers surge down to the water's edge ahead of him. Some of them plunged headlong into the sea to retrieve small casks and boxes which were already beginning to wash ashore. Those who took them from the water did not keep them for long. As they waded ashore they were set upon by groups of stick-wielding men and robbed of their prizes. Even then, permanent ownership had not been established and fights broke out along the length of the beach as items from the sea changed hands again and again.

But as the boats drew closer the cottiers forgot their fighting and crowded down to the shore. Their faces showed neither compassion nor simple curiosity. These were desperately hungry people. They had followed the stricken *Atlantis* for miles in anticipation of finally plundering something of value Something to exchange for food. Nothing had yet happened to thwart their expectations, and suddenly Liam realised the danger his passengers were in.

'Stop pulling! We're going about.' His shout carried above the noise of the wind, and in the boat forty anxious and enquiring faces turned toward him.

'There's a mob waiting for us on the shore,' Liam shouted, for the benefit of the tired Kilmar oarsmen. 'If we land here, we'll have the clothes torn from our backs. We must head for the quay.'

The shipwrecked passengers looked apprehensive as the wind and the tide carried the boat closer to the shrieking cottiers on the beach. They wanted to stay well clear of the hungry mob. *Atlantis* had been no emigrant ship. She was a luxury passenger-vessel carrying wealthy and influential people. Many of those rescued by Liam's boat carried a fortune in jewellery about their persons – enough to feed the largest cottier family for a lifetime.

Liam began to bring his boat about, but by this time it was dangerously close to the surf-pounded beach. The cottiers, suddenly aware that they were about to be cheated, set up a concerted howl that caused the passengers in the fishing boat to tremble with fear.

The turn was half-completed when two short heavy waves bore down upon the boat, one after the other. The first swung the boat broadside-on to the shoreline, frustrating Liam's efforts to keep the craft pointing out to sea. The second spilled inside the overcrowded fishing boat, causing the passengers to panic and unseat two of the oarsmen.

In an instant, the boat was unmanageable and Liam had lost his battle to keep the *Atlantis* survivors from the cottier mob. The next wave to roll in from the sea was relatively small, but it was sufficient to carry the boat to shallow water. Liam felt the keel rasp against shingle and seconds later he and every man, woman and child in the boat were fighting desperately for their lives.

The mob of cottiers went berserk. Those nearest the boat were trampled underfoot in the swirling tide as others clawed their way forward, each of them determined to snatch a share of plunder.

Waves were continuing to buffet the boat and it could be only a matter of seconds before it overturned. The occupants had no alternative. They had to go over the side and face the crazed cottiers.

As Liam fought his way ashore he saw Sir Richard Dudley

staggering beneath the blows of the cottiers. The baronet barely made it to dry sand before he was felled by a club-wielding ruffian, and as he lay sprawled on the sand he was trampled underfoot by the cottiers, who were packed too close together to bend down and rob him.

Liam fought his way in the direction of the prostrate baronet but was twice beaten to his knees before he could reach him. Liam struck out wildly about him, trying to clear a space, but he was surrounded on all sides by a shrieking, fighting mob; and as gold and jewellery spilled out upon the sand brutal and bloody murder was committed again and again upon Kilmar beach.

Someone struck Liam from behind and he fell beneath the feet of the cottiers, feeling rough sand against his face. He tried to rise but the mob surged over him, beating him down again.

But Liam's desperate fight for survival had not gone unnoticed. Nathan Brock had arrived at Kilmar in time to see Liam's boat swept ashore and overwhelmed by the cottiers. Followed by every able-bodied fisherman from the village, Nathan Brock plunged into the near-hysterical mob, felling any man who failed to move out of his path quickly enough.

Help also came to Liam from another source. Tomas Feehan's boat had been only fifty yards from shore when Liam attempted to turn back. The big red-haired man saw the boat go aground and Liam beaten down beneath the murderous blows of the cottiers. Shouting to his own crew, he drove his boat straight for the shore. The power of the waves roaring in behind the boat drove it high up the beach, taking the cottiers by surprise and carving a path through their ranks.

Before the fishing boat had scraped to a lopsided halt, Tomas Feehan was over the side, laying about him with the hardwood tiller. He was no longer a young man, but Tomas Feehan enjoyed fighting and he still carried enough weight and muscle to make him a formidable opponent. Backed by his fishermen crew, wielding oars as though they were pikes, he drove the cottiers from Liam and the prostrate body of Sir Richard Dudley.

Nursing his left arm, broken just above the wrist by a cottier's club, Liam rose unsteadily to his feet only seconds before Nathan Brock and the Kilmar fishermen fought their way to the spot and formed a protective ring about Liam and the surviving *Atlantis* passengers.

'You were a pleasure to watch, Tomas.' Only Nathan Brock's heavy breathing gave any indication of his own exertions on Liam's behalf as he inclined his head toward the big fisherman. 'I am glad you were not fighting for the other side.'

Tomas Feehan spat on the sand derisively. 'On the "other side" are the cottiers you have been pampering.' He swung his arm to take in the still figures littering the sand about them and spoke to Liam. 'Look about you. We might be standing on a battlefield. It was you and the fine lady from Inch House who fed the cottiers and gave them strength to do this. Does that take away the pain from your arm, Liam McCabe?'

Both Liam and Nathan Brock had recognised many of the cottiers among the mob on the beach. Some they had fed and helped back to health. Ignoring Tomas Feehan's words, Liam limped painfully across the sand to where Sir Richard Dudley lay face down, his jacket missing and his shirt torn half-off.

'Nathan, turn him over, see if he lives. It is Sir Richard Dudley.'

Nathan Brock dropped to his knees beside the prostrate body and turned it over. There was blood on the forehead of the baronet and it had spread to the sand beneath him. As Nathan Brock lay him back he stared upward with sand-dusted eyes that saw nothing.

Nathan Brock laid his ear against the baronet's chest and listened.

By now the cottier mob had broken up and moved away, ranging along the shoreline, retrieving items that were beginning to wash ashore from the wrecked *Atlantis*.

For a full minute the men about Sir Richard Dudley stood looking down at him in silence. Nathan Brock stood up and shook his head at Liam.

'He is dead. Lady Caroline is a widow.'

Chapter Fifty-Three

Liam wanted to take the news of Sir Richard Dudley's death to Caroline himself, but in addition to his broken arm he had twisted his knee and for a few weeks was able to walk only with great difficulty.

Instead, Nathan Brock went to London to take his seat in Parliament and then on to France, taking advantage of the newly opened railway linking Paris and Boulogne.

It was a wasted journey. On his return he wrote to Liam, telling his friend that Caroline had been in the south of France when he had reached Paris. He could only leave word with a servant, telling Caroline of the manner in which Sir Richard had met his death.

The letter also contained some very sad news. Nathan Brock had called to see Eugene Brennan, only to be told that the old man had died a week earlier.

Liam limped off to find Father Clery, to break the news to him of the death of his lifetime friend.

The old priest was on his way back to the village from the soup kitchen and makeshift hospital he had set up on Kilmar hill. His efforts to help the cottiers continued, even though the fishermen had refused to help them since the attack upon Liam and the survivors of *Atlantis*. When someone was foolish enough to comment on the priest's continuing support for the cottiers, Father Clery was quick to remind the speaker that there was more than one Kilmar man with cause to be grateful for his ability to forgive human weakness. Instead of criticising, he suggested the fisherman go away and pray that the people of Kilmar might never be faced with the same spectre of starvation and disease.

When Liam broke the news to him, the old Catholic priest was deeply upset.

'It's a terrible thing that he had to end his days so far from Ireland and all his friends,' he said, with tears streaming down his cheeks. 'He was loved by his people as few men have been.'

Liam remembered the pleasure the old politician had gained

from his roses in the garden of the little house in Paris, and he reminded the priest.

'You are right, Liam. We must be grateful that the Lord found a way to reward Eugene for his years of toil. There are few things more beautiful than a flower when a man has time to look at it. I will be saying a Mass for Eugene on Sunday. You'll be there, of course?'

Liam said he would, and Father Clery thanked him for bringing the sad news.

'Perhaps it is all for the best,' he added. 'Eugene was too old to have to accept another change in his way of life.'

When Liam pressed him for an explanation, the priest told him that his Bishop had close links with the Church in France. He had heard that the people there were very discontented, and strong rumours were spreading that King Louis-Philippe was to be deposed.

The news gave Liam something else to worry about, and he was not helped when he received a letter from Caroline. The news had reached her of Sir Richard Dudley's death, and she wrote to Liam in an agony of remorse, taking the blame for his death upon herself. It was the letter of a sick woman.

Liam wrote back to Caroline immediately, but it was only the beginning of a series of letters that did nothing but frustrate both of them. They left questions unanswered and caused misunderstandings and confusion.

It seemed to Liam that Sir Richard Dudley's death, far from solving their problems, had actually added to them. While he lived each letter was filled with their longing for the next meeting. Now nothing was straightforward. The future stretched uncertainly before them, waiting for Liam and Caroline to take up its challenge. For different reasons, each of them was reluctant to accept the invitation, and the knowledge of the uncertainty made them both unhappy.

Then, on 22 February 1848, the people of France deposed King Louis-Philippe in a bloodless revolution that excited Ireland. If France could throw off the yoke of an unwanted monarch without bloodshed, then why could they not do the same?

Nathan Brock and the other All-Ireland Association MPs returned home to damp down the fervour of their younger followers, and Liam was asked to help.

He was grateful for something else to occupy his mind and for almost a month he went from meeting to meeting succeeding in persuading all but a handful of would-be revolutionaries.

The break proved to be the turning-point for Liam and Caroline. Once again hopes for the future crept into their letters. Caroline returned to Paris from the south coast of France and hinted that it might not be long before her doctor would allow her to make the long journey to Ireland.

For his part, Liam worked hard as spring gave way to summer. He fished from dawn to dusk, putting to sea in weather that kept the curraghs leaning against cottage walls, sheltered from the wind. All the fish he caught went by cart to Gorey.

It was no longer necessary for the fishermen to donate a huge part of their catch to starving cottiers. The unfortunate cottiers had relieved the burden on those who had been caring for them by the simple expediency of dying.

Then more rumours about France began to circulate.

The first warning came from London in a carefully worded note from Nathan Brock. The new MP for County Wexford had struck up a most unlikely friendship with Lord Palmerston, the Whig Foreign Minister. The tough old Minister remembered Nathan well from his fighting days – and his interest boded well for Nathan Brock's political future. Lord Palmerston disclosed that the French Socialists were plotting another uprising, this time against the weak revolutionary government that struggled to rule France. It was feared in England that such a revolution would be accompanied by much bloodshed.

When a similar warning came from Father Clery only a few days later, Liam became extremely concerned about Caroline. He tried to tell himself that the Earl of Inch would be aware of the unrest and had probably already taken Caroline from Paris. But then Liam received a letter from her. The Earl had gone to Italy with some of his friends, leaving her behind. He was not expected to return until August. The letter made no mention of the troubles in France, and Caroline seemed unaware of impending danger.

Liam knew he could wait no longer. He must go to France and bring Caroline home to Ireland.

Norah McCabe took the news of his decision in tight-lipped silence. She was fond of Caroline and approved of Liam going to her aid – but she knew matters would not end with Caroline's safe return to Ireland. It would be merely the beginning of a very difficult and unhappy time for Liam.

Norah McCabe was well aware of Liam's feeling for the Earl of Inch's sister, and she did not doubt that Caroline loved him in return, but she could see no happiness ahead for them. It was unthinkable that Caroline should become a fisherman's wife. It was equally unlikely that Liam would allow Caroline to keep him. Then there was Caroline's own family to consider. . . .

She thought of all these things, but voiced none of them to her son. Liam had problems enough on his mind.

Liam had no difficulty in finding Kilmar men willing to work the McCabe boat on a profit-sharing basis while he was away. It was an exceptionally good fishing year and a wooden boat could bring home many times the catch of a curragh. By nightfall on the day he received Caroline's letter, Liam was on his way.

Two days later he arrived in London where he immediately sought out Nathan Brock.

Liam found his friend at a late and noisy sitting of the House of Commons – but this was a very different man from the penniless ex-prizefighter who had arrived in Kilmar in rags, his family supported by parish charity in a County Wicklow poorhouse. Nathan Brock wore new clothes and showed them off to advantage. Tall and broad-shouldered, he carried himself with all the confidence of a successful man.

He greeted Liam warmly, delighted to see him, but when Liam explained his reason for passing through London Nathan Brock's jaw dropped in astonishment.

'You mean you haven't seen Lady Caroline yet? Did you not receive my letter . . . ? But no, you will have been on your way when it reached Kilmar. She is here. . . . Lady Caroline is in London.'

Now it was Liam's turn to show surprise.

'How . . . ? When . . . ? Did her brother bring her here after all? Is she all right . . . ?'

Nathan Brock took Liam's arm. 'We'll take a cab to the house where she is staying. On the way I will tell you all I know. I must admit, I am relieved to see you in London so quickly. Lady Caroline has had a bad time and was fortunate to make her escape. The mobs are roaming the streets of Paris and decent people are frightened to venture from their houses. Thousands of the wealthiest families in France are fleeing to England, paying a fortune for a passage across the Channel. It is said that any man with a boat can grow rich by putting into Boulogne or Calais and bringing out French families.'

Outside the building, Nathan Brock called a hackney carriage from the nearby rank, and when he and Liam were settled in their seats he told what he knew of Caroline's escape from France.

She had been in her brother's house in Paris when the revolution began. At first it was no more than a series of noisy demonstrations through the streets in the centre of the city. Then, when the authorities made no move to restore order, the mob became bolder and began to loot shops and houses. The belated half-hearted attempt by the Army to restore order only served to convince the mob of their own invincibility. The country was lacking strong and decisive leadership, and the lawlessness flourished. The mob spilled out from the heart of Paris and commenced ransacking the houses of the rich on the outskirts of the capital.

The house owned by the Earl of Inch was one of the first to receive attention. When the mob began attacking the entrance gates Caroline was in the house accompanied by only one maidservant, the other servants having fled at the approach of the rioters.

Wearing a servant's cape, Caroline escaped through the tradesmen's gate at the rear of the house and, after a nightmare journey, arrived exhausted and penniless at Boulogne. Here a hard-pressed British consul had obtained a berth for her on an English packet bound for Dover, from whence she made her way to London.

'. . . Such an experience would have tested the strength of the healthiest woman to the full,' ended Nathan Brock. 'And Lady Caroline is still far from strong.'

While Nathan Brock related the story of Caroline's escape from Paris, Liam had been looking out of the carriage window. As they passed through the noisy cheerful streets, his imagination followed Caroline's desperate flight through the riot-torn city no more than two hundred miles away. Now something in Nathan Brock's voice caused him to look quickly at his companion.

'Caroline is ill again?'

Nathan Brock's grave expression gave Liam the answer to his question.

'Is it her heart?'

'I have not been told the details, Liam. She is staying at the home of one of her friends and they are saying nothing. However, I fear it will be a long time before she sets foot in Ireland again.'

Chapter Fifty-Four

After the urgency of Liam's journey from Kilmar, his arrival at the house where Caroline was staying came as a frustrating anti-climax. Caroline's friend was a large and determined lady who informed him firmly that Caroline was sleeping. Until she woke, not even the Queen herself would be allowed to visit the room where she lay.

It was clear to Liam that Caroline's friend disapproved of him but, because Caroline was expecting him, a room had been prepared for him in the house.

Nathan Brock did not stay – he wanted to hear the end of the debate in the House of Commons – and as Liam sank into the comfort of a soft chair in the quiet of the house the weariness of two days and nights of travelling overtook him. Despite his concern for Caroline, he fell asleep.

Liam woke when the warm sun flooded through the window and touched his face. The street noises outside told him it was late and, moments later, a servant entered the room and informed him that Lady Caroline was awake and that he might visit her.

Liam followed the servant filled with a confused mixture of excitement and apprehension. It was many months since he and Caroline had last met. The anxiety of the last few days had served to remind him how much she meant to him – but would her feelings toward him still be the same?

Caroline lay in a huge bed, propped up against a pile of pillows. She was very pale and had lost a great deal of weight, but the loss only served to emphasise the fine lines of her face and neck, giving her beauty a delicate, almost fragile quality.

'Liam . . . !' She held her arms out to him, and suddenly all doubts were gone. He crossed the room to the bed and the next moment was holding her to him. Now he became even more aware of her frailty. He felt that if he were careless she would snap in two like a brittle twig.

Liam stayed with Caroline until her doctor arrived and ordered him from the room, grumbling disapprovingly about visitors tiring his patient.

Liam waited outside the room, and when the doctor left questioned him about Caroline's condition.

'She has undergone a frightening experience,' said the doctor guardedly. 'She is as well as might be expected in the circumstances.'

'But is her heart strong? Will she be well enough to make the journey to Ireland soon?'

'Ask me about that when she has had a few weeks of rest,' replied the doctor. 'For the moment we will think no farther ahead than that. In the meantime, you must stay away from her until this evening. She has had too much excitement, and I have given her something to make her sleep for a while.'

It was the beginning of a pattern that was to be repeated over the next few days. The doctor came every day, and Liam was allowed to visit Caroline morning and evening.

Soon there was a noticeable improvement in Caroline's condition, and as he sat by her bedside one evening she said, 'You must not worry about me, Liam. I am almost well again now. Since my fever I have been so pampered that I was unprepared for the events of those last few days in Paris. I will soon be strong enough to return to Ireland with you. In the meantime, we must enjoy being together again and begin to make plans for the future.'

'How do you see the future, Caroline – for us?'

'Does it matter as long as we are together, Liam? And we can be together, now. I am no longer a married woman. I am a widow. . . .'

Liam stood up abruptly and began pacing the room.

'Yes, you are a widow. A titled and wealthy widow. I am still a fisherman. I own a boat, a horse and cart, and the cottage where I live with my mother. Can you see yourself sharing that life, Caroline? You . . . a fisherman's wife?'

'No fisherman has yet asked me to marry him,' said Caroline quietly. 'You don't have to, Liam. I am not asking for marriage. I only know that without you I am not a complete woman. I need you so much, Liam.'

Caroline suddenly burst into tears, and Liam sat on the edge of the bed beside her and took her hands in his. 'I want you, too, Caroline – with all my being. But it must be more than a bedroom affair for us. I want to marry you more than anything in the whole world, yet I can seen no way for such a marriage to succeed. I cannot change my background, nor you yours. I am Liam McCabe, a Kilmar fisherman. You are Lady Caroline Dudley, sister of the Earl of Inch. People would say that I married you for your money. They would sneer at you for marrying so far beneath you. I don't think I could take that, Caroline.'

To Liam's surprise, when Caroline looked up at him she was smiling through her tears.

'Oh Liam! Do you realise that was practically a proposal – in spite of your protestations that such a marriage could never work?'

Suddenly excited, she struggled to sit up, and Liam helped her by placing more pillows behind her back.

'There *is* a way for us to build a future together, Liam. Start a new life where I can be Caroline McCabe and you can continue to do the things you enjoy. You can fish, own as many boats as you can manage and build up a thriving business for us.'

The idea sounded too much like one of Liam's own dreams and he looked closely at Caroline, fearing she might be delirious.

'There is not a place in Ireland where our past would not catch up with us, sooner or later.'

'That is quite true, Liam – but Ireland is not the only country in the world. There are other lands full of wonderful opportunities just waiting for people like us. I am talking in particular about America. Liam, why don't we go to America? Every day its people are pushing their borders farther and farther westward. Soon it will be the greatest nation in the world. Why not go there and become a part of all it has to offer? All the things we have ever wanted for ourselves could be ours – in America.'

It was a staggeringly bold idea and, as it sank home, Liam's thoughts raced ahead, knocking down the barriers of his earlier doubts and breaking out into the brightness of a real and lasting future together. But there was one major obstacle to overcome.

'Your brother, the Earl. He would never allow you to marry me.'

'He could do nothing to stop us – but he will raise no objection, Liam. You see, Richard's death left me very wealthy. With the Paris house in ruins and his latest gambling debts awaiting settlement, Edward will be in desperate need of money.

'You look surprised, Liam? I can assure you it is perfectly true. This will not be the first occasion on which I have put up money to settle Edward's debts. He and I have always been close, and we are very fond of each other, but I am not blind to his weaknesses. He gambles too heavily and spends more money than he has. I will give him all the money I inherited from Richard and we will set sail for America with his blessing.'

'I couldn't ask you to do that. . . .'

'It was Richard's money. Do you really think I have any right to it?'

Caroline looked at Liam anxiously. Was he seeking a way to say he did not want to go to America?

'I know there are many difficulties, Liam. You will need to consider the idea carefully—'

Liam interrupted her by suddenly hugging her to him. 'I have done all the considering that is necessary.'

She pushed away from him to see his face. 'And . . . ?'

'I think you are a beautiful, scheming woman – and I love you. Lady Caroline Dudley, will you give up this idle life, become Mrs Liam McCabe and come to America with me to found a new family fortune?'

'Liam, my love. I will go with you anywhere and live on lumper potatoes in a sod cabin, if need be.'

For a week, Liam and Caroline made their plans for the future and Liam wrote to his mother to tell her the news.

They would return to Ireland together, and after she had settled her affairs Caroline would marry Liam in Father Clery's little church in Kilmar. Then they would go to America as soon as a comfortable passage could be arranged.

Caroline suggested that Liam might persuade his mother to go to America with them, but Liam doubted whether she would ever leave the village where she had spent the whole of her life. He would make sure she was well provided for, and there would always be a steady income from the wooden boat.

It was a happy time for both of them, and there was such an improvement in Caroline that by the end of the week her doctor allowed her to take a carriage ride with Liam.

Nathan Brock was delighted to witness the happiness they

both shared. He had always been concerned about their association, but was now ready to accept he had been wrong.

Yet it was Nathan Brock who brought the news that broke up their brief period of happiness.

He hurried into the house much earlier than usual, and it was evident from his expression that something was seriously wrong.

'The Government has just received a message from Ireland. The country has risen against the English and the All-Ireland Association is thought to be behind the move. Men are on the march from Bantry to Dublin. Lord Russell has ordered thousands of troops from their barracks to restore order.'

Liam found it difficult to believe the All-Ireland Association had thrown its weight behind such an uprising. It had always been against the use of violence. Even the dissidents who had broken away must know this was not the time to meet the English head-on. Brought to their knees by successive years of famine, the Irish were physically incapable of sustaining the warfare necessary to drive out the English. Nevertheless, Liam knew Lord John Russell would not commit his troops without good cause.

As it happened, Liam's assessment of the situation was correct. There *had* been an attempted rising and for a while it had generated a wild enthusiasm among a handful of would-be revolutionaries who were even now touring the country calling upon their fellows to take up arms and join them. Hailed as heroes, their words were greeted with scenes of wild patriotism. But after a few days the only rumblings to be heard came from empty bellies and the hopeful generals of Ireland's great new army of the people had gained six recruits.

There was never any need for Lord John Russell's troops. Disease and despair had won the war for them.

But this was not yet known to anyone in England. The fear of an Irish rising had been with them for years, fuelled in recent years by the exaggerated reports of an over-fanciful Lord-Lieutenant, who saw revolution in every street-corner meeting.

'What is the news of County Wexford? Has there been any fighting about Kilmar?'

'I don't know,' confessed Nathan Brock. 'The situation is confused. Even Lord Palmerston was unable to tell me anything.'

'Then I had better return home to find out what is happening. Caroline will be all right here for a while longer.'

'No, Caroline will *not* be all right here for a while longer.' Caroline bristled with indignation. 'I will return to Ireland with you.'

'You will be safer here. You barely escaped with your life from one revolution. It would be stupid to walk straight into another. Besides, the doctor said you must rest.'

'I *have* rested. Now I am well. I will be coming to Ireland with you.'

They came very close to a quarrel, but both were adamant. Caroline that she would go to Ireland, Liam that she would not. Eventually, Nathan Brock moved to break the deadlock.

'I think this should be settled by an expert decision. If the doctor is called in, will you both abide by his decision?'

Liam agreed readily. He felt sure the doctor would refuse permission for Caroline to travel to Ireland. Nathan Brock believed the same – but Caroline had other ideas.

When the doctor visited the house he spent a long time in Caroline's room with her and came out wiping perspiration from his brow. Behind him was Caroline, a look of serene triumph upon her face.

'Er . . . yes. Lady Dudley has my permission to travel to Ireland,' said the doctor in answer to Liam's question.

Liam's jaw dropped and the doctor added hurriedly, 'It had been my firm intention to insist that her ladyship remain here. . . . However, I feel that, if she did, her anxiety would far outweigh all other considerations. I . . . er . . . of course, depend upon you to see she does not over-exert herself.'

The doctor dabbed his damp face once again. 'Now, if you will excuse me. I wish you a safe journey. My Lady. Gentlemen.'

Bobbing his head to each of them in turn, the doctor retreated gratefully from the house.

Liam turned to Caroline, but before he could say anything she reminded him, 'You agreed to accept the doctor's decision, remember? Now, we must not waste any time arguing. We both have packing to do. If we hurry, we can take a train this afternoon and be in Ireland tomorrow.'

She smiled at Liam, aware that his concern was entirely for her health. 'I will be all right, Liam. The doctor would not have allowed me to travel had he really believed I was unfit.'

In a sudden burst of enthusiasm, she threw her arms about Liam's neck and kissed him happily. 'Oh, Liam, don't be so solemn. You don't know how I have longed for this day to come. The day when I return to Ireland. It will have none of the dangers of France. They are our people who are fighting, Liam. Yours and mine. We are part of them and we should be there.'

Her arms slipped from about his neck and she took him by the hand.

'We will go and make ready now, Liam. We are going home.'

Chapter Fifty-Five

If Liam and Caroline had expected to find the streets of Dublin barricaded against Irish patriots, they would have been sadly disappointed.

British soldiers there were, in great numbers, but they walked the streets much as they had during Liam's last visit to the city. Moreover, they laughed and joked together as though an Irish uprising was a myth thought up in London.

Liam was both puzzled and relieved by the lack of military activity. As the carriage carrying him and Caroline trundled through the city he looked for guards on public buildings, or discreet signs that all was not as quiet as it appeared to be. He saw nothing.

Outside the city the countryside appeared equally quiet. On the only occasion when the carriage passed soldiers, they were blue-uniformed hussars riding in a relaxed manner, their officer even waving a white-gloved hand at the inquisitive occupants of the carriage.

'They do not look like soldiers who are fighting a war,' exclaimed Caroline as she settled back in her seat.

'Nor soldiers who have won a war,' added Liam. 'But surely the reports reaching London could not have been so wrong?'

Had they only known it, the relaxed attitude of the hussars was due in no small measure to relief. They were the Queen's Royal Irish Hussars, a regiment notorious for their reluctance to fight fellow-Irishmen. Sent out from Dublin to break up a planned meeting called by dissidents at Wicklow, they had learned the meeting had been cancelled. They immediately turned about and rode back to Dublin. Had they taken the trouble to make any enquiries, they would have discovered that the meeting had been moved to Arklow, close to the County Wexford border and less than ten miles from Kilmar. But they did not want to know.

It turned out to be the best-attended meeting held in the area for many years. Cottiers flocked to the hillside site from miles around under the mistaken impression that there was to be a distribution of free food. There were so many of them that their numbers spilled on to the road, a hundred yards from the platform.

By the time the speakers arrived, to urge revolution upon the listeners, they had an audience of at least ten thousand people. The cottiers waited patiently as speaker after speaker urged them to join the fight for the freedom of Ireland. Then, as the hungry crowd was becoming restive, word began to spread amongst them that there would be no food. Confirmation came when a speaker who knew little of the situation in the rural areas called for all volunteers to bring with them a weapon and *four days' supply of food.*

The crowd erupted into noisy anger – and it was at this unfortunate moment that the carriage carrying Liam and Caroline rounded a bend in the road and careered to a stop at the very edge of the frustrated mob.

The howl set up by the cheated cottiers pounded against the side of the vehicle like a storm-driven sea, and the coachman had to fight for control of his terrified animals.

A quick glance out of the carriage window told Liam all he needed to know. 'Turn the carriage and go back – hurry!' he shouted to the coachman. He was no stranger to meetings and he needed no second look at this one to recognise that it was totally out of control.

The coachman brought his plunging horses around in a tight circle, but it was not quick enough for Liam's liking. 'Faster, man! Get them moving.'

The mob saw the carriage turning away from them, and it suddenly became an object on which to vent their ill-humour. They swarmed down the hillside toward it, howling threats and abuse.

Had the road been wider, or the verges more firm, the horses would have pulled the carriage clear of the leading cottiers. Instead, the two rear wheels sank deep into the soft peat earth as the horses slipped and slid, the coachman's whip cracking like pistol shots about their ears.

Finally, the sweating horses pulled the carriage back to the hard road, but not until they were surrounded by shouting, triumphant cottiers.

Hands took hold of the sides of the carriage, rocking it dangerously, and Liam beat in vain against the fingers curling about the open window-frames. Meanwhile, on his high driving-seat, the coachman struck about him with his whip until it was tugged away from him and he was dragged down into the crowd and beaten unconscious.

Now the carriage was being rocked with a frightening rhythm, the wheels on either side leaving the ground as it swayed to and fro.

Liam knew it was no use calling upon the cottiers to stop; they were beyond reason. All Liam could do was to take Caroline in his arms and support her as best he could as the carriage lurched crazily from side to side.

'If it goes over hold tightly to me,' gasped Liam. 'I'll try to break your fall.'

But they had a few more uncomfortable minutes of the violent motion before someone cut the traces of the terrified horses and set them free. Not until then did the wildly cheering cottiers succeed in upsetting the carriage.

It tilted quite slowly at first, allowing Liam to prepare himself for the final crash. Then it fell on to its side to the sound of splintering wood and, with Caroline held firmly in his arms, Liam was upended and fell heavily on his back.

'Caroline, are you all right?'

She stirred in his arms, and without waiting for a reply Liam struggled to free himself from her.

'Stay here. Don't try to move.'

Reaching up with both hands, Liam pushed up the door, and as it fell open he scrambled out on to the side of the carriage. A well-greased wheel spun lazily beside him, and he looked out over a sea of faces.

'Are you satisfied now?' he cried, his County Wexford accent the same as most of those gathered about him. 'Or are you out to murder all your fellow Irishmen and women?'

'We don't ride the countryside in carriages, wearing fancy clothes,' called one of the cottier men, standing well back in the crowd.

'No – and you don't pay for soup kitchens out of your own pocket and look after hundreds of cottiers sick with fever,' retorted Liam. 'But Lady Caroline Dudley does – and that's who is lying inside the carriage you have just overturned.'

Liam's words had an immediate effect upon the crowd. Caroline's generosity was well known to every cottier, and there were many in this very crowd who owed her their lives. There was a sudden upsurge of talk among them.

'Well, are you going to spend all day talking, or will someone step forward and do something?'

'We're sorry, sir.' A black-bearded ruffian pushed his way to the carriage. 'My own child owes her life to her Ladyship.'

'Then get this carriage back on its wheels.' Liam's exasperated words hid the relief he felt that the mood of the mob had swung his way.

Shamefaced men shuffled into position about the overturned carriage, and as they prepared to set it on its wheels Liam dropped inside the carriage to Caroline.

The inside of the carriage was in deep shadow, yet there was sufficient light to show Liam that Caroline was still lying exactly where he had left her.

Alarmed, he crouched beside her, and as he lifted her clear of the frame of the carriage her breast rose and fell rapidly as she fought for breath.

'Caroline . . . ? Everything is all right now. There will be no more trouble. Just relax. Everything is going to be all right now.'

The carriage rose an inch or two, sliding for a way along the ground. Then, accompanied by much shouting from outside, it rose slowly to topple back on to its wheels.

Inside, Liam had managed to retain his balance and he now lay Caroline full length along a padded seat. She still fought desperately for breath, leaving Liam with a feeling of total helplessness.

The shattered door that had been resting against the road swung open on broken hinges and an anxious bearded face peered inside.

'Is her Ladyship all right, sir?'

'No, she's far from right. Send someone for a doctor – and hurry!'

The door swung back to hang half-open at a crazy angle, and Liam pulled it shut and secured it against the curiosity of the cottiers. When he turned back to Caroline her eyes were open and she was looking at him.

'I am sorry, Liam,' she whispered.

'You have nothing to be sorry for. Don't try to speak. Just lie there and rest. A doctor will be here soon.'

'It is too late . . . this time.' Tears suddenly welled up into her eyes. 'Liam . . . I don't want to die. I have so much to live for.'

Liam had not even realised he had taken her hand, but now he felt her fingers tighten in his.

'We'll have no more talk of dying. We've a whole lifetime ahead of us – you told me so yourself. Just rest and don't tire yourself.'

Her eyes closed and she whispered, 'Yes, Liam. I will rest. Tell me . . . tell me what we are going to do in America.'

Taking Caroline in his arms, Liam told her of the voyage they would be making. That they would have the best cabin in the finest ship on the Atlantic run; of their landing in New York and the sights she would see there; the journey across the vast land of America and the house he would build at their journey's end. He described the boat he would have and told her of the happiness they would find together.

He spoke in desperation, frightened to stop, ignoring the cottiers staring in at the windows and doors. It was as though he believed that by talking to her of the future he could make it come true.

He was still talking when the carriage door opened and a red-faced perspiring doctor clambered inside the battered carriage. Pushing Liam roughly to one side, he took Caroline's wrist, then laid his head against her breast.

Straightening up, he said cruelly, 'You've wasted my time bringing me all this way. She's as dead as we will all be, one day.'

Chapter Fifty-Six

The cold northerly wind tugged at Father Clery's flat round hat, threatening to snatch it from his head and pitch it into the brown and evil-smelling waters of the Liverpool dock. Beside him, Nathan Brock talked earnestly to Liam, and all three men had their hands pushed deep into the pockets of their overcoats.

They were standing on the timber-planked deck of *Leviathan*, a giant paddle-steamer that was about to make one of her regular transatlantic crossings to New York.

The decks were crowded with emigrant family groups, many of them saying their goodbyes to relatives, the women tearful, the men serious and filled with importance. For the children it was a time of excitement as they embarked on a half-understood adventure.

'It is not too late to change your mind, Liam. Kilmar's welcome home would be just as warm and honest as its farewell.'

'No, Father. I am going to America. But you'll keep an eye on my mother and write to me with all the news.'

'Of course, Liam. Of course. But I wish you would stay. There is so much to be done here. With yet another disastrous potato harvest I don't know what we are going to do. If there is a single cottier left alive this time next year, it will be a miracle, sure enough.'

Liam's tired face took on a set expression. 'I don't want to hear of the cottiers' troubles, Father – not just yet. I know you and Nathan will work yourselves into the ground for them, yet I wonder whether it will make any difference at all. Some of them will live, many more will die. I doubt if anyone will care – not even the cottiers themselves. Perhaps Trevelyan was right; this is meant to be. If we had not interfered with the way of things, Caroline would still be here.'

Despite his harsh words, Liam felt no anger toward the cottiers now. It had somehow drained away during the long sleepless nights since Caroline's death. He had come to realise that the cottiers themselves were suffering for all that was wrong in Ireland. In an overpopulated little country they were at the end of the long food chain. When times were hard, land-owners, landlords and other tenants used the cottier as a buffer against personal hardship, taking everything he had to give before casting him out to starve. To the Irish politician, the cottier was dying proof of English misrule. To the English politician, no more than an example of Irish improvidence.

The truth was that the cottier was largely responsible for his tragic situation by his own ignorance and fear of change. He was a serf, in a society that had cast off its medieval responsibility toward those who were born to serve. The cottier had become an anachronism, doomed in the rapidly changing world of the nineteenth century.

Yet, although Liam realised all these things, he could not forgive the cottiers for causing the death of Caroline. It would take a new land and a new way of life to bring that to pass.

'All ashore who's going ashore. All ashore who's going ashore.'

A sailor moved about the deck shouting the words in a sing-song voice.

'All visitors leave the ship now, please.' To add emphasis to his words, the first mate of *Leviathan* tugged at the cord of the ship's steam-whistle and produced a bass note that might have come from a cathedral organ.

'Goodbye, Liam. Take care of yourself and return to Ireland a rich man.'

The moment of departure had arrived. Liam said goodbye with a lump rising in his throat as he shook hands with the men who were his last links with the tiny village of Kilmar.

He picked them out in the crowd on the jetty as the huge paddles churned the sluggish waters of the Mersey. The gap between ship and shore widened, but Liam did not lose sight of them until distance took them from him.

He stayed on deck until the wind began to chill him and the approach of darkness hid the lights of land from view. Then he went below to his cabin. The cabin he should have been sharing with his wife . . . with Caroline.